ORIGIN

A SCI FI FANTASY ROMANCE

ALL IS FAIR IN LOVE AND GALACTIC WAR

LORI LIND

Linds Publishing, Inc.

ISBN eBook 978-1-960962-05-8

ISBN Hardback 978-1-960962-03-4

ISBN Paperback 978-1-960962-04-1

LCCN 2023940148

Cover and Book Design: Lori Lind

Publisher Contact:

Lori@lorilind.com

www.lorilind.com

In our quest to decipher existence, we must accept that the furnaces of the stars not only forged but also gave birth to humanity in all its splendid complexity. As stardust, we find ourselves tethered to a grand cosmic symphony, navigating the endless ebb and flow of the universe, our humble abode. We're not just observers; we are progeny, echoes of ancient cosmic fires, carrying the legacy of the universe in our very DNA. Thus, we are not merely in the universe but intrinsically of it—a testament to the power of creation, witnessing, and taking part in the unending dance of existence.

~ Lori Lind

MAFFEI
DRACORE
DRAZANIUM
AURORA 33

QUINDARIAN FEDERATION LOCAL UNIVERSE REALM
GRYMROCK
TERRASTRIA
F1R3X WORMHOLE
ANDROMEDA
TERRAINITIUM
EARTH
MILKY WAY

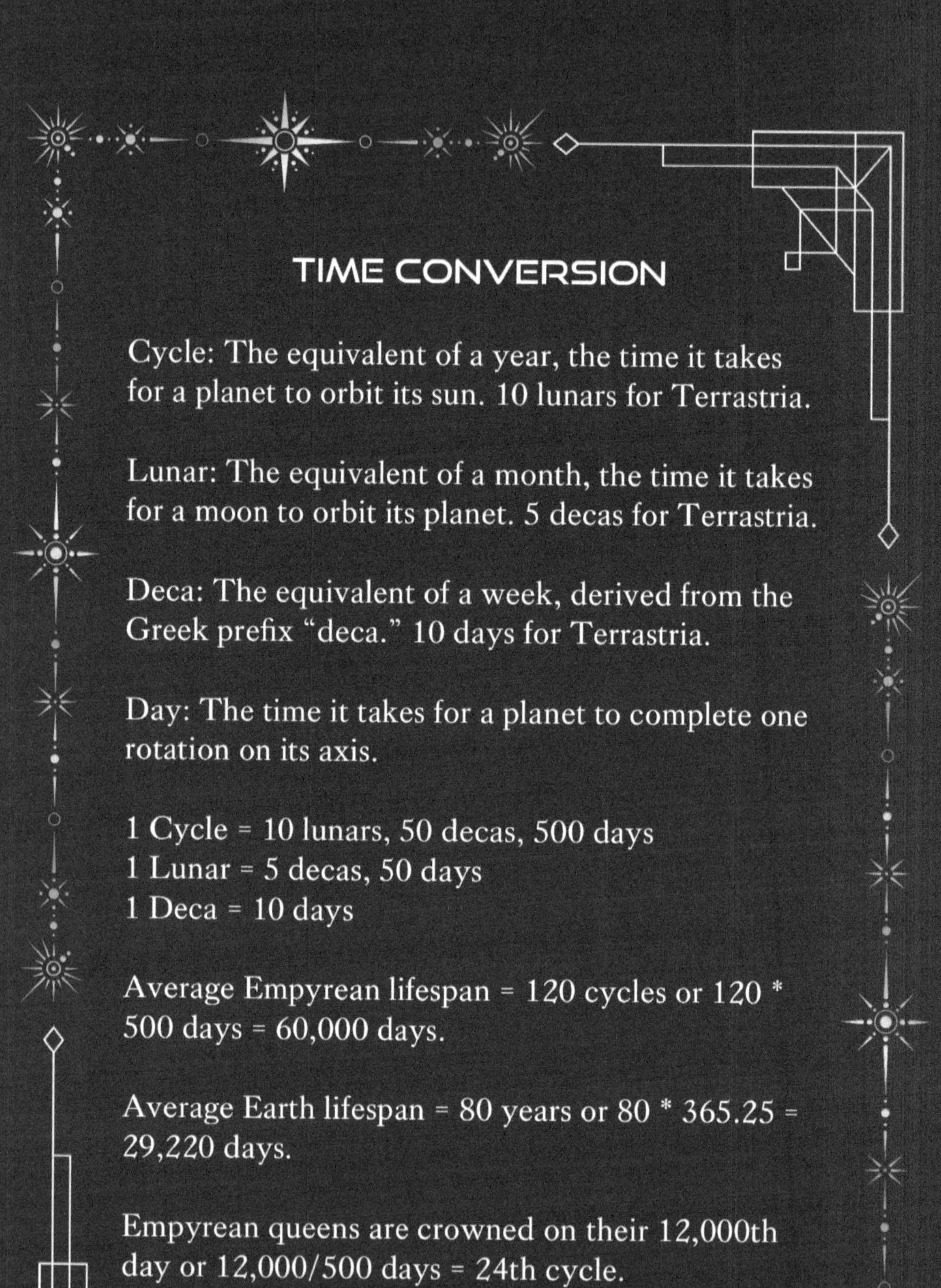

TIME CONVERSION

Cycle: The equivalent of a year, the time it takes for a planet to orbit its sun. 10 lunars for Terrastria.

Lunar: The equivalent of a month, the time it takes for a moon to orbit its planet. 5 decas for Terrastria.

Deca: The equivalent of a week, derived from the Greek prefix "deca." 10 days for Terrastria.

Day: The time it takes for a planet to complete one rotation on its axis.

1 Cycle = 10 lunars, 50 decas, 500 days
1 Lunar = 5 decas, 50 days
1 Deca = 10 days

Average Empyrean lifespan = 120 cycles or 120 * 500 days = 60,000 days.

Average Earth lifespan = 80 years or 80 * 365.25 = 29,220 days.

Empyrean queens are crowned on their 12,000th day or 12,000/500 days = 24th cycle.

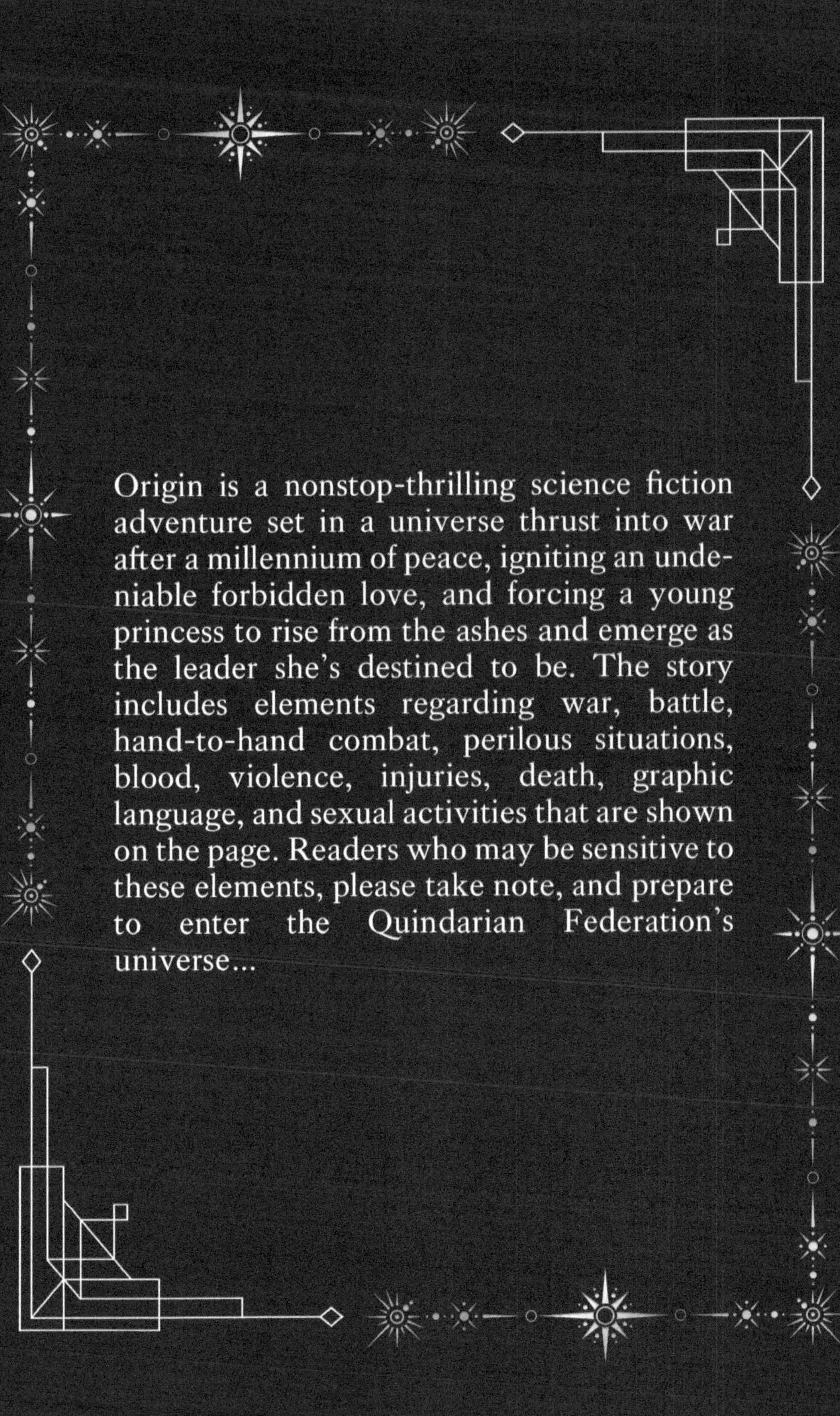

Origin is a nonstop-thrilling science fiction adventure set in a universe thrust into war after a millennium of peace, igniting an undeniable forbidden love, and forcing a young princess to rise from the ashes and emerge as the leader she's destined to be. The story includes elements regarding war, battle, hand-to-hand combat, perilous situations, blood, violence, injuries, death, graphic language, and sexual activities that are shown on the page. Readers who may be sensitive to these elements, please take note, and prepare to enter the Quindarian Federation's universe...

CHAPTER ONE

ELZARIA

It had been peaceful for far too long...

I should feel happy and excited today of all days. But I wasn't. At a time meant for celebrating the most significant milestone of my life, an insidious unease curled within me. I looked out from the castle's highest balcony across the city of Arcadia as the sun barely peaked above the horizon and knew my reign may be the end of my people.

The cool morning air brushed against my face as I stood in silence, absorbing the city's beauty and tranquility, stirring a strange blend of pride and dread within me. Drenched in sweat from the latest nightmare staining my unconsciousness, my heart pounded so hard I thought it was going to explode from my chest. I had fled the comfy confines of my bed to the chilly air along the balcony's edge to clear my head. The thought of jumping nagging at the far corners of my mind.

Gripping the edge of the baluster, I felt the doubt that clouded my thoughts well up. I wanted desperately to be the leader my people deserved. But my heart was heavy knowing that the entire Quindarian Federation's prosperity and safety would become my responsibility. The Empyrean Alliance alone was vast and complex, comprising countless planets from the Andromeda galaxy, all relying on Terrastria's leadership.

Tradition dictated that the first-born daughter of the Queen ascend to the throne upon her twelve-thousandth day. The twenty-fourth cycle of my existence.

Such has been the way of the Empyrean, an unyielding decree since ancient times. It's believed that the ascendancy of youthful queens bestows upon the realm fresh perspectives, innovation, and adaptability. A younger sovereign's energy and enthusiasm were expected to drive change and strengthen interplanetary relations, resulting in better governance. With a longer reign ahead, the queen could focus on long-term planning, ensuring succession stability and reducing potential conflicts and uncertainties during transitions.

Not to overlook the undeniable truth that, at this very age, a queen is most fertile. The Eridani matriarchy, a lineage that hasn't been broken since the time of The Creators, deems soul-binding and the birth of an heir not as mere expectations, but a non-negotiable duty.

Queen Elindra Eridani and her consort Prime Minister Helion Stellatyro Eridani are my parents. They're a lot to live up to.

My mother is a politically cunning ruler. She's determined to protect the Terrastrian people and uphold the values of the Empyrean Alliance. She possesses great power but also carries the burden of duty that comes with it. Having lived in an era of relative peace, my mother is well-versed in the politics of the Quindarian Federation and its member galaxies.

While she is undoubtedly an influential leader, my mother remains a detached figure in my personal life. As her daughter,

I've always found myself standing in the cold shadow of her regal countenance. In private, her eyes are filled with distant worries instead of motherly warmth. Her mind constantly engrossed in state matters, even our personal time echoes with the rustle of documents and the soft whispers of council discussions. Though we share blood, I often feel like just another subject to her, receiving her commands in respectful silence. I don't get motherly advice, just orders to follow.

We might share a meal, but she dines on intelligence reports and military dispatches, her mind feasting on a constant stream of information. Her responses to my requests often feel scripted, like declarations read from a teleprompter. There's love, I'm certain, buried beneath the layers of responsibility, but it's an abstract, aloof sort of affection.

There's an iron wall between us, unseen, built not by disdain but by duty. Emotions, for her, are a luxury afforded only to those who do not bear the weight of an entire galaxy. In this universe filled with intergalactic politics, there's little room for the gentler art of parenting.

Today, I must rise to the challenge as the new leader of Terrastria. I stand on the precipice of destiny, my mother's legacy heavy on my shoulders, the weight of an entire kingdom threatening to crush me.

Sometimes, I feel a flicker of confidence, a small flame born from my birthright and nurtured through cycles of royal tutelage. Yet it wars with a treacherous whisper of fear. A fear that I might not be good enough, that I might not be the queen my people need, the leader my mother has been.

The nightmares that have plagued me of late only amplify my anxiety. Visions of a vast, destructive war creep through the recesses of my mind like a dark phantom. The scale of this devastation shakes me to my core, seeping into my waking thoughts and tinging my every decision with a haunting undercurrent of dread.

I worry that if these nightmares become our reality, I won't be able to steer the Empyrean people through the storm. Can I match my mother's unyielding resolve? Can I stand firm in the face of an overwhelming foe, as she has done time and again?

In the depths of my heart, I fear I might falter, that I might fail. I'm not my mother, not the stoic and unflinching leader she has proven herself to be. And the thought that I might not measure up to her, that I might not be enough for the Empyrean people, sends an unnerving wave of terror coursing through my veins.

My father is every bit as politically astute as my mother. He moves through the complex dance of intergalactic politics with the grace of a seasoned performer, his every step measured, his every word calculated. In the grand theater of the Empyrean Alliance, he's a master playwright, weaving narratives that hold audiences from Terrastria to the furthest reaches of the Quindarian Federation in rapt attention.

His role, like my mother's, demands a certain emotional distance. Yet, with me, he manages to bridge the gap my mother never quite could. He might be a powerful political figure, but to me, he's simply my father.

His eyes, so often stern and scrutinizing when engaging with his peers, soften when they meet mine. The strategic tactician, the hardened negotiator, melts away, replaced by a loving father who treasures his only child. When he smiles at me, it isn't the politician's practiced grin but a genuine expression of paternal affection. His love doesn't feel like a distant galaxy; it feels close, real, tangible. He might not always be physically present—the affairs of the Alliance often demand his attention—but his influence is a constant presence in my life.

In the peace of the last millennium, a calm where battles were few and far between, the prized currency among the Empyrean

Alliance's leaders isn't firepower, but knowledge, diplomacy, and political strategy. Raised in this era of order and stability, my parents meticulously molded me with every enlightened lesson to become a queen worthy of such an alliance.

A princess during a time of peace; I'm no fearsome warrior. Instead, I'm an Empyrean of the scholarly kind, more acquainted with quantum equations and celestial cartography than laser rifles or battle arenas. Given to the life of the mind rather than the sword or shield.

You wouldn't pick me out in a crowd even though I'm the heir to the throne. Nothing extraordinary, really. I'm about as tall as the next girl you meet, with a fit, but by no means muscular build.

Despite hailing from a long line of interstellar warriors, I'm not an imposing figure. My lean arms—lacking the brawny strength seen on our seasoned knights—are more familiar with the weight of digital devices and stacks of archaic books, not the robust recoil of a plasma rifle or the cold, unyielding grip of a blade.

My days mostly involve analyzing complicated data and figuring out tricky quantum problems instead of fighting or learning how to use energy weapons. I may engage in intellectual pursuits, spending long nights decoding alien languages and interpreting star maps, but I'm not weak. At least I don't think so. Cycles of private dance lessons have helped me develop strength, grace, balance, and endurance, all behind the palace's protective walls, away from prying eyes and Vaith assassins.

The Vaith, spawns of the Maffei galaxy, embody the universe's darkest elements. Their reputation as cutthroats and murderers is well earned, for they don't simply dip their toes in vice, they dive headlong into it. They take what they want, using brutality and deceit as their weapons, their vile acts an affront to all that is fair and decent. These misogynistic marauders, these agents of chaos, live to cause harm.

In the chronicles of history, they scorched their heinous acts in the blood of millions. They kindled the flames of the ancient wars, their lust for power and domination leaving a path of desolation in their wake. That bloody stain, that gruesome heritage, it's not just history; it is their mainstay. Their echo of torment still reverberates in the hearts of Empyreans.

As a princess and a scholar, the realm of ideas, theories, and educational pursuits has been my safe harbor, but my parents have allowed me one secret pleasure: clandestinely training in the shadows of our space force.

Our pilots mostly ignore me as long as I don't get in their way. In the cockpit of a strike fighter, my true self comes alive. I'm adept at the controls, a skill born from cycles of intense training and an innate passion for flight. But for me, the allure of space isn't just about the exhilaration of flying or the precision required for tactical maneuvers. It's the intoxicating freedom I taste each time I break through our atmosphere and into the infinite expanse of all that's beyond, an independence I seldom experience within the palace walls. I'm not judged by my lineage, my education, or my potential as a queen, but by my skills and my courage as a pilot.

The dangerous thrill that accompanies flying a strike fighter, the only form of risk my royal status allows me to indulge in, adds an enthralling layer to its pursuit. It contrasts starkly with the typically academic and risk-averse life I lead. The whole thing's one big mental and physical workout. It pushes me to the limit and keeps me on my toes, encouraging me to grow in ways no cushy royal upbringing ever could.

In the solitude of space, it's just me and the raw, unfiltered universe. In its vastness, I'm more than a bookish princess; I'm a capable pilot, yes, a lover of astrophysics, but above all, I'm an individual defined by my own abilities, far removed from the complexities of court politics and harsh judgments. It doesn't matter how socially challenged I am.

But there's a menace, a dark shadow looming over me, though, a call to arms that reverberates in the silent depths of my soul, forcing my feet to stay grounded. A part of me shudders at the distant drum of this war song. Is there a warrior queen inside me, dormant under the skin of an astrophysicist, waiting for the stars to align? It's a daunting thought, both unsettling and intriguing. Yet, there's a flame in me, too. An ember of strength that quietly simmers under the surface. It's a peculiar notion, almost surreal.

The Empyreans are born warriors. Our knights' hardened gazes often cast doubt over my potential. They look at me with bemusement. Could this cerebral princess, they smirk, lead us into an intergalactic conflict? Can this studious girl, they question in hushed tones, bear the weight of our survival? Their jabs send ripples of insecurity across my mind.

Often in the privacy of my chamber, I catch my reflection on the sleek surface of a mirror. An ordinary girl stares back, her blue eyes filled with uncertainty. Will she, the girl who is called "a delicate flower," one day lead an army through the unforgiving expanse of the galaxy?

My heart resonates with a distant 'yes' but my logical mind wages war against it. I'm Elzaria, the analyst, the scholar, who so far hasn't uncovered any dormant warrior queen inside of me.

None of this will matter when the shadow of war descends upon us if my nightmares become a reality. I have no actual experience. I've lived a life of privilege within my gilded cage. I know that I'm vulnerable, as we all are, having lived for a millennium during mostly peaceful, well-controlled times. Those who visit my dreams expect me to heed their warnings, but how I don't know.

The Empyrean people are the oldest known beings. Long ago, we formed an alliance of Royal Houses made up of planets from the Andromeda galaxy where there are thousands of solar systems with inhabitable planets. The home base for the Empyrean Alliance is the planet I call home, Terrastria. Our matriarchal monarchy thrives, and others recognize the Empyrean kingdom as the most diplomatic and technologically advanced realm.

All Empyreans have telekinetic powers, but the royal family has the ultimate power over all elements. I have kept the powers I possess mostly hidden, not wanting to attract the wrong kind of attention. Powerful Empyreans are the favorite targets of Vaith assassins.

For months, The Creators, the original conscious beings that all humanity comes from, have visited me in my sleep. They're omniscient, godlike beings and only speak to a select few through a mental connection. What they've shared with me is terrifying and I try not to think about it too much, but it's still always there nagging at my mind.

Standing at the edge of the balcony, gazing out over Arcadia, storm clouds gather on the horizon, a warning of what my reign will bring. The people in our capital city, with its stunning architecture and beautiful scenery, have no idea of the grim fate that awaits them. The buildings are an exquisite blend of futuristic and classical design, each one boasting intricate details and patterns etched into their smooth surfaces. From afar, the cityscape looks like something straight out of a dream a maze of soaring towers, spires, and beautiful arches, all arranged in a stunning symphony of shapes and colors.

At the heart of Arcadia, towering above all other structures, stands the Empyrean Castle, the home of my family. The castle, a city in and of its own, is a masterpiece of design, made of the finest white stone and glass, with hues of blue and green that give it the appearance of a calm ocean within the bustling city. Its courtyard is a sight to behold, with lush gardens, serene fountains, and intricate pathways leading to various parts of the estate.

Arcadia is a city known for its vast greenery and sustainable infrastructure. It's the heart of a thriving, technological multi-planetarian society that has found a way to balance urbanization with the preservation of natural resources.

Looking out at the city I love, I'm reminded of the nightmares The Creators have sent me. Instead of Arcadia's grandeur, I see plumes of smoke, crumbled buildings, and the looks of terror on innocent faces. The dreams have haunted me. I've tried to push them aside, to focus on my duties as the soon-to-be future Queen and my coronation, but every time I close my eyes, I see the same thing.

Arcadia engulfed in flames. The once-beautiful skyline reduced to rubble and ash. The people I love, my friends, my family, all gone.

I know the citizens of Terrastria are in danger and that it's up to me to protect them. But how? The Creators have given me hints, but they're always vague and cryptic. I needed more information, a clearer picture of what's coming.

The Creators expect me, of all people, to lead our guardian knights, soldiers, and aeronauts into battle against the most powerful enemy the galaxy has ever known and emerge victorious. What are they thinking?

Power has made the Empyreans spoiled. No one dares think of the universe at war once more. Everyone thinks that their way of life is everlasting. No serious plans or preparations have been made in hundreds of cycles for an attack by the Vaith or any others. The peace we think we live under has made us arrogant and lazy. We sing praises of what a mighty people we are. We rule as if no other will ever dare challenge us. We are the mighty

Empyreans, keepers of the peace, the most developed, those who know best. We rule from the shining city on the hill. Our alliance has grown apathetic to the plight and desires of the many vastly different nation-groups of the universe.

The Creators demand for me to become the hero my people need. In my heart, I'm willing, but I know that I'm unprepared. I'm no leader. Neither am I a warrior. What the fuck are they thinking? The heartbeat in my neck thrums at a staccato pace, making my ears ring.

My thoughts grew dark as I agonized over today's coronation. Maybe there's a way I can stop the foretold future events from happening. If I don't become queen, if I no longer exist, or maybe disappear, it would force the future to change.

I leaned out over the edge of the baluster. Certain death awaited me if I were to fall from the dizzying height over the cliff's face. A matter of seconds could change everything...

CHAPTER TWO

ELZARIA

The sudden gust of a cool breeze sent shivers down my spine and ruffled my disheveled hair, startling me from my morbid curiosity. Engrossed in my thoughts, I barely registered the clicking of the heavy balcony doors until Adelaide flung them open. The loud clang made me jump back from the edge.

Adelaide, my closest royal aide, was an older woman who had been my governess since I was a child, her kind guidance shaping my understanding of our universe. She was a pillar of the community within the royal house and a source of constancy in my life. Despite her stern countenance, adhering steadfastly to the rigid code of royal decorum, Adelaide oversaw me with a nurturing warmth that my own parents often failed to provide amidst their myriad obligations.

With a delicate blend of strict discipline and genuine care, Adelaide had been instrumental in molding me into the woman I was becoming. She possessed a profound understanding of the duality of my existence: a princess groomed to wear the crown, while at the same time, a girl, now a woman, yearning for the love, care, and attention that everyone deserves.

Where my parents were often absent, lost in the labyrinth of diplomatic alliances and state affairs, Adelaide stepped in. She was there during my first solo flight, cheering me on with a pride that rivaled any parent's. She was there during my countless schooling sessions, pushing me to question, to learn, and to grow. And she was always there during my moments of doubt, offering words of encouragement and reminding me of the strength that lay within me.

I felt Adelaide's eyes on me, but I couldn't bring myself to meet her gaze. I knew the sunset coronation was only hours away, and I had yet to begin my preparations. Instead, all I wanted was to jump back in bed, drag the covers over my head, and forget about all of this.

Adelaide must have sensed it, because she stepped closer to me. "Elzaria, you must go now and have yourself cleansed and purified according to ancient tradition."

"I can't," I admitted quietly, my voice barely carrying over the gentle rustle of the wind. I turned to face her, my eyes locking with hers. "Adelaide, I'm scared."

There was a moment of silence as my words hung in the crisp morning air. I half-expected Adelaide to chide me for showing weakness, to remind me I was to be Queen and needed to act accordingly. But she didn't. Instead, she softened, her usually strict eyes filled with understanding and compassion.

"I know, Elzaria. It's alright to be afraid, to worry if you're enough." Her voice was gentle, soothing. "Becoming a Queen isn't an easy task. It's daunting, and it's terrifying. It's even more difficult because you're so young. But remember, you aren't alone."

Her words, meant to comfort, only made the tight knot in my stomach twist even more. "I feel alone, Adelaide. More than ever. I don't know if I can do this."

There was a pause before she replied, "Elzaria, you're stronger than you believe. I have seen it. I've seen you face adversity and challenges head-on and conquer your fears time and time again. There's no doubt in my mind you will do so again."

"But what if that's not enough?" I whispered, my gaze dropping to the stone floor of the balcony.

"It will be. Live in the here and now. Don't borrow trouble from tomorrow."

I turned towards her, her calm, authoritative voice interrupting my tangled thoughts. She was right, of course, and I knew I had to focus on the imminent coronation. "Yes, Adelaide," I responded with a reluctant nod.

"You're right. The coronation won't wait for my doubts and fears to disappear." I forced a smile, though it felt empty. I knew Adelaide could see through my facade, but I didn't want to worry her more than necessary.

She nodded, her eyes softening with empathy. "Remember, Elzaria," she started, her voice taking on a gentle tone, "you have prepared for this role all your life. They've taught you to lead. You're the rightful heir to the throne, and I know, without a doubt, that you have the courage and the strength to face whatever comes your way."

Adelaide moved closer, her warm hand gently cupping my cheek. Her touch was comforting, a sense of home amidst the chaos. "Be yourself, Elzaria," she replied, her voice steady and assuring. "You are intelligent, kind, and brave. You have a heart full of love for the Empyrean people. And most importantly, you have the willingness to learn and to adapt. That's what makes a good Queen."

"I appreciate your faith in me, Adelaide," I replied, touched by her words. "The weight of becoming queen feels... overwhelming, to say the least." I looked back at the cityscape, the bustling city unaware of my inner turmoil.

Her words washed over me like a soothing balm, easing some of the tension from my shoulders. I had to force myself to move on. To suck it up and put on the mask my mother wears so flawlessly.

"You're right, Adelaide. I have to trust in myself and my abilities. I... I just hope it's enough." Adelaide's unwavering faith in me, her steadfast belief in my abilities, brought a semblance of comfort to my turbulent thoughts.

I steeled myself, inhaling a deep breath and letting it out slowly. I knew what I had to do. This was my duty, my destiny. And while the looming threat of war filled me with fear, I had to be strong, for the sake of my people and the Empyrean Alliance.

"Thank you, Adelaide, for reminding me of who I am, of what I can do. I needed to hear that," I admitted, grateful for her presence.

"Now, let's get you ready for the coronation, shall we?"

I sighed heavily and nodded in agreement. As much as I didn't want to face it, I knew this was a sacred ceremonial ritual, and I had to undergo purification in order to connect with the energy of our planet and the universe—only then would I be ready for tonight's coronation.

I stood at the entrance to the purification chamber, my heart pounding with nervous energy. This was it—the moment I had been preparing for my entire life was underway. I had prepared for this day for as long as I could remember, and now that it was finally here, I couldn't help but feel a little intimidated. The anxiety was normal, right?

"One step at a time, Elzaria," I murmured to myself, pushing past the threshold into the warm, enveloping space of the chamber. The room basked in a soft, ethereal glow, shimmering tiles reflecting the blue light that emanated from the large bath in the center. It was filled to the brim with water, glimmering like liquid silver.

Attendants, all extraordinarily beautiful women from a mix of cultures around the galaxy, rushed forward to greet me, their movements graceful and fluid. They helped me out of my robe, revealing my naked body to their gazes.

"Breathe, Elzaria," one of them murmured, a gentle reminder that echoed my own. The warmth of a blush stung my neck, but I squared my shoulders, standing tall, the weight of tradition a comfort against the exposure.

The attendants guided me to the bath's edge. With their assistance, I carefully descended into the welcoming waters. As I slid into the large pool, I sank into the warm embrace of the liquid. I felt a sense of peace wash over me, soothing my muscles and calming my nerves.

The room was dimly lit, with candles placed strategically around the perimeter of the bath, casting flickering shadows on the walls. I took a deep breath, inhaling the sweet scent of herbs that filled the air.

The attendants washed my body, using soft brushes and fragrant soaps to cleanse my skin, scrubbing away the unseen impurities, leaving me feeling refreshed and renewed. As they worked, I felt the tension of the past few days melting away.

All too soon, it was time to begin the purification ritual. The attendants helped me rise to the edge of the bath, where they stood ready to begin. Dressed in long white robes, their faces were serene and calm. One of them approached me, holding a small bowl filled with fragrant oil. She dipped her fingers into the oil and massaged it gently into my skin, starting from my feet and working her way up. The oil was warm and soothing, and I closed my eyes, letting out a sigh of contentment.

Another attendant washed my hair, carefully untangling the knots and snarls. She worked her fingers through my long blonde tresses, lathering them with a sweet-smelling shampoo. As she rinsed my hair, I could feel the water running down my back.

Once my hair was clean, they carefully combed it out, working through the tangles with gentle fingers. As I emerged from the bath chamber, I felt renewed and refreshed. The attendants wrapped me in a soft white robe and braided my hair into intricate patterns, weaving delicate beads and crystals into the strands. These braids were more than an accessory; they were a symbol of my purity, my pledge to The Creators, a testament to the transformation within me.

The attendants then led me to a small chapel, where I meditated and prepared for the ceremony. I closed my eyes and breathed slowly, deeply.

The high priestess entered and approached me. She had a serene expression on her face and her eyes glinted with an inner light. I had seen her before, at various religious events. She radiated such calm and confidence that I felt drawn to her.

"Elzaria, the time has come. Are you ready to take on the mantle of leadership?" she asked in a voice that was kind but firm.

I took one more deep breath, trying to steady my nerves. "I'm ready," I said, my voice barely above a whisper, knowing it was a lie.

The priestess handed me our most sacred ancient artifact, the Codex Conscio. A tome that contains immense knowledge of the universe, information from the beginning of time. The Codex was not to be taken lightly. Generations of Empyrean Queens passed down the powerful artifact, diligently protecting it.

The priestess placed her hands on my shoulders, closed her eyes, and began to chant. She led me to stand in front of a statue of an ancient Empyrean Queen. Her voice was low and melodious, filling the chapel with a sound that was both soothing and invigorating. As she chanted, I felt the energy in the room shift, becoming more intense and focused. I could feel her near me, and a shiver ran down my spine. Her soft chant became more intense. Her voice vibrated through my body, and I felt a sense of unease wash over me.

This was a spiritual ritual, meant to connect me with the energy of the universe and awaken my inner power. I felt a surge of heat course through my body, from the ancient tome, awakening the long-dormant parts of my being.

The priestess leaned in closer, her breath warm against my ear. "Let go, Elzaria. Let go of all your doubts, your fears, your insecurities. Surrender yourself to The Creators."

I nodded, feeling the weight of the priestess's words sinking deep into my soul. I closed my eyes and focused on the sensations in my body—the warmth of the oil on my skin, the sound of the priestess's voice, and the gentle pressure of her hands on my shoulders.

"War is coming," I heard a voice, unsure if it was only within my mind. "A great conflict that will shake the very foundations of the universe. It will trap the Empyrean people in the middle, and their fate will rest on the shoulders of their future Queen."

My heart sank as I heard their words. The visions of death flooded my mind as they spoke to me, as if I was seeing them firsthand. "Many will die, and you will suffer horrific loss. This is only the beginning. It will forever change your galaxy and the universe." Blood and laser fire tore through Arcadia, as if the gates of hell had opened up. Sweat ran down my back and I shook.

"Elzaria, the key to victory will lie within you." I gasped in surprise, my fingers tightening around the book's edges. The Creators had spoken to me directly, by name.

"You are the only hope for the survival of your people. You must accept this responsibility. Only then can you lead your people to safety."

The Creators fell silent, and I opened my eyes, taking a deep breath. The weight of the responsibility was almost suffocating.

The priestess continued to chant, her voice growing louder and more fervent. I felt a jolt of electricity shoot through me, igniting a fire deep within my core. I let out a soft yelp, unable to contain the raw emotions that were pulsing through me.

The priestess leaned in close, her voice low and urgent. "Embrace the power, Elzaria. Let it consume you."

I could feel my body responding to her words with each passing moment. Suddenly, I felt a surge of energy course through me, as if a dam had burst within me. I cried out, feeling myself surrender to the power of The Creators. It was as if all of history from the moment of creation flowed through my mind. The meaning of it all a vague understanding of everyone whose DNA I shared.

For a moment, I was lost in a sea of sensations, my mind completely consumed by the burning force. Weak in the knees. But then, gradually, my senses returned. The priestess was now standing before me, her hands outstretched, supporting me by my forearms.

"Welcome, Elzaria," she said, her voice filled with warmth. "You have taken your first step on the path to true enlightenment. The Creators give every queen counsel for the future of her reign. It's a private conversation between you and your makers. May you succeed in fulfilling their requests." She smiled serenely and guided me out of the chapel. Did she know the fate they predicted?

And with that, my journey as an Empyrean leader had begun, shaken and unsure.

I returned to my chambers to find the sweet scent of flowers filling the air with their heady fragrance. Laid out across several tables was a feast fit for a queen, with platters of delicious food and pitchers of sweet fruit wine. Adelaide was waiting for me, bustling about, preparing for my coronation.

Still visibly shaken by the experience, Adelaide handed me a glass. "Drink the wine, Elzaria. It will give you courage."

My coronation gown was a beautiful regal dress, with a long train that flowed behind me as I walked. The fabric was soft and silky, with intricate beading and embroidery that glittered in the light. I wore the finest royal jewelry, with a necklace of diamonds and sapphires that sparkled around my neck. Ornate slippers with tiny pearls and crystals adorned my feet.

As I approached my dressing table, Adelaide turned to face me, her eyes wide with admiration. "Elzaria, you look positively radiant!" She exclaimed; her voice filled with awe.

I smiled, feeling a sense of pride as I gazed at my reflection in the mirror. I was never one to wear fancy clothes or have the latest hairstyles or makeup. Mostly, I was plain and very average, average looks, average weight, average everything except for maybe my high cheekbones. But today, my reflection took me aback by how striking I appeared. I'm not sure why, but my eyes gleamed like blue ice crystals.

Then a wave of insecurity came crashing down on me. I knew that even though I may shine on the outside, on the inside smoldered the ugliness of self-doubt. What was wrong with me? Why was I allowing these dark feelings to overshadow a happy day, one I was born for?

Adelaide moved closer, adjusting the folds of my gown and straightening my necklace. "You truly are a vision of beauty. The people will adore you. Everyone at the banquet tonight will want to talk to you. You'll shine brighter than the stars above," her voice rapid and excited.

As we finished our preparations, we could hear music outside, signaling the start of the coronation procession. Adelaide reminded me to practice the oath one last time.

"I, Elzaria Eridani, do solemnly swear to uphold the traditions and laws of the Terrastrian people and the greater Empyrean Alliance. I vow to protect and defend our planet against all threats, foreign and domestic. I will wield my power with wisdom and integrity, always mindful of the needs of the Empyrean people. To serve with honor, integrity, and courage. To never waver in my duty, even in the face of great adversity."

The words echoed through the chamber, their weight seeming to settle upon my shoulders like a heavy cloak.

"To this end, I offer myself wholly and completely to the throne. To serve as its shield and sword, its voice and its will. To put the needs of the realm before my own, to sacrifice all for its safety and prosperity."

I could feel the power of those words, the magnitude of that responsibility, sinking deep within my soul. It was a burden that I would carry for the rest of my days.

"I will be a righteous leader, upholding the principles of truth and justice, and ensuring that all who seek refuge within our borders will be treated with fairness and compassion. I will be a champion of the oppressed and a defender of the weak, using my power to bring hope to those who have none. I pledge my life and my honor to the throne, to serve and protect our people, to lead with courage, and to do whatever it takes to ensure the survival of our planet. It is with a solemn heart, but also with great pride, that I take this oath. May the goddesses above bear witness to this vow, and may they grant me the strength and wisdom to fulfill it with honor and distinction." My voice was but a whisper as I finished.

My cheeks burned from the lies I felt I was telling. I desperately wanted each and every word to be true, and I could be that person. But I knew deep down I wasn't able to fulfill this role. My heart pounding in my ears, I felt my breathing become shallow and hitched.

I could hear the crowd drifting in from outside. The people of my planet had gathered to witness my coronation, to celebrate the beginning of a new era. I thought of the challenges that lay ahead and the dreams of war and death that my reign would bring.

Lost in a haze of terror, Adelaide guided me down the staircase and out through the massive glass doors to where the procession began.

At first, my legs felt like lead weights, unable to move. Then, panic overcame me and I bolted away from the procession line, heading in the opposite direction from the cathedral. The planet seemed to spin faster as I ran, my heart hammering in my chest. I could hear the fabric of my gown tearing as I stumbled and fell over a broken grate in the road. My heart sank, my legs felt unsteady, but I continued to run.

Leaving my train behind, I raced down alleyways, corridors, and back streets, desperate to escape. Someone was close behind me, their footsteps echoing loudly through the corridors. I could feel the fear and panic rising within me as I ran. My breathing labored; I scrambled over obstacles, never daring to look back.

The next thing I knew, I found myself at the spaceport. I often sought refuge from the constant public scrutiny of royal life in the cockpit of my sleek strike fighter. In space, I'm not Elzaria, the soon-to-be Queen, but Elzaria the pilot—the loner. Out there, amidst the awe-inspiring beauty of the universe in the boundless expanse of space, is where I'm at peace. I yearned to be there, to be free.

CHAPTER THREE

ELZARIA

The ladder to my strike fighter was still retracted, hanging tantalizingly out of reach. With a determined leap, I jumped for the lowest edge of the wing, just as a powerful arm clamped around my waist, wrenching me back to the ground. We landed in a heap, my breath hitching as I looked up into the face of my captor.

Nexion. The name echoed in my mind, along with the recognition of the man atop me. Even though he was only ten cycles older than me, he was the most formidable Empyrean Knight ever known, a force to be reckoned with. His reputation as a consummate warrior was undisputed, his devotion to the knighthood unwavering. Rumors in the halls often hinted at his likely future as Knightmaster.

Now, here he was, pinning me to the ground with a grip that left no room for escape. His eyes locked onto mine, a myriad of unspoken words passing between us. I could only wonder at what lay ahead, with my coronation abandoned, and Nexion, the likely future Knightmaster, holding me captive at the spaceport.

The few times I had been around him, he had been aloof and standoffish. Nexion was highly sought after and considered quite the prize by all the ladies on the court. For that matter, all women. I couldn't help but feel captivated by this warrior as his chest rose and fell inches from my face. His chiseled, muscular body appeared as if carved from stone, and his colossal stature commanded attention. His powerful arms and warm, tanned skin spoke of long days spent training under the sun. The clean-cut, tight-on-the-sides haircut framed his handsome features, adding to his authoritative presence. And then there were his massive hands, seemingly capable of wielding the heaviest of weapons with ease or ripping off his enemy's head. I felt awkward and almost insignificant in his presence, wondering if someone as plain as myself could ever attract the attention of such an attractive man.

Even though every woman fell at his feet, I had never heard of him showing any interest in any of them. I guessed it was because one day he wanted to become Knightmaster and would let nothing stand in his way. He's one of those that are married to the knighthood.

Nexion loomed over me, his jaw flexing in irritation. I gasped as I felt his weight shift, moving lower to settle in a more intimate place, his hard body pinning me to the ground, roughly grasping my wrists to either side of my head. His eyes were a piercing shade of green, and his lips were set in a firm line as he stared down at me. He had a look of stern resolve, and I could tell that he had no intention of letting me go. I couldn't help but notice the way his muscles rippled beneath his dress uniform as he pressed me against the pavement. His eyes bore into mine, cold and unyielding.

"Princess Elzaria, what in the name of The Creators are you doing?" He demanded, his voice low and dangerous.

I struggled to free myself from his grasp, but his hold was too strong as he trapped me beneath him. "I... I couldn't do it. I couldn't go through with the coronation," nervously stuttering my words, and as much as I didn't want it to, my lower lip quivered. "I'm not cut out for this. I can't lead our people into war."

Nexion's expression grew darker, and as he shook his head, his iron grip didn't waver. "You can't just run away from your responsibilities, Princess," he admonished, his tone leaving no room for argument. "You are the rightful heir to the throne. The only heir."

He paused, his eyes drilling into mine, letting the weight of his words sink in. "It is your duty to lead our citizens, to protect them from harm, and to ensure their survival." His voice resonated with unwavering resolve, his eyes unblinking. "You can't abandon them. You have an obligation to your people." The intensity of his words made my heart pound against my chest.

"I know," I swallowed hard, my voice barely above a whisper. The weight of my confession threatened to crush me. "But I'm not ready. I don't know how to rule a planet, much less the Empyrean Alliance."

Tears threatened to spill from the corners of my eyes. I blinked them back, locking my gaze with Nexion's. The vulnerability in my eyes reflected the turmoil within me, but I refused to let him see me cry.

"I don't want to lead our people into war and death." The words fell from my lips like a prayer, the plea of a frightened princess staring down a destiny she felt ill-prepared to face.

Nexion's fingers loosened slightly, but he still held me down. "You think I chose to be orphaned as a baby? You think I wanted to fight and kill for a living? No, *Princess*, I didn't. But sometimes we have to deal with things we don't want to. We have to play the cards life dealt us. It's the mark of a true leader. It's a part of life, your life."

"You have no idea what my reign will mean for Terrastria. I've had dreams foretelling a great war, ripping our planet to shreds and killing millions of innocent men, women, and children. A war that will spread across the entire universe, greater than those of our ancient ancestors. I will only bring death and destruction to our world. I must not become Queen!" I screamed as I hyperventilated.

Nexion looked down at me as if I had lost my mind. "You're running away from dreams? How weak and pampered are you if a bad dream can make you crumble?" He didn't even try to hide the disgust from his voice.

I didn't dare tell him The Creators had spoken to me through my dreams and then directly to me only a short while ago. He would think I was completely psycho.

I stared up at him, feeling a strange mixture of fear and admiration. Nexion was everything I wasn't—strong, confident, and self-assured. He knew exactly what he wanted and was willing to die for the throne. He valued duty and honor above all things and saw me as a fragile child.

Nexion yanked me to my feet as I twisted and bucked, trying to free myself, and cuffed my hands behind my back. My pulse hammered in my veins, fear and rage fueling a futile struggle against his iron hold. But Nexion was too strong, and he held me in place, his grip like a vice around my wrists.

I couldn't believe what was happening—the man was treating me like some common criminal. The cuffs bit into my flesh, a sharp, agonizing reminder of my predicament. A cry of pain escaped me, cutting through the tension like a knife.

"You're a traitor, Princess Elzaria," he hissed, his voice low and dangerous. "Abandoning your people. If what you claim to foresee happens, then you are leaving them to suffer and die in their time of need while you whine and complain. You're nothing more than a coward, a spoiled child who cares only for herself."

The audacity of his accusation ignited a fire within me. "How dare you accuse me of being a traitor!" I shot back, my voice trembling with rage. "I'm the rightful heir to the throne, and I have every right to decide whether or not I'm fit to rule!"

Nexion's eyes blazed with fury, his jaw clenched tight. "You are not fit to lead, Princess Elzaria. You're weak, self-centered, and cowardly. Rather than face your responsibilities, you choose to run away. You're a disgrace to the Empyrean Crown."

His scathing words caused tears to prick at my eyes, their weight crushing me. I had never felt so small and helpless in my life. As I stood before Nexion, I felt like a failure—a pathetic little girl who had never known true hardship or sacrifice.

I glared at him, my eyes burning with resentment. "You don't know anything about me," I seethed, my voice edged with venom. "You don't know what it's like to be in my position. You have no right to judge me."

He yanked me towards him, his solid frame pressed into mine, his words reverberating with a chilling threat. "I know more than you give me credit for, *Princess*," he intoned, his voice graveled and menacing. "And I won't let you run away from your responsibilities. You will face the consequences of your actions, and you will ascend to the throne, regardless of what you want."

I once more thrashed against him, trying to break free from his hold, but it was no use. Nexion was too strong, too determined, and he dragged me back towards the palace, his grip unrelenting.

Flipping around to face the giant, I stared defiantly into his eyes. "I'm no traitor! I must rewrite the course of history, alter the course of the future, or else many Empyrean people will suffer and die. The deaths of our babies, for goddesses' sake!" My voice reverberated with panic and raw emotion as I struggled to restrain my burgeoning telekinetic powers.

He took a step back, his eyes scanning my face as if truly seeing me for the first time. "What are you talking about, Elzaria?" His tone softened, betraying a hint of confusion. "What do you mean by changing the course of history?"

I took a deep breath, trying to gather my thoughts. "I've been plagued by visions," I admitted, my words barely rising above a whisper. "Visions of a cataclysmic war that will ravage our planet, its wrath spreading across the universe. A war that will destroy everything in its path, leaving only death and destruction in its wake. It will dwarf any war our ancestors have ever fought. Countless innocent lives, including our own people, will be lost. The Creators have spoken to me, revealing the horrors that await if I become queen."

Nexion's eyes widened in disbelief, and for a moment, he seemed to be at a loss for words. "The Creators?" He finally echoed, his voice matching my earlier whisper. "You mean the ancient beings responsible for the genesis of all worlds?"

I nodded, a strange cocktail of fear and excitement coursing through me. Nexion was the first person I had ever told about my visions, and it felt liberating to speak the truth. "Yes, they have spoken to me," I confirmed, my voice growing stronger. "They have shown me the grim fate that awaits if I become queen, and it's not pretty. I must find a way to prevent it, to alter the course of history."

"That's a lot to take in, Elzaria," he admitted, his voice filled with trepidation. "How do you expect me to believe such a thing? Why didn't you tell someone like the high priestess sooner?"

Swallowing hard, I desperately wanted to make him understand. "I didn't know how to explain it. I didn't want to sound like a lunatic. But I know what they forced me to see, the horrors I've witnessed. I know what will happen if I take the throne. I shouldn't rule, not when so many innocent lives are at stake."

Nexion looked at me for a long time and offered a slow, understanding nod, his voice quiet. "But we can't just ignore our responsibilities, Princess Elzaria. You can't run away and hope for the best. If these dreams, these messages from The Creators, are your reality and you believe them, then *you* need to find a way to prevent this war from happening."

"I know," nodding in complete agreement. "And I'm willing to do whatever it takes to prevent it. This is the only thing I could think of. If I cease to exist, if I don't become queen, then the future will be compelled to change. I'm more than willing to die right here, right now if it means altering the trajectory of the future The Creators have shown me." My body shuddered beneath his grasp.

Nexion looked at me with a mixture of disbelief and empathy. "You truly believe this, don't you?" He murmured, his voice softening. "You genuinely believe that if you didn't exist, it would change the course of history and prevent a war."

I bit down on my lip, stopping it from quivering as I nodded in response.

He took a step closer to me, his eyes unwavering. "Princess Elzaria, you were born for a reason," his voice poured over me, low and reassuring. "You are the only one who has seen this vision, and that means you are the only one who can fight back. Destiny has chosen you."

Nexion placed a comforting hand on my shoulder, his grip gentle and reassuring. "You can't just outrun fate, Princess," he insisted with a gentle intensity, his voice soft but firm. "You were born to lead the Empyrean people, to protect them from harm. This is your burden to bear, far beyond the glimmer of the throne or the weight of the crown. It's about safeguarding innocent lives." Spoken as the loyal knight he was.

His words echoed in my ears as I looked at him, my heart thundering in my chest. "But I'm not ready," I murmured. "I don't know how to rule, how to lead. I'm not strong enough."

Nexion pulled me closer to him, holding onto both of my arms.

"Strength isn't a prerequisite, Princess," he consoled, his voice a gentle sigh. "You need to have the will to learn." He drew a deep, thoughtful breath. "I've witnessed the aftermath of societies left without a strong leader and seen the chaos, the destruction, the grim reality of other planets at war. I know personally what it's like to be powerless, to be at the mercy of others. That's why I joined the Empyrean Knights. I wanted to make a difference, to protect innocent people from harm."

He paused, his eyes searching mine. "Elzaria, I was a filthy, hungry orphan before the Knights took me in. I had nothing, nobody. I was a scraggly kid, a scrawny street rat, stealing food and always living in fear that I would get caught or beat up. I was never loved or cared for as you have been. But when I found my place among the Knights, I found my destiny. I found a purpose. And I know you can too."

Silence claimed my voice as my mind buckled under the avalanche of conflicting emotions and thoughts. Nexion must have sensed my hesitation. Gently, he removed the handcuffs and turned me to face him. Without realizing it, my hands gripped my chest. The thought of Nexion as a starved, lonely child sliced my heart in two. If he could rise from those desperate circumstances, then maybe I could make a difference?

"I may not agree with everything you've done or said, but in destiny, I'm a firm believer. I believe that you have the power to change the course of history and prevent this war from happening. You have a unique gift, Princess, and it's time to embrace it. It's time to take your rightful place as queen of the Empyrean people."

My eyes found his as a surge of resolve stirred within me. He was right. I could no longer afford to evade my fate. It was time to come to terms with it, to master the art of ruling and guide the Terrastrian people towards safety. What other choice did I have?

"I'll do it," my voice soft but resolute. "To prevent this war from happening, I'll do whatever it takes, and I'll send prayers to the goddesses for the strength and wisdom to make a difference."

A grin warmed Nexion's face as his hands cupped my cheeks. "May your prayers become reality."

Nexion's eyes bore into mine and he leaned in closer, his lips teasingly close to mine. Captured within the emerald depths of Nexion's gaze, I felt the boundaries of our separate existences blur. A silent force seemed to pull us towards each other, an invisible thread woven by the hand of destiny, drawing us inexorably closer. The air between us crackled, and I felt a jolt of electricity shoot through my body, and before I knew it, our lips met in a tender kiss. I felt a raw hunger rising within me, a need that I had never experienced before.

His lips were warm against mine, and I felt a sudden rush of desire course through my body. Nexion's arms wrapped around me, pulling me closer to him as the kiss deepened. His firm hold anchored me in the tumultuous sea of sensations as I savored his unique taste on my tongue. My heart raced with an unfamiliar rhythm. His lips, an exquisite blend of softness and strength, sent waves of hunger surging through my core. It was an innate craving, deep-rooted and insistent, that stirred the very essence of my being, a hunger that no feast could satiate.

An invisible force seemed to pull us together, not merely a product of desire, but the manifestation of something older and more profound, as if the universe itself knew that somehow we were intrinsically linked. The magnetic intensity, the almost palpable energy that hummed in the air around us, it was more than just physical attraction; it was the resonance of two souls intertwined.

But as quickly as it had started, the kiss ended, and Nexion pulled back slightly, his expression unreadable.

My heart raced, a mixture of emotions coursing through my entire being as Nexion stepped away. The lingering taste of him on my lips was both troubling and tantalizing. His gaze spoke volumes as the regret turned his skin ashen. "I'm sorry," he murmured, his voice so soft I could barely hear him. "I shouldn't have done that. Knights don't kiss their queens."

For a moment, I was stunned, unsure of what to say or how to react. Part of me wanted him to kiss me again, to lose myself in the intoxicating desire that was still pulsing through my most intimate places. However, I knew we couldn't afford such distractions, not with the coronation looming ahead.

"It's okay," I reassured, forcing a smile. "We don't have time for distractions right now, anyway. We have work to do."

Nexion snapped his head up, his eyes flickering with a mixture of shame and craving. "You're right, forget that ever happened," he said, stepping further away from me. "We need to focus on the coronation."

The words were like a bucket of ice water being poured over me, shattering the moment and plunging me back to cold, harsh reality. His words echoed in my mind, a haunting reminder of the stark, impenetrable barriers that kept us apart.

It was a law as old as time, etched in the hallowed scripts of the *Celestial Creed*. The Empyrean Knights were forbidden from any form of romantic involvement with the royal family. It was a rule meant to prevent the dilution of power, the crossing of political and class lines that could lead to chaos and disorder. It was meant to keep a clear hierarchy and separate roles to ensure the smooth functioning of our society.

If he was promoted to Knightmaster, he would lead and oversee all other knights. He would be the chief military advisor to the queen and would be involved in all military planning and decision-making. He would also be responsible for training and educating the up-and-coming knight candidates, ensuring that all knights within our realm followed the *Celestial Creed*.

Every Empyrean Knight, like Nexion, had sworn an oath to abide by *The Creed*. They pledged their allegiance to the throne and vowed to uphold the honor and integrity of their position. Any violation of these sacred principles would be met with severe consequences.

Nexion, despite his formidable stature and unmatched prowess on the battlefield, was no exception to this rule. A knight like him kissing a royal, even in a moment of shared vulnerability, blatantly defied *The Creed*. It was a transgression that could lead to the ruination of his career and service in the knighthood. He could face severe penalties and even a death sentence for treason if he was caught.

His apology hung heavy in the air between us, an echo of regret and a stark reminder of the barriers that kept us apart. But in his eyes, I saw something that contradicted his words. A depth of emotion that belied his stoic exterior. A hint of desire, quickly masked behind the stern countenance of a knight duty-bound to his *Creed*.

It was clear that Nexion was torn between his sworn oath and the unspoken chemistry brewing between us. He had always been one to uphold the rules, the dutiful knight whose dedication to the knighthood was unwavering. His disobedience was an anomaly, a momentary lapse that could cost him everything he had worked for.

Yet, as I looked into his eyes, I couldn't help but wonder if this transgression held more than a momentary lapse of judgment. If, beneath the disciplined facade of the promising future Knightmaster, there was a spark of rebellion ignited by a longing that threatened to upend the order we were both shackled to. It was a spark that, however enticing, could only lead to disaster.

As much as I longed for a man like Nexion, for the touch that had sent ripples of warmth coursing through me, I knew we were walking a dangerous path. This was a forbidden road, one lined with harsh consequences and irrevocable damage. Yet, as I gazed into his emerald eyes, a part of me dared to hope that perhaps there was a way around the *Celestial Creed*, a way for our paths to converge without leading to ruin. But I also knew that it was an audacious thought, a dangerous desire that could destroy us both. We were captives of our positions, bound by the chains of our respective duties, forever separated by the unforgiving edicts of the *Celestial Creed*.

I nodded, feeling both disappointed and relieved. The kiss had been exhilarating, but it was better to focus on the tasks at hand. We had a war to prevent, and I needed to be the best leader I could possibly be to make that happen.

Together, Nexion and I hurried back toward the palace, my mind racing with thoughts of the coronation and the future of our planet, our galaxy. As we walked, we found the train from my dress and a stab of regret tore through my heart. I had ruined the beautiful work Adelaide and all those who had worked so hard for this sacred day had done. My face flushed with embarrassment.

Nexion, seeing my discomfort, guided me into a private back entrance to the castle I had never seen before. As we walked through the dimly lit hallway, I couldn't help but feel a sense of unease. The walls were lined with flickering torches, casting eerie shadows on the stone walls. He had a firm grip on my arm, rapidly steering me through the twists and turns of the castle's hidden passageways.

Ascending a steep, uneven stairway, the smooth sole of my shoe slipped. Nexion caught me in his arms, protecting me from falling.

He held me for a moment longer than necessary, his eyes locked onto mine. His normally stoic expression replaced with a look of pure longing. He gently let me go, stepping back and creating a distance between us. But even with the space, I could feel the magnetic connection. Magnets hold an irresistible attraction that compels them to seek one another out. There's a tangible force between them, an invisible bond that neither can deny. When they're near, they seem to resonate in anticipation, a magnetic intensity of subtle vibrations as they inch closer, drawn by the magnetic pull.

I could feel the attraction, the positive end of one magnet being drawn to the negative end of another. There's a spark, an electrical charge that passes between them as they near. It's a force of charged particles, a sensory symphony that ends with the gratifying 'click' of connection, a union that feels as natural as breathing.

Nexion cleared his throat, breaking the silence. "Princess," he began, his voice filled with a potent mix of thirst and contrition. His eyes, those emerald green eyes, bore into mine with an intensity that was almost unbearable. "There's something I need to say to you."

"Yes, Nexion?" His name breathlessly escaping my lips for the first time. It was as if his name was an expensive bourbon, smooth and rich gliding over my lips, leaving them warm from the caress of its heat eliciting my tongue to moisten them.

The air around us seemed to hum with the potency of that utterance in our quiet surroundings. His eyes widened in silent surprise, the emerald depths reflecting the torchlight, capturing my gaze. I watched as an almost undetectable shudder passed through him, his powerful frame momentarily weakened by the unexpected thrill of hearing his name spoken with such raw desire. There was a pause as he savored the sound of his name.

His jaw clenched as he gathered his thoughts. When he spoke, his voice brimmed with a sincerity that made my heart stop in anticipation.

"I can't explain what's just happened between us, but I burn for you, Elzaria," he confessed, the words coming out in a rushed breath, his gaze never leaving mine. "But as much as every fiber of my being screams to be with you, I can't betray my oath."

His words hung heavily in the air between us, every syllable echoing off the stone walls.

"My duty defined by the *Celestial Creed*, my allegiance to you as your protector—it's a responsibility I can't neglect. It's a burden I chose to carry when I swore to serve and protect the Queen," he continued, his voice filled with the want of something he knew he could never have. "I would be doing you and our people a great disservice if I allowed my personal feelings to interfere with my duty."

I could see the truth of it in his eyes. His staunch commitment to the knighthood.

"I can't allow myself the luxury of love, not when there's so much at stake," he finished.

As he stepped back, there was a finality in his eyes, a resolve to uphold his duty, no matter the cost. And I knew then, the hands of fate might have connected us, but it was our duties that were destined to keep us apart.

We moved quickly and before I knew it; I was standing at the door to my chamber, my hand on the lever, nervous to enter. I knew I must apologize to Adelaide and hoped that she would forgive me and could repair the damage I had done to my gown and appearance.

As I pressed my hand down on the lever, I realized Nexion had vanished without making a sound. His sudden absence was jarring, leaving me somewhat disoriented. A pang of longing twisted in my chest, an unspoken wish that things could be different.

I lingered in the hallway, letting the cool metal of the door handle seep into my skin. The reality of our situation hung over me like a cloud, and I felt the weight of it all pressing down on me. His touch, his voice, the shared understanding of our precarious positions, all gone, replaced by the silence and solitude of the empty hallway.

As I prepared to face Adelaide's disappointed gaze, I sighed, releasing the breath I hadn't realized I'd been holding, and pushed the door open.

Immediately, I saw her sitting on the chaise at the foot of my bed, sobbing. I ran to join her. Kneeling at her feet, I begged her forgiveness.

"Adelaide, I'm so sorry." My voice trembled, struggling to stay composed as tears threatened to spill from my eyes. I held her hands, my apology as sincere as the pain that filled my voice. "I was wrong to flee. To let fear dictate my actions, which was far from acceptable. I was scared and overwhelmed, but that's no excuse. I hope you can forgive me for my behavior."

Adelaide looked at me, her eyes red from crying. "Oh, Elzaria," her voice a mix of relief and happiness. "I'm just glad you're back. We were all so worried about you."

Guilt gnawed at my heart, knowing I made Adelaide worry. "I'm sorry to have caused you so much trouble. Can you help me fix my hair and makeup? And my dress, too."

Adelaide rose, her fingers deftly brushing away her tears. "Of course. Now, let's get you ready for the coronation." With that, she led me to my dressing table, where she set to work fixing my makeup and hair. Soon, I looked almost as good as before.

Just as she was adding the final touches, Adelaide's hand paused on the train of my dress that had been cruelly torn away. "Oh no," panic filled her eyes. "What happened?"

Shame washed over me as I confessed how the fabric had been caught on a sharp grate during my flight. "I'm so sorry, Adelaide. I'll understand if you can't fix it in time."

Adelaide gave me a reassuring smile. "Don't worry, Elzaria, I've got this." With nimble fingers, she quickly sewed the train back onto my dress, and within minutes, I was ready for the coronation.

As I stood in front of the full-length mirror, I couldn't help but feel a sense of awe at the transformation. I looked every inch the queen, regal and powerful. Adelaide had truly worked her magic.

"Thank you, Adelaide," I turned to her and squeezed her hands.

"Your Highness, you're going to be a wonderful queen," she said, tucking away a small strand of stray hair. "You have the strength, the intelligence, and the compassion to be an outstanding leader. And you have the sworn support of the Empyrean Knights and the other nobles. You're not alone in this, Elzaria."

CHAPTER FOUR

ELZARIA

Once again, Adelaide escorted me down the grand staircase, out the glass doors, and to the beginning of the procession line. This time, I was ready for the coronation, or as much as I would ever be.

The cheers of the people lining the street echoed in my ears as I made my way down the line, trying to keep my spine straight. I felt a sense of commitment, hoping that I was ready for the challenge ahead and that The Creators would give me the guidance I needed. The sun smoldered in the late afternoon cerulean sky, casting a golden glow on my skin as I walked. Along the way, I noticed faces filled with joy and hope, and I realized they had faith in me.

At the end of the procession line, I saw the grand doors of the cathedral standing wide open, beckoning me inside. The enormous cathedral towered over everything in sight, its immense spires reaching up towards the sky. The walls were crafted with intricate stone carvings, paintings, and stained-glass windows that reflected the light of the sun in prismatic hues. Intricate carvings and sculptures adorned the walls, telling a story of ancient battles and triumphs.

I took a deep breath, feeling a surge of nervous energy, as I stepped forward, ready to take my place as queen.

As I walked up the steps leading into the cathedral's narthex, I could feel the eyes of everyone upon me, their gazes filled with curiosity. The high priestess, her acolytes, and various elders proceeded forward.

As I crossed from the narthex into the nave, the Empyrean Knights greeted me, standing at attention on either side of the aisle with their swords drawn and held in front of their faces. Nexion was at the forefront, his expression solemn and self-assured.

"Are you ready, Your Highness?" He asked, his voice so low that no one else heard.

I nodded, feeling the weight of his gaze on me. "I am," I said, my voice steady and only for him to hear.

Without another word, Nexion and the other knights presented their swords in a fluid movement, pointing them in front of me a few inches off the stone floor. In unison with precise and synchronized movements, the knights raised their swords high into the air, creating an archway of gleaming blades. I walked slowly beneath this symbolic gesture, my head held high as I passed under.

I could feel the significance of tradition bearing down on me. The sword ceremony was a symbol of loyalty and allegiance, a tradition that dated back centuries. As I passed beneath the archway, I knew I wasn't just accepting the support of the knights, but was walking in the footsteps of history itself.

As I emerged from the arch, I proceeded down the aisle toward the dais. Deep blue sapphire and white fabrics adorned the intricate silver filigree-covered dais standing in the center of the cathedral. Tall white marble pillars surrounded by a low railing with steps leading up to it framed the dais. Candles flickered on either side of the altar and two tall lanterns provided additional light. An ornate stone throne sat in the center of the dais, inlaid with silver ornamentation.

The high priestess, who stood before the altar, held her hands clasped in prayer. Behind me, nobles and commoners alike filled the cathedral, their eyes fixed on me, awaiting the ceremony to begin. The silence was deafening, a blanket of stillness stretched across the cathedral. Only disrupted by the occasional sound of rustling fabric as someone adjusted in their seat. It was a thick, palpable blanket that wrapped around the room and smothered any hint of sound. It picked at my nerves and heightened my senses.

The priestess motioned for me to approach her, and I did so, feeling the soft velvet of the sapphire blue carpet beneath my feet.

I kneeled before her, clasping my hands, joining her in silent prayer.

After a long period of quiet reflection, the Priestess guided me, "Rise, Elzaria, servant of The Creators and chosen by divine providence."

I stood as the Priestess summoned me forward with the ancient Codex Conscio open and resting upon her palms. I placed my hands on the ancient tome and felt the energy from it enter me. A surge of power coursed through my veins. It was a sensation unlike any other—a mix of fear and exhilaration that left me feeling both alive and terrified all at once.

Through a mind link, The Creators once again showed me the horrors of the prophesied war. The destruction and chaos that will ensue—it was almost too much to bear. As the images of devastation flooded my mind, I felt a fire ignite within me. A burning determination to do whatever it took to prevent this future from coming to pass. But despite the overwhelming sense of dread that threatened to consume me, I refused to falter. I refused to show any signs of weakness in front of those assembled.

I knew they were counting on me to be a stalwart queen. I knew they expected me to be the leader they needed through this unforeseen dark time and to emerge victorious on the other side. And so, I stood tall, my emotions locked away behind a wall of iron will.

With a final command to be faithful, The Creators withdrew their mind link. And as their presence faded from my consciousness, they left me alone with my thoughts and the weight of the world upon my shoulders.

Despite the monumental task ahead of me, I refused to give up. I would do whatever it took to ensure our survival. Even if it meant sacrificing everything I held dear.

The Priestess's expression told me she knew what I had just endured. She smiled and took a long, deep breath, allowing me a moment to regroup.

"Your Royal Highness, raise your right hand and make your oath of fealty to the Empyrean people as you stand before The Creators, the Royal House, and all those you serve." The Priestess demanded.

I raised my right hand and began the oath that just hours before I had practiced in my chambers. This time, my voice was loud and robust. Unwavering as I punctuated each command with a strength of will. As the last words left my lips, the cathedral filled with our anthem. The Priestess closed the tome and handed it to my mother, the now former queen, for safekeeping.

She took my left hand as an attendant draped a heavy deep blue velvet robe trimmed in white fur over my shoulders and fastened it closed with a large sapphire brooch. Other attendants held the edge of the robe and my train as the Priestess and I made our way to the throne. Reaching the throne, I still couldn't believe this was happening to me. It all seemed so unreal, and I wondered if this was how my mother had felt. I carefully turned and sat upon the throne, seeing my parents' proud expressions.

The Priestess took the crown from its pillow and held it high, calling upon the congregation to witness the crowning of their new queen. She approached me with the crown in hand, and

I sat with my shoulders square to receive it. She affixed it to my head, using the braids to secure it. The crown was heavy, made of xenochronatium, the universe's most valuable alloy, and encrusted with precious gems. As it settled onto my head, I felt the weight of responsibility intensify.

"May The Creators bless you and crown you with glory and honor, so that through your leadership you spread goodness, righteousness, justice, and peace throughout the universe. May your reign bless all who serve under it. I am at your service, Your Majesty." The Priestess blessed me and bowed deeply before me.

Trumpets blared, announcing my coronation to the kingdom. The sound echoed through the cathedral, reaching the far corners of the room. The congregation erupted into cheers, their voices lifting up in unison as they celebrated me as their new queen.

I looked out over the crowd, feeling a sense of awe and overwhelming gratitude. These were my people, and I was their leader. It was a responsibility I didn't take lightly. I made a silent vow to do everything in my power to protect them.

Despite the weight of the crown and the responsibilities that came with it, I felt a spark of something unfamiliar.

I found myself unable to shake the feeling that had taken root within me. I felt a call to walk through a door that had been opened. And though I didn't yet know where that path would lead me, I knew I had to follow it.

Next, it was my duty to declare the successor to the role of Knightmaster. He would be my stalwart guide through the evil that The Creators had foretold. I had received comprehensive dossiers on several of the most senior members of the Knights of the Empyrean Crown and had chosen the knight with the most battle experience over the more politically connected ones. An attendant carefully handed over my freshly forged royal sword, its unexpected weight surprised me, reminding me of the responsibility I was about to shoulder. The murmurings in the crowd stilled once more, anticipation hanging thick in the air.

I cast my eyes over the row of Knights before me, standing rigid, their faces a collection of calm resolve and silent expectation, mindful of the counsel my advisers had given me on whom to select. Yet, as I lifted the sword, an inexplicable force seemed to guide my arm, diverting from the course laid out by logical choice. I felt a power pull me towards the unassuming Knight. Deep within my mind, I felt The Creators' unseen hands molding my decision, nudging me towards a path that defied all conventional wisdom. The tip of my sword came to rest, aimed at the heart of an unsuspecting figure amidst the seasoned knights—the one they least expected—Nexion.

His eyes widened in surprise as I continued to point the sword at him. I wasn't only naming the new Knightmaster, but I was also defying the norms, choosing a less experienced knight over seasoned veterans. The Creators' will flowed through me, their invisible strings tugging at the edges of my consciousness, leading me on this scandalous path. And in that moment, under the watchful gaze of The Creators, Nexion wasn't just a junior knight anymore; he was my Knightmaster, the one chosen by fate and the higher powers that governed us. His hand instinctively went to his chest, as if to protect himself from the sharp point of the blade. Nexion's face grimaced in shock and disbelief as he realized what was happening. The nobles and my family looked at each other questioningly, unsure of what to make of this unexpected turn of events.

But as he saw my intention, his expression yielded into one of understanding. As I stood steadfast with the sword pointed towards him, I was certain that this was the right choice. I felt the approval of The Creators deep within my mind, and I knew Nexion was the one who would lead our Knights into battle and protect our kingdom against any threats. I had no doubt that Nexion was the right choice for the role of Knightmaster, but at what cost? The Creators had intertwined our paths even further, making the choice for me, a choice that seemed to resonate with the rhythm of my heart. But how would I explain this to my court, to the people of Terrastria, and most importantly, to Nexion himself?

Nexion slowly stepped forward, his eyes fixed on me. As he kneeled before me, I placed the flat of the sword's blade on each of his shoulders, naming him the new Knightmaster.

"By the power vested in me by The Creators and the Royal House, I name you, Nexion Fortisbellator, Knightmaster of the Empyrean Crown. Rise now as the leader of our Knights and protector of our people."

The crowd applauded reticently, and even though I knew this choice was a surprise to everyone, I felt a sense of satisfaction at having complied with the decision favored by The Creators. Nexion rose to his feet, and I handed him my sword as a gift.

"May this sword serve as a symbol of your duty and honor. May it always guide you in your quest to protect our kingdom and our citizens."

Nexion took the sword and bowed deeply to me. "I am honored to serve as your Knightmaster, Your Majesty. I will do everything in my power to protect you, the Royal House, and our kingdom."

When the ceremony reached its conclusion, I proceeded down the nave. The congregation, nobles, and Knights bowed and curtsied in my honor, expressing their congratulations and well-wishes. I couldn't help but feel overwhelmed by the sheer magnitude of the moment. I proceeded through the narthex, out the grand doorway, and descended the steps to a hover-car awaiting me. The attendant held the door open for me, and I stepped inside, taking a seat, the heavy velvet robe trailing behind me. Aides gathered my robe and train, wrapping them in a tight bundle, and laid them around my feet. My parents joined me, and the car rose into the air and soared towards the castle. I looked out across the city, taking in the beautiful sights of its shimmering light. The sun was setting, casting golden light over the spires and stone buildings, and I felt a sense of joy at the beauty of it all.

My parents hugged me, their eyes shining with pride.

"You did it, my dear," my mother said, embracing me tightly. "You are now the Queen of our Empyrean people."

I hugged her back, feeling happy that the formality of the coronation was over. My father turned to me, a somber expression on his face. "Remember, Elzaria," he said, his voice low and serious. "With great power comes great responsibility. You must always put the needs of your people before your own."

I nodded, understanding the weight of his words. "So long as I can look to you two for direction, I'll be all right." I knew that being the queen wouldn't be an easy task and wanted all the help I could get.

The hover-car pulled up beside the enormous glass doors and our staff greeted us. Several of my aides swept me out of the car and up to my chambers, where they helped me out of all the royal regalia and into a new gown for the banquet. The new gown was much less formal and hugged my curves in all the right places. They freshened up my makeup and restyled my hair, allowing my long blonde tresses to flow down my back.

Adelaide came into my room and curtseyed deeply. "Your Majesty, how may I be of service?"

"Adelaide, please don't be formal. You've always been family to me. I need you to be the caregiver and confidant you've always been. Oh, and always call me Elzaria, that's an order." I giggled as I tugged her into a bear hug.

She hugged me back, and I saw the tears of love and devotion well in her eyes.

"So, you chose Nexion to be Knightmaster, huh?" She questioned as she gave me a sideways glance.

"You know I hadn't planned for him to be my choice, but as the knighting ceremony began, I felt drawn to him in a way I can't describe. I think the choice is the right one and that The Creators will bless him."

Adelaide burst out with a loud, boisterous laugh, causing her body to shake with the force of it, and she doubled over in amusement.

"What's so funny?" I couldn't help but ask.

"The thought of him tackling you in all your finest and slapping handcuffs around your wrists. I guess your pre-coronation jitters paid off after all." She said, still laughing and drawing out the giggles of the others in the room.

"So, someone told you about that, hmm?" I asked. My face instantly turning a bright shade of red, but I couldn't help myself as I too broke out in uncontrollable laughter.

Barely able to breathe, I told them all about our encounter except for the parts about how he kissed me, and the doomsday talk of war. They especially loved hearing about when my train ripped off and about when he jumped up, caught me by the waist and slammed me to the ground. Followed by how he sat on me with my wrists held against the pavement next to my ears. They had a hard time imagining the always serious and dutiful knight ever doing something like that.

After our fits of giggles subsided, we all relaxed and fell back into our comfortable roles. I loved these women as if they were family.

"I bet you're excited to see Nexion at the banquet tonight. I wonder if he'll ask you to dance?" Bethany wondered as she organized and tidied away the accouterments of my previous gown and regalia.

I had to admit; I was looking forward to seeing him and finding out how he felt about being named Knightmaster; it had to have been a shock.

"Ooh, I know, Seraphean will be jealous! She has had her eye on Nexion for a long while now. She can't stand it when you get something she doesn't." Adelaide reminded me of my cousin on my father's side.

Empyreans don't usually have cousins since our birthrate is so incredibly low. Most Empyreans feel blessed if they can have one child. My father, though, has twin siblings, a younger sister and a younger brother, which is even rarer. Long ago, a virus attacked the reproduction organs of Empyreans, causing a change in our molecular structure. Now, most Empyrean babies are boys. The rarity of girls only strengthened our esteem and value for the Empyrean matriarchy.

"I think Seraphean's mother has always been jealous of your father because he was first born and rose to not only become Prime Minister but also the Queen's consort. Seraphean and her mother have some serious issues!"

Nodding, I agreed with Adelaide. "I've noticed that Seraphean hasn't been around as much lately. I hope she's found better uses of her time other than annoying me with her spiteful words."

I sat and watched as Adelaide and the others dressed up and primped for the banquet. The royal stewards invited those of the household staff, who weren't needed to prepare or provide help, to attend the banquet.

Once ready, the group of us headed for the banquet hall, laughing and holding hands as we approached. Suddenly, everyone went silent, dropping their heads and standing back. I knew the reason. Protocol. As soon as we neared the public space, I straightened my posture and put on my *queenly* demeanor. I took a deep breath, preparing myself for the grand entrance. The doors opened, and the sound of trumpets filled the room. The formality of it all sent an exasperated shudder down my back. I stepped inside with an unapologetic stride, my heart pounding in my chest. All eyes were on me as I made my way to the head table, where I would sit with the most important and inevitably dull guests.

My eyes scanned the room, looking for the Knightmaster, and didn't see him.

The banquet was a lavish affair, with tables overflowing

with food and drinks. I tried to engage in small talk with those at my table, but my mind kept wandering—to Nexion. I felt a strange mix of excitement and nerves to see him again. To my disappointment, though, he never arrived. Feeling a bit dejected, I excused myself from the table and wandered over to the balcony overlooking the city.

Lost in my thoughts, the echoing rhythm of footsteps approaching from behind snapped me back to reality. I turned, expecting to see Adelaide or one of the other girls, but instead, it was Seraphean.

"Elzaria, have you heard the news?" She shot the question at me, a spark of mischief glinting in her eyes.

My brows furrowed, a touch of anxiety fluttering within me. "What news?"

A smirk tugged at her lips. "About Nexion. Word is he's left the castle, and has decided to live at the training academy, in the Citadel Avendel. You know the place, practically on the other side of the planet." She released a teasing giggle.

"What? Why would he do that?" A knot tightened in my stomach as a lump formed in my throat.

Seraphean gave a shrug of arrogant amusement. "I'm not sure, but I heard a rumor that he wanted to focus on his duties as Knightmaster. Gossip has it he felt he couldn't do that while living here in the castle with all the distractions."

I nodded, as my heart sank, a grim certainty clutching me. There was more to it than his newfound duties; this move was about me, it had to be.

"Did he say anything else?" My voice wavered despite my effort to sound steady.

Seraphean hesitated for a moment before answering. "Well, I heard he felt ashamed of what happened between you two before the coronation. He's a knight, believes he should have shown more restraint. He doesn't know why you chose him as Knightmaster and feels bad that he overstepped the more senior knights. You've caused quite a rift amongst the knights in order to get a man's attention. Desperate much?" Her words laced with poison, she let out a shrill laugh, taking another sip of her drink.

I felt my cheeks flush with embarrassment. Had Nexion really left because of me? I couldn't believe it. I'd been hoping to see him again, to talk to him and maybe even dance with him. But now, it seemed like he had misconstrued everything. I knew there was more to it than that, but I didn't press her for details. She was already so smug.

"Thank you for telling me," I responded, trying to keep my voice unaffected.

Seraphean nodded and left me alone on the balcony. I stood there for a few moments, ruminating over how things could've gotten so twisted. The evening had started off so well, but now I couldn't shake the feeling that this was a bad omen.

Walking through a side door, hoping to sneak away from the banquet, a sweaty hand grabbed my face, covered my mouth, and pulled me to his chest. While he was bigger than me, he wasn't very large for a man. I struggled to free myself and he kneed me in the back.

"Don't move, bitch." He commanded, as I felt the blade of his knife press against my throat.

I grabbed onto his arm with both hands, trying to keep the blade away from me. He shoved me forward, and I struggled against him. His legs tangling in my long skirt, we fell, the knife slicing open my shoulder. Losing his grip on my mouth, I let out a blood-curdling scream for help. Just as he swung the knife at my face, a huge guy grabbed him and threw him against the wall. I scurried to my feet and ran back toward the banquet hall, shouting for help.

Chaos broke out as three guards whisked me away to my chambers and others went to capture my assailant.

One of the guards held a towel over the cut until our onsite doctor could come.

"Your Majesty, do you know the man who attacked you? Have you seen him before?"

"No, it all happened so fast. I don't remember much about him, and I don't think I've ever seen him before. Thank the goddesses for the guy who got to me so fast and threw him off. Who was that? Is he okay?"

"Yeah, he's fine. I heard on my comm that he beat the shit out of the asshole who attacked you. Oh sorry, forgive the language, your Highness."

"Don't worry about being formal with me. So, who is he?"

"He's a young guy who's working here until he leaves for the Knights Academy, starting in a couple of days. He's a good kid. I can't remember his name."

"Please find out who he is and give him my thanks. Let the Captain of the Guard know I want to reward him for his bravery. He'll know what to do. Have they determined who the guy is that tried to kill me or why?" I asked, as the reality of what happened began to sink in.

Before he could say more, my father burst in with the doctor close behind.

"Oh, my goddesses, Elzaria, are you okay?" He started to hug me when he froze, seeing the blood seeping up on the towel. He turned to the doctor and shoved him toward me.

The guard let go, and the doctor took over. Even though the cut was fairly deep, it wasn't an issue for our Empyrean medicine. Before I knew it, the doctor had numbed the area and applied a nano patch.

"You should be mostly healed by the morning," he assured me and everyone else milling about my rooms. "I think it's time for the Queen to get some rest." He demanded, clearing the room, leaving only my mother and father.

"Elzaria, I want to know exactly what you were doing before

the attack. How the hell did that guy get you out the side door with no one noticing? Someone has got a hell of a lot of explaining to do." Father was livid.

"I went out onto the balcony to get some air. You know, it's been a stressful day. Not long after I went out, Seraphean joined me and was her usual nasty self. I wanted to leave the banquet without causing a fuss, so I headed for the side door and that's when the guy grabbed me. It all happened so fast."

"Seraphean? Her mother told me she was out of town and wouldn't be taking part in the coronation or banquet. That's odd," Mother replied.

"You never know with Seraphean. But I'm exhausted. We can worry about this more tomorrow."

"Of course, sweetheart. I've posted extra guards in the area. You'll be safe, don't you worry."

I closed the door behind my parents as they left and leaned back against it. Finally, I was alone.

It had been a long day with a lot of unexpected twists and turns. I couldn't believe how defenseless I was against my attacker. It was only by chance that someone was near enough to save me. I hated knowing that I had to be saved and had no means of protecting myself. Maybe I am as delicate as everyone treats me. The thought unnerved me.

My emotions were on edge and spilled over as silent sobs wracked my body. I knew I couldn't keep up the facade of a strong Empyrean queen any longer. I flopped down on my bed and let the tears fall freely down my face. When there was no more to shed, I dampened a cloth with cold water and pressed it against my swollen eyes, blackened with streaks of the makeup that no longer defined them.

I had only been the Queen for a few hours and had already made a mess of things. Now everyone thinks I'm an emotional child that runs away, that I give promotions to those who do me favors or to men I'm attracted to, and that I'm helpless, unable to defend myself in my own home. To top it all off, I feel like an idiot for selecting Nexion as Knightmaster, even though the choice wasn't mine. The Creators had practically forced my hand. Of course, only I knew that.

What a mess and, as usual, Seraphean had brought out the worst of my insecurities. I don't know why I've always let her get to me. Since we were little kids, she's always known how to trigger me.

I couldn't believe that Nexion had left without even saying goodbye. It felt like a betrayal, even though I knew it was his duty as Knightmaster to focus on training the other knights. I don't know why his leaving even bothered me. I hardly knew him. Sure, I'd seen him around the palace, but he was just another knight, at least until today.

Undressing, I felt vulnerable and alone. I slipped into my nightgown. Every little sound in the room seemed to echo in my ears, and the replay of everything that had happened in my mind only made me feel worse. As I closed my eyes, I remembered the feel of Nexion's lips on mine, his touch, his scent. The memory of our encounter filled me with a desire I couldn't explain. I couldn't help but wonder if things would've been different if he hadn't kissed me. Would he still be here?

But deep down, I knew that there was more to it than that. Maybe he regretted kissing me, or maybe he thought I was desperate for his attention. Oh, goddesses, how embarrassing, and now he was my Knightmaster. The advisor I would need to rely on most during a time of war. Now... now he thinks I'm just some foolish girl.

As I lay there in the darkness, I couldn't help but think about all the things I wanted to say to him. But it was too late. He was gone.

Eventually, I drifted into a restless sleep. In my dreams, I saw Nexion's face, his eyes filled with regret.

CHAPTER FIVE

ELZARIA

The sound of urgent knocking on my chamber door jolted me awake from a restless sleep.

"Elzaria, wake up," the voice demanded.

I stumbled out of bed groggily, rubbing my eyes, which were still clouded from sleep and swollen from last night's pity party. When I opened the door, Adelaide stood there, her eyes wide with fear.

"What's happening?" I asked.

"The Vaith have attacked a small Empyrean outpost near the outer edge of the galaxy. You need to hurry and get down to the war room," she said in a flustered tone.

I felt a knot form in my stomach as the news sank in. The Vaith were notorious for their violence and their disregard for the Federation's laws. If they were attacking Empyrean outposts, it could only mean trouble.

"Adelaide, how do you know this?"

"You know how the rumor mill is around here. Someone

from the waitstaff probably overheard when delivering drinks to the officers gathered down there. They've been meeting for a little while."

"What? Why are you telling me this and not someone from the military or one of my advisers?"

"Oh, ah, I don't know. Maybe they thought you needed your rest after yesterday's big events. How are you? How's your shoulder?"

"I'm fine. Stop babying me." I said, taking out my frustration on her.

"If my mother were still queen, would they have woken her with the news?"

"Yes, of course."

"Ugh."

As I dressed, my mind raced with thoughts of what could be happening. Were the Vaith planning an all-out attack on Empyrean territory? Were they looking to start a war? Why was Adelaide the one informing me of the attack?

I rushed into the war room, and I saw the senior military officers were already there, huddled around a large holographic display. They snapped to attention and gave me a quick bow, annoyed by my arrival. I had the sense that they weren't happy about having to report to me. They probably believed that I was incompetent and that they should report to my mother and father, the now Queen Emeritus, and the Prime Minister.

I couldn't really blame them. I'd only been the Queen for half a day. Although I had studied military warfare and tactics in school, I had zero experience.

"What's the situation?" I asked, trying to assert my authority.

One officer turned and looked at me with a dubious expression. "The Vaith attacked a small outpost on the outer edge of the galaxy. We've sent a team on a reconnaissance mission."

He and the others resumed their conversation as if I wasn't there.

"What are the casualty reports? How long before we hear back? What do we know so far about the objective of the attack? Is it normal for you to make these decisions without consulting with the Queen?" Echoing their annoyance, unable to hide the sarcasm from my tone.

The officials exchanged glances, clearly taken aback by my questions. But I refused to let their condescension get to me. I refused to back down and was determined to prove myself as a capable leader, even if it meant ruffling a few feathers.

"We're still awaiting reports on casualties, Your Majesty," the officer replied, his tone more respectful now. "The reconnaissance team has not yet arrived at the outpost, but we expect to hear from them within the hour. As for the purpose of the attack, we're not sure. The Vaith have been known to send assassins after people at Empyrean outposts in the past, but it's unusual for them to attack so brazenly in a public place and to do so at the same time as your coronation. I think they're sending a message." One replied.

"They've been encroaching on our territory for some time now, and tensions have been rising between the Vaith and those living along the outer rim," another officer explained.

I nodded, taking in the information. "And why wasn't I consulted before sending out the reconnaissance team?"

There was a moment of uncomfortable silence before one officer spoke up. "Your Majesty, we didn't consult with you because we thought you would be busy with the coronation festivities. And, er, the attempted assassination. We didn't want to bother you with details of military matters. We apologize for this misunderstanding."

I clenched my jaw, feeling a surge of anger. Did they really think so little of me? "I am the Empyrean Queen, and as such, I expect to be informed of any matter that concerns the safety and security of our people. Is that clear?"

The officers nodded, looking chastened. "Yes, Your Majesty."

"Good. Now, let's get to work," I said, taking a seat at the large conference table. "We need to come up with a plan before the Vaith make their next move."

The officers quickly got to work, discussing possible strategies and tactics.

A couple of hours later, the reconnaissance team finally reported in, sharing that the Vaith had left the outpost and four members of one family were dead. The attack didn't seem to be part of a larger, more nefarious plot, but rather a personal vendetta between some lower levels of the Vaith and some individuals on the Empyrean outpost. It appeared to be a personal score to settle between Vaith bottom feeders and members of a corrupt Empyrean family who had a deal go bad. It was a relief to know that it wasn't an all-out attack on our territory, but I couldn't help but feel uneasy about the situation. The fact that the Vaith were conducting personal vendettas within our galaxy made the situation even more unpredictable.

As the officers relaxed, I remained tense, ever cognizant of The Creators' warnings. I requested they provide me with all the details regarding the current military needs around the galaxy. It was clear to me that we needed to be better prepared for future attacks, even if they were just personal scores.

"I want to know about any potential threats or conflicts, and be informed of any military actions taken in the future," I said, my voice firm and confident.

"Of course, Your Majesty." One General replied.

On my way back to my chambers, I stopped by the Captain of the Guard's office to follow up on last night's attack.

Captain Draven was so absorbed in his reading that he didn't notice me at his door, so I knocked. "Sorry to interrupt, but I wanted to touch base with you about the guy who attacked me last night."

"No interruption at all, Your Majesty. I was just reviewing the evidence we had collected. Looks like the guy is a well-known psychopath. He's got a troubled past but never tried to kill anyone. He claims he was paid to get you last night and was given instructions on how to enter undetected, but can't tell us who hired him. Says they paid him in loose credits and never met the guy. He's locked up and won't be causing any more trouble. I'll keep you updated on the search for the guy who did this and we've increased palace security."

"Thank you, Captain Draven." The thought that someone paid a guy to kill me and that they knew how to get in and around the palace sent an icy chill down my spine. I hated feeling vulnerable.

I returned to my chambers and asked Lorentzian Svenzen, one of the greatest Empyrean minds ever, to come to see me. He was a historian and physicist, along with being one of my closest friends. He was a straight shooter, and I always respected his opinions.

When Loren arrived, he gave me a big hug.

"Good to see you're okay. I heard about the attack."

"Sounds like the guy was a nut-job. He's in custody, but now I've got even more babysitters watching over me." Laughing, I tried to play it off as no big deal. Changing the subject, I explained to him the situation at the Empyrean outpost. I also told him how our military officers lacked faith in me. "I think they're accustomed to working with my mother and father. They didn't think I would be interested in the Vaith attack, if you can believe that."

"Give it time, Elzaria, they will come to know you," Loren replied, knowing I could be a bit of a hothead.

"Loren, there's something else you need to know."

He raised one eyebrow, recognizing my tone of voice.

"Before the coronation, I panicked and ran away. I almost left in my strike fighter."

"What?" Loren demanded, shocked to hear that from me. "How did I not hear about this already?"

"I don't know. Everyone else seems to know. And just wait. There's more." I cautioned him, shaking my head and rolling my eyes. "Nexion is the one who came after me. I tried to fight him off and leave, but he threw me to the ground. Even though I continued to fight back, he had his orders to return me and was hellbent on doing so. I don't want to get into all the details of our conversation, but suffice it to say he understands why I ran, and I came to my senses and returned."

"Ok, so what's the big deal? A little embarrassing maybe, but cut to the chase. What's really bothering you?"

"Promise not to tell a soul." He nodded, giving me the side-eye. "Nexion kissed me. It's hard to explain, but it felt like much more than a simple kiss and I know he felt it too. Although, his eyes filled with regret almost immediately, and he apologized. We both brushed it off like it was nothing, but then he left Arcadia directly after my coronation. So, maybe he's more upset about it than I thought, you know, *The Creed* and all."

"Maybe he needs a little time to clear his head. I doubt a man like him would think much of a simple kiss. Maybe he's a little overwhelmed because you unexpectedly named him Knightmaster." Loren replied, never one to judge me, but still curious enough to say something.

"I think he believes the kiss was a major mistake on his part because I'm royalty. Someone told me he felt embarrassed and that he believed he had failed to live up to *The Creed*. But they didn't mention a kiss, so I don't know. Maybe it was because he handcuffed me. And worse still, I was also told that I had caused a huge riff between Nexion and the senior knights because I named him Knightmaster. The person accused me of only promoting him to 'get a man,' which tore the heart out of me." I tried to explain it all to Loren the best I could.

"Why did you promote him, Elzaria? We hadn't discussed him. Do you have any idea if he is even qualified?"

"Loren, do you remember me telling you about those bad dreams of war and destruction that I've been having?"

He tilted his head and nodded slowly, uncertain of what was to come.

"Well, I haven't been completely honest with you. They weren't just dreams. They were messages sent from The Creators."

Loren looked at me like I was nuts. I knew he would. Wouldn't anyone? I put my hand up in front of his face to stop him from saying anything.

"Now hold on, before you think I'm crazy, let me explain. I have always felt connected to The Creators. I think that's why I can read the ancient Codex or at least some of it. In the last few decas, they've been much more direct but never addressed me personally until yesterday when they mind-linked with me."

I knew I was blowing Loren's mind. I grabbed his hands and implored him to believe me.

"You have to trust me. I need you to believe in me."

"I do Elzaria. We've been best friends since we were kids. There's no way I think you would make this shit up. Go on. Please finish. I promise, I've got your back."

The relief of his words gave me the assurance I needed to continue.

"During the coronation at the Knighting ceremony, I lifted my sword, and it was as if it had a will of its own. It pointed squarely at Nexion's heart and that's when I felt The Creators guide me to select Nexion as the next Knightmaster. I knew it was the right thing to do. It was the only thing I could do. I can't explain why, and you're right, I have no idea what his qualifications are."

Loren and I sat on the sofa in my living room, me on the armrest and he in the center. We didn't speak for a long while.

"I don't know how this got so complicated so fast, but obviously it has. I need your help. It's important that I have my Knightmaster nearby to provide me with counsel regarding security matters and military affairs, but I also need your help as well, Loren. I want you to give up your position at the university and become my Chief

Advisor, responsible for providing me with strategic guidance and advice on matters of state, diplomacy, and policy, as well as overseeing the work of other advisors and staff. My mother's team is so much older and I don't trust them the way I do you. Will you do it?"

Loren's mouth fell open. I had overwhelmed him with all the information and by my request. He dropped his face in his hands and rubbed his temples.

I held my breath in anticipation of his response.

Out of nowhere, and so out of character for him, he dramatically dropped to one knee and bowed his head. "Your Majesty, Queen Elzaria Eridani, I am at your service. My allegiance to you will never falter. I will follow you to the ends of the universe and always do my best to advise you wisely."

Laughing, he rose and pulled me to my feet, hugging me so tightly I couldn't breathe. I couldn't help but giggle at his teasing sincerity.

"Dammit Loren! Look what you've done. You've got me giggling like a little girl."

"Don't worry, I'll always be here to put my queen in her place." He poked me in the ribs, making me squeal.

He laughed and so did I. I already felt the tension drop a few notches. With Loren by my side, I felt more confident and relaxed.

"Thank you, Loren. I couldn't do this without you."

"You won't have to. I'm always here for you. Oh, and I don't think you should tell anyone about The Creators speaking directly to you. That kind of power may draw the wrong type of people to you."

There was a loud knock at the door and when Loren opened it, an Ensign I recognized from my earlier meeting burst into my chambers.

"Your Majesty! We have a situation. An unknown vessel has entered our territory and is heading towards us. We've tried to hail them, but they're not responding."

I felt my anxiety rise. Was this another attack?

We rushed down to the war room where other officers had gathered.

"Bring up the visual on the main screen," I directed.

An image of a sleek, white spaceship filled the screen. I didn't recognize the design, but it was definitely not an Empyrean vessel.

"Have you scanned for weapons and shield strength?" I asked.

"There's no sign of weapons or shields, Your Majesty," an officer reported.

That made no sense. Why would a spacecraft enter our territory with no defenses?

"Send a team to board the ship and bring their leadership to me. And make sure they're not armed," knowing the risk.

The officer nodded and left to carry out my orders.

I turned to Loren, who was already by my side. "What do you think this could be?"

"I don't know, Elzaria. But we need to be cautious," Loren replied.

We waited anxiously for the team to board the ship and return with whomever it was. As we waited, I couldn't help but wonder what kind of trouble was ahead, but was determined to face it head-on.

Eventually, the team returned with a group of alien people I had never seen before. They were humanoid in appearance, with silver skin and glowing blue eyes. As they walked into the room, I could feel the tension rise.

One of them stepped forward, bowing deeply before me. "Your Majesty, I am Prime Minister Mortimer Vexor. We come in peace from the planet Dracore located in a small galaxy that you include in the Quadran Alliance," he said, in perfect Empyrean.

I raised my eyebrows in surprise. "You speak our language?"

"Yes, Your Majesty. We have been studying your culture and

language for some time now. We've traveled a great distance to meet with you."

I couldn't help but feel skeptical. "And why have you come to meet with me unannounced and without invitation?"

The Dracorian hesitated before replying. "We come with a plea for help. Our planet is in great danger, and we require your assistance. We came in desperation. I have sent multiple communiques requesting to meet with the Empyrean Queen and have had no response."

I exchanged a look with Loren. He was skeptical, too. "What kind of danger?"

"Our planet is under attack by a powerful enemy force. We believe they are your enemy as well." He cleared his throat before continuing. "It all began when they discovered we have a plentiful amount of tritanzium. As you know, the rare and highly sought-after mineral is used to develop explosive devices, as well as advanced energy weapons. Initially, they paid us, and we delivered their orders to a substation not far from our world. But now, they have moved their own people and equipment onto our world in a hostile takeover. They're devastating our planet and stealing the tritanzium. We have been fighting them for a couple of cycles, but our resources are running low. We need your military aid to help us evict them from our planet."

"Who are these invaders? Why do you think they need so much tritanzium?" I asked, concern growing in my gut that the Vaith were taking steps to build massive weapons caches.

"They aren't who they told us they were when we first started doing business with them. They've gone to great lengths to hide their true identity by using shell corporations and operating secretively. However, we managed to infiltrate their shipping facility and found deliveries headed to the Maffei galaxy." He needn't say more. We all knew the Maffei galaxy had long been a stronghold of the Vaith.

I frowned, unsure of what to do. I didn't want to ignore the plight of a people in need, but I couldn't risk putting the Empyrean people in danger by provoking the Vaith.

"I'll need to discuss this with my advisors before deciding on how to proceed. Please, make yourselves and your crew comfortable while we deliberate," I said, dismissing the Dracorians and instructing one of our officers to see to their needs.

It was late, and I hadn't eaten all day. I turned to Loren. "Please arrange for a meeting first thing in the morning with the war council and my senior advisers. Ask my parents to attend as well. I'm sure they're trying to let me take command and not get in the way, but if the premonitions I told you about are on the horizon, we're going to need everyone's help. Request Nexion to return from Citadel Avendel to take part as well. My Knightmaster should be with me, helping me analyze intelligence reports, seeing what our forces and those of the Vaith's are capable of, and making plans and strategies for if the Vaith up their attacks. All of us need to discuss how to respond to the Vaith's hostile takeover of the Dracorian tritanzium mines and the possible buildup of weapons caches. First, though, verify what Prime Minister Vexor has told us. We need hard evidence if we have any chance of convincing the legislature to take any action."

"Will do. I'll send you an update on what time we'll meet."

We each went our separate ways. It had been a long day, full of uncertainty.

Before I opened the door to my chambers, I smelled the savory aroma of a hearty stew wafting into the hall. Hopeful my nose was correct, my stomach growled. I entered and found a covered dinner on a small table near the window. Next to it was a gorgeous bouquet of white flowers, which I recalled seeing at last night's coronation banquet. Adelaide always took such good care of me.

I ate way more than I should have and collapsed in my bed.

CHAPTER SIX

ELZARIA

The door to the private meeting room closed behind us, plunging the room into a hushed silence. I stood at the head of the table, feeling the weight of my new role as Queen of the Empyrean Alliance. My parents took their seats on either side of me, their faces etched with concern. Loren stood at the back of the room reviewing a holographic display, his eyes scanning the files with an intensity that belied his calm demeanor. While the others filled the remaining seats around the conference table. Nexion was notably absent.

I cleared my throat, drawing everyone's attention to the matter at hand. "As you all know, there has been a recent attack on one of our outposts, as well as reports of a hostile takeover of the Dracorian planet. We have confirmed much of what Prime Minister Vexor has shared with us to be truthful." My voice was steady despite the worry. "These incidents demand our immediate attention and a powerful response. For more reasons than these alone, I believe the Vaith are preparing for war. One that will cause devastation across the universe."

After a moment of silence, Mother spoke up, her voice heavy with concern. "Elzaria, I share your worries about the recent attacks. The danger is real, and we must be prepared to respond. And I agree that our kingdom's security should always be our top priority, but doesn't that seem extreme?"

How was I going to convince them to take me seriously? Convincing them that The Creators had spoken to me when not even the High Priestess had ever claimed such a privilege. It seemed an impossible task. How would they ever believe The Creators had spoken to me, directed me? It was a risk I was going to have to take. The alternative was unbearable—a war like those of the olden times, which horrors had been immortalized in our songs and history lessons. The memory of these lessons painted a grim image of death, a past I couldn't allow to repeat.

Yet, I steeled myself, prepared to face their reaction to what I was about to say. After all, everything hung in the balance, and it was up to me to tip the scales towards peace.

"I know I'm inexperienced, but all I can do is be honest and forthright with you. The reason I'm concerned about a war against our Empyrean people is because The Creators warned me of its coming. At first, they sent me harrowing dreams of battles and the falling of our great cities. Then on my coronation, they addressed me directly. Yes, I know this sounds almost impossible to believe since The Creators haven't spoken with anyone since the ancient wars a millennium ago. But they did, and we need to prepare if we have any hope of changing the hands of fate."

The room fell into stunned silence as my words hung in the air. Even my parents and most trusted advisers looked at me with skepticism. I could see the disbelief etched on their faces, but I knew what I had experienced. I took a deep breath and continued, "I know it's a lot to take in, but we can't ignore the warning signs. We need to prepare now before it's too late." I knew they all thought I was out of my mind, but I couldn't let that stop me from doing what I believed was right.

Loren was the first to break the silence. "I understand that this may be difficult to swallow, but we can't ignore the possibility of war. Our history is riddled with conflicts. We must take this seriously. And I believe her when she says The Creators spoke to her. Why would she dare say something this provocative otherwise? The Vaith have always been drawn to violence and corruption. They have mostly kept to themselves within the confines of their own galaxy, but we've recently seen the Vaith aggressively pursue their wants by moving out beyond their own territory. They've taken over the Dracorian mines and we suspect they're amassing weapons. We must prepare for the worst-case scenario."

He walked beside me, leaning on the conference table. "And let's not forget about the ancient wars. The Creators spoke then, and they're speaking to us now. We can't afford to ignore their warning."

I felt a swell of gratitude towards Loren. He was always there to back me up when I needed it most. I knew I could always count on him.

My mother looked at Loren with a hint of surprise, and my father remained silent while several others mumbled questions about what I had divulged. Finally, Father spoke up. "While it may be a stretch to believe The Creators have spoken to you, Elzaria, I will agree that we need to look into the matter and see what we can learn about the Vaith's intentions."

I let out a sigh of relief. At least my father would listen to me, even if he didn't fully agree with me. "Thank you, Father. I know it's hard to believe, but I wouldn't lie to you about something this important. In the meantime, I feel we must prepare our forces for any eventuality."

"Yes," Father agreed, his firm jaw staunchly set. "We can't afford to be caught off-guard. We must strengthen our defenses and remain ever vigilant against those who wish to do us harm."

The military officers and advisers in the room exchanged uneasy glances as they listened.

"Your Highness, with all due respect, we have no concrete evidence of Vaith aggression. We can't mobilize our armies based on a dream and a vision from The Creators." General Aron, a grizzled veteran, was the most vocal opponent. "We don't need to waste our resources and disrupt our economy just because a young Queen claims to have had a vision from The Creators," he said, his voice dripping with sarcasm. "There's no evidence that the Vaith are preparing for war. They could just be expanding their territory. We don't need to jump to conclusions."

Commander Kiera, on the other hand, disagreed. "The Vaith have always been a threat to our security, and now they're openly attacking our outer-rim planets and most likely amassing weapons. We can't afford to be caught unprepared. We need to fortify our defenses and make sure we have the firepower to repel any potential attack."

The other military officers and advisers were split between the two sides, each arguing passionately for their position. Heated debate filled the room with angry voices.

But as the discussion went on, it became clear we couldn't ignore the possibility of war. The Vaith were a threat and were becoming more aggressive. The Empyrean Alliance couldn't afford to ignore the aggression.

In the end, they agreed to consider that the Vaith were up to no good and to move forward with additional reviews of the potential for war. Unfortunately; however, I didn't convince any of them to make concrete plans for protecting Terrastria or our Alliance partners. It wasn't a full endorsement of my concerns, but at least it was a start.

As the meeting wound down, we agreed to send a small research team to evaluate the Dracorian situation. To prevent the Vaith from moving tritanzium through Quindarian Federation space, a patrol fleet would monitor the shipping lanes and intercept their ships. We also agreed to establish the Dracorians as trading partners, putting the Vaith on notice that we would take a close interest in their tritanzium production. Their reaction will be very telling.

Everyone except my parents and Loren left with their assignments.

Mother reached out to place her hand on mine, offering her support. "Elzaria, we have confidence in your abilities to lead us through these difficult times. We'll stand by your side, whatever course of action you decide to take, but tread lightly, sharing information about The Creators speaking to you. You wouldn't want people to think we have a *Mad Queen*."

"Thank you, Mother," I sighed, wishing there was some way to earn her confidence and the respect of those in Empyrean leadership.

"Yes," Father chimed in. "We're ready to do whatever it is you need."

"Elzaria, perhaps it is time to consider sending a patrol fleet to protect other vulnerable outposts and planets within our alliance as well," Loren offered.

"An excellent suggestion," Mother agreed. "But we must also be mindful of our own defenses and the cost to our economy."

"I agree," Father said, his brow furrowed in concern. "We must maintain a balance between offense and defense at a reasonable cost."

I nodded, my mind racing with thoughts of potential strategies and the concern no one was taking me seriously. The anxiety over the threat of war, coupled with everyone treating me like I was a child with an overactive imagination, had my telekinetic powers buzzing. Now wasn't the time for them to become known. A worry lingered in the back of my mind. I had never trained to use my telekinetic abilities and wielding out-of-control powers came with significant risk. If I wasn't careful, I could pose a danger not only to myself but also to those around me. I knew I needed to learn how to control my powers better, especially when I was stressed. The assassination attempt was a wake-up call for me to take my safety seriously, which meant I must learn how to defend myself. Not rely on others for my safety.

After today's meeting, I realized it was going to be a struggle to earn the respect of my knights, military members, and advisers, when suddenly an idea hit me. The Empyrean Knights were the most respected and brave warriors in the universe, their training legendary, and I remembered hearing that this cycle's class would soon start. What if I were to train as a knight? I don't recall a queen ever doing something like that, but... why not? In ancient times, there were warrior queens.

Becoming a knight would give me the confidence and skills to lead the most formidable Empyrean warriors into battle. If they saw I was willing to train and fight alongside them, they would be more likely to respect me. But more importantly, though, this could be my chance to master my untamed telekinetic powers. I've got them—somewhere in me, that power is there—but it's like a sleeping dragon. I've no clue how to wake it up without causing havoc. The Empyrean Knights were known for their discipline and focus, and I knew they could help me develop my skills. Perhaps they could guide me, teach me control, so I could use my powers rather than fear them. But did I stand a chance of surviving? I've heard some insane stories about their training. My muscles ached just thinking about it.

My athletic record was, to put it mildly, less than what it would take to be a fierce warrior. The prospects of handling energy blades, high-tech bows, sleek daggers, and swords were more than intimidating. How would someone like me, more of the bookish type, a dancer, survive the brutal training?

This decision was fraught with risks, of course. What if I didn't have the mettle, the endurance, the sheer will required? The thought of failure was daunting. And yet, the potential benefits were too tantalizing to ignore. If I could actually pull this off, it would be a radical achievement. Of course, it could also be a spectacular failure. It was a decision that could well change the course of my reign. There was an allure to the thought of testing my limits, pushing my boundaries, and proving that I was more than just a "young Queen". Yes, there was uncertainty and fear, but there was also opportunity.

At that moment, I decided I would become an Empyrean Knight.

One thing was for sure, this wouldn't be a walk in the park. But if I managed it, if I could prove to myself and everyone else that I could do this, it might be worth every terrifying, exhilarating moment. I'd become a decent pilot, secretly flying beside those in our space force. If I could do that, how hard could the Knight's Academy be? Deep breath, Elzaria, here goes nothing.

"Wait, before you leave," I called out, halting them as they pushed back their chairs, "I would like to propose one more thing. Considering the current situation and the assassination attempt, I believe it's crucial that I attend the Knight's Academy in the Citadel of Avendel."

My parents froze, gaping at me in disbelief as I continued, "I believe it is my responsibility as the new queen to protect Terrastria, not just through diplomacy, but by becoming a strong and skilled warrior that our knights and military will respect."

My declaration hung heavily in the air, and I could see the surprise written across everyone's faces. They exchanged glances, no doubt trying to process the unexpected announcement.

"Absolutely not! That would be politically scandalous." Losing her normal cool demeanor, my mother's voice rang out sharp and clear. "Our knights have sworn to protect the royal family, not the other way around. They serve the crown. This notion of yours, it's unthinkable, it's a foolish idea. You can't be serious, Elzaria!"

I met her gaze squarely, strength surging within me. "Yet, Mother, our ancient queens and even our revered Creators were elite warriors. The tales of their valor are part of our history, immortalized in our songs. I refuse to be just a protected little girl anymore. I can't—won't—be that person."

"Elzaria, this is absurd! Training as a knight is no easy task, it's brutal. You've never shown any aptitude for such... rigor," Father's worry-laden voice added to the dissent, his gaze wary. "You're a scholar, not a fighter. You can't just decide to become a knight."

I took a deep breath, ready to make my point. "And that's exactly why I need to do this. Yes, I'm a scholar. Yes, I have a ton to learn. But isn't that what we've always talked about? Never stop learning, right?"

"But this, Elzaria," he gestured helplessly, "this is extreme."

"Is it, though?" I insisted, mustering every ounce of resolve. "You taught me to confront my challenges, not shy away."

"But Elzaria," he replied, "This is completely different."

"No, it isn't!" I shot back. "You taught me to never be afraid of a challenge. To face it head-on. I need to do this. Not just for me, but for Terrastria. For us."

There was a pause before Loren spoke up. "Elzaria's right. This might not be the traditional path for a queen, but it could be good for her. Good for a royal family whom many think are out of touch with the citizenry." Loren's voice cut through the tension. "Elzaria, you're the queen. It's uncharted territory, but if anyone can navigate it, it's you. If this is what you believe is best for Terrastria, then you should do it."

His words felt like a lifeline amidst the storm of their resistance. I smiled at him, grateful for his support.

Looking from my father to my mother, I added, "I'm not asking for your permission. I'm telling you my decision. I will train with the Empyrean Knights."

"Elzaria, are you certain?" my mother asked, her voice softening, her eyes searching mine for any hint of doubt.

"Absolutely," I replied, my voice steady despite the flutter of nerves in my stomach. "I know the training won't be easy, but I'm more than willing to face the difficulties."

Loren was quick to voice his approval. "Elzaria, the value of your sharp mind and academic accomplishments has already been proven throughout your studies at the university. Now, I think it would be beneficial for you to undergo a physical training regimen so that you can become proficient in combat and warfare tactics. This way, you will know how to protect yourself and others if ever needed."

"May I remind you all," Father cautioned, "attending the Academy comes with its own risks, and we must consider the potential impact on our kingdom's stability if anything happens."

"Father, I understand your concerns," I assured him. "But I truly believe that this is the best course of action for me."

Mother hesitated before speaking up. "Elzaria, your safety is our utmost priority. However, if you are determined to go, we will support your decision. Somehow, we'll figure out a way to make this happen. We were young once, too. I remember when your father was a young knight before entering the political fray." I swear she blushed and gave my father a flirtatious glance, batting her eyelashes. I couldn't believe it. It was so out of character for her.

"But there must be a formally declared temporary regent in place to oversee the kingdom in your absence." She finished, regaining her normal cool demeanor.

"Your mother can serve as regent. It will almost be as if she had never left. We have long served as a powerful duo," Father suggested. "This would ensure continuity in leadership and decision-making."

"Thank you both. I know how hard this is for you to swallow. I know I can rely on you each to assume your previous duties and oversee the alliance during my time at the Academy. Everyone respects you both and will hardly notice my absence." I said, grateful for their willingness to support my decision even though they disagreed with it. "Loren, I trust you will continue to advise and assist them in their roles on my behalf."

"Of course," Loren pledged. "I will do everything I can do while you're away."

As our meeting ended, I felt more confident in my decision to attend the Knight's Academy. The support of my parents and the encouragement from Loren only strengthened my resolve. I knew that, with their help, I could focus on becoming a skilled warrior, a leader to respect.

Leaving the room, I took one last look at the faces of those closest to me. I knew my decision would change not only my life, but the fate of our entire kingdom.

CHAPTER SEVEN

ELZARIA

Later that evening, on my way to dinner, I ran into Loren in the passageway as he was leaving his office. Just a couple of days had passed since Nexion's promotion to Knightmaster, and we hadn't exchanged a single word. The memory of his kiss lingered in my mind. I wanted to talk to him about not only the kiss we shared, but, more importantly, his resentment towards me for naming him Knightmaster. I wondered what he would think about me attending the Knight's Academy.

"Loren, any word from Nexion? Why did he skip out on the meeting?"

Loren fell in step beside me, his face serious. "I've reached out to him, Elzaria. Even requested he return to Arcadia."

"And?" I snapped my fingers impatiently. "So? What's the deal?" My voice tight with apprehension.

"He declined," Loren replied, his face darkening with frustration.

The floor seemed to shift under my feet. "He... what?"

Loren sighed. "Turns out, you were right. Nexion felt the kiss was out of line for a knight." Loren looked everywhere but at me as he continued. "Also, he's not thrilled about his promotion. He thinks you overlooked more senior knights, causing hard feelings among them. He's worried they might think his promotion was due to... your feelings for him."

I exhaled loudly, feeling my cheeks flush with embarrassment. I knew my decision to name Nexion as Knightmaster had been controversial, but I believed in his abilities and never doubted his loyalty. It hurt to know that he might think otherwise.

"Feelings for him? What feelings? He kissed me! This is ridiculous. And since when does the Knightmaster just flat out refuse his queen?" Hoping there was some way to compel Nexion to return.

Loren rubbed the back of his neck, a sure sign he was uncomfortable. "Normally no. This situation is different. Nexion's always played by the book. He has a reputation for steering clear of romantic entanglements, especially those with the Royal House. Can you blame him?"

Shutting my eyes, I absorbed his words. Yes, it was a bitter pill to swallow, but it made sense. Despite the sting of rejection, I understood, I guessed. Nexion needed space, time to process his new responsibilities as Knightmaster. I could give him that, couldn't I?

"Very well," I conceded, forcing myself to accept the situation for what it was.

"You know he will never in a million cycles allow me to enter the Knight's Academy. I'm going to have to figure a way around the Knightmaster." I said, changing my direction to my father's office as an idea popped into my mind. "Let him know not to worry about it and to continue his duties from the Citadel," I said over my shoulder, leaving Loren to go the other way.

I quickly made my way to my father's private office, knowing that he would be the only one who could help me with my plan. As I walked in, he was buried deep in his datapad, oblivious to the world. Clearing my throat, he looked up.

"Father, I need your help," I said, coming to stand in front of his desk.

He lifted his gaze, eyes glinting with worry. "What seems to be the matter, Elzaria?"

"You know I want to attend the Knight's Academy, right?

"Yes," he nodded.

"Well, I must do so undercover," I declared, inhaling deeply. "I don't want anyone to know of my true identity."

Father leaned back in his chair, his expression growing curious as he considered my request. "And why is that?"

"Because I don't want Nexion to find out who I am," I explained. "I think it would be better if he didn't know that I was attending the Academy."

"Elzaria, attending the Academy under an assumed name carries a great deal of risk," His tone cautious, he leaned back in his chair. "You won't have any protection, and no one will know who you are. What if something were to happen to you?"

"I understand the risks, Father," I replied, determination in my voice. "But I need to do this."

"You understand you won't have guards to protect you, nor any comforts of home. No one will know you're a royal. And worse, I'm worried you may be injured or even killed."

"I understand the risks, Father," I repeated, my voice steady. "But I can't let fear hold me back from my destiny. Becoming a skilled warrior, and attending the Academy, is the only way I can do that. I have to stand on my own two feet and not receive any special treatment if anyone is going to take me seriously. I know that in the past a few women have completed the knight's training, so I know it's doable. We both understand that if anyone at the Academy knows who I am, they'll act differently towards me. Which one of the guys would be willing to punch their queen in the face?"

"Very well," Father said, nodding his head thoughtfully. "Let me see if I can help you with your plan. I'll try to create a fake identity for you to ensure that no one knows who you really are. I've done this for your mother and I in the past so that we can travel more freely."

"Thank you, Father."

"But you must promise me one thing."

"What is it, Father?" I asked, anxious to hear his request.

"You must promise me that you will stay safe, no matter what," he said firmly. "And if at any point you feel that your life is in danger, you must tell the Academy's Headmaster and return home immediately."

"I promise," I said, feeling a weight lifted off my shoulders.

Father sighed, running his fingers through his hair. "Very well, but we need to be careful. We can't have anyone finding out who you really are in the middle of training. That would embarrass us all."

I nodded in agreement.

"We need to move fast, and we can't let anyone know what we're up to," he said. "I'll talk to your mother and get her help."

"Alright, let's meet tomorrow night so I can slip away under the cover of darkness," I said as I walked around the desk and gave him a peck on the cheek.

The next morning, I got to work changing my appearance. I began by sending Adelaide and my other attendants to run errands throughout the city. They would be gone all day, giving me the privacy I needed to transform myself into someone unrecognizable. As I watched Adelaide leave, I let out a sigh of relief, happy to have some time alone.

I started by dying my hair a dark brown color, dried it, and tied it in a simple tail at the nap of my neck. I quickly shed my clothes, exchanging them for a simple worn tunic and breeches. Then I headed for the castle's military barracks to find clothing a typical knight would wear. Hopefully, some small enough for me.

As I made my way through the bustling corridors of the castle, I felt a sense of excitement growing within me. This was my chance to prove myself, to show that I was more than just a pampered princess. I felt driven to hold my own at the academy, to earn the respect of my fellow knights, and to prove to Nexion I could stand on my own two feet.

When I arrived at the barracks, a group of knights who were busy cleaning their weapons greeted me. They looked up as I entered, their eyes narrowing as they took in my worn clothing and unfamiliar face.

"What do you want?" One of them asked, his voice gruff with suspicion.

"They sent me to gather the dirty clothing. Should I come back another time?" I asked, dropping my head submissively.

"No, but be quick." He demanded.

Stuffing random items into the bag I had brought, I slipped into the supply room unnoticed. There were shelves of everything a knight could possibly need. It felt good knowing that we took such good care of them. I searched the shelves, finding all the necessary items to complete my transformation. On the bottom shelves, I found the smallest sizes, and luckily for me, most knights tended to be quite large, leaving lots of the smaller sizes, which were still going to be big on me, but it was the best I could hope for. I found some other useful gear and ran out of the back door straight for my chambers using the secret passages Nexion had shown me the day of my coronation.

As soon as I entered my room, I found my mother in full action, gathering various items and preparing to help me change my appearance. She turned to me, her eyes shining with excitement as she gestured to a small table in the center of the room.

"Ah, there you are," she said, beckoning me forward. "We have much to do if we are to make you unrecognizable."

My mother, standing there, with an unexpected excited energy, was a sight I'd never thought I'd see. She's the embodiment of stoicism, always carrying an air of royal sophistication about her. An expert in masking emotions for the sake of politics, seeing her enthusiasm was surprising.

"Mother?" I asked, curious about her unusual eagerness. "You seem... excited?"

She paused, a thick leather belt dangling from her hands, and looked at me. It was a rare expression, one of unfiltered understanding and solidarity.

She paused for a moment and looked at me with an intensity that was both comforting and alarming. She was always an enigma to me, her thoughts and feelings hidden behind a mask of indifference. It was rare to see her drop that facade.

"Well, Elzaria," she smiled, her tone lighthearted yet sincere. "This is something new, isn't it? And it's a path you've chosen willingly."

My eyes widened in surprise. I had been expecting her to be concerned, worried, or even disapproving. But this? It was like she was genuinely supportive of my choice.

"Let's face it," she continued, her gaze holding mine. "It's not every day that a royal decides to leave the comforts of the palace for the sweat and grime of knight training. It's a brave choice, one that I respect. I never imagined you as a warrior, but I agree with Loren that you branching out from your studious ways could be good for you. I'll tell you a secret... I always wondered what life would've been like as a normal person. Being born into this family certainly does limit our choices. The Academy won't know what hit it."

It was a side of my mother I'd never seen before. This wasn't the stoic Queen, but a mother acknowledging her daughter's ambitions and cheering her on. Her enthusiasm filled the room and fueled my own excitement. It wasn't just her approval, but her heartfelt support that bolstered my spirits. This newfound encouragement steeled my resolve, strengthening my determination for the challenge I was about to undertake.

"Sit down, Elzaria," she said, indicating a chair in front of the table. "We must start with your hair. I see you've already changed its color."

I sat down in front of the table, watching as my mother went to work. She deftly braided my hair in a series of intricate warrior braids, each one perfectly made and designed to keep my hair out of my face. I watched carefully so that I could repeat them once at the academy.

Next, my mother applied temporary tattoos, using her skilled hands to create a range of intricate designs that would help to disguise my true identity. No Empyrean Queen has ever had tattoos. As she worked, I watched in awe, marveling at her skillfulness and the way she seemed to transform me before my very eyes. She carefully applied the tattoos to my face and arms, her fingers moving with precision as she made sure every line was perfect. As she worked, I couldn't help but wonder where she had learned to do this so well and why. Maybe I didn't know my mother as well as I thought.

"Perfect," she said at last, stepping back to admire her handiwork. "You look like a true warrior, Elzaria. No one will recognize you. You can't remove these without Elyspur oil, which is very rare. I will leave a bottle on your dressing table for when you return."

Finally, I slipped into the basic fatigues I had found in the barracks. I wore a simple black tunic with matching pants and boots and added a belt with a small pouch for my essentials, including a small knife and a few credits of currency. Even though I had to leave behind my royal life, I was determined to make this work. Never before had I dressed like this. It was comfortable and practical, and I hoped it was enough to blend in at the Academy. I packed the other things in a backpack that was small enough for me to carry easily.

Looking at myself in the mirror, I couldn't help but think that I looked like a completely different person. I could hardly recognize myself staring back at me.

"You look so exotic, Elzaria," my mother said, her eyes shining with pride. "I am so proud of you for following your heart and pursuing this path. Our world needs more strong and capable women like you. Be fearless and always remember who you are and where you came from. I have no doubt that you will do great things." She reached out and placed a hand on my shoulder, giving it a reassuring squeeze. "Now go out there and show them what you're made of. We'll be waiting for you when you return, ready to celebrate your success."

Before she left, dinner arrived. My father entered, taking the cart from the server while I slipped into my bedroom to hide. He had arranged for my favorite dinner to be brought up for us to share. When he saw my new look, his eyes widened as he took in my appearance. "Elzaria?" He asked, his voice a mixture of shock and disbelief. "I hardly recognize you, even though I know who you are."

He circled around me, looking at my mother, shaking his head in disbelief. "I see your handiwork Elindra, what a magnificent job you two have done. Reminds me of when we were young." They shared a private laugh but didn't elaborate.

"Let's eat our meal while I tell you about the false identity I've created for you," he said as he pulled out a chair and began filling his plate with food.

Mother and I joined him.

"They will know you as Zalara Galen, the daughter of Dax Galen, one of the wealthiest Empyrean shipping magnates and my long-time friend."

I listened closely as my father outlined the details of my new identity. My heart raced with nervous restlessness as I realized my plans were actually coming to fruition. I was to live a double life, pretending to be someone else, while also training to become a knight. It was a lot to take in, but it motivated me to succeed.

After dinner, my father inserted a chip into my arm a little above my wrist, which would serve as my identification, banking, and travel files, allowing me access to the funds in my new bank account under the name Zalara Galen. It was a strange and bit painful sensation, feeling the chip slide under my skin, but I knew it was necessary for my mission. Everyone throughout the Alliance had them from birth, except the royal family.

After inserting the chip, he handed me a data pad. "I've developed a cover story to explain your absence."

I read through it carefully, committing the details to memory. According to the story, I left on a covert mission to visit some of the Empyrean outpost planets that had been experiencing unrest. As the new Queen, it was my duty to gain first-hand knowledge of my people and their needs. I would travel in secret, with only a handful of trusted advisors accompanying me. The trip was expected to take close to an entire cycle, during which time I would be out of contact with the rest of the kingdom. Secrecy of my location was paramount to my safety.

It was a risky cover story, but it was the best he could come up with. If anyone asked about my absence, the story would hopefully satisfy their curiosity without raising any red flags. My father had even arranged for a few select individuals like Loren to leak information about my supposed mission, adding to the credibility of our story.

With a deep breath, I closed the data pad and looked up at my parents. "I'm as ready as I can be, I guess." My voice a little nervous. "I'll do whatever it takes to make this work."

My parents nodded, their faces filled with pride and love. "We know you will," my mother said.

They hugged me tightly, and I was on my way.

"Hold up, Elzaria. I almost forgot to give this to you," Father unrolled a leather bundle. Inside, tucked in rows, were glistening xenochronatium throwing knives. "These have been in our family for many generations. In this roll is also a vest with pockets for you to sheath the knives in supple leather. Think of them as a second set of ribs."

Stunned, I didn't know what to say as I slid one of the small knives from the bundle and weighed it in my hand. Light and perfectly balanced.

"They're not all that different from that game you and Loren like to play all the time with the darts. Practice every day, any chance you get. They're the best weapon for your size."

I wrapped them up and added them to my pack. "Thank you, Father. These mean more to me than you know." I hugged him tightly and set off through the hidden passages.

As I stepped out of the castle, I felt a thrill wash over me. I was Zalara Galen now, a new identity that felt both empowering and terrifying. I scanned the surroundings, taking in the castle's beauty, where I had spent most of my life. It was a strange feeling, knowing that I was leaving behind everything I had ever known to embark on a new journey.

I set out for the academy, ready to start my new life. As I walked through the bustling streets of the city, I felt like a completely different person. The tattoos on my face and arms helped to mask my identity, and the simple dark clothing I wore allowed me to blend in with the crowd. It was liberating to be free from the constraints of my royal status.

I made my way to the Hyper-Rail, a sleek and futuristic mode of transportation that promised to get me to the Academy in record time.

As I approached the station, I noticed its sleek, aerodynamic design, which was built with intelligent, self-cleaning materials that kept it looking pristine. The station had lush greenery and vertical gardens integrated into its architecture, providing a serene and inviting atmosphere for commuters.

I swiped my new identification chip and entered the station, my heart beating fast with nervous energy.

Upon entering, a holographic assistant greeted me and helped me purchase my ticket. It then guided me to the correct platform. They designed the platforms with safety barriers, which opened in sync with the train doors, ensuring passengers remained secure until the train arrived.

The Hyper-Rail vehicle itself was a streamlined, elongated pod with a silver, metallic finish. Its design minimized air resistance, allowing it to achieve incredible speeds with minimal energy consumption. As the train arrived, it glided silently into the station, producing only a faint hum as it levitated above the tracks. The Hyper-Rail was a marvel of modern technology, a network of vacuum-sealed tubes that used magnetic levitation to propel passengers at incredible speeds.

I boarded the train and settled into my seat, taking in the sights and sounds. The interior was spacious and well-lit, with ergonomic seats that adapted to my body shape for maximum comfort. Advanced noise-canceling technology was installed in the vehicle for a quiet and peaceful ride.

As the Hyper-Rail accelerated, I felt a gentle push against my seat, but the motion was otherwise smooth and seamless. The train reached its cruising speed of over 1,000 km/h with ease, allowing it to cover vast distances in little time. The ride was so comfortable that I barely noticed the speed at which I was traveling. Large panoramic windows allowed for breathtaking views of the landscape as it whizzed by, and interactive displays provided information about my journey and the world outside.

During my travel, I had access to an array of on board amenities, including high-speed communications, augmented reality entertainment, and a selection of gourmet food and beverages. The Hyper-Rail also had sleeping pods for the overnight trip, ensuring I arrived well-rested and ready to head for the academy. I knew this would be the last time for a long time that I would enjoy the privileges of royalty.

CHAPTER EIGHT

ELZARIA

A stern-looking guard standing sentry duty met me outside of the secure entrance portal. He eyed me suspiciously. I held my breath as he examined my credentials, praying that my false identity would hold up under scrutiny. After a few tense moments, he nodded and allowed me to enter.

Within seconds, Orion-9 greeted me. He was a dedicated and intuitive hospitality droid designed to guide new knight candidates upon their arrival.

"Welcome to the Terrastrian Order of the Empyrean Knights Academy, an elite institution nestled in the heart of the majestic Valarian Mountains on the planet Terrastria." I heard as I strode through the portal.

Orion-9 was a state-of-the-art, semi-humanoid droid with a sleek, metallic body and an illuminated, holographic face that displayed an array of friendly expressions. He stood at a modest height of 1.5 meters, exuding an approachable and non-threatening presence.

O-9's frame was constructed from lightweight materials, allowing him to move gracefully and silently through the Academy's corridors. They equipped his limbs with advanced articulation and dexterity, enabling him to interact with objects and environments with almost human precision. The droid's sensory systems, including high-resolution cameras and auditory sensors, allowed him to perceive and analyze his surroundings in real time, ensuring he could effectively navigate the Academy and avoid obstacles.

O-9 explained he used advanced artificial intelligence, which allowed him to communicate with the knights in a natural, intuitive manner. His language processing capabilities enabled him to understand and speak multiple languages, and his vast internal database contained information about the Academy's history, facilities, and training regimens. This wealth of knowledge allowed O-9 to provide personalized guidance and support to each new knight, making sure they smoothly integrated into the Academy. There would be no room for human error with this guy around.

"Please extend your arm so that I may register you and download your personal details." O-9 requested, and I complied.

"Interesting; you are female. We rarely admit females. Hmm, you are also the smallest candidate ever to attempt to become a knight. That will require adjustments. I will ensure that we make them. Good to see you have extremely high academic marks. Perhaps that will be enough to carry you through the training."

"Gee, thanks for the show of confidence."

"You're welcome." O-9 replied, obviously not programmed well enough to catch my sarcasm.

O-9 and I then started out for a tour of the campus so that he could ensure I knew my way around the various facilities, training areas, and common spaces as well as the places they prohibited candidates from going.

"This ancient academy has trained generations of Empyrean Knights, who are renowned throughout the galaxy as the mightiest warriors and defenders of peace and justice," he shared.

I plodded along behind him, listening to his long and detailed descriptions of each area. Although I love history, it was more than I wanted to listen to.

"The Academy's architecture is a blend of traditional Terrastrian stone and advanced crystalline technology. A shimmering energy shield surrounds its fortress-like structure, ensuring the safety and privacy of its esteemed occupants. The Academy is accessible only through the portal. If you earn your knighthood, you will always be able to access the portal by the scan of your Knight's Empyrean Sigil—an emblem in the shape of a shield and embedded with an encrypted nano-chip unique to each knight," he explained. I remembered seeing Nexion's pinned over his heart.

We eventually made our way to the Grand Hall, a vast, awe-inspiring chamber with a high, vaulted ceiling adorned with intricate celestial murals depicting the legends of the Empyrean Knights. The Hall was lit by ethereal, floating orbs that cast a soft, calming light, creating an atmosphere of tranquility and reverence similar to the cathedral in Arcadia.

Next, O-9 guided me to the Academy's state-of-the-art training facilities.

"The builders tailored these facilities to enhance the physical, mental, and mystical abilities of the Empyrean Knights. The Combat Simulation Arena uses advanced holographic technology to create realistic and challenging scenarios, allowing the knights to hone their martial arts skills and strategic acumen. While the Arena adapted to each knight's specific needs, providing customized training experiences." O-9 could barely contain his excitement as we walked through. I could barely contain my heart rate passing by the racks of dangerous-looking weapons.

"Over there, we have the energy blades," O-9 gestured to an array of slender, hilt-like devices arranged neatly on a rack. Each of these benign-looking hilts held the potential to become a deadly weapon capable of cutting through almost anything. Their activation would ignite a blade of pure, scalding energy. The thought alone sent shivers down my spine. It was hard to look at them without imagining the damage they could inflict.

Beyond the energy blades were rows of intimidating traditional swords. Some were broad and heavy, designed for knights who relied on brute force. Others were slender and lightweight, intended for knights with swift, agile fighting styles. The polished blades gleamed menacingly under the stark overhead lighting.

Then came the daggers and throwing knives—small, sleek, but equally lethal. Concealed weapons designed for subtlety and precision. I could almost feel their cold, unyielding touch against my palm, the weight of responsibility they carried. They reminded me of the gift from my father tucked inside the bag, weighing heavily on my back as we trudged along.

Further down the aisle were the more exotic weapons, the kind I had only heard about in stories like what I think might be monomolecular whips—weapons that used advanced technology to inflict damage.

My heart was racing like crazy, I was so nervous and impressed at the same time. These weapons, each more intimidating than the last, were tools of the Empyrean Knights. I was here to learn how to wield them, to master them, and the thought was utterly terrifying.

O-9 went on to tell me that besides physical training, the Academy also focuses on the development of the knights' psychic and telekinetic powers, collectively known as "quantum resonance." The Meditation Chambers amplified these abilities with crystal-infused walls and floors that resonated with the knights' inner energy. Here, knights learn to harness the power of the cosmos, mastering techniques such as telekinesis and energy manipulation.

After touring the training facility, we walked through a beautiful garden that led to the Great Library of Terrastria, a treasure trove of knowledge that spanned millennia.

O-9 explained that the library held ancient tomes, scrolls, and holographic archives containing information on the history, culture, and sciences of countless worlds. "Knights spend innumerable hours studying these archives, seeking wisdom to aid them in their quests." O-9's partiality towards the library was clear in his excited words.

Then, in a more somber tone, he cautioned me about the Empyrean Knights' code of honor, known as the *Celestial Creed*. "It is central to a knight's training. The Empyrean Knights teach the virtues of courage, compassion, and wisdom, and instill a deep sense of duty to protect the innocent and uphold justice. The knights complete their training with the Rite of Ascension, a sacred and challenging ritual to prove their mastery and commitment to the *Celestial Creed*.

As we left the library, we headed for what was obviously the barracks.

O-9 continued on, "Once a knight has successfully completed their training, the Academy gives each newly ascended knight an Empyrean Saber—a legendary weapon that harnesses the power of the quantum resonance. These energy blade weapons are imbued with the essence of their wielder, allowing them to channel their Empyrean powers and perform incredible feats of skill and force. The Terrastrian Order of the Empyrean Knights Academy has, for millennia, produced the most formidable warriors in the galaxy, ensuring the continued safety and prosperity of the people of Terrastria and beyond," he said as he concluded the campus tour.

Stopping abruptly just before the door, O-9 turned to me. "Knight candidate Zalara Galen, do you honestly believe that you are up to the challenge of becoming an Empyrean Knight?" O-9 bluntly asked.

"I wouldn't be here if I didn't believe so. Are you questioning my integrity?" I snapped back.

"No, not at all. It was a question based on the condition of your physical state."

I just shook my head and followed him on into the barracks. I couldn't believe I had only been here for a short time and already felt totally inadequate.

Finally, O-9 led me to my new quarters, a private and comfortable living space designed to segregate the women from the men. It was small, but had everything I needed for the time I would be here. The droid provided yet another exhaustive introduction to the room's amenities, from the adaptive sleep pod and eating area to the personal cleaning station and small area for studying. O-9 also thoroughly familiarized me with the communication and security protocols, emphasizing the importance of maintaining a safe and supportive environment for all.

Finally, he left. I quickly unpacked my small bag. In the wardrobe, I found various fatigues and other athletic clothing that actually looked like they'd fit. O-9 must have had someone stock these items for me while we were touring the academy.

I sat nervously in the common area, waiting for the other knight candidates to arrive. I was thankful for having arrived early enough to get my bearings before the others moved into our quarters.

The door to the barracks swung open, and a group of candidates entered, chatting and laughing amongst themselves.

They fell silent as they spotted me, their eyes scanning me with curiosity and skepticism.

"Who's this?" one candidate, a tall, muscular guy, asked mockingly. "Is this someone's little sister?"

Another candidate, with a wicked grin and a ruddy complexion, chimed in. "Maybe she's here to make us sandwiches while we train."

A few of them laughed. I just rolled my eyes, determined not to let them get to me.

Several more guys made their way into the barracks. I tried to blend in with the furniture and not attract any more attention than I already had. Then, in he walked. The giant that had saved me from my attacker at the coronation banquet. I couldn't believe it, but then remembered the guard telling me they had accepted him into the academy. I peeked up through my eyelashes at him. He came to a dead stop when he saw me. Confusion written across his brow.

I turned away, but in my peripheral vision I saw him shake his head. As if he was convincing himself what he saw was impossible.

Before he could look more closely, the door slammed open, and a towering figure strode in. It was Master Sergeant Torin Killdare, his face set in a permanent scowl.

"Attention!" He barked, and the room instantly fell silent. We all jumped up and snapped to attention, their laughter forgotten.

"Welcome to the Empyrean Knight's Academy, maggots!" the Master Sergeant roared. "You're here because you think you have what it takes to become a knight, but I assure you, most of you will fail."

He paced the room, scrutinizing each candidate. When he reached me, his scowl deepened. "And what do we have here? A pathetic excuse for a human, much less a knight. You better prove me wrong, or you'll be out of here in a heartbeat."

The Master Sergeant ordered us to change into our training gear and form up outside. We spent the rest of the day doing endless physical training—running, push-ups, sit-ups, and more—while he screamed insults and threats at us.

"You call that a push-up trainee? My grandmother could have done better, and she's dead!" He bellowed at one candidate.

As the day progressed, he led us to an obstacle course designed to test our physical and mental limits. The Master Sergeant ordered us to scale a tall wall, and I saw the skepticism in the eyes of the other candidates as they glanced at me. My heart raced as I approached the wall, knowing that all eyes were on me.

I tried to hoist myself up, but my arms and legs trembled with exhaustion. My fingers slipped on the cold, wet rope, and I fell back to the ground, rope burns across my palms. Mocking laughter erupted around me.

"What a joke!" one guy sneered. "She can't even climb a wall. How's she supposed to become a knight?"

Another chimed in, "I heard she's the spoiled little girl of the wealthy shipping magnate Daz Galen."

How the hell did he know that already?

There was more laughter when I heard another guy say, "I bet she's here to score a husband. She probably thinks one of us will be desperate enough to be interested in her."

Anger and humiliation surged within me, and I refused to let them win. With a deep breath, I summoned every ounce of strength I had left, and I tried again. And again, I failed. I kept trying and failing until finally, my fingers found purchase, and I slowly made my way up the wall. When I reached the top, my arms felt like they were on fire, but I'd proven them wrong. They all moved on to the next obstacle, but the Master Sergeant took note.

After the grueling day of training, they herded us into the mess hall for dinner. We ate in silence, backs straight and eyes forward, as per the Master Sergeant's orders. The food was bland and unappetizing. It consisted of a simple meat dish, boiled vegetables, and some sort of starchy side.

Around me, I could hear the sounds of retching as some candidates struggled to keep the food down. Their bodies were pushed to the breaking point, rejecting the sustenance they desperately needed.

I took a deep breath and forced myself to chew and swallow each bite, my stomach churning in protest. I knew I needed to eat and drink plenty of water to maintain my strength, so I focused on my mission and reminded myself of the war I was trying to prevent. Finishing my meal, despite the discomfort, was the least I could.

As we finished and the mess hall emptied, I knew this was only the first of many challenging days. I'd have to do a lot more to prove myself to these guys and the Master Sergeant.

As the day ended, my muscles burned with exhaustion, and every fiber of my being screamed for me to give up. But I refused to let them see me break. I remembered the reason I was here, and I accepted the pain. I knew my lack of athleticism would be my undoing.

Finally, as night fell, the Master Sergeant dismissed us. I stumbled back to the barracks, my body aching and my clothes drenched in sweat. The only thing I wanted was to collapse onto my bunk, but I had to tend to my raw, blistered hands. I wrapped them with bandages coated in nano biotech that sped up healing. Too exhausted to even change out of my clothes, I face planted on my bed. Sleep claimed me.

CHAPTER NINE

ELZARIA

Day two was mostly a repeat of day one except for more screaming, more insults, and much more pain. And so began my living hell.

Day three, at 4:00 am, the beating of a metal container reverberated next to my ear, jarring me awake and freaking me the fuck out. I was disoriented from exhaustion and the lack of sleep from the pain I felt all over my body.

"Rise and shine infants. 5k run before breakfast." Master Serg bellowed.

"Let's go, let's go. This run will be timed. Line up and go when your name's called."

Still dazed, my head throbbed like the worst sort of hangover. I could barely move, much less run. Maybe this was a huge mistake. But what else could I do? If I quit this early, I'd be a joke. My reputation, such as it was, ruined forever. Go until I dropped. That's the only plan I had.

"G... Galen!" Master Serg's bellow echoed through the still morning air, filled with pure venom that sent a shiver down my spine. Shit, I hadn't been listening.

A brutish shove from the guy behind me sent me stumbling forward. An impatient grunt from him reminded me I was in his way.

"Move your ass, princess!" he growled, shoving me harder. Here "princess" was the worst sort of insult.

With an attempt at steadying my shaking nerves, I straightened my shoulders and forced my aching legs into a pained jog.

Master Serg, however, wasn't finished with me. He matched his pace with mine, his face twisted into a mask of disgust, his eyes like the edge of a sharpened blade. His words bit into me, "What, you need a bloody invitation, girl? Maybe a little red carpet?"

I kept my gaze ahead, ignoring his taunts.

"What's this, Galen?" he snarled, his voice dripping with scorn. "Waiting for your fucking fairy godmother to carry you?"

Ignoring the bitter taste of humiliation, I focused on each stride, my jaw clenched.

His next words were spit out like venom, his voice a seething hiss that seemed to claw at my resolve. "You're nothing but a weak, pampered little girl trying to play soldier. You're a disgrace. You don't belong in this academy. You're pissing away our time, our goddesses' damn resources. Do you think this is a fucking joke?"

The stark, unmasked hatred in his voice stung worse than any physical blow, but I bit back the retort that threatened to spill out. I wouldn't give him the satisfaction.

"I ought to ship you back to your daddy with a bow in your hair," he threatened, a wicked grin twisting his features as he imagined the scene.

I forced my feet to move faster, each step pounding in sync with my heart. His words echoed in my mind, but I forced them into the background, focusing instead on the rhythm of my footfalls, the harsh rasp of my breath.

I ran. I ran harder than I ever had, ignoring the searing pain in my legs and the raw burn in my lungs. I ran because, in that moment, I had everything to prove—to the academy, to Master Serg, to the world. But most importantly, to myself. Because in the end, I wasn't just the 'little girl' they saw. I was more, much more. And I'd be damned if I didn't prove it.

The rest of the day was a blur. Covered in sweat and grim, I dropped onto my bunk. That's when I realized that somewhere along the way I'd gotten a busted lip. The last thing I remembered was a salty metallic taste threatening to make me puke before the darkness claimed me.

Day four started once again at an ungodly early hour, except this time a gentle nudge woke me to the cautious look of one of the giants. The giant who had saved me from the assassin, Ganthion, that was his name.

"Hey Zalara, get cleaned up. It's the rules not to hit the sack like... well, er, that." He lowered his head, shaking it back and forth, looking at my disgusting form on top of the covers, one foot still on the ground.

Swinging my other foot to the floor, my calf cramped, and I couldn't help the soft cry that escaped my lips before I bit the side of my mouth, forcing myself to rein in any emotion. Ganthion closed the door as he left, not saying more. Did he know who I was? If he did, he never admitted it or said a word.

I had just enough time to clean up in the personal sanitation chamber and dress before we all had to haul our asses back out for another day of inhumane torture.

The rest of the day was a fresh set of miseries, but who knows? Maybe the tasks were the same as the day before. Who can tell when every movement of one's body was sheer agony? At least I was able to clean up and shower before exhaustion claimed me once again. In the back of my mind, my father's words echoed, reminding me I had to practice throwing the knives he gave me every day. Tomorrow, yeah, I would start in the morning...

Day five was different. I got up early and turned on the shower to disguise the sound of the knives clunking into the back of the wardrobe. They'd send me home if they knew the damage I was causing with weapons no one was to keep in the barracks. I took the risk because what other choice did I have? I had to learn quick, or I was out of here. Father was right. The stance and throwing motion were like that of throwing darts, but the grip and release were very different. These knives didn't have handles and were one smooth blade perfect for accuracy. Or at least they would be accurate if I were any good at throwing them. Mostly they fell not finding purchase in the wood. I promised myself to practice each morning and before I'd sleep. Like everything else, it was about putting in the work.

Today didn't start off with cruel calisthenics. Instead, we waited in the common area for our orders. The room silent, everyone too tired to speak. After a little while, an instructor I hadn't seen before directed us to the mess hall for breakfast.

"What's up?" I heard Ivarian ask Zarek.

"Don't know. Don't care. Best if you don't go asking for trouble." He mumbled around a piece of meat he'd stuffed in his mouth.

There was nothing out of the ordinary. The officers sat at their table while we filed through, heaping food on our trays. Filling my cup with piping hot *plasmafuel*, the nickname for the bitter caffeinated drink we all craved, I turned to find a table to sit at when I saw him, Nexion. He stared through me, expressionless. Like I didn't exist. He never ate in the mess hall. For that matter, I hadn't laid eyes on him once since I arrived.

Did he recognize me? No, that would provoke some reaction. I was too insignificant. Then his gaze raised to meet my eyes. I immediately looked down at my tray.

My pulse spiked, and I felt a blush creeping up my neck as I stood under his cold scrutiny. I willed my feet to move, to make a swift U-turn and find a seat far away, when Zarek, the insufferable toad, deliberately stuck his foot out. My legs tangled, and my balance betrayed me. Time seemed to slow as I tumbled forward, my tray of food and steaming plasmafuel hurtling through the air ahead of me.

A gasp ripped through the mess hall as I landed flat on my face. The cold slop from my tray soaked my uniform instantly, and the hard floor stung my cheek where it kissed it.

Before I could lift my head, a scalding shower of plasmafuel splashed over my back. Turning to see where the hot spray had come from, I saw that the cup had ended up in Nexion's lap. His face turned a frightening shade of red, the scorching liquid dripping from his uniform where the cup at landed before he batted it away. His stony stare turned murderous as he stormed out of the mess hall, leaving a deathly silence in his wake.

"Fuck you! Watch where you're going, why don't you?" Zarek's cruel voice echoed through the hall as raucous laughter erupted from the guys around me.

Their laughter echoed around the room, turning my face scarlet from humiliation. My eyes squinted closed, wishing the floor would swallow me up.

"Galen... Galen... Candidate Zalara Galen! Don't you know your own fucking name?" Master Serg's voice boomed above me.

Dammit to hell. In the chaos, I had forgotten my new name.

"Galen! You fucking clumsy waste of space!" Master Sergeant Killdare's voice thundered in the sudden silence. My heart dropped further, if that was even possible. "How the hell did you even get here? Did you pay your way in?"

"No, sir, I—" Trying to stand, I slipped again, landing with a thud on my butt.

"I don't give a rat's ass about your excuses! Look at this fucking mess you've made!" He gestured to the spilled food and drink on the floor and soaking into my uniform.

"Is this how you intend to represent the Empyrean Knights by making us the laughingstock of the galaxy?" The furrow in his brow was deeper than I thought possible, and the vein on his temple throbbed ominously.

"If you can't even carry a fucking tray, how do you expect to hold a weapon? Or are you here to make us all look bad? Because if that's the case, I can gladly arrange your transportation back to your daddy's mansion!"

His tirade continued, each word a lash, leaving me with metaphorical welts. The mess hall was a symphony of snickers and whispered insults. As I lay there, soaked in humiliation and plasmafuel, I realized this was just another test, and like the rest, I would conquer it. No matter how many times I fell, I would always stand back up. Fall down seven times and get up eight, right?

Eventually, I got everything, including myself, cleaned up and returned to the squad. Ensuring I didn't miss a minute of training the Master Serg had me stay late and dinner brought to my room. As if I wasn't already shunned enough already, now, no one would dare have anything to do with a loser hated by the Knightmaster himself.

After a deca of indoctrination, which main purpose was to break us down mentally and physically so that they could rebuild us in the way of the Empyrean Knights, we entered the next phase of our training. I was exhausted. I didn't know if I could survive and worried that maybe I was in over my head.

The days fell into a routine, alternating between physical training, hand-to-hand sparring, weapons training, academics, and quantum resonance training. I felt my body developing muscles in places I didn't even know I had. I'd shed a lot of blood and sweat, but I refused to shed any tears. I wrestled my emotions into a steel box and locked them away. The other candidates and trainers always treated me differently because I was, well, me, an awkward girl, and a small one at that.

One night after a particularly grueling day, I sat alone in the barrack's common area covered in scratches and bruises. Bent over my knees, I held my face in my hands, forcibly trying to shove the tears back when I felt a warm hand on my shoulder. It was Ganthion, one of the few guys who hadn't spewed insults at me. He was a good guy, worked hard and kept his head down. I'd overheard him talking about the small remote town he was from and how he sent most all his pay to his family. Becoming a knight and taking care of his parents was everything to him.

"Hey, Zalara, don't let those guys get to you," Ganthion said, his voice full of concern. "They don't know anything. You've come a long way since we started. I've seen it with my own eyes."

I looked up at him, grateful for his kind words. "Thanks, Ganthion," I sighed. "It's just hard sometimes, you know? I feel like I don't belong here."

He shook his head. "That's not true. You belong here just as much as anyone else. You're strong and smart. That's what it takes to be a knight. Don't let anyone tell you otherwise."

He sat down next to me and put his arm around my shoulders. "You know, Zalara, I've been watching you since you got here," he said, turning to look at me. "You're tough, and you never give up. I admire that about you. You're going to make a great knight someday."

I looked at him, my eyes searching his face for any hint of insincerity, but all I saw was warmth and kindness. "Thank you, Ganthion," I said, my voice barely above a whisper. "You have no idea how much your words mean to me."

He smiled and squeezed my shoulder. "Anytime, little sister. I'm here for you."

As the days passed, I grew stronger. My body adapted to the grueling training regimen, and my mind sharpened with each new challenge. I learned to control my breathing and focus my thoughts, allowing me to push past the pain and exhaustion.

My saving grace was our hours spent in the schoolhouse or library. While the math and astrophysics were demanding for most all the guys, for me, it was a basic review. I used the time to study combat techniques and watch holographic projections of elite fighters teaching how to fight and use various weapons. I hoped mentally rehearsing and visualizing the moves would somehow help me improve at a quicker rate.

I was alone, though. The other candidates shared camaraderie and found solace in each other's company, bonding over their shared struggles and triumphs while they mostly ignored me.

The Master Sergeant continued to be a constant source of fear and intimidation. His insults became more cutting, and his punishments more severe. One day, he ordered us to stand at attention for hours on end, without moving or speaking. My legs shaking and my throat burning, I refused to falter. I remembered the prophecy and stood tall.

Eventually, the Master Sergeant dismissed us, and I stumbled back to my quarters, my muscles screaming in protest. My body was a wreck.

After several decas of relentless training, I was totally beat up. There wasn't any part of me that didn't ache or have some sort of injury. Each morning, I woke with the sort of stiffness that made it feel as if they had thrashed me with sticks during my restless sleep. My limbs felt heavy, my muscles strained to their limit, protesting with throbbing spasms whenever I moved.

My skin was no better. It bore the marks of countless scratches and welts, a map of my hardships. Cuts, scrapes, and bruises in various shades of healing marred my flesh, each with their own painful memory. There were rope burns on my palms, a testament to my failed attempts at scaling the training wall, mixed with the newly forming callouses and rough skin.

Then there were the blisters. They adorned my feet like cruel jewelry, the result of endless miles run in boots that seemed designed more for torture than practical use. Each step sent stinging shocks of pain through me, yet every day I somehow pushed through it.

My knees were swollen, a constant, dull ache radiating from them due to the countless falls, knee drops, and abrupt stops. There were times I feared they might give out on me altogether, but they held up a grudging testament to my stubbornness.

The worst, though, were my ribs. A brutal sparring session had left me with a deep, purple bruise that made every breath a painful endeavor. I could feel the sharp twinge with each inhale and exhale, a grim reminder of my current state.

Physically, I was wrecked, a shell of the woman who had walked into this academy with her head held high. Despite the pain and exhaustion, I refused to break. Every bruise, every scrape, every blister, was a battle scar, proof of my resolve. This pain was the price I had to pay for the safety of my people. But by the goddesses, was it a steep price.

O-9 greeted me as I slumped down in a chair. "Hello candidate, Zalara Galen. You look more disheveled than usual."

"So? Is there a problem?"

"I have been tracking your progress, and you are doing well."

"You're the only one who thinks so."

"Might I offer you a small piece of information?"

"O-9, I don't think there is any information that can help me. I'm black and blue from head to toe and every fiber of my being hurts. Thank you, but I'm heading for bed."

"Follow me." O-9 insisted.

It was late, but I complied. We walked to a small building behind the headmaster's home hidden down a path in the woods. It reminded me of a hunting lodge back in Arcadia, near our summer retreat.

O-9 opened the door and led me into a warm room that smelled of herbs. A woman dressed as a medical assistant greeted us.

O-9 told her, "We have a candidate in need of repair. Please see she is taken well care of." He spun around and was gone.

"Hello, I'm Tatiana. Please use the room through those doors to shower and relax for a bit. I will let you know when I'm ready to care for you."

After a hot shower, I sat in the sauna wrapped in a thick fluffy white towel, waiting for Tatiana to return.

"Come this way," she said, startling me from my near sleep.

"Rest there," she said as she pointed for me to lie in a small pod-like chamber. She closed the overhead door, and I felt the warmth of the scanner move up and down my body. The chamber filled with gas, and I was out.

When I awoke, I felt the best I had ever felt in my entire life. Nothing hurt and all the new muscles I had developed buzzed with strength and resilience. I sprang from the pod, curious to find out what Tatiana had done to me. She was nowhere to be found. The building was empty. Looking around, I saw a couple of other pods and a cabinet with various medicines. This must be used to aid knights in their recovery after a hard battle. I made a mental note to thank O-9 the next time I saw him.

The next day, the training regimen changed yet again. Instead of physical training, we now worked on learning how to harness and control our telekinetic powers over the elements. It was a new challenge, and I was eager to learn, even though I was nervous about what might happen.

As the Master Sergeant demonstrated controlling water, he explained the importance of suppressing our emotions and thoughts in order to manipulate the elements. I focused on his words, trying to push aside the doubts and fears that swirled in my mind.

When it was my turn to try, I stepped forward. I stretched out my hand, trying to connect with the element, but nothing happened.

"Come on, Galen! Use your goddess given powers!" the Master Sergeant shouted, his voice roaring across the training grounds.

I closed my eyes, trying to focus, and remember what we'd learned in class. And then suddenly, a burst of energy streamed from within my chest and exploded from my hand. A jet of water shot up from the pool in the garden where we were standing and out towards the Master Serg, spraying him powerfully in the face. Choking and sputtering, the Master Sergeant's face flashed with anger.

"What the hell, Galen? Are you trying to kill me?" He bellowed.

He split us up based on our elemental strengths and I ended up in the water group. The other guys in my group eyed me warily as we began our training.

I'd never used my telekinetic powers before, so I was nervous about what was to come. As a royal princess, I had never needed to use them. The royal family was the most well protected and cared for in our galaxy. Besides, I didn't like drawing attention to myself; I didn't like the spotlight. Give me a stack of books and a hammock in the woods and I would be lost in my stories for hours.

I knew both my parents, especially my father, wielded enormous power over the elements and my mother could summon a bolt of energy at the snap of her fingers. Several times I had overheard them discussing my lack of powers and speculating that they may have skipped a generation which was known to have happened. In reality, though, I knew they were strong; too strong, and they terrified me.

I watched as the other candidates expertly manipulated the water, forming it into various shapes and even making it dance in the air. I tried to mimic their movements but was clumsy and untrained, and my attempts were met with mocking sneers.

"Look at her flailing about. She's pathetic," Urias sneered.

Zarek added, "Why would she think she could be a knight with powers like those?"

I felt humiliated and angry, but refused to give up. Concentrating with all my might, I attempted to channel my powers, when suddenly, the water in front of me rose into the air. I gasped, surprised by the sudden surge of energy, and then lost control. The water crashed down around me, drenching me from head to toe.

Everyone burst into laughter, taunting me, but I didn't let them get to me. I tried again, and this time, controlled the water a little better, lifting it in the air and shaping it into basic columns and flows. It felt exhilarating, and I was excited to explore my newfound abilities.

But as the day wore on, mishaps continued to happen. I accidentally drenched several of the other guys. So, the Master Serg ordered me to practice alone far from the others until I had better control over my abilities.

Several days later, we were preparing for various tests outside in the gardens. Next to me, Ganthion was practicing shooting his bow and guiding his arrows with his powers. I heard a loud crack as a sharp spear of flame burst out of a tree. It tore through the air directly at Ganthion's back. He didn't know it was coming. I threw myself in front of the flame and, without thinking, surrounded us both in a torrent of wind deflecting the flame around us.

For a second, everyone stood there in stunned silence. Then turned to focus on squelching the fires erupting around us from the incident.

"Thanks, sis," Ganthion nudged me with his shoulder.

I couldn't help but chuckle. "Now look who's not able to control his powers." I said, pointing to Urias, one of the jerks who was always quick to throw and insult my way.

After days of practice, I finally felt like I had a semblance of control over water. I could lift it into the air and shape it into various forms, and I could even make it dance in the air like the other candidates in my group. I discovered the ability to shoot it in a tight stream with enough force to slice a piece of wood in half, something I hadn't seen anyone else do. The Master Serg seemed pleased with my progress and even complimented me on my newfound abilities. Now, if I could just figure out how to apply my water skills to the other elements, then maybe I would get somewhere.

Despite the progress I'd made, I still felt isolated from the other candidates. They continued to treat me with contempt and mockery, refusing to acknowledge my accomplishments.

The hand-to-hand combat training was brutal. Every day, they pitted us against each other in the ring, and the trainers would shout at us to fight until one of us was down. It was ruthless, and I hated every second of it.

The rules were simple: limit our strikes to firm taps, no heavy contact, and don't cause intentional injury, but our competitive natures prevented us from adhering to them. No one wanted to lose. Inevitably, there were nasty wounds. Even with the best medical attention, the lasting effects of a powerful punch or kick still lingered in my mind.

My small size made it easy for the others to push me around. I hated it when they would toy with me. It wasn't only painful, but humiliating.

But then, one day, something changed. Perhaps it was the anger that had been simmering inside me for so long, or maybe it was just time for me to show what I was capable of at last. Whatever it was, I felt a surge of energy flow through me, and I knew I was about to do something unimaginable.

The sound of fists hitting flesh echoed throughout the training room from matches taking place as I prepared to square off against Zarek, the most formidable knight candidate and hateful asshole. His muscles bulged as he paced around me with an intensity that stole my breath away. The smell of sweat hung heavy in the air, and I felt drops rolling down my forehead while we silently sized each other up, waiting to see who would make the first move.

I felt my heart pounding in my chest, and my muscles ached from the grueling training I'd endured over the past lunars. But I knew that this was my chance to prove myself, to show them all what I'm truly capable of.

We circled each other, and then he lunged at me. I dodged his punch easily and then countered with a blow of my own. It landed squarely on his jaw, and his head snapped back a bit. He smirked, and I saw the rage in his eyes.

He came at me and surprised me by sliding beneath me, knocking my legs out from under me. Just when my head hit the canvas, he punched me in the face, barely missing my nose. The adrenaline shot through me, and on instinct I rolled away from him and sprang to my feet. Breathing heavily from the exchange, I bounced back and forth on my toes, re-centering my composure.

The Master Serg shouted for us to continue, and we resumed. He came at me again, and again I dodged him, but this time I could feel my telekinetic powers stirring within me. They were always there, lurking beneath the surface, but I'd never known how to control them.

Now, though, I felt them surge forward, and I raised my hand. With a flick of my wrist, I sent Zarek flying across the ring, crashing to the ground in a heap.

The other candidates gasped, and even the Master Serg looked impressed.

Without hesitation, he charged at me again. I dodged his blows, my body moving with a fluidity that surprised even me. And when I struck, I struck hard. The force of my punch, backed by my inner force, sent him reeling, and he stumbled back, struggling to regain his balance.

For a moment, there was silence in the room as we both caught our breaths, waiting for the other to make a move. And then, in a flash, he charged at me again.

With a quick movement of my hands, I sent him flying across the room, and he crashed into the wall, this time dazed and disoriented. No one spoke, the shock of what they'd just witnessed still settling in.

Master Serg's voice, gravelly and stunned, broke the silence. "Well done, Zalara. You've shown us all what it means to wield the quantum resonance of a knight."

His words were like music to my ears, and I felt a sense of pride swelling inside me. For the first time since I arrived at the training camp, I felt like I might measure up.

Over the next few days, I continued to hone my skills, practicing my telekinesis and learning new combat techniques. The other candidates treated me with more respect, and I sensed a shift in the dynamic between us. I was no longer an outcast; I was one of them.

Days turned into lunars as I continued to train. I grew strong and controlled my telekinetic powers over the elements better each day. I felt the energy within me, humming with a level of quantum resonance I had never thought possible. The elements responded to my inner command, and I could mold them into whatever I needed them to be. My newfound strength had earned me the respect of the other candidates, and I had even made a few friends, especially Ganthion. But I knew I had many more tests yet to come, not to mention our final trials. We had all heard stories about guys failing the last trials and being sent home or, worse, killed.

One day, the Master Sergeant called me into the training room. "Zalara, today you will face off against one of our top trainers in a sword match." I felt my heart sink. I had never been good with swords, and the thought of facing an opponent in a sword fight terrified me.

I donned my protective leathers, my lightweight chain mail, and gloves as I prepared to enter the dueling arena. I stumbled over my own feet when I saw Nexion walk up to the edge of the arena.

The other candidates in the dueling arena looked on in awe as the Knightmaster strode in, his long black coat billowing behind him, his presence filling the space with an air of authority. The Master Serg and other trainers straightened their posture, showing their respect for the man who was considered one of the greatest knights of their time.

As Nexion approached the edge of the arena, his eyes scanned the group of candidates. When his piercing green eyes landed their gaze on me, I could feel the weight of his scrutiny. His eyes took in my protective gear, the sword in my hand at my side, and the intensity in my focus. I could sense his curiosity as if he was trying to piece together why I had been attracting so much attention from the trainers. I felt his gaze on me, probing and assessing, so I straightened my spine, determined to show him what I was capable of.

The trainer I was facing, a burly man with a bushy beard, approached me, his sword held loosely at his side. "Are you ready, Zalara?" He asked, a hint of amusement in his voice.

I swallowed nervously, feeling a bead of sweat trickle down my forehead. "As ready as I'll ever be," I replied, trying to keep my voice steady.

The trainer chuckled and then raised his sword, signaling the start of the match. I dodged his first few swings, but he was quick, and I knew I couldn't keep it up for long. I lunged forward and swung my sword, but he parried it easily, knocking me off balance.

I swallowed hard, fighting off the nerves that threatened to overwhelm me. My opponent was a tall, muscular man with a wicked glint in his eye. He had a fierce reputation as one of the best trainers at the camp, and I knew that this would be a true test of my skills.

The sound of swords clashing filled the air as we continued our dance. I was quick on my feet, darting in and out of his reach, trying to find an opening. He was skilled, though, and parried each of my strikes with ease.

I stumbled backward, trying to regain my footing, but he pressed his advantage, raining blows down on me. I could feel the weight of the sword in my hand, and I knew he outmatched me.

My heart pounded in my chest, and the sweat from my forehead ran into my eyes, but I refused to give up. I had come too far to let this opportunity slip away. I focused all my energy on the sword, feeling its balance and the power of my telekinetic abilities. Suddenly, I felt a surge of energy within me, and I knew this was my moment.

I raised my sword, and with a flick of my wrist, I sent a wave of telekinetic power towards my opponent. He stumbled back, surprised by my sudden attack.

Seizing the opportunity, I charged forward, my sword flashing in the light. He raised his blade to meet mine, but aided by my powers, I was too quick. With a swift movement, I disarmed him, sending his sword flying across the arena.

The other candidates murmured, and even Knightmaster Nexion nodded, looking fascinated. The trainer stared at me in shock, his eyes wide with disbelief.

The Master Sergeant stepped forward, a proud smile on his face. "Well done, Zalara," he said.

Before I left the arena, Knightmaster Nexion approached me, his eyes still fixed on me. "Well fought, Zalara," he said, his voice low and measured. "I can see why the trainers have been talking about you."

A shiver ran down my spine at his words, a mix of fear and excitement coursing through me. "Thank you, Knightmaster," I managed to reply, trying to keep my voice steady and dropping my gaze to the floor.

I wondered if he had any idea who my true identity was. I had been at the academy for lunars now and had hardly seen him and thought he had left. Standing this close to him, I couldn't help but remember the kiss he had given me before my coronation and worried that he would never forgive me for promoting him to Knightmaster over the other more senior candidates.

Now that I had studied the *Celestial Creed* and understood more about the duty and honor of knights, I knew how difficult it was for Nexion to face his fellow knights and those senior to him. I now doubted my decision to promote him, but there was nothing I could do.

Nexion cleared his throat, bringing my attention back to him and those incredible emerald-green eyes, which were so intense and captivating. His eyes drew me in and left me mesmerized. I couldn't help but notice that the hue was striking against his golden-brown skin and almost seemed to sparkle with energy.

"I would like for us to spar tomorrow first thing in the morning," he said, interrupting my thoughts. "Let's see firsthand how well you've developed your skills during your time here."

My heart skipped a beat at the thought of sparring with the Knightmaster himself. I knew how skilled he was, and the idea of facing him in the arena both terrified and excited me. There was no way I could say no, not to him, not when he was the only one who had ever sent scorching heat through my veins.

"Of course, Knightmaster. I'll be ready."

He nodded and stepped back, the faintest hint of a smile on his lips. He said nothing, and his gaze lingered on me for a few seconds too long before he broke away to leave. As he walked away, I studied the back of his head and wondered what he saw when he looked at me. Did he see a warrior, or did he see the girl that he had once shared a forbidden kiss with?

I shook my head, trying to push those thoughts away. I couldn't let my feelings become a distraction. My goal was to become a knight and prove to myself and everyone else that I could stand on my own two feet.

As I left the training room, unease settled in the pit of my stomach. I knew that the next day's sparring match would be a genuine test of my skills, but more than that, I knew it would be a test of my heart.

CHAPTER TEN

ELZARIA

I woke up before dawn, my muscles already feeling tense in anticipation of the match to come. To relax and quiet my mind, I took a hot shower before getting dressed in my training clothes. I grabbed a protein bar and ate it on the way to the arena, my eyes fixed on the path ahead of me. I knew this would be a chance to prove myself to the Knightmaster.

As I arrived at the arena, the inky blanket of night was giving way to the first hint of dawn. The stars, which had been twinkling brightly, were yielding to the approaching day. Hues of deep indigo and navy blue had yet transitioned to a palette of purples, pinks, and oranges. I always loved the breaking dawn's promise of a new day, when everything is still, and the air's cool freshness embraces the world.

I could see Nexion already waiting for me as he moved to the edge of the arena. The golden rays of the morning's dawn gleamed on his bare torso, causing my breath to catch. It was the first time I had seen him without a shirt, and the sight was halting.

The large black ink tattoo of an angel with its wings spread wide in a beautiful yet solemn display of power was etched into his skin on his right side and instantly drew my attention. One wing extended from his hip, curving up under his arm, while the other unfurled across the plane of his chiseled abdomen, leading to the center of his chest. It was a chaste image against his dark, tanned skin, the angel seeming almost lifelike amidst the ridges and valleys of his muscular form that, for me, provoked lascivious thoughts.

I traced the intricate lines of the tattoo with my eyes; the design radiating an intriguing mix of power and tranquility. Each detail was meticulously rendered, from the feathers on the wings to the fervent expression on the angel's face. It was hard to pull my gaze away.

My fingers twitched with a desire to trace the tattoo, to feel the heat of his skin under my palm, and experience the contours of his impressive body. I wondered about the story behind the tattoo. What had compelled Nexion to choose such a solemn and potent image to paint his body permanently? Was it a tribute, a promise, or a reminder? I could only speculate, each possible explanation adding layers of depth to the already complex man before me.

The sight of Nexion, shirtless and emblazoned with the powerful image, was undeniably sensual. I could feel an unfamiliar heat curling in my stomach, a pulse of arousal that seemed to echo the rhythm of my heart. It was a powerful feeling, one that both thrilled and unnerved me in its intensity.

Yet, it was the unspoken allure of the man behind the ink that truly captivated me. His disciplined physique, coupled with his fierce yet principled demeanor, embodied a unique blend of strength and restraint. As I continued to drink in the sight of him, I realized my attraction to Nexion went far deeper than physical desire—it was an undeniable pull.

He looked up as I entered, his eyes narrowing as he studied me.

"You're early," he said, his voice low and measured.

"I wanted to make sure I was properly warmed up," I replied, trying to sound confident.

Nexion nodded, a small smirk on his face. "Very well, you warm up and stretch. I'm ready when you are."

I kicked off my shoes and pulled off my shirt, wearing only a sports bra and fitted-cropped pants. Nexion watched as I stretched and warmed up, never dropping his gaze. I could feel the intensity of his focus on me, as if he were searching for clues about what made me tick. He seemed to be carefully studying every move I made. His eyes traveled from my head to my toes, scrutinizing me as if he were trying to discover some hidden truth.

I wiped the sweat from my face and entered the arena. The canvas was rough beneath my feet, and all I could hear was our breathing. Grateful no one came to watch.

NEXION

She tried to hide her nervousness as I stepped onto the canvas. The difference in our size alone would back most opponents down, but not her. Zalara squared her shoulders, expecting the worst, as if I was a wild beast ready to rip her throat out.

I took a step forward, locking my gaze with Zalara's. "Remember," I reminded her in a measured tone, "we're not here to hurt each other. We're here to spar, to test our skills, and learn from each other."

Her nod, combined with the quiet determination in her eyes, set my heart racing. It was a potent mix of respect and intense attraction that was hard to dismiss. I had been watching her progress since her first day, not expecting her to have made it this far. She may be small, but she has proven to be a mighty opponent to her classmates and instructors alike. I couldn't stop myself from seeing first-hand what it would be like to go up against her in such close quarters.

"Understood," she replied.

And with that, we began.

We circled each other warily, both of us waiting for the other to make the first move. I could feel the tension in the air, the energy between us almost tangible.

I made the first move, launching towards her, my fist aimed at her face. She was swift and ducked out of the way. I attacked with a barrage of punches and kicks, which she mostly dodged. She was small, but her agility and knowledge of the craft were commendable, her movements fluid and calculated. Continuing to test her, I landed a glancing blow to her cheek, snapping her head back, hard enough for it to sting darkening her blue eyes.

Her focus heightened; she took a deep breath, steading herself. "Is that all you've got, Knightmaster?" She taunted, hoping she could throw me off. Her smart-ass little mouth and defiant look made me laugh to myself.

I lunged forward, using my weight to push her back into a corner with a couple of side kicks. She wasn't about to give in and hit the deck with her shoulder. Rolling out from under the left hook headed her way.

This time, it was her turn. Agile and flexible like a cat, she spun jumping in the air, knocking me in the chin with a sound hook kick, causing me to lose my footing for a second. She saw her advantage and moved with a quick cross punch aimed at my nose. Not anticipating my speed, I grabbed her fist and held it long enough to remind her who was dominant. Her telekinetic powers simmered beneath the surface of my hand. I remembered watching how she only let them come out when her fight-or-flight instincts were triggered.

We traded blows back and forth, both of us landing hits and taking them, always holding back just enough to not cause injury. Sweat trickling down Zalara's face, I continued to push her nonstop, checking her endurance. I wanted to know who she truly was and draw out the wild animal I suspected she hid deep within her core.

The sparring match intensified in both speed and contact. Slowly, I brought her to the brink. Her frustration mounting as I provoked her by toying with her. Moving quickly to smack her in the face, then landing a harsh side kick to her gut followed by an immediate round kick to the head ringing her bell. I saw her pupils grow large and black and hoped she would allow her inner demon to break through.

Her breathing suddenly changed to a deep, slow rhythm. In an instant, her blows now flew with the heated energy of her powers. It was all I could do to block and counter her onslaught. It was time to force them back into their cage.

As she swung at my face with a left hook, I captured her arm, spinning her around, using the momentum to throw her on the ground, knocking the breath from her. I dropped to the ground, pinning her with my body, trapping her wrists and jamming them to the mat on either side of her face. Fuck, she was beautiful, the tattoos along her face projecting her fierceness.

Our chests heaved as we tried to catch our breath and she writhed beneath me, trying to free herself. My face inches from hers, the intense attraction between us became a force of its own, a mix of arousal and longing that was hard to resist. The heat rolled off me as I felt sweat run down my sides. I couldn't help but notice how good she smelled, a mix of something floral and something uniquely her.

Zalara seemed to be caught in the same spell, her clear blue eyes turning into stormy oceans as she stared at me. Succumbing to the irresistible pull between us, I leaned down and kissed her. The world around us seemed to fade as I lost myself in the taste of her. She returned my kiss, her lips hard and demanding against mine.

I explored her body, relishing her responses to my touch, the hunger between us growing. Sliding my hand down her side, I explored the curves and dips of her waist and ass. We both became more and more consumed by the passion that flared between us. I could feel her heart beating against her ribs and was sure she could feel my hardness pressing against the apex of her legs. She released a soft gasp at the suddenness of it all, fueling my carnal desire.

I growled deep from within my throat, taking great pleasure in her reactions. My hand slid up her side as my lips moved to her neck, nipping and licking as I worked my way down towards her chest.

She moaned softly, unable to contain the pleasure that coursed through her from my touch. As I explored her body with gentle yet demanding hands, she ran her fingers through my tangled, damp hair. I felt a fire burning inside of me, a desire like nothing I'd ever felt before.

The intensity between us only increased as my mouth captured one of her nipples over the fabric of her top. My teeth teased and tantalized, causing her to shudder.

As I felt her body yield to my advances, the reality of our situation, our ranks, hit me hard. The guilt crashed over me like an icy wave, the *Celestial Creed* echoing in my head. I abruptly pulled away, breaking our passionate embrace. Mad as hell, I had let this happen, echoing the mistake I had made with the princess. "I'm sorry," I apologized, my voice hoarse with guilt and regret. "That was a mistake. I shouldn't have taken advantage of you."

Rolling away from her, I scrambled to my feet.

"I acted out of line," I began, my voice grating with anger and regret. "I violated your trust, violated my position as your trainer."

Her eyes widened slightly, but she remained silent, waiting for me to continue. Each word tasted bitter in my mouth as I continued, "My desires clouded my judgment."

Hating myself, I paced back and forth. Tore my fingers through my hair, wanting to rip it out. "I betrayed my duty, my oath. I am sorry, Zalara."

The confession hung heavily in the air between us, its stark truth making my stomach churn.

She sat up; her face flushed with a mix of embarrassment and desire, her voice barely audible. "It's okay, Knightmaster," she whispered, trying to hide her feelings. "It won't happen again."

Her words echoed in my mind as I nodded, the guilt clutching my chest as I struggled to regain my composure. "You're right," I agreed, forcing my voice to be as cold and distant as I could manage. "It won't happen again."

And with that, I left the arena, leaving behind the lingering resonance of a passion that should never have surfaced.

I stormed away from the arena, my thoughts a whirlwind of confusion and guilt. Each step was heavy with regret, my mind replaying the events of what happened in vivid detail.

The door to my quarters slammed shut behind me, the noise echoing off the stone walls. I leaned against it, clenching my fists in an attempt to control the surge of anger coursing through me. The image of Zalara, flushed and breathless beneath me, refused to fade.

With a growl of frustration, I turned, pacing the room in an effort to shake the memory from my mind.

"What the hell was I thinking?" I growled, my words bouncing off the stone walls. "I took advantage of her. I let my desires take control. Dammit, Nexion, you're her trainer, her guardian!"

The guilt gnawed at me, my stomach clenching in shame. As much as I wanted to blame Zalara for the irresistible allure she held over me, I knew I was the one at fault. I was the one who had crossed the line.

The room fell silent, save for my harsh breathing. I raked my fingers through my hair, desperately trying to regain control of my emotions. But the dishonor remained, a heavy burden on my conscience.

With a sudden surge of anger, I kicked the chair by the desk, sending it crashing against the wall. The noise echoed around the room, providing a brief release for my frustration.

"I swore an oath," I reminded myself, my voice filled with self-loathing. "An oath to protect, to guide, to keep my emotions in check. But I've failed."

My reflection stared back at me from the mirror on the wall, a harsh reminder of the man I had become. The *Celestial Creed* was burned into my soul, a constant reminder of my duty and my failures.

"I have to make this right," I said, my voice firm with determination. "I owe it to her, to myself."

But as I stared at my reflection, the image of Zalara remained, a haunting reminder of the line I had crossed, the trust I had broken. The guilt was an unwelcome guest, one that would linger until I could find a way to make amends.

CHAPTER ELEVEN

ELZARIA

I never once laid eyes on Nexion again. I knew that like before, when he left Arcadia, he was avoiding me like the plague. His loyalty to the crown and sense of honor and duty to the knighthood came before all else to Knightmaster Nexion. Thankfully, I didn't get any sense that he had recognized me through my disguise.

The training never let up. I was constantly dirty, tired, and beat up. If I wasn't doing some form of physical training, I was spending hours studying or practicing the use of my telekinetic powers. My new life differed completely from what it had been before as a princess and newly crowned Queen. Those grueling hours gave me callused hands and a lean, muscular body.

Mostly, I kept to myself. The other candidates respected me but didn't feel comfortable working with a female. The Master Sergeant kept a cool distance from me, too. Making sure no one thought he was giving me an easier time because I was a girl. He pushed me hard and expected me to be perfect, like I was his secret project. If he was going to have a girl become a knight, he would make sure no one questioned it.

We faced our final set of trials before the Rite of Ascension, the test that would determine whether or not we would be accepted into the knighthood. The Master Sergeant had designed a course that was nearly impossible to complete, filled with traps, obstacles, and challenges that would challenge even the most skilled knights.

I stood at the starting line, my heart pounding in my chest. It was a long and winding path that led through the forest, over the mountain's top, across the river in the steep valley below, and finally, returning to the academy's AI simulation room before finally crossing the finish line. The other candidates had all gone before me, and a couple of them had failed to make it to the end. I knew I was the only one left, and my chances of success were slim.

The starter's pistol rang out, and I ran, my feet pounding against the dirt as I raced toward the first challenge. It was a wall, nearly twenty feet high, with no visible handholds or footholds. Using my telekinetic powers to create a makeshift ladder, I levitated rocks and tree limbs to create steps I could climb up.

The next challenge was a rope bridge that spanned a deep ravine. I crossed it while dodging arrows and fireballs that instructors hurled at me. I used my telekinetic powers to deflect the projectiles, and with steady feet and hands, I made it across the bridge.

The obstacles kept coming, each one more difficult than the last. I climbed sheer rock faces and swam across treacherous rapids. Then came the wild boar that had been set loose in the forest. The boar surprised me just after leaving the stream.

Distracted by the cold of the water and the wetness of my clothes, I didn't see it coming. Just before he gored me, I reacted by flipping around, but lost my footing and fell, slamming my face into the rocky ground. My lip burst open as it smashed into a sharp edge. I was still sitting on my ass when the boar came roaring back. The adrenaline from my injury and the terror of seeing him come at my face provoked my base instinct for survival. A bolt of energy shot out from my hand exploding the beast, leaving me covered in a disgusting foul-smelling gunk. I trudged back into the stream and washed off the best I could. The cold water helped stop my lip from bleeding, but I could already feel the swelling setting in.

I tried to shake off the incident as I headed back to the AI simulation room. I had fought my way through every challenge that had been thrown at me. No matter how hard the last test was, I refused to give up.

After a long slog back to campus, exhausted and beat-up, I faced the ultimate test. The AI chamber was an advanced and highly sophisticated training facility used by our knights to hone their combat skills. Upon entering, the warriors found themselves in a fully immersive and adaptive environment.

The chamber used high-resolution holographic projectors to construct and deconstruct virtual environments rapidly. This allowed the sim to create any imaginable battlefield scenario in real time, from dense urban environments to vast alien landscapes. The chamber was also equipped with an advanced climate control system that could mimic various weather conditions, including rain, snow, wind, and extreme temperatures.

The AI running the simulation was a highly adaptive system that could learn and respond to the warriors' actions, providing them with a tailored training experience. It analyzed their strengths and weaknesses, pushing them to their limits and helping them improve their skills. The AI also created realistic and intelligent virtual enemies for the warriors to face, simulating the tactics and abilities of actual adversaries they might encounter in combat situations.

To further enhance the realism of the training, the simulator used advanced haptic feedback suits and specialized weaponry. The suits simulated the sensations of impact, temperature, and weight, while the specialized weapons mimicked the feel and function of real-world counterparts. This allowed the warriors to become fully immersed in the simulation, forgetting they were in a controlled environment as they engaged in high-stakes combat scenarios.

I connected the neural link behind my ear, donned my haptic feedback suit, and entered the AI simulation room, which was set up to look like that of a small war-torn civilian town. The buildings appeared real, and I could hear the distant sounds of people going about their daily lives.

The Master Sergeant's voice echoed through the room, instructing me that my objective was to locate and apprehend a dangerous insurgent hiding in the town. I had to complete this task while minimizing civilian casualties and making morally sound decisions.

I made my way through the town, my senses heightened, and my heart pounding in my chest. The civilians seemed to go about their daily routines, unaware of the danger lurking in their midst. I knew I had to be cautious, as any wrong move could have dire consequences.

I turned a corner and found myself faced with two impossible choices. On one side of the street, a group of children played in the yard of their home, innocent and carefree. On the other side, a woman was being held hostage by a man in a mask, his weapon pointed at her head.

The man with the weapon was the insurgent they had tasked me with apprehending. I knew that if I attacked him directly, he would likely kill the woman, and if I hesitated, the insurgent might escape, putting even more lives in danger.

I had to decide, and I had to make it fast. With my telekinetic powers, I carefully lifted a rock from the ground and hurled it toward a nearby trash can, creating a loud noise that distracted the insurgent. In that split second, I moved swiftly and used my powers to disarm the insurgent, knocking the weapon out of his hand.

The weapon fell, and I rushed forward, shielding the hostage with my body. As the insurgent reached for the laser-pistol, I flung myself over it. He kicked me in the back, but I held tight. Seizing the pistol, I used my powers to bend the barrel, rendering it useless. As he continued to attack me, all the lunars of difficult training kicked in. I sprang to my feet. He went for my throat. I shoved his elbows down and head-butted him in the nose, causing him to loosen his grip. I grabbed him by the shoulders, and using all my weight, I side-kicked him in the knee. The sound of his knee snapping and breaking was gruesome, but didn't stop me from jumping on top of him and punching him in the jaw, knocking him unconscious.

I ensured the children across the street remained unharmed and freed the woman from her captor. I had resolved the situation with no casualties, and made sound decisions.

As I stood there, panting and exhausted, the AI scene around me faded away. The Master Sergeant's voice rang out once more, informing me I had successfully completed the final test. I had proven that I had the strength, skill, and moral compass necessary to become a true knight.

As I exited the simulation room, my fellow candidates and the instructors applauded my performance. I felt a swell of pride and accomplishment, knowing that I hadn't only endured the grueling physical and mental challenges, but had also upheld the high standards of the knighthood.

The Master Sergeant approached me, and we made eye contact, acknowledging the other's presence. He then extended his right arm to me, reaching out and firmly grasping my forearm just below the elbow. I knew this greeting served as a symbol of our mutual dedication to the Empyrean Knighthood and our commitment to stand by one another in the heat of battle, as well as our willingness to support and protect one another in times of need. This simple yet meaningful gesture was a universal sign of respect and loyalty among those who have chosen the path of the warrior.

"Candidate Galen, I would have you at my back anytime," he said, giving me a short crisp bow.

"Thank you, sir." I replied. At the same time, I saw Nexion whip around and head out the door, evoking a raised eyebrow from the Master Sergeant and a few curious looks from the others.

How dare he ruin this moment for me? Perhaps it was because I was exhausted from the final trials, but it pissed me off. I resolved to confront him the next day. It was long overdue for him to deal with the attraction we felt for each other and his reaction to me each time he kissed me. I was determined to make him understand why I chose him as Knightmaster, too. For now, though, I was going to celebrate with my fellow knights.

CHAPTER TWELVE

ELZARIA

I awoke from the best night's sleep I had had since arriving at the Academy. The anxiety of needing to succeed was a heavy weight now lifted from my shoulders. My confidence was running high, and I was determined to confront Nexion and bend him to my will, after all, I was his Queen. I laughed out loud, wondering what Nexion and everyone else at the Citadel would think about having the Empyrean Queen working alongside them during training. I had endured more than my fair share of insults and humiliations at their hands. Would they be angry? Would they take my deception as an insult? I hoped not. I desperately wanted their respect and loyalty.

I took a gloriously long hot shower, braided my long hair in one thick tail, and found a black form-fitting training suit to wear. For the first time in lunars, I allowed myself to reminisce about all the beautiful clothes and shoes I left behind. I missed my parents, Adelaide, and everything about my former life. It would never be the same as before. I was a different person and liked my new strength. Since today was a well-deserved day off for all the knight candidates, the dining hall was empty. I took my time eating breakfast and rehearsed in my mind what I was going to say to Nexion. Although I dreaded it, I knew it was time to find him and get this over with.

The Citadel was a ghost town. Following tomorrow's graduation, the academy would close, and they would spend a few decas preparing for the next class of candidates. Today, it seemed, everyone was gone, and I worried I wouldn't be able to find Nexion. He wasn't in his office, the library, the Grand Hall, the arena, or the garden areas. That left only his residence or the AI simulation center. I didn't want to discuss these matters with him in his residence, no matter what. So, I headed for the AI simulation center, not having much hope that he would be there.

As I entered, I heard the simulator was active. I quietly crept into the control room to see who it was and what they were doing and found Nexion holding a weapon that was a cross between a bo and an energy blade. Knights often used them to train with because they could adjust the level of force from nothing but the tap of the weapon to the highest lethal level. Typically, during training, knights used a moderately high level to motivate their opponents to avoid getting hit. It stung and left welts on your skin. The pain could be intense. I despised the feeling of it, how it made me feel weak and vulnerable; a strong negative motivator that I had grown to resent.

I watched Nexion move from one practice drill to another. For such an enormous guy, he was agile, like a big cat. His movements were fluid and lethal. I pity the fool who thinks it would be a good idea to piss him off.

Wanting to ensure our privacy, I instructed the simulator to lock all the exits and then shut the simulation down.

Nexion shouted, "Who's there?" As he disconnected the neural link from behind his ear and shrugged off the haptic feedback suit, leaving him in only fatigue pants, his chest bare and covered in sweat.

I walked into the room, which was barely lit, and stood with my arms crossed, tapping my right foot against the floor.

"Hello Zalara, I didn't know anyone remained in the Citadel today. Let me take this opportunity to congratulate you on your success yesterday at the trials and on tomorrow's ascension to knighthood."

Nexion crossed the room, taking hold of my right arm in a respectful grasp. "Sure, thank you," my voice dripped with sarcasm. "I saw how proud you were of me when you bolted out of the door as soon as I had made it through the last trial."

Nexion quirked his head to the side, surprised by the tone I was taking with him; the almighty Knightmaster.

"It's time we talk, *Knightmaster*." I squared my shoulders toward him, determined not to let him intimidate me. "You remember our encounter after sparring in the arena, don't you?" I spit out the question with venom lacing each word.

He eyed me cautiously but didn't speak.

"You had the audacity to kiss me and then ran away like a scorned child. You hid from me, too weak to speak your mind. And you call yourself Knightmaster!" I spat at him.

Coming to stand within inches of me, in an effort to intimidate me, I could feel the heat rolling off his body.

"Young knight, you may have completed your training, but you had better watch your tone." His voice deepened. "I do not tolerate insolence from anyone."

"Oh? How about the Empyrean Queen? I hear she found you quite *delicious?*" I knew I was pushing every button he had. It wasn't how I had planned for this conversation to go, but I had kept all my anger and frustration bottled up for far too long.

Nexion's eyes radiated with fury as he clinched his jaw, the tension from grinding his teeth, causing a slight tick. I instinctually stepped back a few inches, still trying to hold my ground against this formidable angry giant.

He shoved his bo into my hands and stomped to the rack, holding more, ripping one from its harness. "We will settle this like the warriors we are. Simulator set scene for complete darkness. Weather of the Sarvian desert. No other constructs." He commanded the simulator.

Instantly, the room darkened to an inky blackness, and the heat rose. I stood motionless, waiting for what Nexion would do next.

"So, you wanted to turn up the heat, little girl?" He whispered next to my ear.

Where he had come from or gone to, I had no idea, but I swore under my breath I wouldn't back down.

"So, what? Are we going to stand in the darkness and hurl insults at each other?" I said with more confidence than I felt.

"A well-trained knight can confront his opponents under any circumstances. Are you afraid of the dark, little one?"

His absolute arrogance grated on my last nerve. How dare he reduce me to "little girl, little one." I continued to stand motionless, refusing to rise to the bait. The hair on my neck stood on end as I felt him stalking me. I just knew he had a smug expression. Oh, how I wanted to smack it clean off of him.

The slightest bit of air moved to my right side. I lashed out with my bo but didn't connect. In a split second, he smacked me on the ass. He had increased the pain level, making me jump. Damn, that hurt, but I refused to let him know.

He laughed low in his chest, which gave me the opportunity I needed. Swinging out, aiming for what I hoped were his knees, this time, I connected. Then silence. The heat was oppressive.

As I crept to the left, I refused to let him bully me or be afraid to call him out about his actions towards me. "Are you always a hit-and-run kind of guy? Kiss a girl and flee? Not man enough to have a conversation? Are your feelings really hurt that easily?" Oh, man oh man, I knew my verbal jabs were hitting their mark.

Again, out of nowhere, he struck me on the ass this time much harder, taking my breath with an audible hitch. He knew that one had hurt.

"Am I that repulsive to you?" I said, unable to hide the quiver in my voice. The air stilled, neither of us breathed.

"You're not repulsive."

"What did I do to deserve your scorn? Why do you hate me so much that you refuse to speak to me or acknowledge my presence?" Then, barely audible, "*You* kissed me."

"I'm a knight, now the Knightmaster; not that it was my time to be, but a responsibility I take most seriously. By *Creed*, I'm to be honorable and display the highest level of integrity. My behavior wasn't acceptable, and *you* agreed. That was the end of it."

Once again, the heat of anger flooded through me. Like a cat, I swung my bo, closing my eyes and acting on pure instinct. Two hard hits, one to the body and the other to the face, I hoped. "True knight? I agreed? Are you fucking kidding me?"

I knew I had drawn blood. I smelled the tangy iron metallic scent mixed with the slightly salty odor of his sweat. The sweltering heat mixed with my rage as I swung again, this time missing and giving away my position.

Nexion used it to his advantage, swiping my feet out from under me, feeling the sting of his bo against the back of my ankles. I tried to swing myself back up, but he caught me by the waist, slamming me to the floor. The force knocked the breath from me as the memory of him doing the same when I had run away from my coronation came rushing back. He straddled my waist and pinned my hands to the floor next to my cheeks.

I wished I could see his face. To read his expression, but the impenetrable darkness concealed everything. The inability to see heightened all my other senses. The pulse in his thighs was a slow drumbeat against my skin. His raspy breaths echoed in my ears.

Nexion's lips crushed against mine. He took my lower lip between his teeth and tugged roughly, making me gasp. His tongue plunged into my mouth, and I responded fiercely, wrapping my legs around him. There was nothing gentle about this kiss. It was raw passion and desire. I sucked on his tongue, biting it lightly, causing him to growl into my mouth. His hand slid up my side, rough and calloused, sending shivers down my spine. I moaned into his mouth; the sound swallowed by his lips covering mine.

I couldn't deny the intense arousal I felt, even as my anger towards him simmered beneath the surface. It was like my body was betraying my mind, responding to his every touch and kiss.

As the kiss deepened, I could feel his hard cock pressing against me. I ground my hips against him, wanting more. His hand found its way to my breast, squeezing it brusquely over my top, making me whimper with need. I clawed at his back, trying to get closer, demanding to feel every inch of him.

As he broke the kiss, I couldn't resist biting his lip in retaliation.

He growled in response, grabbing my hair and pulling it back forcefully. "You want to play rough, little knight?" He murmured in my ear, his hot breath making me melt. "I can play rough, too."

Before I could even process what he meant, he was kissing me again, harder than before. His hands roamed my body, trailing over my breasts and hips.

He ripped himself away from me, leaving me feeling cold even in the sweltering heat.

"Oh, great, here we go again. Seriously, if kissing me is so bad, why do you do it?" I rambled as I started to get up.

"Don't move, Zalara," he commanded, "or else I will have to punish you." Nexion ordered from behind me. How he moved so silently was a mystery. I felt his hands wrap around my waist as he slid them up and slowly stripped me of my top. He pushed my shoulders down to the floor and then peeled off my pants, leaving me naked yet unseen in the room's blackness. I heard him unlatch his belt and drop his pants to the floor. As he lowered himself next to me, I felt his cock on my thigh and couldn't resist sliding my fingers around it, eliciting a groan.

"Zalara! I told you not to move." His shout took me by surprise and made me jump.

In one motion, he swept me up and threw me over his lap. I landed hard. His massive forearm holding me in place. His hand smacked down on my backside with a sharp sting. As he spanked my bare bottom, I screamed a continuous stream of profanity and struggled to get away.

A soft chuckle from him made me freeze. "Mindless cursing, Zalara? Don't tell me you're in over your head. Does a little spanking hurt so much?"

"Fuck you," I hissed.

His laughter filled the dark space. "I'm aware of the fact that you want me to fuck you, little one. I can feel it in every fiber of your body."

I opened my mouth to argue, but his hand came down on my ass again and again. It felt like it was on fire, a pain I had never experienced. He reached down and squeezed, kneading my ass in his calloused hands, sending a streak of pain through my skin and a shot of desire to my center. I didn't stay there long. He flipped me over back onto the floor, straddling my waist once again, except this time the heat of his skin threatened to consume me.

He brushed his lips across my chest and across my throat, so gently I could barely feel them. The sensation of the stubble on his chin against my soft skin was nothing less than intoxicating. He worked his way up my jawline while the rest of him stayed perfectly still. "Now let's see what we can do about that smart mouth of yours, little knight." His lips crushed against mine once again as he took my breast in his hand, squeezing and toying with my nipple.

Nexion trailed kisses down my collarbone and to my breast, sucking gently on one while he caressed the other. Sliding down my body, he laved kisses down my stomach and over my hip.

He pulled my knees up and apart, settling in front of me, cupping my ass in his hands. Then his lips found my center, wet, hot, and open. The first touch of his tongue to my clit made me arch my back and dig my fingers into his head. I tugged at his hair, pulling his mouth to me.

"Mmmm, yes," I moaned, lifting my hips and forcing his mouth harder against my clit.

It was an experience unlike anything I had ever had. I'd never been with a man.

His fingers spread my folds, his warm breath on my wet lips. He flicked his tongue over my clit, then swirled it around the sensitive nub. With his mouth on my clit, he slid two fingers into me.

I was tight, and his fingers stretched me, once more blurring the line between pleasure and pain.

He grunted in approval as I writhed against him. He nibbled on my clit, sending delicious shock waves through my body. Sliding his tongue into my opening, he pumped it in and out of me, stretching my wet flesh. I was so close to the edge. I felt myself tightening around him, signaling my impending release.

He once again slid his fingers in and out of me as he sucked my clit. My orgasm overtook me, and I threw my head back as I came crying out in a hoarse scream.

Nexion moved back up my body, scattering wet kisses from my hip to my breast. As he settled between my legs, I felt the hard length of his cock pressing against my entrance. I wanted *this* more than I wanted to hate him.

The heat was intense, but I didn't want him to stop. I wanted to feel his body against mine. I needed to feel him inside me, to know what it would feel like.

His hand slowly trailed down my body. As he slid his hand over my bottom, the roughness of his fingers against the tenderness of my skin from the spanking mixed with his touch and felt amazing. I groaned and pushed myself into his hand. He just held me there for a moment, not moving, almost as if he were focusing on something.

I pressed my hips up, begging him silently to take me. I felt him hold back, but he wasn't going to deny me this. He was going to give me what I wanted. I couldn't control my body, no matter how hard I tried. I bit my lip in frustration, trying to rein in my raging libido.

I wanted him inside me, now. The thought of Nexion in that way surprised me. Would we have a casual encounter, or would he just bang me hard and fast and then leave?

As if he could read my mind, he growled in my ear, "I will take you, take all of you, my little knight, not just fuck you. You will be mine and I will give you pleasure; unlike anything you have ever experienced."

His head dipped down and he kissed me again, hard and raw. I slid my hands over his back, feeling the tension he was holding onto.

"Are you sure about this, little one? If I take you, there will be no going back." I felt the strength of his erection pressing against my center. I wanted him to fill me, to make me his.

"Yes," I begged.

"I want you, Zalara," he said between kisses. "Your body is screaming for me. You're so fucking wet," Nexion grunted as he moved his cock, sliding it along my wet lips. "It's fucking soaking. I can smell your arousal."

The thought of him smelling me made me blush profusely. My face went hot and if he could see it, I was sure it was bright red. His thumb played across my clit and pressed it hard, sending a wave of pleasure straight to my core.

"Oh God, Nexion," I moaned. "Please."

"Please what, little one?"

"Please, please fuck me," I moaned. I trembled, fearing how it would feel for the first time. Nexion didn't know I was a virgin, nor did I want him to. I was already obsessed with the pleasure-pain combination he had introduced me to.

I felt the head of his cock push against the slick entrance of my body. The tip of it slid into me; it was huge. I'd never felt something there before. He held still for a moment, letting me adjust.

"So tight, little one," Nexion muttered. He slid back out and pumped his hips going in a little deeper, a little faster with each stroke. I buried my face in his neck as I felt every inch of him enter me.

I squeezed my eyes shut. It burned, but it also felt so carnal, so sensual, so right. He was touching me where no one had ever been.

"Fuck, Zalara," he groaned, sounding pained. "You feel like heaven."

Propped up on his elbows, he rocked his hips against mine, making me feel every inch of him sliding in and out. The feeling was amazing, as I pushed my hips up to meet his.

He groaned and leaned down, kissing me. As he plunged his tongue into my mouth, I sucked it hard in time to his thrusts. He pushed up to his hands, giving him more leverage against me.

"So, fucking perfect," Nexion growled. He picked up a steady pace, his massive body hovering over me.

He slid a hand down my belly and over my hip. With his thumb, he massaged my clit as he thrust into me. I moaned in pleasure as my orgasm built again. My fingers traced along his sides, feeling the muscles rippling underneath his skin.

His hand on my clit, his cock inside me; the pain I had felt was long forgotten. Once again, the tension rose inside me. My body coiled tight; I was so close.

Nexion lowered himself back to his elbows and growled in my ear. "Cum for me, little one," he demanded, thrusting harder against me, rocking his hips so that he rubbed against my clit. My entire body tensed as I let out a primal scream that echoed off the walls, and the waves of pleasure washed over me as my orgasm ripped through me. Nexion groaned as I came convulsing around him.

His body tensed against mine and with another groan, he thrust once more, holding himself deep within me. I could feel him throbbing as he came.

I lay there panting, trying to find the strength to move.

"How do you feel about me now, little one?" His voice had lost its edge.

"I thought you hated me. That you regretted kissing me," I mumbled, my voice shaking.

Nexion climbed off me and sat on the floor as he lifted me into his arms. He settled me onto his lap as I straddled his hips, my knees on the floor, and my throbbing folds against his skin. "I never hated you. You are one of the best students the academy has ever had. Now, the finest knight." He stroked my back with a tender touch. "You surpassed all my expectations. No one thought you'd come so far when you first arrived."

He pushed my braid behind my back and stroked my throat with his thumbs. "Tell me, Zalara, why does a spoiled little rich girl, the daughter of a wealthy shipping magnate, want to be a warrior? I thought at first this was just some game you were playing, but I watched you closely and saw how hard you fought for each and everything you achieved. As if driven by some force within you." His voice was soft as he ran his fingers over my face. I felt shy and was still coming down from my post orgasmic bliss. I wasn't sure how to respond or how to tell him who I really was.

"It's complicated. You're right, I did grow up as a privileged, spoiled girl. But that's not who I am. I don't want to be defined by my birth no more than you would." I kissed him softly, hoping he would accept that much for now.

"Mmmm, I guess." He said, not sounding convinced.

"Now, answer me something. Why did you go so cold and shut yourself off to me? Why ignore me?"

"It's complicated. I serve at the pleasure of the Queen. You've studied the *Celestial Creed*. Our duty must always come before our needs or wants. We are loyal to our knighthood and our Empyrean royal house. We vow to protect and defend our realm above all else. That doesn't allow for personal relationships."

"The former Queen Elindra has a very happy marriage to Prime Minister Helion, who rose through the political structure from starting out as a knight and eventually becoming Knightmaster before he was elected as Prime Minister. Did he not act in accordance with *The Creed*?" I questioned.

"That's different, my little knight. You are no Queen, and I should never have been named Knightmaster. It wasn't my time."

I gasped at his blunt revelation. "Why do you question the authority of the new queen?"

"She's no queen. She's a spoiled brat. She tried to run away from her coronation, and I had to haul her back. And then, *Queen Elzaria* spouted a bunch of nonsense about how she dreamed of war breaking out across the universe, killing millions. She tried to convince me The Creators had spoken to her. If you can believe that."

As soon as the words left his mouth, my body tensed. The sting of Nexion's barbs hit me like a slap in the face, the impact jarring and sudden. The reminder of my deception made me panic. I practically jumped off his lap and searched blindly, desperately for my clothes.

"What's wrong Zalara?" He asked, confused by my sudden reaction.

His words, the heat, the utter darkness, bore down on my chest. I wrapped my arms around my shins and dropped my forehead to my knees. My anxiety rose, unleashing the images of war savaging the Empyrean people. The responsibility to protect and serve the Empyrean people crushed me. I could hear the cries of children. Violently shaking, I covered my ears and screamed.

Nexion lifted me into his lap, brushing my damp hair from my face. "Simulator, lights twenty percent."

He held me against his chest. His slow, strong heartbeat calmed me. "What's wrong, Zalara?"

When I didn't reply, he cupped my face in his hands, making me look at him. We saw each other for the first time. His brows furrowed, his lips tight with concern. His thumb traced the tattoo that led from my forehead around my eye to along my cheekbone as he studied the intricate pattern.

I was bare to his gaze. It wasn't only that I was naked, but that the truth of who I was demanded to be told.

"I'm so sorry, Nexion."

"For what? You have done nothing wrong. It is I who should apologize to you for the way I have mistreated you during the most difficult times of your training."

"No, no, please don't apologize. You have every right to hate me."

He was so confused.

Fighting back the tears, I refused to let him think I was weak. I saw my shirt and pants near us and rolled off his lap as I was engulfed with the embarrassment of my nakedness; or maybe it was the untold lies.

Turning my back to him, I quickly slipped my shirt over my head and down over my torso. Still sitting on the floor, I struggled to pull on my pants over my damp legs. I knew his gaze never left me.

Before I could stand, he was there, lifting me to my feet by my arms. His glistening abs rippled with tight muscles. Not wanting to look him in the eye, I had nowhere else to look except down. My breath caught in my throat as I laid eyes on him, on all of him. Going weak in the knees, I reached out and seized his hips.

Using one finger, he raised my face, forcing me to meet his eyes.

"Explain." He didn't ask, he commanded.

I couldn't speak, much less think, standing this close to him. Crossing my arms over my body, I turned and paced back-and-forth biting at my thumbnail. He didn't move.

"What I'm about to say will shock you. You will rightfully hate me more than you ever imagined you could. Please know what I've done was born out of a deep desire to protect our Empyrean people and to become a better person." I stood before him as he braced himself for what I said next.

Staring into his eyes, refusing to blink, my chin held high, I softly said, "Nexion, I am Queen Elzaria."

His head shifted as he looked at me intently. "No, this can't be. No queen has ever dared enter the Empyrean Knighthood. No queen would ever allow herself to be humiliated and beaten by those who serve her."

Studying me closely, I saw the instant he recognized my eyes.

"No queen has ever allowed herself to be tattooed or worn the braids of a warrior. No..."

I tried to take his hands. He jerked them away from me and turned his back on me. "I'm so sorry, Nexion. Please, I beg you to forgive me. I became a knight to earn the respect of the people of Terrastria and our Empyrean Alliance, to defend myself when the war reaches our doorstep, to be strong in the face of the coming devastation."

I tried to walk around to face him, to no avail. He kept his back to me, every muscle in his body tense, vibrating with anger. I grabbed his wrist, forcing him to turn towards me, but he still turned his face away.

"I asked you to come to Arcadia and meet with me, and you refused. I wanted to explain why I promoted you to Knightmaster. I knew you thought it a mistake, and that I was... how did you put it, 'a spoiled brat... spouting a bunch of nonsense.' I thought I could prove myself worthy of my position if I became a knight. That *you* would respect me."

He didn't respond. He flung my hand off his wrist and, without even a glance, he swept up his clothes and headed for the door.

"Nexion, stop. Say something!" I screamed, but he was gone.

My heart was cleaved in two. The noise in my head deafened me. The image of my betrayal etched across his face before he turned away, burned like acid in my gut. I knew I had to open my eyes, but I was too weak, too defeated to do anything but scream. I knew he would never forgive me.

"Simulator, lights out. Play Screamo music at maximum level."

I dropped to my knees, first screaming, then wailing until all that was left was dry heaves.

Love and hate raged around me in a torrent. One moment I felt loved in his tender embrace, the next, his searing hatred. Like when the same charged ends of magnets repel each other, the closer they get, the greater the tension forcing them apart. The two of us, the same as two magnets, locked in this dance of attraction and repulsion. I now understood what was meant by the fine line between love and hate, two intensely passionate emotions, with a paradoxical relationship. They're polar opposites, yet their intensity ties them closely together.

CHAPTER THIRTEEN

ELZARIA

Closed up within the walls of my small room, I could hear the excited voices of the other candidates returning to the Academy after being released for the first time since training started. They had spent the day with their families and friends, celebrating tomorrow's graduation and ascension to knighthood. I stood across the room, chucking my knives at the back of the wardrobe. My daily practice had become a release for my angst. I often imagined whoever or whatever was pissing me off at the back of the wardrobe. I had long since decimated the original wood and scrounged around campus for new planks to use. 0-9 helped me find the wood, hammer, and nails, believing the story I concocted as to why I needed them. Today, I wasn't sure if I imagined Nexion's face or my own as I brooded about the mess I had gotten myself into.

I felt like I had nobody. My family and I all agreed that once I stepped into my new identity, there would be no contact between us for both my safety and to prevent any potential embarrassment to the royal house. I don't think anyone expected me to complete the training. I had to give it to my parents; they'd held up their end of the bargain. No one had contacted me. And as far as I knew, the press didn't know what was happening either.

I packed the few things I owned, and they were ready to go. As the class valedictorian, I had finished my speech a few days ago, not knowing if I would pass the final trials but wanting to be prepared. There was nothing left for me to do. My excitement about graduating was gone after that confrontation with Nexion, and I wished I could just leave.

Sitting on the edge of my bed, I thought back to my first day at the academy. I'm such a different person. I wondered where I would go from here. My royal life seemed like a foreign concept to me now. The Knightmaster gave all ascending knights new duty assignments, but I knew my father would meet with the academy's upper echelon and explain my situation. I didn't want to have him speak for me, but what alternative did I have? The chip in my arm identified me as Zalara Galen and I had no means of proving otherwise.

With nothing else to do, I fell into a fitful sleep. Eventually, my alarm rang, and I dragged myself out of bed. I didn't want to go. I didn't want to face life hated by Nexion and the other knights. Surely, I could think of something to right this unbearable situation.

A bunch of the guys were hanging out in the common area. Laughter filled the air, a stark contrast to the turmoil brewing in my chest. Ganthion, all 6'7" of him, lumbered towards me, his grin broad and boyish. The infectious joy in his eyes was hard to resist, but I couldn't shake the war raging within me.

"Zalara! Come here, lil' sister!" He swooped me up in a bear hug, his muscular arms lifting me off the ground. His excitement was palpable, making the storm inside me feel even more tumultuous.

I managed a halfhearted smile, patting him on the back. "You look happy, Ganthion."

"Damn right, I am! We made it, Zalara. We're about to become knights! Can you believe it?" His voice echoed around the room with pride.

I pulled back, meeting his bright gaze. His eyes sparkled with ambitions of daring deeds and honor, oblivious to my private turmoil.

"I wish I could, Ganthion," I sighed.

His eyebrows furrowed, his grin fading slightly. "Hey, what's the matter, Zalara?"

I gave him a half-hearted shrug. "Just nerves, I guess."

"You've got this. Be yourself, your true self. Everything will work out as it's supposed to." He winked at me and turned to Quin, grabbing his arm and shaking it hard.

He knows. Somehow Ganthion knows my secret...

One by one, the guys joined our little circle, their faces beaming with anticipation. They slapped me on the back, their congratulations rang hollow in my ears. I tried to mirror their laughter, their enthusiasm, but it felt fake.

They talked about the ascension ceremony, their recent assignments, and their new lives. My stomach churned. I wished I knew what tomorrow would bring. For me, there weren't going to be any cool assignments. I faced the truth. A stone-cold reality only I would be accountable for.

A sudden wave of loneliness washed over me. I missed my family, my old life. But most of all, I would miss the new life I had built alongside these men. The feeling that we were all in this together, that we were all working towards the same goal. But now, I was on my own.

The bitter rift between Nexion and me only amplified my feelings of isolation. His icy demeanor, his cold, unfeeling eyes, the betrayal of his trust all hammered at my conscience.

As the guys continued to chat and laugh, I left. My room seemed like the only place where I could escape from the sharp sting of happiness that I couldn't feel.

Retreating to the quiet solitude of my room, I sank down on my bed, my mind a whirlwind of thoughts. There was a lump in my throat that I couldn't swallow, a sadness in my heart that I couldn't shake. Sure, I was graduating, but what price had I paid?

The ascension ceremony loomed over me like a dark cloud, and the thought of facing Nexion and the other knights filled me with dread. I had to find a way out of this mess, to reclaim my identity, my dignity. But for now, all I could do was steel myself for the storm that was sure to come.

I spent the next two hours perfecting how I looked. The knight's graduation was one of the biggest events of the cycle. The media would broadcast the event throughout the universe, not only our galaxy.

I wore my hair down in soft curls. Usually, I kept it in a high braided tail or bun. The Master Serg nagged me about cutting it short so that it couldn't be used as a hold when sparring, but I kept it long. It was the one personal luxury I allowed myself, even though it had cost me several times when one of the guys would grab it and yank my head back. I soon learned, and so did they, that the motion put me in the perfect position to punch them just under their ribs or in the tender spot of their armpit. Keeping my hair brown was a constant extra effort. I had the liberty of buying female products as a woman, and no one ever raised any questions about the contents of the delivered box.

For the first time since arriving at the academy, I applied makeup. I had grown so used to my tattoos that I had almost forgotten they were there. The memory of Nexion's fingers tracing the pattern on my face made my heart ache.

Finally, it was time for me to dress in my Empyrean Knight's formal regalia. The magnitude of what every inch of the uniform stood for wasn't lost on me at this moment as my hands nervously removed each item from the smaller wardrobe I used for my clothing rather than knife throwing.

I carefully took the crisp white dress shirt with a high collar off the hanger and unbuttoned it. I slipped my arms into the sleeves, pulled the shirt over my shoulders, and straightened it out. My hands shaking, I struggled to fasten the buttons.

The Regalia included a sleek, form-fitting jacket in deep midnight blue, adorned with silver embroidery. The trousers were tailored in the same midnight blue fabric as the jacket, with a sharp crease down the center of each leg. A thin silver stripe ran down the outer seam. On my feet, I wore polished black dress boots.

I hardly recognized the person standing before me in the mirror.

O-9 greeted me as I entered the Grand Hall.

"This way, knight candidate Galen," he directed me forward. "Your seat is located in the first-row center, giving you easy access to the dais for your speech."

"Thank you, O-9."

He abruptly stopped in front of me; I almost ran into him.

"Knight candidate Galen, I would like to congratulate you on your success here at the Citadel. I doubted your ability to finish the training, yet here you are at the top of your class. Job well done."

I leaned over and whispered to the droid. "I had my doubts, too. Thank you, O-9, for all your help."

He chirped and led the way to my seat. Soon everyone was seated listening to hypnotic music softly echoing off the towering ceilings. Sitting in the front row made it difficult to see who all attended the graduation. I tried to sneak a few glances, but never saw the Knightmaster. He was an integral part of the presentation, responsible for pinning each knight with their Empyrean Sigil. Surely, he wouldn't skip this because of me.

The Headmaster spoke first and directed the ceremonies with precision. Before I knew it, he introduced me as the class valedictorian. I carefully approached the lectern. The Headmaster's assistant placed a wooden box in front of me to stand on so that the crowd could see me. Placing my data pad in front of me, I realized that this was the first time I spoke publicly as the Empyrean Queen. I had left so quickly following my coronation that there hadn't been enough time for me to perform any of my public duties.

I cleared my throat, and it echoed throughout the hall.

"My fellow knights, esteemed instructors, honored guests, and all of you who are watching across the universe,

Today, we knight candidates stand here, united as a testament to our hard work, our perseverance, and our unwavering commitment to the principles of the Celestial Creed. We have successfully completed the rigorous training, and now prepare to be inducted into the Terrastrian Order of the Empyrean Knights, the mightiest of warriors who protect the Andromeda galaxy.

Our journey has been far from easy. We have faced challenges that have pushed us to our limits, both physically and mentally. But through it all, we have emerged stronger and more prepared than ever to serve and protect the Empyrean people, the Quindarian Federation, and all others who seek truth and justice.

As we take our place among the ranks of the Empyrean Knights, we pledge our loyalty to the Royal House, and we dedicate ourselves to the service and protection of the people of our great galaxy. It is our solemn duty to uphold the values of honor, integrity, and selflessness that are the foundation of the Celestial Creed.

We must always remember that our actions have consequences and that we bear the responsibility of our choices. In the face of adversity, we will stand firm, guided by the unwavering principles of our Creed."

My heart raced as I spoke, knowing that the next words were a lie. The guilt I felt for the deception I had carried out pressed heavily on my conscience. The entire universe would soon know that I had misled them by assuming a fake identity. Forcing the panic down, I swallowed hard and continued.

"Honesty, in all our endeavors, shall be our guiding light. We shall be truthful in our words and actions, not only to ourselves, but to those we serve. We must remain transparent in our intentions, as it is only through honesty that trust can be established and maintained."

I looked up and saw Nexion standing behind the center of the back row with his arms crossed over his chest. Even from the distance, his anger was clear. I knew he was aware of my deception, and yet he remained silent. It was the same look he had given me the day before when I had admitted to my lie.

"Duty is the cornerstone of our knighthood. We must remember that our purpose is to serve and protect, not just the Royal House, but the entire Empyrean realm. We have been entrusted with the lives of trillions, and we must honor that trust by fulfilling our duty to the best of our abilities.

We stand together as one, a united force that will face any challenge with courage, determination, and unwavering loyalty. We will not falter, nor will we turn away from our sacred duty to serve and protect. We are the shield that guards the realm, and we are the sword that strikes down its enemies.

As we embark on this new chapter in our lives, let us remember the teachings of our instructors, the camaraderie of our fellow knights, and the importance of the principles that have guided us thus far. We are the future of the Empyrean Knighthood, and it is our responsibility to ensure that the Andromeda galaxy remains a beacon of peace, prosperity, and justice.

May the Celestial Creed continue to guide us, and may we always remain true to our purpose. Here's to our shared journey, and to the bright future that lies ahead.

Thank you"

The room broke out in loud applause and still, Nexion stood like a statue glaring at me. I felt like a fraud uttering these words while I myself had been guilty of dishonesty, my identity a complete fraud.

"Wait! I have more to say," I exclaimed.

Going off-script, I had to say what needed to be said. It had to come directly from me. An apology.

I gripped the edges of the podium, my knuckles turning white. I took a long, slow breath and looked out at all the many faces. Finding Ganthion's he nodded reassuringly.

"As I stand before you all today, I feel a deep sense of gratitude for the opportunity to train alongside you, to learn from you, and to call you my brothers in arms. However, I must also address a matter that weighs heavily upon my heart, a deception that I have carried with me throughout our time together."

A gasp echoed throughout the silent hall.

"You have known me as Zalara Galen, a fellow recruit, and friend, but my true identity is that of... Queen Elzaria Eridani of the Empyrean realm. When I first ascended to the throne, I was filled with uncertainty and doubt about my ability to lead and protect our people. I felt ill-prepared and undeserving of the loyalty and devotion of the knights who had pledged their lives to the Royal House.

With the support of my mother, your former queen, my father, the Prime Minister, and my closest advisers, I made the difficult decision to assume a new identity and attend the knight's academy. My goal was to learn the true meaning of strength, honor, and duty, so that I might better serve and protect the Empyrean people."

Looking directly at Nexion, I implored him to forgive me.

"I understand that my deception may have caused hurt and confusion, and for that, I offer my deepest and most heartfelt apologies. My intentions were never to betray your trust, but rather to earn it through my own merit and hard work, with no special treatment or favors.

I stand before you today, not as a weak and spoiled queen, but as a warrior who has fought and bled alongside you, who has faced adversity and emerged stronger for it. I am proud of my accomplishments, but I am prouder still to call you my fellow knights and comrades.

I pledge to you, my Empyrean people, and to all those in the knighthood, that I will continue to serve and protect you with the same courage that I showed during my time at the academy. I will strive to be a queen worthy of your loyalty and devotion, and together, we will protect the prosperity of the Empyrean realm.

Thank you for your understanding, and for allowing me the honor of standing among you as a true Empyrean knight."

The audience erupted into loud cheers as everyone rose to their feet. Nexion was gone. I bowed my head in a brief silent prayer and as a display of gratitude. I was stunned by the warmth of those in front of me. Descending from the dais, I joined in behind the line of knight candidates as we marched towards the chancel to be pinned with the Knight's Empyrean Sigil.

The Knight's Empyrean Sigil is a unique emblem bestowed upon each knight during their graduation and ascension to knighthood. The pin is crafted from xenochronatium, a rare metal found only within the Andromeda galaxy, and features an intricate design that represents the knight's bond to The Order.

Shaped like a shield, the pin symbolizes the knight's duty to defend and protect the people of the Andromeda galaxy. In the center of the shield is an engraved representation of the Empyrean Alliance's symbol, signifying the vast territory that The Order of the Empyrean Knights is sworn to protect.

One by one, each of us kneeled before the Knightmaster to receive our Knight's Empyrean Sigil. Holding my chin high and back straight, I approached the Knightmaster, my thumbs tight along the seams of my trousers with my palms facing inward, towards my thighs. My focus was on his sigil, unwilling to look him in the eye. As I stood before the Knightmaster, I could feel the weight of the moment upon me. This was the culmination of all my hard work, when my transformation into a knight would be complete. My heart pounded in my chest, and my breathing grew shallow.

I carefully lowered myself to one knee, placing my left foot forward while keeping my back straight and head held high. My right hand rested gently on the hilt of my sword, and my left hand lay open on my left thigh, palm up, symbolizing my willingness to serve.

As I kneeled there, the reality of the situation washed over me.

"Rise, Queen Elzaria," Nexion commanded, pointedly using my real name, his voice piercing my heart as the memories of the simulation room flooded my mind.

I rose, keeping my line of sight fixated on his sigil, and stood at attention before him. The warmth of his hands against my left breast just above my heart elicited a slight gasp only he heard as he pinned my sigil. Still refusing to look at him, I stood unmoving, unable to breathe. He stared at me for a long moment. Beyond my control, a single teardrop rolled down my cheek. As was custom, he reached out his right hand, grasping mine almost at the elbow in a firm embrace that lingered longer than it should have. I didn't move, eyes frozen on his sigil. He gently let go and I pivoted in the opposite direction.

CHAPTER FOURTEEN

ELZARIA

As I stepped out of the Grand Hall, a sea of people and the press immediately swarmed me, all eager to catch a glimpse of their queen. The air was thick with expectation, and the atmosphere was electric as countless cameras flashed and holographic recorders hummed, capturing my every movement.

I could feel the weight of their gazes on me, each person analyzing my posture, my attire, and my expression. I did my best to maintain a calm and composed demeanor, even though I felt the pressure of their scrutiny. Master Sergeant Killdare appeared by my side and guided me to an awaiting hovercraft.

Seated within were the Headmaster and several other dignitaries. As I settled into the hovercraft, I could feel their eyes on me, their expressions a mix of shock, awe, and confusion.

The Headmaster, a thin and gaunt man, was the first to speak. "Well, I'll be damned," he said, his eyes widening in disbelief. "Zalara was our Queen all along?"

I nodded, my eyes scanning the faces of those around me. "Yes, Headmaster. I've been posing as Zalara Galen since I entered the academy."

"Your Majesty," the Headmaster began, his voice filled with a mixture of respect and confusion. "We had no idea... we didn't know that you were actually Queen Elzaria."

The other dignitaries nodded their agreement, their faces etched with surprise and disbelief.

One of them, a tall, muscular man with a thick beard, spoke up. "You're very different from the young princess portrayed in the media and we assumed you to be, Your Majesty. To think that you could achieve what you did while pretending to be someone else. It's truly remarkable."

I could feel their eyes on me, watching my every move.

"My deception may have caused confusion, but please understand that my intentions were pure," I replied, keeping my tone even and controlled. "I needed to learn the true meaning of strength, honor, and duty, so that I might better serve and protect the Empyrean people. And I believe that my time at the academy has given me the readiness and knowledge necessary to do just that."

The Headmaster nodded, his expression softening slightly. "Yes, Your Majesty, we have seen the progress that you, as Zalara Galen, have made during your time here at the academy. You showed remarkable dedication, courage, and skill, and have earned the respect of your fellow knights."

We arrived at the Headmaster's residence and were treated to a lovely dinner. Foods I had missed during the many lunars I had trained. The night wound down, and I said my polite goodbyes.

Walking back to the barracks, the Master Sergeant followed behind. I turned. "There's no need to walk me to the barracks. Stay at the party and enjoy yourself."

"Your Majesty, I have been assigned to protect you until you are returned home to Arcadia."

"What? You have got to be kidding me. You know that's unnecessary." I insisted.

"I'm following orders."

"I understand." I said, turning to face him. "Thank you for making me a knight. Earning your respect was the hardest thing I've ever done. You've changed my life. Made me better."

He swallowed hard and flushed with embarrassment. "You were a lot tougher than I gave you credit for at the beginning. You have a lot to be proud of, Your Majesty."

"Oh, by the way, where is the Knightmaster this evening? Why wasn't he invited to this dinner?" I asked candidly.

"He was invited, Your Majesty," the Master Sergeant replied, his voice betraying a note of reluctance. "But he was called away on urgent matters."

"What kind of matters?" I pressed, my curiosity piqued.

"The worst kind, I'm afraid," he replied. "There have been reports of Dreadnaughts, the most notorious space pirates, attacking Empyrean shipping vessels close to Grymrock, an outpost located at the far reaches of our galaxy. Nexion offered to lead a fleet to intercept them since our Empyrean flagship, the Phantom Resolute, is based at the Citadel Avendel's spaceport."

My heart sank at the thought of Nexion volunteering for this mission. Especially since I assumed it was partly to avoid me. "Where is he now? How can I reach him?"

"He's currently preparing the Phantom Resolute for service, Your Majesty. But I'm afraid it's not safe for you to join him on this mission."

"Why not?" I demanded, my emotions getting the better of me. "I'm an Empyrean knight. It's my duty."

"I understand, Your Majesty," the Master Sergeant said calmly. "But this is a dangerous situation. The Dreadnaughts are heavily armed, and the risks are too great."

"Okay, I understand," I replied, dropping the conversation. "I'm packed and ready to return home tomorrow. I'll be waiting right here in the morning so that you can escort me to the spaceport. No need to hang out here all night. The academy is one of the most highly secured places on Terrastria. Tonight is no different from any of the other days I've been here."

He agreed and left me.

I waited to ensure he was long gone. Then I grabbed my bag and headed to the military spaceport not far from the academy. At the portal, O-9 greeted me. "Hello, Zalara. How may I help you?"

"I'm heading for the train station. Open the portal, please."

"I'm afraid you are not on the exit list this evening. Request denied."

"O-9, who am I?"

"You are Knight, Zalara Galen, daughter of Dax Galen."

"No, O-9, you are wrong. Check your information more closely for an update. I am Queen Elzaria."

O-9 whizzed and chirped. "Yes, you are correct. My apologies. How may I help you, Queen Elzaria?"

"Open the portal, now, please."

"I'm sorry to inform you, Your Majesty, but you are not on the exit list."

"O-9, I am your Queen. The highest-ranking person in this galaxy. You are programmed to follow my commands. Now open the portal."

I thought O-9 was going to bust a chip. Finally, his overloaded neuromorphic systems came to the only conclusion they could. I outranked everyone.

"This way Queen Elzaria." He guided me to the portal's edge. Before I stepped through, I turned to O-9, "Thank you, O-9. Your hospitality and special help during my stay will never be forgotten."

I heaved my bag on my shoulder and stepped through the portal.

I hadn't used my NeuralComm device since coming to the academy. The comm snapped in place behind my left ear. A neural interface linked directly to my nervous system, allowing me to control the device with my thoughts and receive information directly into my brain. It offered augmented reality, which overlayed digital information onto the user's real-world environment, providing contextual data enhancing their interaction with the surroundings. It was also a universal translator instantly translating most any spoken or written language, facilitating seamless communication between people of different linguistic backgrounds. It was also an advanced AI assistant, a highly intelligent, personalized virtual assistant capable of learning from the user's preferences and anticipating their needs.

Lucky for me, we had never changed it to reflect my Zalara identity. I requested a transport which arrived surprisingly fast, perks of being royal I had forgotten. I debated about contacting my parents and decided to touch base with them, since they might help me gain a little cover over my actual plans.

"Hi Mother, it's me, Elzaria," I spoke quietly, unsure of her response to my universal public disclosure of my identity.

"Elzaria! It's you. I've missed you so much! Quick, Helion, join me." I smiled at her genuine excitement.

"I did it. I'm an official Empyrean Knight."

"We know, congratulations! We're so proud of you. Your speech was breathtaking and so professional." Father responded with a rarely seen broad smile.

My parents insisted I tell them all about my time at the academy, but I was in a hurry, so I gave them a brief rundown, leaving out anything related to the Knightmaster, injuries and insults. It thrilled them to hear about my achievements, and they congratulated me profusely. They were also eager to know when I would be returning home, as they had been worried about my safety as a knight-in-training.

"Mother, Father, I have to go," I said, cutting our conversation short. "There's something I need to do."

"What is it, Elzaria?" My father asked, his tone serious.

"I can't explain it right now, but I need to help someone. And I need to do it alone. Please don't try to stop me."

My parents exchanged quizzical looks, and I could tell they were worried. But they also knew me well enough to know that once I had made up my mind, I wouldn't change it.

"I need your help. I need you to lead the media and the academy to believe that I am on my way home, arriving tomorrow. That will give me cover so that no one will look for me or wonder where I am."

"Okay, I guess another few days away from your royal duties won't hurt anything. But we need you back soon. There's been more unusual incidents that lead back to the Vaith." Father replied.

"Be careful, Elzaria," my mother said, her voice hesitant. "And come home to us safely."

"I will. Love you both," I promised, before terminating the communication.

I boarded the transport and instructed the AI to take me to the spaceport where the Phantom Resolute was located. As the Empyrean's flagship vessel, it was heavily guarded and fortified against any possible attack. I knew I couldn't just walk in and announce myself as the Empyrean Queen. That would only cause chaos and confusion.

Instead, I used my neural interface to tap into the spaceport's security systems and request that it disable the sensors and cameras in my path while I crossed through them. As the queen, I had the topmost security clearance. Royalty did nothing without it being planned and almost always public, so no one ever thought that the queen would be sneaking onto a vessel, much less a military warship. Maybe that would be something to change in the future if I ever had a child. But for now, it seemed to work for my needs.

I had the transport let me off on the side of the road nearest the back of the spaceport, where a loading dock was located. Waiting for the transport to be gone long enough to not be able to trace me, I commanded my NeuralComm assistant to place me in absolute incognito mode, not allowing even the highest-ranking military commanders or my parents to trace me. Jogging to the fence line felt good after having no physical training for a couple of days. My Empyrean energy blade made quick work of the fence. Relying on my ability to control the security systems and my knight's training, I carefully made my way to the loading dock.

Once there, I removed the civilian jacket I wore, revealing my knight's uniform. My hair was in a tight braid down the center of my back. I looked like I belonged on the base. Striding confidently, I moved swiftly, making my way towards the docking bay where the Phantom Resolute was berthed.

As I slipped through the entrance to the vast hangar and looked around, I made sure no one was watching me. I couldn't help but feel a mix of excitement and anxiety. The enormous hanger stretched out before me, the metallic walls gleaming under the bright artificial lights. I was about to do something that was both reckless and daring, but I knew it was necessary.

I knew the risks of my secret mission were high, but I couldn't just stand by and watch Nexion put his life on the line while things were so mixed up between us. And as the Empyrean Queen, it was my duty to understand what dangers lie within my realm.

Dominating the center of the hangar was the Phantom Resolute, the pride of the Empyrean fleet. The engineers crafted the ship's sleek, streamlined hull from a highly advanced alloy that allowed it to withstand the rigors of deep space travel and combat. Its edges were sharp and angular, with a series of strategically placed thrusters that would enable it to maneuver with incredible agility. The Phantom Resolute's matte black finish made it blend into the darkness of space, a fitting attribute for a vessel that struck fear into the hearts of our enemies.

As I cautiously made my way toward the ship, I activated my neural assistant, ensuring it had disabled the sensors and cameras in my path. I knew I couldn't afford to be detected; although I was the highest-ranking commander of the military, my presence here was strictly off the record.

Moving gracefully and silently, I navigated through the labyrinth of crates, machinery, and fuel lines that filled the hangar. My heart raced as I narrowly avoided a group of crew members who were busy prepping the ship for takeoff. They were performing last-minute checks and loading supplies, completely unaware of my clandestine presence.

I paused for a moment, allowing my neural assistant to scan the ship's layout and identify a suitable hiding spot. It highlighted a small, rarely accessed maintenance shaft near the rear of the Phantom Resolute. I knew it would be the perfect place to remain undetected.

With time running out, I quickened my pace, finally reaching the base of the ship's towering hull. Using my telekinetic powers, I jumped onto a high platform, which granted me access to a discreet hatch. I moved towards the hatch and activated my neural interface to hack into the ship's security systems. I bypassed the lock and slid inside, closing the door behind me. As I crept inside the Phantom Resolute, I felt a surge of adrenaline course through my veins.

Following the directions of my neural assistant, I crawled through a series of narrow passageways, dragging my bag along with me. My heart pounded with every twist and turn. I could hear the muffled voices of crew members as they went about their duties, each one a potential threat to my mission.

Finally, I reached the maintenance shaft, and with a sigh of relief, I squeezed into the cramped space. As I settled in, it wasn't long before I felt the powerful engines of the Phantom Resolute rumbling to life; the vibrations reverberating through the ship's structure. I braced myself for the sensation of takeoff, knowing that I was about to embark on a dangerous journey.

CHAPTER FIFTEEN

ELZARIA

I had been stowed away in the cramped maintenance shaft of the Phantom Resolute for longer than I had expected. My limbs ached and my stomach grumbled, but I couldn't risk being discovered by any of the crew members. I had already come too far to be caught now.

Finally, after what felt like an eternity, the ship's engines slowed, and I knew we were far enough away from the spaceport that Nexion wouldn't be able to return me. I took a deep breath and gathered my courage, preparing myself for the confrontation that lay ahead.

With a sense of purpose, I emerged from the maintenance shaft and made my way to the command deck. As I strode down the narrow passageways, I could feel the tension building inside me. I knew Nexion would be angry that I had snuck onto his ship.

My neural assistant led me to where I knew I would find him, the bridge. As I entered, I could feel the eyes of the other officers on me. They were all staring at me, their expressions a mix of surprise and curiosity. I could tell that they knew something was amiss, but they didn't want to make a scene in front of their commanding officer. I tossed my bag in the back corner and turned toward the bow.

Nexion was standing at the front of the bridge, his back to me as he barked orders at his crew. He was so focused on his mission that he didn't even notice me enter.

I took a deep breath, trying to push down the feelings of anxiety and guilt that were threatening to overwhelm me.

"Knightmaster," I said, my voice ringing out across the room. "We need to talk."

Nexion spun around, his eyes locking onto me. His shock was palpable as he saw me standing there. I could tell from the way his jaw tightened and his muscles tensed he was angry, hurt, and embarrassed all at the same time. Without a word, he strode towards me, his eyes blazing with a mix of emotions.

"Queen Elzaria," he growled in a low voice meant only for me while grabbing me roughly by the arm. "What the hell are you doing here? You had no right to sneak onto my ship."

I winced as his grip tightened, but I refused to back down. "I had to come, Knightmaster," I said, my voice firm. "I understand you feel betrayed by me hiding my identity from you. But you gave me no choice. You refused my request to return to Arcadia so that we could discuss the reasons I promoted you to Knightmaster. My decision to become a knight had already been decided upon by not only my advisors but also by my mother, the former Queen, and my father, the Prime Minister. The only reason I used a false identity was because *you* refused to speak with me, and I knew *you* would never allow me to train as a knight." I tried to keep my voice low, but my frustration was oozing out.

"This isn't a discussion to be had here," he hissed through gritted teeth. Nexion's eyes narrowed, and I could see the anger building inside him. "You had no right to do this," he said. "You may have put the entire mission in jeopardy."

He unceremoniously pushed me out the door and into the corridor, eliciting several raised eyebrows from the crew.

"I know, and I'm sorry," I said, my heart pounding in my chest. "But I had to do something." Not far down the corridor, he shoved me through a door that slid open as we neared. It was his personal quarters.

As I stumbled in, I couldn't help but be impressed by the sophistication of the space. The living room was spacious and decorated with sleek, modern furniture and intricate metallic accents. The kitchen area was equally impressive, equipped with state-of-the-art appliances and a fully stocked bar. But it was the bedroom that caught my eye; with its plush bedding, soft lighting, and massive windows that provided a stunning view of the stars outside, it was the epitome of luxury.

Nexion closed the door behind us. He turned to face me, his eyes dark with anger and frustration, gripping me at arm's length until he was all but hurting me.

"I don't know what you're expecting to accomplish by coming here," he said, his voice cold and clipped. "But I can tell you one thing, this changes nothing between us. I don't trust you, *Queen Elzaria*, and I never will."

I took a step forward, determined to make him understand my point of view. "Nexion, I know I messed up by not telling you the truth about my identity, but you have to understand that I had no other choice. I couldn't risk your judgment clouding your decision to train me as a knight."

He let out a harsh laugh, shaking his head in disbelief. "You don't get it, do you? It's not about your identity or you becoming a knight, Elzaria. It's about the fact that you lied to me. You made me question everything I thought I knew about you. And now, you expect me to just forgive and forget?"

"I know it's not just my dishonesty. I know you think I promoted you because of the attraction we have for each other, but in fact, that has nothing to do with my choice to name you Knightmaster." My anger rose and my face flushed with heat.

"I know you won't believe me because you think it's *all nonsense*, but The Creators guided my decision and although your actions towards me have made me doubt my decision, I know in my heart it was the right thing to do whether or not you like it. Just so you know, I had selected a different person to name as Knightmaster before my coronation. But when I lifted the sword to point towards him, it took on a will of its own. The sword pointed to you and The Creators made their choice. I am but their vessel. If you don't like it, then you need to take out your anger on them, not me. But then you don't seem much like the praying sort of guy." Once again, I knew I was poking at him, inflaming his temper.

Nexion shook his head, his expression one of exasperation. "I can't believe you would do something like this," he said. "You, of all people, should know the importance of honesty and integrity. You took the knight's oath of the *Celestial Creed*, and yet you lied to everyone at the academy, including me. You should have come to me as soon as you arrived."

"If you will recall, *you* avoided me. Halfway through my training, you showed up at the arena to find out why the instructors were talking about my strong telekinetic skills. Then the next day, you ordered me to meet you alone for a sparring match, which ended when *you* kissed me. I never saw or spoke to you again until I confronted you in the AI simulator... and, well... you know how that ended!" I shouted in frustration.

For a man who never showed his feelings, I always seemed to emotionally trigger him. His expression betrayed his thoughts, as

I knew he was recalling the steamy, hot sex we had in the inky black darkness of the simulator.

"I wasn't avoiding you, er, well, Zalara, that is. New to my role as Knightmaster, I wanted to allow the instructors and others an opportunity to get to know me, and I wanted them to know I respected their knowledge and experience. I kept close tabs on every one of the candidates. Like the day you first started to harness your telekinetic skills and practically drowned everyone, including yourself. What I still don't get is how someone with your innate powers never learned to wield them." He shook his head in disbelief.

It shocked me to learn that Nexion had been watching me so closely. I hadn't thought about how difficult it was for him to assume a powerful position over those he had previously reported to.

"I'm sorry that your promotion to Knightmaster has made things so uncomfortable for you. If I had known more about you and the knighthood, I would have resisted the direction of The Creators. But then, they knew that, and they knew I would follow their direction. How could I not? As far as my telekinetic powers go... I hid them. I've always avoided drawing attention to myself and knew that people would judge me, or the telekinetic powers would make me a target. Believe it or not, I hate attracting attention to myself. If I had an older sister and was in the role of the spare, I would be more than happy. I've always been a nerdy loner. You're probably right that *I'm no queen, and just a spoiled brat,* as you said."

Nexion loosened his grip on my arms as he took a step back, his eyes locked with mine. "I don't doubt your abilities as a leader or a knight, Elzaria," he said, his voice husky. "You have proven yourself time and time again. But you have also awakened something in me I thought I had buried long ago. I can't deny the intense desire I feel for you. I can't deny that you've made me angrier and more frustrated than anyone ever has. You've got one hell of a smart mouth on you."

I could feel the heat rising in my cheeks as I took in his words. Despite everything, I still found myself drawn to him, unable to resist the pull of our mutual attraction.

"As your Queen, I demand that you forgive me for lying and betraying your trust. It's an order." He raised his eyebrows, but before he could speak, I put my finger on his lips. "In return... I will submit to your command over this ship and its mission. I will submit to you." I said, biting my lower lip.

"You will submit to me in all things?" Nexion's green eyes gleamed with the fire of lust.

"In all the ways that matter to you." I promised, looking up through my eyelashes.

Nexion yanked me close to him as his lips crashed down on mine, with a fierce hunger that left me breathless. I moaned into the kiss. My arms wrapped around his neck as I pressed my body against his. He swept me up in his arms, carrying me to his bed in a blur of motion. He ripped off my uniform with a roughness that left me dizzy with desire.

"Don't move." He ordered.

I lay still in his bed, naked and a little nervous about what he would do next as he stalked around the room, slowly removing his own uniform. The intensity of his gaze, as he paced, reminded me of a wild, out-of-control beast.

"Your lies made me look like an idiot. You embarrassed the entire Empyrean Knight's academy. How are any of us to explain that we didn't know our Queen was in our midst? We treated you like any other candidate. We insulted you. We made you bleed. We made you suffer."

"You made me strong. You made me powerful. You made me a knight." I softly replied.

He stood in the center of the room angrily, or maybe it was nervously, snapping his belt between his hands. I could see the hurt in those simmering emerald eyes. I sat up and swung my legs over the edge of the bed. Wanting to go and comfort him. Before I could stand, he growled, "I ordered you to not move."

"Does that mean you forgive me?" I purred.

"Do you submit?"

"Yes."

In the blink of an eye, he was on me. He flipped me over the edge of the bed, placing his massive palm on my lower back. I heard the sudden sharp crack slice through the air before I felt his belt lash against my bare bottom.

I cried out. The pain was unlike any I had ever experienced.

"I would punish any knight who lied or damaged the reputation of The Order as you have done. For you, though, punishment has a different meaning. Do you understand?"

"Yes."

"You must submit under your own free will and can leave at any time. Do you agree?"

I felt the heat of his massive palm pressing against my back.

"Yes, I agree." Eager to put this behind us and curious to see what he had in store for me, I couldn't help but question him. "Are we just going to stand here?"

I opened my mouth to make another snarky comment, but was cut off by another lash of his belt.

"Oh shit, that hurt!" I cried out, wriggling under his grasp.

He laid the belt across my hips and caressed the fiery lashes gently.

"You lied to me, little knight. You willfully made a mockery of our most sacred oath."

"I'm sorry. I didn't intend to cause anyone harm. Well, maybe you a little."

He chuckled, "The path to hell is paved with good intentions." He once more picked up the belt.

"Please, no, please, just forgive me already." I bit out.

Smack!

"Just get over it already!"

Smack!

"No more," I begged, panting and unable to take anymore.

Without another sound, he stood behind me, placing his hands on my hips and sliding them up my sides. His hot chest rested on my back as he kissed my neck and licked the edge of my ear, sending a wave of chills all over me. I felt his hard cock between my legs.

He trailed kisses down my back, dragging my hips away from the edge of the bed, giving him access to my breasts. With only my shoulders and head remaining on the bed, I clung to the blankets to keep from falling. He wrapped both of his arms tightly around me and gripped a breast in each hand. I groaned as he pinched and rolled my nipples between his fingers. He growled in my ear as his cock grew even harder between my legs. I started to rise up, but with one hand, he gently pushed my head down until my forehead rested against the bed. I gasped as he spread my legs with his thigh and surrendered to him as he kissed a path down my spine.

With one hand, he reached around and circled my clit with his fingers, and with the other, he lightly traced circles over my buttom, eliciting the sensation of fire and ice. He sank two fingers into my wetness as the heel of his hand rubbed against my clit. I could feel my arousal climbing as his fingers pumped in and out. I was on the precipice of my orgasm, writhing against his fingers when he stopped and held me tightly. He slid two of the fingers from his other hand in drawing my wetness up the back side of me. Circling my back opening, I moaned and then he pressed a finger against the opening, pushing it in a little and eliciting a gasp as I pushed up off the bed.

"I told you not to move."

"Please," I begged, not knowing what I was begging for, but wanting so much more.

"Please what?" He asked, his voice husky. "Please forgive you? Please don't spank you? Please fuck you?"

"Yes, yes, all of them."

"I will forgive you, Elzaria. But first, I must ensure you remember not to lie to me again."

He dove the two fingers that had been holding me from the front deep within me while using his other hand to spank my tender cheeks.

I cried out as he slapped me a second time, his hand coming down heavy and hard on my already blazing bottom.

"I'm going to spank you until I feel you cum around my fingers."

Another and another smack rang out, amping up my arousal.

"Cum for me, little one."

I felt the waves of pleasure building to a crescendo and was completely under his control. I lost count of the slaps against me. They were hard, each one forcing me to ride his fingers deeply. My need for release was becoming desperate. On his final slap, he pressed his finger into my back opening. My hands gripped the bed as my body shook with the force of pleasure and I spasmed around his fingers, making them slick with my arousal. I felt his fingers pushing in and out of me as I continued to orgasm.

As I came down from my high, I collapsed against the bed, only to be rolled onto my back. Opening my eyes, I looked up into Nexion's ravenous face. His eyes smoldered with desire as he leaned in for a kiss. It was wild, hot, and demanding. My body was still shaking as he pulled his lips away.

My throbbing ass was on the edge of the bed and Nexion stood in front of me. He pulled my knees up and spread my legs with his hands as I felt his hard cock teasing my clit.

It was so sensitive from the intense orgasm I had just experienced. With no warning, he thrust into me hard and fast as I gripped the edge of the bed.

"Oh, my goddess." I cried out as he pounded into me. Again I begged, "Please."

"Please, what?" He grunted as he increased the pace of his thrusting.

"Please, don't stop."

With a growl, he pushed me back and planted his hands on each side of my head. Leaning down, he kissed me savagely, never taking his lips from mine. He pumped into me again and again; I felt my body climbing toward another orgasm.

"Don't cum until I tell you to." His face was dark with desire.

"I won't, I won't." I panted.

He picked up speed, and I gripped the bed tight as his thrusts became more erratic. The tension was building up as he pressed on a spot deep inside me with each thrust.

I was close. I could feel it as he gripped my hands above my head.

"Cum for me, little knight. Cum for me."

I felt the tension peak as he fucked me faster and faster. I screamed as my orgasm hit. With one final deep thrust, he exploded inside me. I felt his breath fan over my lips before he crushed them against mine. He kissed me with more passion than I had ever felt before.

Nexion sat up unexpectedly and the heat between up dissipated. I knew he had received a communication. "I have to return to the bridge." Leaving me on the bed, still in the throes of my orgasms, he gathered his clothes and disappeared from the room. After a quick shower and just before heading out the door, he turned to me and commanded, "Be naked in my bed when I return."

Sore and sweaty from his *spicy punishment* and after spending hours in the cramped maintenance shaft, I knew I needed to clean up. To my surprise, I found a large tub, surely a rarity aboard a military space vessel. After a long luxurious hot soak and a snack, I returned to his bed, naked as he requested. Mesmerized by the view from the enormous windows, as I gazed out at the magnificent display of the Andromeda galaxy's spiral arm filled with stars, gas, and dust, I fell into a deep sleep.

I awoke to the sensation of fingertips tracing circles over my shoulder and Nexion's body spooning snuggly against my backside. Glancing over my shoulder, I smiled.

"Sleep well, little knight?"

"Mmmm, I did," I said, turning to face him. "Everything okay on the bridge? How long have I been out?"

Ignoring my questions, he traced the tattoo on my face with his finger. "I'm astonished by the efforts you made to hide who you really are."

"It's nothing I can't undo. Although I've grown to like my tattoos."

"Me too. I like the wildness of them." He said, kissing my forehead.

His hand gently caressed my arm, then my waist and hip. I shuddered in response.

"You like my touches, don't you? I see how your body always responds." His hand glided up to my breast, teasing my already-hardened nipple with his thumb.

He leaned in; this time he kissed me tenderly. He kissed my cheek and then my neck while his hand carefully roamed over my body. This was a different side of Nexion. Sweet and kind, he worshiped my body, taking his time.

He started to go down on me, but I stopped him. I sat up, pushing him on his back. I desperately wanted to give him pleasure. To make him feel the words neither of us could utter.

I kissed and licked my way down his chest and shredded abs, feeling his shaft slide across my wetness. I traced his tattoo with my tongue. As my kisses reached his hip, I took his cock in my hands and stroked him up and down its length. I felt it jerk in my hand.

I guided his cock into my mouth, and he moaned as I ran my tongue over and around the tip. Gripping his shaft and stroking him as I ran my tongue down to the base and back up, I alternated between long slow licks and sucking hard on the tip. Taking him deep into my mouth, he buried his hands in my hair, pushing me down his length. My head bobbed up and down, taking him deeper and then sliding back up.

"Oh, my goddess." He groaned. "Suck me. Suck my cock, little one."

I grew bolder, pressing on his thighs, forcing his legs to spread a bit more, opening him up. I licked the underside of his cock and traced my tongue around his balls.

His cock grew harder, and the veins were pulsing as I stroked his shaft with my tongue. I took him back between my lips again, sucking harder as I stroked him with my hand. I felt his body tremble as he let out a low moan. He was ready to cum. I quickened my pace, sucking harder, stroking him quicker.

I looked up and found his eyes were closed and he was biting his bottom lip.

Oh, how I loved making him feel good.

"I'm going to cum, little knight. I'm going to cum in your mouth." He drew in a deep breath and let out a loud groan.

I felt his shaft pulse as he came hard and the salty taste of him exploded on my tongue.

He collapsed onto the bed, his chest heaving as he struggled to regain his composure. "Thank you, little knight," he managed to say.

He rested his forearm over his eyes, taking long, deep breaths. I climbed up beside the now gentle giant and rested my head on his chest.

Running his hands through my hair, we lay quietly for a long time. He pulled me up so that we were face to face. His eyes were serious, and he stared at me intently. "Did I hurt you?"

"No," I murmured. "You didn't hurt me." Confused why he would ask me.

"No, before. I hurt you; I should never be rough with you."

"I wanted it," I sighed softly.

"No." He said strongly. "I couldn't control myself. I was rough. You should've told me to stop. I'm sorry."

"You're my first; how would I know?" I rested my head back on his chest. "I enjoyed the pleasure-pain combo." I giggled.

Raising up and looking down at me, "What do you mean, I was your first?"

"I mean, I've never had sex before you."

"You were a virgin?"

"Yes," I confessed.

"What the fuck is wrong with me? How could I have not known? I'm so sorry. I would have been different... taken my time and guided you through. It's my responsibility to take care of you. You deserved so much better than a rough fuck."

"I guess I'm a good liar. I don't lie on purpose. It's something you must bring out in me. Besides, you were amazing and made me feel things I never imagined possible. Promise me you won't freak out and start ignoring me." I demanded, pushing him back down and curling up on his chest.

"Okay, okay." He laughed, "But I won't tolerate liars." He said, draping his arm over my waist and giving me a little squeeze.

"I know. I know… I won't lie to you."

"No more lies, my little knight."

"No more lies," I mumbled against his chest.

"I will pleasure you often, and I will punish you when needed. I can't guarantee that you'll always like it, but I will never hurt you."

"Promise me?" I asked.

"Rest, little one. We'll continue this discussion later." He said, stroking my back.

He rolled over, wrapping his arm around me and tucking his thighs against my buttom as he gathered me tightly against him and held me close. I felt safe. I felt loved.

I was falling in love with Nexion.

CHAPTER SIXTEEN

ELZARIA

A siren shrieked throughout the ship, waking us from a deep sleep. Nexion flipped me over and ran, yanking on his clothes as he headed out the door.

Tangled in the sheets, it took me a bit longer to free myself and dress, but I wasn't far behind him. I ran onto the bridge as I tied my hair back in a tail.

"Commander, six Dreadnaught ships decloaking off Grymrock!" The sensor operator shouted, his voice strained.

The situation was fluid and chaotic. I wanted to help but didn't know how. I watched Nexion. His authority was unquestioned by the crew.

"Status report," he ordered, watching the information scrolling on the command control console.

Everyone strapped in. The Phantom Resolute's crew was preparing for battle. I found an unoccupied seat in the back corner, but at least I was close enough to see firsthand what was happening.

As I sat in the shadows of the Resolute's bridge, the vast emptiness of space outside was interrupted by the appearance of six previously cloaked Dreadnaught Pirate ships. I could hardly believe my eyes. The element of surprise was on their side, and they wasted no time in commencing their attack on our ship.

The Dreadnaught pirates assembled to attack the Empyrean outpost. Their cloaking tech kept them invisible to us until the Resolute had nearly reached the planet.

I watched as the officers focused and responded swiftly, following established protocols and Nexion's orders. I paid close attention as one worked to raise the ship's shields and adjust their strength to prioritize the areas of the ship facing the most imminent threats. While another activated and calibrated the ship's weapons systems, preparing them to fire on the enemy vessels. My buddy from the Academy, Ganthion, worked to communicate with the ship's engineering team to optimize power distribution between propulsion, shields, and weapons systems. Others analyzed data from the ship's sensors to determine the enemy's position, trajectory, and possible tactics.

Nexion seemed to interact with all of them at once while he coordinated with the ship's tactical officer to devise countermeasures against the enemy's attacks, such as deploying decoys, evasive maneuvers, or electronic warfare maneuvers.

He strapped into the commander's chair and allowed the neural connections to form. Nexion and the ship were now as one.

"Six ships approaching, three hundred klicks, weapons armed. We're taking on heavy fire. Watch those shields," Nexion demanded.

The lead pirate vessel was immense, dwarfing its five smaller counterparts. They all looked to be older ships that had undergone a patchwork of repairs, but their highly advanced cloaking tech gave a hint as to who was really behind the attack. Their ships were a stark contrast to our own flagship, the Phantom Resolute, which was larger, newer, and more sophisticated. A thing of beauty. I could feel my heart pounding in my chest, wanting to help, but I had to remain out of the way, knowing that my presence would only add confusion to an already dire situation.

"Red alert! Battle stations, everyone!" Nexion barked, his voice filled with authority. "Deploy countermeasures and bring the forward cannons online!"

"Let's give them a warm welcome," Nexion sneered. "Return fire. Focus on the Dreadnaught's lead ship, then the strike fighters."

I could hear the crew's hurried movements and the hum of the ship's systems powering up. The tension in the room was palpable. Despite their surprise, the crew of the Resolute was well-trained and ready for action.

"Shields holding at 90%, Commander!" Reported the tactical officer.

"Keep our bow pointed at the lead vessel," Nexion ordered, a steely edge to his voice. "Divert auxiliary power to the shields and bring our aft cannons online as well. We'll have to deal with those smaller vessels, eventually."

"Commander, the strike fighters are moving to flank us!" The sensor operator warned.

"Dammit! It's like taking down a group of angry cats." Nexion cursed under his breath. "Helm," Nexion directed the ship itself, "initiate evasive maneuvers! Keep us out of their firing arc as much as possible!"

The Resolute lurched and shifted as Nexion, through the ship's neural connection, expertly maneuvered the massive vessel to avoid the incoming fire from the pirate spacecraft. I gripped the edge of my seat, holding on tight as the ship rocked violently from side to side.

A sudden explosion shook the bridge, sending sparks flying over the shields and crew members scrambling. "Damage report!" Nexion demanded, his voice barely audible above the cacophony of alarms and the ship's groaning metal.

"Direct hit to our port side, Commander!" The tactical officer yelled. "Shields down to 60%."

"We can't take much more of this!" Nexion growled. "Target the lead ship's engines and fire everything we've got!"

The Resolute's cannons roared, unleashing a torrent of energy toward the pirate flagship's engines. The smaller vessels continued to harass us, but Nexion's focus remained on the lead ship. I could see the determination etched on his face, unwilling to let these pirates succeed.

As the battle raged on, the Resolute's weapons found their mark, disabling the lead pirate ship's engines and leaving it vulnerable. With their flagship crippled, the smaller vessels hesitated, momentarily unsure of their next move.

"Commander, they're retreating!" The sensor operator exclaimed, relief evident in his voice.

"Stay sharp, everyone," Nexion warned. "They'll be back. Keep an eye on that lead vessel; we'll have to deal with it before we can safely approach Grymrock."

As the battle continued, the Dreadnaught fighters regrouped and attacked once more. The Resolute took some damage, but it paled compared to the devastation inflicted upon the lead pirate ship.

"Sir, the lead ship is diverting all energy to their key weapons systems. Looks like they're taking aim at Grymrock's capital city, Astralys."

Nexion, driven to end this conflict before they could kill millions within the unsuspecting city, made the decision to forcibly dock with the crippled Dreadnaught vessel.

"Prepare for immediate docking maneuvers with the hostile vessel," he commanded, his voice firm, ringing with authority.

"Helm, bring us within docking range. Steady, but swift." His gaze fixed on the main screen, the pirate ship looming larger as we rapidly approached.

"Armaments, stand by. If they so much as twitch in a way I don't like, I want you to be ready to fire. Engineering, maintain full power to the engines. Be ready to give us a boost if we need to make a quick exit," he added, his tone unyielding, allowing no room for doubt.

"Prepare for boarding!" Nexion commanded, his voice cutting through the chaos on the bridge. "I want all available knights to assemble at the airlock, and I mean now. We're taking this fight to them."

He unstrapped the neural connections. "Captain Selene, the helm is yours." He ordered.

I stood beside Nexion. "I'm coming too," I declared. He started to argue, but he knew it wouldn't change my mind. The bag I had dragged with me from the academy sat in the back corner of the bridge where I had dropped it when I first arrived and confronted Nexion. I threw on my leather vest, fully sheathed with knives, strapped on my holster, attached my energy blade, and shrugged on my leather jacket. My Empyrean Sigil over my heart. In what felt like an instant, Nexion and the others readied themselves, strapping on gear and weapons.

Just then, we heard metal scrapping and a dull thud as our ship joined the Dreadnaught's ship. We took off running.

As the Resolute docked with the hostile ship, a team of Empyrean knights, including Nexion and me, gathered at the airlock, weapons at the ready. The doors hissed open, revealing the dimly lit and smoky interior of the pirate vessel.

"Stay close and watch each other's backs," Nexion warned as we entered the enemy ship.

Almost immediately, the pirates met us with a hail of laser fire. We ducked for cover, returning fire as we pressed forward through the narrow corridors of the Dreadnaught ship.

"Elzaria, watch out!" Nexion shouted, pushing me out of the way of a pirate's energy blade and landing on my knees. I rolled to my feet and engaged my attacker in close combat.

Our blades clashed, the hum of energy filling the air as we traded blows. I parried and counterattacked with the grace and skill instilled in me during my training at the Knight's Academy. Finally, I saw an opening and struck, taking down my opponent with a swift, decisive blow.

"Good work, Elzaria!" Nexion praised, already engaging another pirate in a fierce hand-to-hand duel. I moved to help him, my blade flashing through the air as I sliced through the throat of another enemy.

Around us, the knights of the Resolute fought valiantly, carving a path through the pirate crew. The battle was brutal, but our persistence and skill turned the tide in our favor.

Just then, I felt the heat of an energy blade pass much too close to my shoulder. Realizing there were attackers behind us, I screamed "They're at our 6." Ganthion met the first bad guy head on, grabbing him up and tossing him into the incoming pirates. I unsheathed a knife and flung it into the eye of one still standing. The attack coming from both sides raged on.

"Hostile vessel weapons at 92%, you guys better get a move on." We all heard over our comms.

"Push forward!" Nexion roared, his voice echoing through the ship. "We're almost at their command center!"

We fought our way through the ship, the sounds of battle and the cries of the fallen ringing in our ears. As we reached their command center, we found the pirate captain and his remaining crew waiting for us.

"I won't allow you to take my ship!" The pirate captain snarled, his eyes blazing with rage.

Nexion and I exchanged a decisive glance. "Then you leave us no choice," he said, raising his weapon and charging toward the captain.

I found myself face-to-face with a particularly skilled marauder. He moved with a predatory grace, his movements fluid and deadly. I could tell this wasn't an ordinary pirate; he was well-trained and experienced.

Our eyes locked, and without a word, we engaged in a savage hand-to-hand fight. The pirate swung his energy blade at me with incredible speed and precision, forcing me to rely on my reflexes to keep up. We exchanged blow after blow, our blades clashing in a brilliant display of sparks and light.

During the fight, the pirate landed a solid hit. His fist connected with my face and sent me reeling backward. I could taste the blood in my mouth from my split lip, but I refused to let the pain slow me down. I gritted my teeth and lunged back at him, my rage fueling my every move.

Despite my best efforts, the pirate continued to press the attack. His blade found its mark, slicing through my leather jacket and the fabric beneath it and in between the sheaths of my vest. He'd gotten lucky. His blade cut a deep gash into my ribs. I gasped in pain but by the grace of the goddesses parried his next strike, retaliating with a swift kick to his chest that sent him staggering backward.

As we fought, I noticed a pattern in his movements, a slight hesitation that I could exploit. I waited for the perfect moment, and when it came, I feigned a stumble. The pirate, sensing an opportunity, lunged forward to deliver the final blow.

But I was ready.

With a burst of telekinetic energy, I propelled myself to the side, narrowly avoiding his blade. As he stumbled past me,

I swung mine, slicing a deep gash into his thigh. The pirate howled in pain, his blade faltering for just a moment—that was all the opening I needed.

With a last surge of strength, I drove my energy blade into his chest, piercing his heart. The pirate's eyes widened in shock before he crumpled to the ground, lifeless.

Breathing heavily, I stood over my defeated foe, my body aching from the brutal fight. I wiped the blood from my lip and pressed a hand to my wounded ribs, adrenaline coursing through my veins.

"I will not be defeated," I vowed, turning my gaze back to the surrounding battle.

Together, our knights fought against the pirate captain and his crew, their blades and telekinetic powers clashing in a dance of destruction. Despite their tenacity, the pirates were no match for the combined might of the Empyrean Knights. With the pirate captain finally defeated, the remaining crew surrendered, and the battle was won. Ganthion raced to disengage the weapons programmed to blast the city below.

As we stood amidst the wreckage of their command center, Nexion turned to me, pride and admiration in his eyes. "You fought like a true Empyrean warrior today, Queen Elzaria."

I smiled, my heart swelling with pride. "We fought together, Nexion. The strength of the Empyrean people lies not in one warrior, but in the unity and courage of us all."

As the adrenaline faded and the reality of my injuries set in, I felt my vision blur. I tried to keep moving, but my strength was rapidly waning. Nexion noticed my faltering steps and rushed to my side.

"Elzaria!" He shouted, concern etching his face as he took in my bloodied condition. "You're losing too much blood. We need to get you to the sick bay, now!"

I tried to protest, to tell him I could manage, but the words caught in my throat as darkness closed in. My knees buckled, and I would have fallen if not for Nexion's muscular arms wrapping around me, hoisting me up before my body hit the ground.

"Nexion," I whispered, but my voice was weak, barely audible.

"Save your strength, Elzaria. I won't let anything happen to you," he reassured me, his voice fierce as he carried me through the chaos of the battle scene.

Nexion barked orders to the crew as he ran towards sick bay. "Detain any Dreadnaught survivors! Undock from their ship and prepare to pursue the remaining fighters! I want every single one of them destroyed!"

Rage filled his voice with anger and something else I had never heard before... fear. I could hear the underlying worry for my safety. As we entered the sick bay, Nexion's tone shifted from commanding to frantic.

"Doctor!" He yelled, laying me gently on a medical bed. "Elzaria's been injured—she's losing blood fast! Save her!"

The ship's doctor rushed to my side, his eyes widening as he assessed the extent of my injuries. He quickly worked, his hands moving with practiced efficiency as he treated my wounds.

Nexion paced the floor, his eyes never leaving my battered form. His fear for my life was tangible, and I could see the tension in every line of his body. He had always been a formidable warrior, but at this moment, I saw the depth of his devotion to me, the lengths he would go to protect me.

As my consciousness faded, the last thing I heard was Nexion's voice, filled with desperation. "You're going to make it, my little knight. I swear it."

NEXION

As I paced back and forth in the sick bay, anxiety gnawed at me. I couldn't take my eyes off Elzaria, who lay unconscious on the examination table. The steady hum of the ship's engines did nothing to calm my nerves. I couldn't shake the feeling that I should have stopped her from joining the fight on the hostile ship.

The sick bay was a sterile environment, filled with state-of-the-art medical technology that seemed to blend seamlessly with the ship's design. An extensive assortment of medical supplies and devices lined the walls in sleek storage compartments. The lighting provided a soft, calming glow meant to soothe anxiety, but only set me on edge.

The medical assistant, who was prepping the necessary equipment, noticed my distress and approached me. "Sir, I understand you're worried, but I assure you that Dr. Xanderian is one of the best. He has served as a field medic in countless battles, and he has even developed some of the groundbreaking medical technology we use today. The Queen is in expert hands."

Glancing at the doctor, a tall slender man with sharp features, a steady hand, and an air of quiet confidence, he worked swiftly to address Elzaria's wounds. I wanted to believe the assistant's words, but my worry for her was overwhelming. I couldn't help but feel responsible for her injuries.

Dr. Xanderian worked with exacting movements, utilizing advanced medical equipment that seemed almost miraculous. He applied a nano cell bio-patch to Elzaria's deep wound in between her ribs, which would speed up the healing process and reduce scarring. A holographic display showed the doctor her vitals and an internal map as he monitored her condition closely.

"She's lucky you brought her to me so quickly. The sword went between her ribs and pierced her lung. Another couple of centimeters and it would have sliced into her heart."

I never knew the pain those words could incite. It was all I could do to remain standing.

Time crept slowly, the minutes feeling like hours. When the doctor finished his work, he finally spoke to me as he washed Elzaria's blood off his hands. "Commander, I'm confident that Queen Elzaria will make a full recovery. The nano cell bio-patches have already begun the healing process. I've sealed all wounds, and she'll regain consciousness soon."

Hearing this, my anxiety subsided a fraction. I walked over to Elzaria's side and fell to my knees, my eyes welling up with tears of relief. Gratitude and concern mingled together, "Thank you, Doctor. Thank you for saving her." Despite the good news, I couldn't shake the guilt I felt for letting her get hurt in the first place. The Knightmaster must protect his queen at all costs. I resolved to do everything in my power to protect her from now on, even if that meant protecting her from herself.

With a heavy heart, I forced myself to leave Elzaria's side in the sick bay. I knew I had to return to the bridge and resume my duties as the commander. My concern for her was immense, but I couldn't let it cloud my judgment or impair my ability to lead the crew during this critical time.

As I stepped onto the bridge, the tension in the air was palpable. The crew was hard at work, diligently monitoring various systems and maintaining communication with the rest of the fleet and any allied forces. They were sharing information and coordinating our response to the attack, ensuring we remained one step ahead of the enemy.

I approached the communications officer, who was busy relaying updates between our ship and the others in the fleet.

"What's the status of our transmissions with the fleet and our allies?" I asked.

The officer looked up from his console, concern etched on his face. "We're maintaining contact with the fleet, but we've lost contact with a few of our allied ships, sir. We're working to re-establish communication."

I nodded and moved on to the engineering station. The engineer was monitoring the ship's structural integrity and vital systems, ready to alert me of any significant damage or potential system failures. "How's the Phantom Resolute holding up?" I inquired.

The engineer wiped the sweat from his brow and replied, "We've sustained some damage, but our shields are holding and all our systems remain operational. We're working to repair any minor damage and reinforce our defenses."

I appreciated the update and made my way to the tactical station. The officer there was responsible for providing me with situational awareness, which helped me make informed strategic decisions during the battle. "What's the latest on the enemy ships?" I asked, bracing myself for the answer.

The tactical officer quickly responded, "We've taken out three of the smaller enemy fighters, but the remaining two are proving to be more challenging. The Dreadnaught ship we were docked with earlier appears to be disabled, but we're monitoring it just in case one of the hostiles thinks they can re-board."

I took a deep breath, processing the information. Despite our losses and the challenges we faced, I knew we had fared well. Elzaria's courage in battle inspired me, and I owed it to her and the rest of my crew to stay on the bridge and see this fight through to the end, protecting Grymrock from any further incursions.

As I mulled over our next steps, Ganthion, Elzaria's friend from the Knight's Academy, approached me, his expression full of concern. "Sir, I heard about Elzaria. How is she? Will she be alright?"

I nodded slowly, remembering the relief I felt when the doctor told me she would recover. "She's going to be okay, Ganthion. Dr. Xanderian has treated her injuries, and she should regain consciousness soon."

Ganthion's face lit up with relief. "Thank you, sir. That's good to hear."

After I reassured Ganthion, I turned to my communications officer for an update on the rest of my knights.

"Sir," he began, "we have seven injured and one dead. We lost Ivar. We recovered his body, but sir... he's got a wife and kid. A young son."

"Dammit, I hate that it happened. Those fuckers will pay." I swore as I tore my hand through my hair. "Give me his wife's contact information and I'll let her know. How are the injured?"

"Most of them have minor injuries—cuts, bruises, and a few sprains. They've been treated and are resting in their quarters. However, Valdorion sustained more serious injuries during the battle."

My brow furrowed with concern. "What happened to Valdorion?"

The communications officer hesitated before continuing. "He was caught in an explosion during the fight on the ship, sir. He suffered burns and some shrapnel wounds. Dr. Xanderian treated him right after you left Queen Elzaria. He's stable now and recovering in the sick bay."

"Thank you for the update, officer," I replied, relief washing over me that Valdorion was in stable condition. "Keep me informed of any changes in their status."

"Yes, sir," he responded with a nod.

Ganthion, who had been listening to the update, clenched his fist. "We'll make those pirate bastards pay for what they've done, Commander."

I looked at him, fury strengthening my resolve. "Yes, we will. We'll crush and obliterate any who dare threaten our galaxy from threats like these. That's our sworn duty as Empyrean Knights."

Ganthion nodded in agreement, and our attention turned back to the work that needed to be done.

I focused my attention on the hostile ships. "Alright, let's finish this. Find and target the remaining enemy strike fighters and prepare to engage."

"Aye, sir!" The tactical officer replied. It didn't take too long for us to find the other two pirate strike fighters and unleash a barrage of fire upon them. One was obliterated in a brilliant explosion, while the other was disabled and captured. Its pilot held for interrogation.

As we secured the captured pirate ship, two large, modern Empyrean vessels arrived to provide support and keep watch for any further hostile activity. With the situation finally under control, I ordered the crew of the Resolute to take some much-needed rest and get some food in their bellies.

Exhausted, I returned to my private quarters, the weight of the day's events pressing down on me. As I closed the door behind me, I couldn't help but feel the emptiness of the room without Elzaria by my side. I longed for her presence. Dr. Xanderian's update reassured me she was healing well and semiconscious from the meds he used. Mostly, she needed time to recover.

As I stared at the empty space in the bed where she would have rested, I realized just how much she meant to me, and how much I wanted her to be part of my life.

I tried to sleep, but it was no use. I snatched up a bottle of Arcanix, a honey-colored elixir that flowed as smooth as melted butter, but packed a fiery punch that scorched your throat all the way down. It was the real deal, the kind of badass hooch that could make you grin like a maniac for a night or put the toughest son of a bitch on his sorry ass; no questions asked. I didn't bother with a glass. I sank against the wall behind the bed, my gaze losing itself in the black abyss beyond the window, bringing back images of the sweltering darkness within the AI Sim back at the academy.

Elzaria. Damn her. How had she crawled under my skin? Better yet, how had she burrowed her way straight into my heart? It was as if she'd blown a cannon through the fortified walls I'd built around myself, not caring about the defenses I'd put up.

I couldn't help but shake my head, a bitter smile tugging at my lips. A few lunars ago, I would've laughed at anyone who suggested I'd have anything but disdain for the spoiled royal. Yet, here I was, consumed with worry for the stubborn woman who had shown she was more than capable of holding her own in a fight.

Elzaria was a force, a tempest that had swept into my life, leaving nothing untouched. She was smart as hell, witty, and as stubborn as they came. I'd thought of her as a bratty princess, a porcelain doll, but how wrong I'd been. She was a warrior, my queen, my little knight.

I clenched my fists, nails digging into the bottle. The guilt was a living thing inside me, gnawing at my insides. I should never have let her face the Dreadnaught pirates. I should have been the one to take that hit. But then, I knew the truth—she would've gone into that ship whether or not I liked it. That's who she was, who she'd always be. She was a force of nature and I'd be damned if that didn't spark a flame in me.

I've seen a lot, been through hell and back, but nothing, and I mean nothing, could have prepared me for this onslaught of emotions. Every time I thought of her laying there in the medical bay, her life almost snuffed out, it was like a gut punch. It wasn't just the physical pain that had me drinking Arcanix; it was the raw, twisted fear of losing her.

What was this? I didn't do love. But the depth of my feelings for Elzaria was like nothing I'd ever known. Was this what they called love? If so, it was one hell of a sucker-punch.

Elzaria, with her sharp mind, her incredible power, and her quick wit, had a way of making me feel seen, really seen. And that mouth of hers, always ready with a retort, a jab, a sarcasm. Sometimes, the only way to silence her was to kiss her. And damn, did I want to kiss her. Her curves were irresistible, and her sharp tongue kept me coming back for more.

She's the kind of woman that'd make a man forget his own name. I know now not to let that royal facade fool me. There's a wild, fiery spirit under that crown. That look she got in her eyes, like she dared me to step up or step off.

She's got this natural beauty about her, untouched and unspoiled; she's a strange cocktail of naivety and sharp intellect, an enticing blend that makes my blood heat just thinking about it. Makes a man think... dangerous thoughts. But what can I say? I've always been one for danger.

As I sat there, staring at the vacant expanse of black dotted by the stars, my thoughts were a whirlwind, a storm of doubts and revelations. Protecting her, that was the priority, but how? How could I shield her from a universe of threats? From the seedy Dreadnaught pirates to the treacherous Vaith, danger was a constant, an ever-present shadow.

A wild idea crept into my mind, a solution so outrageous it felt like I'd been smacked upside the head. Make her mine, forever. But the idea of commitment, of letting someone in, it wasn't just foreign to me; it was downright alien. I'd been a knight all my life, a lone wolf, not bound by the shackles of emotions.

Being an orphan, love was a concept as elusive as the edge of the universe. I had no blueprint, no guide on how to love a woman, least of all a queen. The thought of it was as daunting as it was tempting. But Elzaria wasn't just any woman, and she certainly wasn't just a queen. She was a warrior, a leader, an energy to be reckoned with. She deserved someone who could match her strength, her spirit, not someone fumbling in the darkness of his own emotions.

Damn the Celestial Creed. It had been my guide, my compass in life. But love, it seemed, followed no creed, no rules.

Could I be a lover and a leader? Could I lead my warriors into battle, my heart tethered to a woman I feared losing more than life itself?

What would they think? The knights, the court, the Empyrean people. I was a Knightmaster, not some love-struck fool. But maybe, just maybe, I could be both. For her.

I'd spent my life fighting, defending, always on the hunt. But this, this was a battle of a different kind. This was a battle not for victory, but for happiness, for love.

I loved her.

I fucking loved her with a ferocity that startled me. It was a love that consumed me. I'd move galaxies to keep her safe, to make her happy.

I exhaled, forcing myself back to the present, back to the Arcanix. One last swig and then I could get some shut-eye. I had a job to do and needed to get back to the bridge soon. I had to keep us all safe. But one thing was certain: I'd protect Elzaria, no matter the cost. For my little knight, I'd storm the gates of hell. Because for the first time, I had something worth fighting for. I had someone worth fighting for. Elzaria. She'd changed everything. And there was no turning back.

CHAPTER SEVENTEEN

NEXION

As I left Elzaria in the capable hands of Dr. Xanderian, I couldn't shake the feeling that something far more sinister was at play. With a small crew, I boarded the planetary shuttle to descend to the surface of Grymrock. It was crucial to gather as much information as possible and coordinate our next steps with the local authorities.

Upon our arrival, we were greeted by Nobleman Alastar Pendleton, Grymrock's highest-ranking official, and a team of security officers. We exchanged formalities and were escorted to a secure conference room to discuss the recent events.

The command room in the spaceport on Grymrock was all cool tones and sharp angles, mirroring the anxiety that hung heavy in the air. Nobleman Pendleton, flanked by his officials and my officers, stared at the tactical holograph, concern etched across their hardened faces. As I entered, their eyes snapped to me, each one searching for answers I wasn't sure I had.

"I can't understand why the Dreadnaughts would target a small Empyrean outpost like ours," Pendleton began, a puzzled expression on his face. "What could they possibly hope to gain?"

"Gentlemen," I began, my voice steady but layered with a deep sense of foreboding. "We are standing on the precipice of a situation that requires our full attention and nothing less."

"Let's all be seated," Nobleman Pendleton gestured for us to be seated around a large table. I sat at the end opposite of Pendleton.

"I don't want to panic you, but your city was the target of the lead Dreadnaught ship. If we hadn't stopped them in time, your citizens would have been decimated. Their cannons were armed, aimed, and almost deployed."

A collective gasp echoed against the walls of the silent room. Everyone at the table was taken aback in disbelief.

I nodded in agreement. "The advanced cloaking technology they used is particularly troubling. We've got to find out how they acquired such tech and what their ultimate goal is."

At my direction, my communications officer rolled out a holographic device in the center of the table. The image sprang to life, showing us the F1R3X wormhole, with its location and travel portals displayed on a map of our local area of the universe. The wormhole, this cosmic snake, twined its way from a distant spiral galaxy that had yet to be explored by the Empyreans, through Andromeda, brushing past Dracore in the outer rim, and all the way to the Maffei galaxy. And right smack in its path sat Grymrock, a pearl of military strategy. A pearl the Vaith could easily seize.

"This," I said, pointing at the swirling holographic image, "isn't just a pretty light show. This is our critical flaw."

A murmur swept through the room. Pendleton's brows knitted even tighter, his gaze piercing the holographic image as if trying to glean its secrets.

A few of the officers exchanged worried glances. No doubt they were pondering the same strategic implications I had been grappling with.

"It's a double-edged sword," I continued. "A way for us to move quickly, yes, but it could also be a path straight to our door for the Vaith. It's faster than light travel in its rawest form."

"What about the other wormholes?" One of the younger officers asked, his voice shaky with underlying tension.

"None of them offers such strategic value," Pendleton spoke, the enormity of the realization quieting the room. "This one... it's a universal linchpin. A key to the entire star map."

"Agreed," I responded. "Most wormholes are unstable, unpredictable, or they're out in the hinterlands, away from key strategic points. This one... this one's different."

"It is a conduit to the heart of Empyrean territory," I continued, my gaze steady on the hologram. "Our defense of Grymrock isn't just about one planet. It's about protecting our entire realm. If we lose control of this wormhole, the consequences will be cataclysmic."

The conversation shifted to the possibility of the Dreadnaught pirates being backed by a more nefarious force.

"It's becoming increasingly clear that the Vaith are involved in this attack," I suggested, gauging Pendleton's reaction.

He frowned, mulling over the implications. "The Vaith... I should have known. They're a ruthless, cunning lot. Never to be trusted. The Vaith society is an embodiment of anarchy, rooted in violence and corruption. They're infamous as ruthless opportunists, ready to spill blood for power. With a history stained by brutality."

"You're right. The Vaith have always been power-hungry, untrustworthy," I continued, my gut churning at the implications. "Supreme Commander Skarnak is no fool. He knows the tactical advantage this wormhole provides, and by the stars, he'll exploit it. If they move through, it's not just Terrastria they'd hit. Every planet in the path could be under their boot."

"The worst-case scenario," Pendleton said, his voice resonating through the cold command room, "is that we don't just lose Terrastria, but our foothold in the entire sector."

"Let's not forget," I interjected, "that Terrastria houses our primary communication relays. We lose those, we're practically fighting blind. Losing Terrastria would be a devastating blow to the Empyrean Alliance. A bastion of cultural and scientific development, its fall would leave us teetering, scrambling to regroup."

I watched as realization dawned on Pendleton's face. The holograph flickered in the middle of the table, highlighting the intergalactic chessboard on which we were all merely pawns.

The room was silent, each man absorbing the enormity of the situation. Decades of peace had made us soft, unprepared for the taste of war. But the Vaith weren't interested in the sweet fruits of peace. They craved power, domination, and the wormhole provided an all-you-can-eat buffet.

As we exchanged information about the Vaith, the room grew increasingly tense. "Their men dominate women, treating them as little more than property," one officer commented. "They even allow slavery, despite its being outlawed by the Quindarian Federation's Supreme Judiciary ages ago. The Vaith are tyrannical leaders, and always looking for ways to expand their power." Pendleton reminded everyone; the disgust thick in his voice.

I clenched my fists, feeling a surge of anger at the thought of the innocent Empyrean people on Grymrock and elsewhere suffering at the hands of the Vaith. "We cannot allow them to to go unchecked. For starters, we must find out who among the

Dreadnaught pirates is working with the Vaith and put an end to this alliance." Everyone nodded.

"We've been asleep at the wheel, gentlemen," I stated, the reality biting into me like a winter's chill. "But the time has come to prepare, to secure this sector, and safeguard our people."

"We must prepare for war," a gruff voice boomed from the back. A veteran general, his countenance hardened from decades of service, stood with his arms crossed over his chest.

"But are we prepared for the costs of such a war?" A lieutenant asked, his youthful face pale under the harsh lights. "The ancient wars claimed millions of lives, laid waste to whole planets..." His voice trailed off, swallowed by the chilling silence that followed. The memories of those wars were etched into our collective history, a grim reminder of the cost of conflict.

"Indeed," I replied, my gaze sweeping over the room. "We must not forget the horrors of those wars. Our ancestors fought so that we might know peace. The last thing we want is to repeat those mistakes."

"But," I continued, "we must also not forget that the cost of inaction can be just as devastating. If the Vaith attack, and we're not prepared, we're looking at casualty figures that dwarf those of the ancient wars. It's a grim reality we must face."

The weight of the situation hung heavy in the room, a quiet dread echoing in the silence. But at that moment, I saw not just fear, but determination. The Empyrean spirit wasn't so easily quelled, and we were prepared to defend our people, our Queen, and our way of life.

"The ancient wars taught us the value of peace," I said. "Now, we must show the Vaith the cost of war."

A hardened resolve passed through the room, mirrored in each pair of steely eyes that met mine. They were soldiers, officers, warriors at heart, and they knew the cost of freedom. There was a storm brewing, and we were standing right in its path. The Vaith might have started the game, but by the stars, we'd be the ones to end it.

Pendleton nodded solemnly. "Agreed, Commander. We'll coordinate our efforts with your crew and the security forces here on Grymrock. Together, we'll uncover the truth behind this attack."

We began strategizing our next steps, knowing that the safety of Grymrock and the entire Empyrean realm may depend on our success.

Upon our return to the Phantom Resolute, I immediately called for a meeting with the commanders from the other two Empyrean ships that had joined us. The situation had become increasingly complex and required the attention of all our highest-ranking officers.

Commander Zyrana Velor of the Empyrean ship "Stalwart Protector" and Commander Daltus Thren of the "Sovereign Dawn" joined me on the bridge of the Resolute. As we exchanged greetings, I noticed the ferocity in their eyes, reflecting our shared animosity toward the Vaith.

Before we could delve into the discussions, my sensors officer notified us he identified an inbound Xanthra ship coming directly toward us. I watched as the unknown ship approached the Resolute, my apprehension growing with each passing moment. The ship was unlike any I had seen before, with sleek, silver curves that seemed to shimmer in the light of the nearby star. As it drew closer, my communications officer informed me of an incoming transmission.

The message was from Xanthra Queen Cassia herself, requesting permission to board the Resolute via a transport shuttle. I hesitated for a moment, unsure of the queen's intentions, but ultimately agreed to her request. We needed all the allies we could get in our fight against the Vaith and the Dreadnaught pirates.

As Queen Cassia and her entourage made their way to us, I arranged for a secure conference room to be prepared, with welcoming food and drink.

I made my way to the airlock as the shuttle docked with the Resolute to greet Queen Cassia and her entourage. The queen emerged from the shuttle, dressed in a formal deep green gown with gold trim. Her beauty was breathtaking, with incredible red hair that cascaded down her back. But her expression was worried, and I could sense the tension in her body as she approached me. Queen Cassia, leader of the Xanthra Alliance, had come to address an urgent matter. Her presence was a clear indication of the gravity of the situation we faced.

I shared with her a Universal Translator, or UTran, an advanced wearable device facilitating real-time communication across various languages of the universe.

The translator housed a vast database of known languages, constantly updated through a subspace communication network. Long ago, the Empyrean had developed the device which transformed inter-species communication, leading to greater understanding, cooperation, and peaceful conflict resolution across civilizations.

"Commander," she said, offering a small nod. "Thank you for allowing my ship to dock with yours and agreeing to meet with me. I know my visit is a surprise to you."

"It's an honor to have you on board, Queen Cassia," I replied, returning her nod. "May I ask what brings you to our ship?"

She hesitated for a moment before speaking. "Our spies have infiltrated the Dreadnaught underground and we believe the Vaith may be planning an attack on the Xanthra Alliance and possibly the Empyrean as well. I came to you on a secret mission based on our intelligence. There were no specifics, only rumors or else I would have sent you an urgent communique. I had hoped we were wrong, but we witnessed the tail end of the attack that you just fought off as we exited from the second wormhole we had to journey through to get here. I came in person, not trusting this information to be shared by any other means."

We quickly made our way through the ship's corridors and gathered in the conference room. Not having needed this space in the past, its grand design surprised me. Luxurious fabrics decorated the room, and detailed maps of the galaxies lined the walls, revealing the vastness of our universe. The large round table at the center of the room was made of a shimmering, dark ebony wood that seemed to reflect the stars themselves. The architects had been mindful of the many demands of this ship.

Queen Cassia began the meeting by sharing her concerns about the Dreadnaught pirates. "These pirates have been attacking and harassing our outer fringe planets and stealing from our merchants," she said, her voice firm and laced with concern. "As you know, the Xanthra Alliance comprises worlds from the small galaxy called Aurora 33. Our galaxy, with its 33 solar systems and inhabitable planets, has fostered fair and balanced civilizations. We may be small, but our worlds are rich in natural resources, making us a target for the likes of the Vaith."

She continued, describing the unique characteristics of the Xanthra worlds. "Xanthrians are artisans, valuing nature and the love between our people. We have been fortunate to live in peace, independent of the needs of outside galaxy civilizations. Yet, it seems our peace and prosperity have now attracted unwanted attention far from their own galaxy."

As the meeting progressed, it became apparent that Queen Cassia was seeking our help. "The Xanthra Alliance is small, and we have never experienced war. We are ill-prepared to face the Vaith's aggression, which we now believe to be the force behind the Dreadnaught pirates you just dealt with. We implore the Empyrean to aid us in our time of need."

Her heartfelt plea struck a chord within each of us present. We knew that standing together against the Vaith and their Dreadnaught allies was the only way to protect the innocent lives at stake.

We all had hoped that Elzaria would be able to take part in the meeting. Only the queen could guarantee the help the Xanthra needed. However, still in the throes of recovery, I wasn't sure if she could join us. Just as we were about to adjourn, the doors to the conference room opened, and there she was, walking in tentatively.

I felt a surge of admiration for her strength, mixed with worry for her well-being as I rushed to her aid, offering her my seat at the massive round table. The room hushed to a silence, all eyes on us, as I turned to address the commanders and Queen Cassia.

"Our Queen has the heart of a warrior," I began, cutting through the quiet. "She took a blade through the ribs during the clash with the Dreadnaughts and still kept fighting." I wanted them to hear the truth, the unvarnished reality, not a diluted version from the media.

"Many of you may not be aware that our Queen kept her royal blood a secret to train at the Empyrean Knight's Academy," I continued. "She didn't just graduate; She excelled."

The commanders' faces registered surprise, morphing into admiration as they absorbed the reality of their Queen's accomplishments. "She's the first Warrior Queen we've had since the Great Wars," I said, my pride for her resonating in every word. "She's strong. She's intelligent. Not just a figurehead, but a leader, and she's earned our respect."

The atmosphere in the room changed. A ripple of assent passed through, with Queen Cassia appearing particularly struck by Elzaria's resilience.

Despite her pain, Elzaria nodded her appreciation for my words and took her seat at the table. As she gathered her thoughts, the room awaited her perspective, knowing that any course of action required her approval.

Elzaria spoke, her voice authoritative. "Thank you, Nexion, for your kind words. Welcome Queen Cassia, it is so nice to meet you. I only wish it was under better circumstances. I value your opinions and unabashed thoughts. Now, let's discuss our next steps in addressing this threat that looms over us all."

Together we discussed all that we knew to this point about the Vaith and their Dreadnaught minions. As we delved deeper into the discussion, Elzaria's mind was racing with the potential outcomes of our actions. She knew this was a defining moment in her reign as the Empyrean Queen. Her eyes flicked across the faces of her commanders, gauging their reactions as she spoke.

"We need to act fast. The Vaith shouldn't be underestimated. We need to strengthen our defenses, warn our allies, and prepare for the worst."

As the meeting progressed, I couldn't help but steal glances at Elzaria. Despite her injuries, she exuded a quiet strength that left me in awe. I wanted nothing more than to wrap her in my arms, to soothe her pain and protect her from harm. But I knew she was a warrior through and through and didn't want my over protection.

As the meeting ended, we formulated a plan of action. Our first step was to gather intelligence on the Vaith and their Dreadnaught allies. We needed to know their strengths, their weaknesses, and their objectives. Only then could we hope to devise a strategy to defeat them.

The room fell silent, the magnitude of the task ahead casting long shadows over us. But there was a resolve brewing, a sense of unified purpose. It was a daunting challenge, but I knew that the men and women of the Empyrean Alliance were ready to face it. After all, there was far more than our peace at stake. The very future of our galaxy hung in the balance.

Elzaria and I returned to our quarters, both physically and emotionally drained from the last two days' events. As she lay down to rest, I joined her, gently pulling her into my arms.

We snuggled together and discussed our next steps. We decided that Commander Zyrana Velor of the Stalwart Protector would remain in orbit around Grymrock, ensuring the safety of the planet and others in the vicinity. The Resolute would return to our home world, Terrastria, while the Sovereign Dawn would resume its normal patrol duties.

Elzaria, still weak but driven, sent a formal communique to Vaith Alliance Supreme Commander Skarnak. Skarnak was a ruthless leader, fueled by a desire for conquest and dominance. He saw no value in mercy or compassion and viewed the suffering of others as a means to an end.

In her message, Elzaria informed Skarnak that we were aware of his use of the Dreadnaught pirates for his nefarious schemes. She warned him that any actions taken by the Dreadnaughts would be considered on behalf of the Vaith and that the Quindarian Federation would not tolerate such attacks.

With the message sent, we could only wait and hope that it would have some effect on Skarnak and his plans.

SKARNAK

Meanwhile, on a distant world in the Maffei galaxy, Skarnak received Queen Elzaria's communique. He laughed dismissively as he relayed its contents to his second-in-command. "The new little Queen doesn't know what's about to hit her," he sneered.

Skarnak continued, arrogance dripping from his words, "Let her send her warnings. They'll do nothing to stop us. Soon, we'll bring the mighty Empyreans to their knees."

Skarnak hissed in delight, "With the intelligence we've gathered from my new little pet, Seraphean, the unwitting rat feeding us all the intel we needed, we'll blindside the entire

Empyrean Alliance. They'll beg for my mercy. And when reality hits, when the shadows of defeat loom over them, their voices will quiver in desperation. But they will learn—mercy is not in the Vaith vocabulary. The age of the Empyrean is over. The order of the Vaith will rise."

As he spoke, the cold, calculating glint in Skarnak's eyes promised a dark future for those who dared to oppose him.

CHAPTER EIGHTEEN

ELZARIA

As the Phantom Resolute approached the atmosphere of Terrastria, I couldn't help but feel excited. It had been almost a cycle since I had last set foot in my home city, and I was impatient to be reunited with my family and everyone I cared for.

Nexion stood by my side, his powerful presence a constant comfort. My wounds had healed remarkably well thanks to the advanced technology, although a silver scar remained under my heart along my ribs, a permanent reminder of the battle with the Dreadnaught and how close I had come to death.

We touched down in the bustling spaceport of Arcadia, on Terrastria. As the airlock opened and we disembarked, the familiar faces of my parents greeted me. Their eyes filled with relief as they enveloped me in a warm embrace. My father took Nexion's arm in a firm warrior's grip. "Thank you for keeping our girl safe. Maybe next time she should stay on the ship instead of the front lines of the fight."

"She took the oath of the *Celestial Creed* as she ascended into knighthood. It's her duty to fight alongside her fellow warriors and as Queen, it's her decision to make," Nexion responded firmly, shaking my father's arm. "I have every confidence in her skills."

My father nodded, surprised by Nexion's words, and glanced at me with a new level of respect in his eyes.

"It's so good to see you, Elzaria," my mother spoke softly, her voice choked with emotion.

"I've missed you both so much," I replied, hugging them at the same time.

As we made our way through the spaceport, Nexion and I filled my parents in on the harrowing events of our encounter with the Dreadnaught pirates and their suspected connection to the Vaith. I also thanked them for allowing me true anonymity during my time at the Academy as the media surrounded us.

"You look so strong and confident now," my mother exclaimed admiringly, as she took in my more muscular and physically fit appearance. "You have truly become a warrior Queen—the first to do so since the ancient wars. I couldn't be any prouder of you."

My father nodded his approval. "The academy has turned you into a self-assured leader. The Empyrean people are fortunate indeed." As we made our way through the spaceport, residents recognized me and shouted their congratulations for becoming a knight. I couldn't help but worry, knowing that I was now both their Queen and protector standing between them and the hands of Skarnak.

When we reached the end of the spaceport terminal, a sleek hover-car awaited us. We climbed in, and the vehicle smoothly lifted off the ground, heading towards the castle. As we traveled, my parents shared other news about what they believed were Vaith incidents they had dealt with during my absence. None of them had any direct ties to the Vaith, but all appeared to be connected.

"I fear the Vaith have been plotting against us for a long time," I said gravely. "I know you have a hard to believing that The Creators spoke to me of a war that would soon engulf the universe, causing destruction and the loss of millions of lives, but we can see their warnings are coming to fruition."

The concern in my parents' eyes deepened. "We must scrutinize these matters," Father said firmly. "Tomorrow, we'll convene a meeting with our highest-ranking military officers and trusted advisors to discuss the potential of war erupting around us and consider our response."

"Thank you, Father. That would be helpful. The trust you show in me will help to convince the senior officials of my credibility. Your support will garner their respect for my decisions."

We arrived at the front entrance to the castle, and I noticed there were many people welcoming me home. Their cheers and excitement lifted my spirits as we neared.

Stepping out of the car, Adelaide greeted me with open arms. She had been a constant presence in my life since childhood and this had been the longest we had ever been apart. It hit me hard how much I missed her. Her eyes filled with tears of joy as she embraced me.

"Your Majesty, you've been gone for so long. I can't tell you how much I've missed you," Adelaide said, her voice trembling with emotion. "I couldn't believe what I saw on the news from the Empyrean Knight's Academy graduation ceremony. Your parents told everyone you had left on a secret mission with a small military contingency to visit different areas of our kingdom across the galaxy. They said you went undercover so that you could get to know the people in each area and gather information about them. None of us suspected you were becoming a knight! I'm so proud of you."

I smiled at her, touched by her devotion. "Thank you, Adelaide. It's so good to be home."

Next to her stood Loren. He had known of my secret journey to the Academy and had kept my identity hidden while I attended. We exchanged a knowing look, and I could see the relief in his eyes at my safe return.

"Welcome home, Elzaria," Loren said, his voice warm and genuine. "I'm so glad to see you again." He grabbed me in a tight hug, swinging me around. I couldn't help but notice Nexion's jealous reaction before he quickly hid it behind his Knightmaster's stern grimace.

As the excitement of my arrival continued, Nexion quietly slipped away, unnoticed by most. I guessed he wanted to let me have time with everyone after being away for so long. Without planning to, we had kept our relationship a secret for now.

Accompanied by Adelaide and Loren, I entered my chambers and was overwhelmed with a deep sense of gratefulness for the life that had been given to me. The room was luxurious, elegantly decorated, and equipped with all the conveniences fit for a queen. I had deliberately blocked out thoughts of my life before the Academy, but now they surged back in waves.

I'd been naïve, cloaked in the protective bubble of my regal upbringing, thoroughly educated but blind to what really matters in life. That naïve girl had weathered the brutal testosterone-filled Academy, had fought hand-to-hand with a Dreadnaught pirate, and emerged, not as an ignorant princess, but a knight, a little wiser to the world's harsh realities.

I turned to Adelaide and Loren, who had followed me inside. "I can't tell you guys how much I've missed you while I was away. Your friendship and loyalty mean more to me than you'll ever know." I couldn't believe how quickly I had gone from knight to sentimental girl. With a Vaith attack brewing, I knew I needed to lock the old me away and fully embrace the warrior within, but it was hard.

As they left me to adjust to my surroundings, I wondered where Nexion had disappeared to. I knew he would be close, always ready to stand by my side when needed, but his absence felt strange after being together so much.

Alone in my chambers, I took a moment to think back on my journey and the incredible transformation I had undergone—from an inexperienced queen to a skilled warrior. I knew that the challenges ahead were great, but at least now I had opened my parent's eyes to a possible attack by the Vaith. There were many more senior officials to convince, but I was ready to confront them.

NEXION

I slipped away from the crowd, quietly making my way to my old mentor's home. Master Sergeant Gareth Glastonbury, now retired, was one of the Knight's Academy's most renowned indoctrination sergeants. He took no bullshit from anyone and was a strict disciplinarian, living and breathing the *Celestial Creed*. For most of his life, he was married to the knighthood and had no family. Well, except for me, I guess.

Thinking back, I remembered how I'd grown up on the streets. With little else to do, I would sneak in and out of the academy by way of a large sewer pipe that ran from a reconstitution plant to a building within. I was a scrawny, dirty little kid and worshiped the knights I spied on. I found the best food in their trash and didn't have to fight anyone for it.

I didn't think anyone ever noticed me, but one day, just as I climbed up a tree to watch the knights spar, an enormous hand yanked me down by the nap of my neck. Master Sergeant Glastonbury was terrifying, holding me like some rat. I was fourteen and small for my age when he caught me. I'll never forget his words to me, "Boy, I've been watching you come here and rummage through our garbage for a long time now. Show me how you're getting in, and I'll make you a knight."

Of course, I didn't believe him. Why would he want to help the likes of me? That's when for the first time in my life I felt the hands of The Creators. For no other reason than an instant connection to this man, I showed him how I snuck in and out. I turned to leave before I got into any more trouble when he grabbed my arm and hauled me back to the academy. From that moment, I was his responsibility, and he ensured I'd be my best. He pushed me beyond my limits and made me earn every success I had. The academy accepted me even though I was underage. Since I began training midway through a cycle, they forced me to repeat the grueling training from the start of the next cycle. No one had ever given me anything in this world until Master Sergeant Glastonbury. I could never repay my debt of gratitude.

Over the cycles, I remained close with him; he was a mentor and the father I never had. He gave his life to the knighthood and married only after he retired, never having children of his own. It felt like ages since I'd seen Gareth and Clara, and I could almost hear their eager questions about my latest scuffles with the scum of the universe and my fresh duties as Knightmaster.

Reaching their house, I knocked gently on the door. Clara was the first to greet me, her eyes widening in surprise as she realized who stood before her.

"Nexion! My dear boy, it's so good to see you!" She exclaimed, embracing me tightly.

Gareth appeared behind her, his face breaking into a broad grin. "Welcome home, son," he said, his voice thick with emotion.

As we settled into the living room, I recounted the battle I had just fought against the Dreadnaught pirates and the suspicions I had that the Vaith were behind their actions and planning more attacks. That, in my gut, I knew the attack had been a test to see how ready we were for something greater.

Their faces grew grave as they listened to my account. Clara grabbed my arm. Her eyes filled with worry. "Be careful, Nexion. The Vaith are a dangerous enemy, and we don't know how far their reach extends."

I gave her a reassuring smile, squeezing her hand softly. "I will." I nodded, my mind already racing with ideas and strategies. But as the conversation turned towards the impending war and our preparations, my thoughts kept drifting back to Elzaria.

Changing the subject, I explained how I met Queen Elzaria just before her coronation and thought she was just a pampered royal. How she had changed her appearance and assumed a new identity so that she could attend the Empyrean Knight's Academy.

"I only knew her as Zalara. She fooled everyone. She's lucky she didn't get herself killed. And what's even more incredible, she never once asked for any favors. I hate to admit it, but everyone treated her badly because we all assumed she was a spoiled girl looking for a husband. The Master Sergeant pushed her hard, expecting her to give up and leave. The only reason I allowed her to stay was because she reminded me of when I was a scrawny kid. She had a look of desperation I never understood...until now." I replied, shaking my head, still surprised by all that she had accomplished.

I explained how she fought by my side against the Dreadnaught pirates. "She took a blade between her ribs. Another couple of centimeters and it would have pierced her heart." I told them. They listened intently; their eyes filled with concern.

Out of nowhere, never having been a man of many words, I blurted out, "I love her."

Their expressions shifted to a mixture of shock and concern. "Nexion," Gareth said carefully, "you must remember that she is your queen."

"I know," I replied, my voice unwavering. "But my love for her is undeniable, and I would do anything for her. I am her Knightmaster, sworn by *Creed* to protect her with my life."

Clara gave me a tender smile. "We can see how much she means to you, Nexion. And we trust your judgment, don't we, Gareth?" He nodded.

Feeling emboldened by their understanding, I took a deep breath, "I want her to be my soul-bound forever committed to her."

Gareth hesitated for a moment before smiling. "Then I may have something you want." He said as he retrieved a small, ornate box from a hidden compartment in the bookshelf and handed it to me.

"This was my mother's. Generations have handed down this family heirloom. It would be an honor for your soul-bound and our queen to wear it as a symbol of your love and dedication." He said, warm with pride.

Inside the box lay a stunning ring. Its band, crafted from an intricate weave of gold and xenochronatium, symbolized the joining of two lives and destinies. At the center of the band sat a brilliant blue sapphire, encircled by a halo of smaller diamonds. The gemstones seemed to shimmer with a celestial light, as if capturing the very essence of the stars themselves, reminding me of her eyes.

My hands trembled slightly as I held the ring, understanding the gravity of the commitment I was about to make. "Thanks to the love and support you have given me, I'm more than prepared to take on the challenges of being bound to Elzaria, in both love and in service."

We talked for a long while, catching each other up on our lives before I hugged them goodbye and headed towards the castle along quiet, dark corridors.

When I arrived, I made my way through the shadowed halls. With my heart pounding in my chest, I carefully made my way to Elzaria's chambers, the ornate box containing the ring concealed within the folds of my cloak.

When I reached her door, I found it slightly ajar, as if inviting me in. I cautiously slipped inside; the room, dimly lit by the soft glow of the moonlight filtering through the balcony doors. Elzaria was fast asleep, her chest rising and falling gently as she dreamed. The lacy top she wore had slipped up, revealing the silver scar on her ribs. It seemed to shimmer in the pale light, reminding me of how close I had come to losing her.

I hesitated for a moment, not wanting to disturb her rest, but knew that this moment might never come again. With a deep breath, I approached the bed and gently shook her awake.

"Elzaria," I whispered, "wake up."

Her eyes fluttered open, and she looked up at me, desire flooding her face. "Nexion? Where have you been?"

"I have something important to ask you," I replied, my voice full of emotion betraying my nerves.

Before she could protest, I scooped her up in my arms, carrying her to the balcony overlooking our breathtaking city of Arcadia. The city lights sparkled like a sea of stars below us. We were alone, surrounded only by the beauty of the universe.

I carefully set her down, our eyes locking as I held her hands firmly in mine. "Elzaria," my voice shaky with the intensity of my feelings, "From the first time our paths crossed, I sensed something exceptional about you. That first kiss jolted me as if by some otherworldly force. It was an arrow to the heart." The heat from my instant arousal flooded my face.

"Mistakes were made; I'd misjudged you. I had misconstrued your actions, your motives. Yet as I witnessed your transformation into a knight, I found myself inexplicably pulled towards you, never once suspecting who you were. Your fierce spirit, your unyielding resolve to succeed in the face of every obstacle, left me astounded."

"When the Dreadnaughts attacked, you didn't hide behind your title. You fought. You were a force, Elzaria," I continued, each word laced with admiration.

"And as you lay unconscious from your injuries, I knew you were my everything. You have captured my heart and soul, and I want nothing more than to spend the rest of my life with you."

Elzaria's eyes widened with surprise. "Nexion, I..."

My heart pounded in my chest as I continued. "I don't care that you're a queen. All I know is that I love you. My love for you is no delicate flower; it's a relentless flame, fierce and scorching. A blaze kindled by courage, tempered in adversity, resilient in the face of any battle we may face. It's a love that lasts, not just for a lifetime, but for eons, unwavering, unyielding."

"Every beat of my heart, every breath I take, I want it to be for you. Protecting you, standing up for you, it's more than just an oath—it's my honor, my privilege. But I want more than just that. I want to be the source of your happiness, the cause of your laughter, the shelter in your storm."

Elzaria's eyes shone with unshed tears as she listened to my declaration. Without hesitation, I got down on one knee, pulling out the ornate box from my cloak and opening it to reveal the ring, the sapphire glinting in the moonlight.

"Will you do me the honor of becoming my soul-bound, forever committed to one another and to the cause we fight for?"

She gasped, placing a hand over her mouth as tears spilled over. "Yes, Nexion! I love you, too!" She exclaimed, throwing her arms around me. "Yes, I will."

I paused, my heart racing as I continued, "I have fallen deeply in love with you, and I want to walk through life with you, not just as someone I vow to protect, but as your partner, your equal, and my one true love."

I carefully slid the ring onto her finger, the gemstones catching the moonlight, sealing our promise with the light of the cosmos. It fit perfectly, as if it had been made for her alone.

Our lips met in a passionate kiss that seemed to meld our very souls together. I felt a surge of hunger course through my body. I picked her up, carrying her back into her room.

I worshiped every inch of her, savoring the taste of her skin and the feel of her soft curves beneath me. Our bodies moved together in perfect harmony. Her moans of pleasure fueled my desire, and I lost myself in the moment, consumed by the fire of our passion.

I kissed her deeply, my tongue exploring every part of her mouth as I moved inside her, thrusting deeper and harder with each passing moment.

Elzaria's body was slick with sweat as we moved together, our arousal growing. Her nails dug into my back and she bit down on my shoulder, as pleasure mixed with pain, flooding my senses with the need for release. Our bodies moved in a heated dance, and I felt myself nearing the edge of ecstasy. With a loud groan, I let go, my cock pulsing as I came deep within her.

As we lay in each other's arms, catching our breath, I knew we had just taken a step forward in our journey together. The rise and fall of her chest against mine stirred a peace deep within me, a serenity I hadn't known I craved. We were no longer only partners in battle, but partners in life, bound by love and commitment.

Elzaria's gentle fingers traced the sweeping wings of the inked angel on my skin, a question in her eyes.

"Tell me about your angel, Nexion," she murmured, her voice soft in the hushed darkness of the room. Her fingertips traced the intricate lines, igniting a pleasant shiver that ran through me.

I hesitated for a moment, caught in the surprising intimacy of the question. No one had ever asked before.

"He's more than just an angel, Zara," I began, the fondness for that past life seeping into my voice. "This tattoo is my oath, my promise to a man who saw something in a lost boy and gave him a second chance."

I paused, my gaze drifting towards the distant stars seen through the window, remembering. "I was that boy, Zara. And Master Sergeant Glastonbury... he was that man. He plucked me out of a destiny that would've ended in a gutter somewhere, and he made me an Empyrean Knight. He taught me *The Creed*, the faith. He gave me a purpose."

Her eyes held mine, encouraging me to continue. "I remember him telling me about The Creators. About the universe being far more than we could comprehend, teeming with life, mysteries, and wonders. He taught me that our lives held meaning beyond the flesh and bone. That even death was just another journey, not the end."

Running my fingers through her hair, I continued, "The idea of a force bigger than us, shaping us, watching over us... it gave me a kind of peace, you know? This angel," I gestured to the tattoo under her fingers, "it's my reminder of that. He's my icon."

Elzaria's fingers stilled, her gaze thoughtful as she studied the inked image on my skin. "So, it's your faith... your belief in something more?" she asked, her voice soft and curious.

I nodded. "Yes, it's my faith. A symbol of my journey, my purpose. My promise to never fear death, to never doubt the path set before me. It's my tribute to the man who saved me, the life I have now, and the belief in something greater beyond the stars."

The silence that followed was comfortable, filled with a newfound understanding. Elzaria pressed a soft kiss to the angel on my skin, and for the first time, I shared the true meaning of my inked angel. For the first time, I wasn't alone. I had shared a part of my soul with her. And it felt right.

As Elzaria's fingers resumed their gentle exploration, tracing the outline of the angel, I felt a sense of peace wash over me. A sense that I had finally found my place in this vast universe. Not as an Empyrean Knight, but as a man—a man in love.

I could feel her warmth against my skin, "I promise to always be there for you, to keep you safe and to love you forever."

We drifted off to sleep, our bodies entwined. I knew that we had found something that was rare and precious. We had found true love, and together, we would conquer the universe.

ELZARIA

The morning light cut through the blinds, arousing me from a deep sleep. Nexion's soft snore next to me in my bed, in my chambers, reminded me of the commitment we had just made. I admired the beautiful ring he had given me, and I didn't want this moment to end or for us to leave this sanctuary, but knew our responsibilities demanded we get moving. I stroked the side of his head, his normally short hair grown out with soft dark curls wrapping around my fingertips.

"Time to rise and shine." I giggled as I trailed kisses from his chest up to the side of his neck. "We have responsibilities..." I turned to leave, dragging the sheet with me, but he had other plans...

He growled like a bear and in one fell swoop, flipped me over. "Responsibilities can wait."

Our lust for each other was insatiable. This time, we both understood the urgency and made quick work of meeting our needs before launching into our day.

As Nexion and I entered the large conference room, hidden deep beneath the castle, I felt a mixture of excitement and trepidation. With my hand wrapped over Nexion's elbow, the engagement ring he had given me gleamed brightly, catching the attention of everyone present. My mother, in particular, seemed ecstatic, her eyes lighting up at the sight of the ring on my finger.

"Elzaria, my dear! Is that what I think it is?" She exclaimed, rushing to embrace me, her normal cool countenance forgotten. "Oh, congratulations! A royal wedding! We must start planning immediately!"

I couldn't help but smile at her enthusiasm. "Mother, please," I said, trying to calm her down. "We have gathered here today to discuss matters of great importance."

"But what could possibly be more important than a royal wedding?" She asked, her eyes still sparkling with excitement.

"An attack by the Vaith that could spark a war across the universe," I replied, my voice composed and a bit frosty, quelling her excitement.

A hush fell over the room as the gravity of my words sank in. My mother nodded, understanding the seriousness of the situation, and took her seat next to my father. Her politician's veneer returned.

As the meeting began, military officers and advisors filled the room, each contributing their knowledge and expertise to the discussion. My father took the lead, his voice steady and commanding.

"We must be prepared for any possible action by the Vaith," he said, addressing the room. "Our intelligence reports following the attack at Grymrock suggest that they have been plotting and scheming against us for some time. We must be vigilant and ready to defend our people and our allies."

The room buzzed with activity as we discussed strategies and tactics, the potential strength of our enemy, and how to bolster our defenses. Nexion offered valuable insight into the Vaith's motivations and tactics.

"We need to strengthen our alliances and ensure that our communication channels are secure," Nexion suggested. "The Vaith will probably try to exploit any weaknesses they can find."

As the meeting progressed, I couldn't help but steal glances at Nexion, wondering how he had come to be in my life.

As I looked over at him, I noticed he was looking back at me, a small smile on his face. Damn, he was so good-looking.

The discussions continued, but through it all, I couldn't help but think about how much I loved the man.

Focusing everyone's attention on the matters at hand, my father broke in. "We must also determine what the Vaith are planning. We need to discover their upcoming targets and make sure that they can't follow through with their plans."

I nodded, my mind whirling with ways in which we could accomplish that task. I turned to Nexion, and he smiled at me reassuringly.

"You know the Vaith won't give up on their quest to conquer this galaxy," Nexion said, his gaze steady.

"The Vaith won't stop at anything to advance their greed once they get started. They're relentless and cunning," Father replied.

Eventually, the meeting ended, and we all knew that there was much work to be done. As we prepared to leave the room, my mother took my arm, her voice full of pride.

"Elzaria, I am so proud of the strong, capable ruler you've become," she said, her eyes shining with tears. "And I know with Nexion by your side, there's nothing you can't face."

I smiled at her, grateful for her support, and squeezed her hand. "Thank you, Mother."

CHAPTER NINETEEN

ELZARIA

Upon returning to my chambers with Nexion, we found Adelaide waiting for us, her eyes wide with excitement. She had already heard the news of our impending soul-binding through the palace grapevine, and she couldn't contain her enthusiasm.

"Oh, Elzaria! Nexion!" Adelaide exclaimed, throwing her arms around both of us. "I'm so happy for you two!" she beamed, her face alight with enthusiasm. "We must start planning your soul-binding right away!"

As we disentangled ourselves from her embrace, I couldn't help but smile at her excitement. "Thank you, Adelaide. We're thrilled too, but there's something you should know." I glanced at Nexion.

Adelaide's eyes sparkled with anticipation. "Yes? What is it?"

"I don't want to wait long for our binding ceremony," I said, my excitement growing. "In fact, I thought that the one-cycle anniversary of my coronation, which is in ten days, would be the perfect day for our binding."

Adelaide gasped, her hands flying to her mouth. "So soon? But there's so much to do!"

Nexion smiled, "It's fitting, don't you think? That was the day Elzaria and I first met."

I laughed, remembering how I had run away from my coronation, and how Nexion had been ordered to return me to the castle. "He tackled me, you know, handcuffed me, and hauled me back. What a mess I was. Remember how I tore my train off and had to have Adelaide help clean me back up?"

Adelaide chuckled; the memory vivid in her mind. "You still looked absolutely beautiful at your coronation, My Queen."

"And it was also the day Nexion first kissed me," I teased, looking at him with a mischievous glint in my eye. "He was so worried, thinking he had overstepped his boundaries as a knight."

Nexion responded by sweeping me into his arms and kissing me deeply, right in front of Adelaide, who squealed with delight. When he finally released me, he grinned. "Now I can kiss you anytime I want."

Adelaide, still giggling, clapped her hands together. "Alright, you lovebirds! We have a binding to plan—and not much time to do it. Let's get to work!"

And so, our whirlwind of a royal binding ceremony preparations began.

Nexion was called away to fulfill his Knightmaster duties at the Academy and elsewhere, leaving me with my mother and Adelaide to tackle the preparations for our ceremony. The palace was a pandemonium of activity, with everyone eager to make the event perfect.

My mother and Adelaide were in a frenzy, overseeing every detail of the upcoming celebration. They enlisted the help of the royal household staff, transforming the castle into a vision of elegance and grandeur. They adorned the grand hall with garlands of fresh flowers, their sweet fragrance filling the air. The royal household staff arranged the tables with exquisite care, set with the finest linens, crystal, and silverware, ready for the grand banquet that would follow our soul-binding.

Slipping away from the whirlwind of preparations that had consumed the days leading up to the soul-binding, I found myself in the cobblestone streets of a small artisans' district. A clandestine mission had sparked in my mind, a personal endeavor that felt as necessary as the beating of my heart. A smile lit up my face as I walked into the tiny tattoo parlor, a secret dwelling hidden in the folds of the city.

The smell of disinfectant and ink wafted in the air, blending with the faint hum of the tattoo gun. I settled into the worn leather chair, nerves flaring at the anticipation of what I was about to do. I handed the artist the sketched image of an angel, like Nexion's, but smaller, yet just as potent in meaning. The artist raised an eyebrow but didn't ask any questions. His silent understanding was enough.

I had chosen a spot on my left side, just under my heart, where the Dreadnaught pirate's blade had once sliced through my ribs. The scar that marred my skin was a mark of pain, a reminder of survival, and now, it would be the canvas for something beautiful, a symbol of love and resilience.

As the artist started his work, the needles against my skin felt like little pinpricks of fire, a dance of pain and purpose that I welcomed. Each stroke felt transformative, as if the ink was seeping into my very soul, etching a promise deep within me.

In that chair, under the humming needles and focused gaze of the artist, the tattoo became my badge of honor, my promise, my tribute to the man I loved. I embraced the pain and the permanence of it, a testament to the irrevocable changes that had led me to become who I was.

The inked angel on my side was smaller than Nexion's, but just as majestic. Its wings spread out, unfolding across the plane of my scar and beyond, like a beacon of hope emerging from past trials. My fingers traced the fresh lines, a mirror of the times I had traced the same design on Nexion.

I left the parlor that day with a quiet sense of triumph, a little secret tucked away beneath my clothes. The angel was a token of love, a totem of faith, and an emblem of the journey I had taken from a sheltered princess to a warrior woman, an Empyrean Knight. It was a promise of the soul-binding to come, another surprise for Nexion on our wedding night, and a symbol of the future we would face together, bound by love and the angels etched into our skin.

Amid all the preparations, Adelaide and my mother devoted particular attention to my wedding dress. Inspired by the iconic gowns worn by previous queens, my dress was a work of art, tailored to fit me perfectly. The ivory satin bodice featured a delicate lace overlay, hand-stitched with intricate floral patterns. The designers crafted the long, graceful sleeves from exquisite lace, lending an air of elegance and sophistication to the design.

They fashioned the skirt of the gown from flowing layers of satin and tulle, cascading down to a breathtaking train that seemed to go on forever. The dress was the epitome of regal beauty, and I couldn't help but be in awe of the craftsmanship that had gone into creating it.

To complete the ensemble, I would wear a stunning tiara encrusted with precious gemstones that had been passed down through the generations. The glittering piece fitted gently on my head, its intricate design a testament to the skill of the royal jewelers. A veil of the finest silk tulle, edged with delicate lace, cascaded from the tiara, framing my face and trailing down my back.

I added my own special touch by placing the Knight's Sigil over my heart where it rested, a symbol of my love for Nexion and my commitment to the knighthood. During my last fitting, I looked at myself in the mirror. My heart pounded with excitement at the thought of finally being bound to Nexion for eternity.

As the day of the royal binding ceremony drew nearer, the entire royal household was consumed with the task of preparing the castle for our special day. The servants meticulously groomed the gardens, and polished and arranged every room to perfection. The kitchens were a hive of activity, with the royal chefs preparing a sumptuous feast fit for a queen and her soul-bound knight.

Throughout the hustle and bustle, my mother and Adelaide were my constant companions, offering their support and guidance as we navigated the final days leading up to our ceremony. I was eternally grateful for their love and dedication, knowing that without them, this incredible day wouldn't have been possible.

The morning of the wedding dawned clear and bright, as if the universe itself was blessing our union. It was a perfect day, and all the arrangements for the ceremony were in place, except for one crucial detail—Nexion still hadn't returned. The looming threat of the Vaith had kept him busy, and I had missed him terribly. Despite his absence, I knew he would do everything in his power to be there for our special day, but be that as it may, I nevertheless worried.

My father assured me Nexion would be at the cathedral on time and ready. "My dear, he would move heaven and earth to be there for you," he said with a reassuring smile, stroking my back gently.

With my father's words of encouragement, I focused on getting ready for the ceremony. Adelaide and my mother helped me into my stunning gown, affixing the tiara and veil to my hair. I could hardly believe the radiant bride gazing back at me in the mirror was really me. A couple of days ago, I had stripped out the brown hair color and returned my hair to its natural light blonde. I also removed the tattoos from my face. I couldn't wait for Nexion to discover my new permanent one over my ribs, and wondered what his reaction would be seeing the old me as I walked down the aisle.

As I stood at the entrance of the castle, a sleek hover-carriage awaited me. Advanced technology powered the gleaming vehicle, allowing it to hover above the ground and travel at incredible speeds without making a sound. Its elegant lines and graceful curves were a testament to the sophistication of Empyrean engineering.

My father helped me into the carriage, and we set off through the streets of Arcadia towards the cathedral.

The city was alive with excitement, as the citizens of Arcadia had turned out in droves to catch a glimpse of their queen on her soul-binding day. As the carriage glided through the streets, I couldn't help but feel an overwhelming sense of joy for the love and support of my people as I waved to the cheering crowds.

My pulse quickened as we approached the cathedral. I could barely wait to see Nexion. The days without him had felt like forever.

As the carriage came to a stop in front of the cathedral, I took a deep breath, feeling a mixture of excitement and jitters. My father extended his hand to help me descend from the vehicle, and I stepped out into the warm sunlight, my veil dancing softly in the gentle breeze. The magnificent cathedral loomed before us, its spires reaching towards the heavens.

Together, my father and I ascended the broad stairs leading to the cathedral's entrance. As we reached the top, the narthex doors opened, and he smiled warmly and kissed me on the cheek, whispering words of encouragement before we entered the nave.

The choir filled the cathedral's vast interior with their heavenly voices echoing through the space. Gasps of astonishment arose from the congregation as I stepped into the nave. For the first time since my coronation, I felt like a queen. I tried my best to carry myself with grace, back straight and shoulders back, as everyone turned to look at me. The love and support from the congregation washed over me like a warm embrace, filling me with a sense of belonging and purpose.

The air was thick with the fragrance of lush, sweet-scented flowers that adorned the cathedral's walls and pews, their petals white with light blue ribbons wound around, stood in contrast to the deep blue velvet carpet that stretched down the central aisle. The carpet led my gaze towards the altar, where I knew Nexion would be waiting for me.

My father offered his arm, and together we began our slow procession down the aisle, each step bringing me closer to the man I loved and the life we would build together. The choir's voices swelled in harmony, providing a poignant soundtrack to this most important moment in my life. I couldn't help but feel as though my heart would burst with happiness, knowing I was about to become soul-bound to my one true love, Nexion.

As we continued our slow procession, my eyes finally found Nexion standing at the altar. Dressed in his knight's dress blues, which fit him impeccably, accentuating his broad shoulders and the strength that lay beneath, I gasped at the sight of him. His dark hair was neatly styled, and his eyes shone with an intensity that spoke volumes. I couldn't help but think of how incredibly handsome he looked, the epitome of a gallant knight.

As Nexion caught sight of me, his eyes widened, and I could see the emotions welling up within him. He looked as though he was on the verge of tears, and the vulnerability he displayed at that moment assailed me with emotion. It was a side of him I'd rarely seen, as he was always the strong, stoic knight, expertly in control of his emotions. But today, on our binding day, the depth of his love for me seemed to break through even the toughest of barriers. As I drew closer, Nexion's composure crumbled completely. Tears streamed down his face as he took in the sight of me in my wedding dress.

As we reached the altar, my father gently placed my hand in Nexion's, symbolically giving me away to the man who would be my partner for life. Nexion's hand trembled slightly as he took mine, and our eyes locked in a silent exchange of love and commitment. His voice was barely a whisper as he said, "You are the most beautiful woman I have ever laid eyes on, my little knight."

My eyes welled up with tears, and I replied, "And you, my love, are everything I have ever hoped for and more than I could ever have imagined."

With our hands joined, we turned to face the priestess, ready to make our vows and begin our lives together. The cathedral, filled with the love and support of our friends, family, and guests, seemed to radiate a warmth that enveloped us, creating an atmosphere of joy and celebration as we prepared to embark on this new chapter of our lives together.

The priestess began the ceremony, her expression solemn, yet filled with kindness. Her voice reverberated throughout the cathedral. *"In this sacred space, we gather here today to witness and celebrate the joining of Empyrean Queen Elzaria Eridani and*

Knightmaster Nexion Fortisbellator in their soul-binding, as they pledge their love and commitment to one another."

Then, she faced us and asked that we state our vows. The sanctuary was silent as everyone held a collective breath. The silence was broken by Nexion's strong and steady voice as he spoke from the heart. *"Elzaria, my queen and my love, I vow to stand by your side, to protect you and honor you, in times of joy and sorrow, triumph and defeat. I promise to be your strength and your shield, your partner and your friend, to shoulder your burdens, and support your dreams, for all the days of our lives."*

I felt a tear slip down my cheek as I listened to his words, and when it was my turn, the words poured forth from the depths of my soul. *"Nexion, my knight and my love, I pledge my loyalty and devotion to you, in happiness and hardship, in victory and struggle. I promise to be your companion and confidante, your rock and your refuge, for as long as we both shall live."*

Next, we exchanged rings, symbols of our eternal commitment to one another. As Nexion slid the band onto my finger, I couldn't help but admire the way it gleamed in the light, a beautiful reminder of the love we shared.

In reciting my vows, I had to acknowledge to the Empyrean people a truth that had become a part of me, a part of my reign. I turned toward the congregation and spoke. *"By stepping onto the path of a knight, I, Queen Elzaria Eridani, have crossed the lines that divide royalty from knighthood. As I took up arms, learned the warrior's ways, and embraced the life of an Empyrean Knight, I did not merely cross a line, but obliterated it."*

I once again turned to Nexion, smiling softly. *"By allowing my heart to entwine with the Knightmaster, Nexion Fortisbellator, I further muddied these once distinct lines. We have mingled not just our lives, but the very essence of our souls. By soul-binding to him, I entangled the fibers of the royalty with the knighthood, the Celestial*

Creed with our our personal vows. Love, in its raw, unyielding form, has led us on a path not walked in a thousand cycles."

Looking out into the eyes of those we shared this sacred ceremony with, I continued. *"I stand here, my hand in his, aware that by this act, I have not only changed my destiny but that of the Empyrean Alliance. By rewriting the norms, we redefine what it means to be a knight, a queen, a servant of The Creators. Our love, our unity, this newfound fusion of roles, it changes the expectations, and moral compass that has guided us for centuries."*

I paused, letting the gravity of the moment sink in. *"Through my actions, my love, and my vows today, I have reshaped the course of history. As the first warrior queen in a millennium, I acknowledge the weight of this responsibility. The path we walk may be unprecedented, even challenging, but it is ours. And with the strength of our love, the power of our unity, and the courage of our convictions, we will forge a different path, setting a new precedent for generations to come. This I promise, this I swear, this is the legacy I wish to leave behind."*

In honor of my unique status as the first queen in a thousand cycles to become a knight, our ceremony concluded with a potent blood oath. The priestess presented us with a handfasting cord, intricately woven from strands of light blue and shimmering silver ribbons, the colors of our kingdom. We extended our hands, and as she bound them together, she pricked our palms with a ceremonial dagger.

Our blood, like our hearts, mingled together as one, symbolizing the unbreakable bond we were forming. Then we recited the ancient oath: *"In the presence of all here, and before the eyes of The Creators, we swear to protect and defend one another, and our Empyrean Alliance. Through trials of fire, darkness, and despair, we stand unflinching. In life as in death, our oath, our loyalty, and our blood bind us. We pledge to share in each other's burdens, to bear witness to each other's allegiance, and to face together whatever our fates may bring. This we swear, bound by our blood, and our shared destiny."*

With the oath completed, the priestess declared us soul-bound, and Nexion pulled me into his arms for a heart-stopping kiss. He dipped me deeply, his powerful arms supporting me, and our love seemed to fill the very air around us. The congregation erupted in cheers and applause, sharing our joy and happiness.

Hand in hand, we walked back down the aisle, our faces aglow. We were now soul-bound partners, ready to face whatever challenges and adventures life had in store for us, side by side, as equals in love and duty.

As we left the cathedral, the sun was setting, casting a warm glow over everything. Nexion helped me down the steps, his strong arm supporting me as I carefully navigated the stairs in my gown and high-heeled shoes. He sweetly gathered my train and veil to ensure they wouldn't be damaged as we approached the waiting carriage.

Once we were safely inside, Nexion pulled me close, cupping my chin in his hand and stroking his thumb along my cheek. He kissed me tenderly and gazed into my eyes. "Elzaria, my stunning queen, it's hard to believe how lucky I am to be soul-bound to you. You look absolutely gorgeous today, like an angel descended from the heavens. Your long blonde hair, your pristine skin—I've never seen you look more beautiful."

He gently brushed a strand of hair away from my face, his touch sending shivers down my spine. "When I left you a few days ago, you still wore the disguise that hid your identity during training with brown hair and tattoos. But now, seeing you as you truly are, I am struck by your beauty and grace."

Nexion's voice grew softer, more intimate as he continued. "I love you more than I can put into words, Zara. I look forward to our life together, building a family with you, and sharing all that lies ahead. Together, I feel like anything is possible."

I smiled, my heart swelling with love for this incredible man who had just pledged his life to me. "Nexion, I feel the same way. I never imagined I could love someone as deeply as I love you. I can't wait to see what the future has in store for us."

As the carriage passed through the streets of Arcadia, we held hands, basking in the love that had brought us to this day.

Our carriage came to a stop at the castle. We heard the sounds of laughter and celebration already in full swing. Nexion helped me down, and together, we were whisked away to my chambers where Adelaide was waiting for us.

Upon entering the room, Nexion pulled me close and kissed me passionately, his powerful arms enveloping me. Our embrace grew more heated, and I could feel my heart racing in my chest. Just then, Adelaide cleared her throat, reminding us of her presence.

Embarrassed, Nexion released me and apologized. Adelaide informed him that his friends and family were waiting for him in the banquet hall, and he reluctantly left my side, promising to see me soon.

Once Nexion had left, I slipped off my shoes and started to change into a different white gown for the banquet. However, before I could undress, a wave of nausea washed over me, and I suddenly found myself retching into a nearby basin.

Adelaide rushed to my side; her face filled with concern. "Elzaria, are you alright? Do you need a healer?"

I wiped my mouth and shook my head, struggling to regain my composure. "No, Adelaide, I'm fine. But I need you to promise me you'll keep a secret."

Her eyes widened, but she nodded in agreement. "Of course, Elzaria. You have my word."

Taking a deep breath, I confided in her. "Adelaide, I'm with child. I took a test earlier."

Her eyes widened in shock, but she quickly broke into a broad smile. "Oh, my sweet girl, that's wonderful news! A royal heir!"

I grinned, my heart swelling with happiness at the thought of having a baby with Nexion. "Yes, but I want to wait until after the banquet to tell Nexion. I want it to be a surprise."

Adelaide nodded, her excitement barely contained. "Of course, Elzaria. Your secret is safe with me."

Together, we started once more to prepare for the banquet, our shared secret adding an extra layer of elation to the already festive atmosphere. I couldn't wait to see the look on Nexion's face when I finally shared the news with him.

The chatter of the imminent wedding reception hummed outside the doors of my chamber. Our conversation drifted to the people who were present at the wedding, but it was the absence of one in particular that had my brows furrowing in worry.

"Seraphean..." I mused aloud, my eyes staring into the reflective surface of the mirror, my mind far from the excited halls of the palace.

"Yes," Adelaide asked, her hands deftly working at the many tiny fastenings on my dress. "She didn't attend the wedding, did she?"

A sigh escaped me, Seraphean's absence stinging more than I cared to admit. "No, she didn't," I mused, a lump of worry forming in my throat.

Adelaide's hands stilled on the fabric for a moment, her gaze meeting mine in the mirror. "Elzaria... I've heard rumors," she began hesitantly. "Seraphean has been gone from the royal court for lunars. Her parents are... distressed."

"Distressed?" The word hung heavy in the air. I knew Seraphean was prone to mischief and bouts of jealousy, but this sounded more serious.

"They thought she was off enjoying herself on one of the neighboring planets, shopping, partying, and the likes," Adelaide continued, her voice dropping to a hushed whisper. "But then, a significant amount of credits were found missing from her accounts."

My heart clenched in alarm. "How significant?"

"Enough to buy a small starship, perhaps even fund a private army," Adelaide replied.

An icy shiver ran down my spine. This was more than just the usual antics of my wayward cousin. The implications of such vast funds being withdrawn unsettled me. It wasn't like Seraphean to involve herself in matters of such high spending. Yet, the suddenness of her disappearance coupled with this large credit withdrawal made it clear that she was up to something, and it could be nothing good.

"Thank you, Adelaide," I murmured, my mind racing as I tried to piece together the scant information.

We fell into a solemn silence, our previous excitement replaced with a sense of unease. Whatever the spoiled troublemaker was up to, it felt like a storm was gathering on the horizon. Little did I know then that Seraphean's actions would soon pull our home planet Terrastria and the entire Empyrean Alliance into the eye of the storm.

As I entered the banquet hall, I saw Nexion waiting for me, looking handsome in his formal uniform. Our eyes met, and a warm smile spread across his face as he approached me.

"May I have your attention please?" The announcer requested, his words echoing off the walls of the hall. "It is my honor to introduce the newly soul-bound couple. Welcome Queen Elzaria Eridani and her Knightlord, Nexion Fortisbellator Eridani." As in the Empyrean tradition, Nexion took his partner's surname and, as the queen's consort and Knighmaster, he took the newly established title of Knightlord.

All eyes turned toward us as the room erupted in applause and cheers, and with that, the festivities began.

Dinner was a lavish affair, with an array of delectable dishes prepared by the royal chefs. I could tell Nexion was watching me closely, noticing that I wasn't drinking during the toasts. He didn't say anything, but I could see the curiosity in his eyes.

My father stepped forward and took my hand, leading me to the dance floor. He looked down at me with a proud smile as we moved to the music. It was a tradition for the bride to dance with her father first, symbolizing the transition from the father's care to the husband's care.

"Elzaria, I am so happy for you. Nexion is a good man, and I know he will love and protect you with all his heart," he said, his voice filled with affection.

"Thank you, Father," I replied, my eyes welling up with tears. "Your love and support mean the world to me. I couldn't have asked for a better father."

My father's eyes grew misty as well, and he pulled me closer. "Remember that no matter where life takes you, you will always be my little girl and you have a home here and a family that loves you."

I hugged him tightly, grateful for his love as we continued our dance. I knew I was ready to embrace this new chapter of my life with Nexion.

As my dance with my father finished, it was time for Nexion and me to share our first dance as a bound couple. Nexion took my hand and twirled me around onto the dance floor. The music swelled around us as we gracefully moved in sync, lost in each other's gaze. It was a magical moment, one that I would cherish forever.

As Nexion and I danced, he pulled me close, "You look absolutely stunning, Elzaria. I can't believe I get to call you mine forever."

I smiled up at him. "You truly are the greatest gift the universe has given me. Not to mention, the only one who could ever get away with spanking me."

Nexion chuckled softly, his eyes twinkling with happiness. "I promise to spend the rest of my life making you feel as loved as you make me feel."

As the night wore on, I felt overheated and stepped out onto the balcony for some fresh air. The cool breeze brushed against my face, refreshing me. Soon, Nexion joined me, concern etched on his handsome features.

"Are you okay?" He asked gently, wrapping his arms around me.

I nodded, leaning into his embrace. "Yes, just a little warm."

Nexion smiled and slowly danced with me on the balcony, the stars above us shimmering in the night sky. Despite my tiredness, I didn't want the night to end. Sensing my fatigue, Nexion made the decision for both of us.

With a loving smile, he swept me up into his arms and carried me back to our chambers. I protested weakly, but he silenced me with a tender kiss.

"There will be plenty of time for celebration later," his love for me was clear in his voice. As he carried me through the castle, I knew we were a force to be reckoned with.

◈—《◍》—◈

Entering the room, the heat between us grew. Our first night together as soul-bound was a moment neither of us would have foreseen a cycle ago. Yet here we were, our souls intertwined, as if fate had intervened and brought us together to share this incredible moment. The room was dimly lit, with soft, flickering candles casting a warm, romantic glow on everything it touched.

I slowly removed my gown, carefully undoing the buttons. Nexion's eyes smoldered with desire as I revealed the delicate, lacy slip I wore underneath. I could see him watching me, savoring every moment as I stood before him, vulnerable and all but exposed.

Laying the gown over the back of a chair, I walked over to my dressing table and picked up my hairbrush. I sat in front of the mirror, gently brushing out my long, now golden locks, and couldn't help but steal glances at Nexion's reflection. He was watching me intently, and I felt a thrill of excitement run through me.

Nexion lounged comfortably in a plush armchair with a snifter of brandy cradled in his large, calloused hand. The candles gently illuminated his rugged features, casting shadows that made his chiseled jawline even more striking.

As I looked at him through the mirror, his emerald eyes met mine, twinkling with mischief. He swirled the brandy gently, letting it breathe. As I watched, he brought the snifter to his nose, inhaling deeply, appreciating its complexities with a quiet reverence. Then, he took a slow sip; the swallow flexing his throat, the glow in his eyes deepening. He savored it, not rushed, the epitome of a man at ease.

All the while, his gaze never left me, those striking eyes tracking each movement of my brush through my hair. There was an undeniable fire between us.

After a few moments, Nexion rose from the chair and approached me, his arms encircling my waist. He gently lifted me from the dressing table and carried me over to the bed.

As he laid me down on the silky sheets, he leaned in and kissed me, his lips soft and warm against mine. The passion between us grew, and soon our kisses became more urgent, our breaths intermingling. I felt my body responding to his touch. I offered myself to him, and he took the invitation, his hands roaming over my body, caressing and exploring every inch of me. My nipples hardened under his touch, and I moaned softly, unable to contain my pleasure.

He pulled away from me and stood up, quickly discarding his clothes. I watched in awe as his carved, bronzed body came into view, his cock proudly standing at attention. I couldn't resist the urge to taste him, so I licked my lips and beckoned him over to me.

Nexion climbed onto the bed, positioning himself above me. I reached up and grasped his hard shaft, feeling the heat of it in my hand. He moaned softly as I stroked him. I licked and sucked, taking him fully into my mouth. His moans were growing louder, and I knew he was close. He withdrew from my mouth and lowered himself next to me.

His hand slid down between my legs, cupping my sex through the fabric of my slip. I gasped as he rubbed his fingers over my clit, sending waves of pleasure coursing through my body. I writhed under him, my hips moving in time with his touch.

He pulled my slip up, exposing me to his gaze when he saw it. His mouth fell open, stunned by the beautifully inked angle across my ribs.

I slowly slid the slip over my head and let it drop to the floor, laying back and stretching my arms above my head for him to appraise.

Nexion froze. His breath hitched, his gaze firmly locked on the tattoo, an echo of his own.

"Surprise," I whispered, my cheeks growing hot under his intense scrutiny.

His silence stretched on, the seconds ticking by like hours. For a moment, I worried I had misjudged his reaction. But then, his stunned expression morphed into one of pure awe. "Zara..."

he breathed out his new nickname for me like a prayer, his voice a mere sigh in the stillness of our chamber.

His fingers gently traced the outline of the angel, sending shivers down my spine. "This... it's... You've... replicated my tattoo," he murmured, his voice choked with emotion.

I nodded, biting my lip. "Yes. Yours means so much to you. I... I wanted to share in that. To hold the same symbol close, the same icon."

He swallowed hard, the muscles in his throat working as he tried to find words. "You have no idea what this means to me, my little knight."

I met his gaze, my heart pounding in my chest. "Maybe not fully. But I hope this shows you, at least in some small way, how deeply I love you."

He gathered me in his arms, pressing me against him. "It shows me that and so much more," he said, his voice rough and husky. "I never thought I could love you more than I already did, but now... this, this is more meaningful than I could ever express." His gaze dropped to my side again, to the black ink, his thumb gently caressing the tattoo, his touch setting my skin aflame.

I could feel his breath, hot against my skin, making me shiver with anticipation. He leaned in, trailing kisses down the lines of the angel to my hip, finding his way to my center. Cupping me from up under in his massive hands, his tongue found my clit, and I cried out in ecstasy. His tongue was like a flame, licking and sucking at my most sensitive parts, driving me wild with desire.

Using my hands for support, I pushed up and rocked my hips against his mouth, wanting more, needing more. He slid two fingers inside me, and I moaned, clenching around him. He pumped his fingers in and out, his thumb rubbing over my clit, and I felt the tension building inside me.

I was on the edge of rapture, teetering on the brink of release, when he suddenly withdrew his fingers. I opened my eyes, confused and disappointed, but he was smiling down at me, his eyes filled with love.

Nexion tenderly pushed me back onto the bed and inched his way closer to me. As he settled into position, his lust-filled eyes locked with mine. He positioned the tip of his cock at my opening and slowly pushed forward, parting my folds as it entered me. I let out an involuntary moan as I stretched to accommodate his size and dug my heels into the bed, pushing against him.

Nexion rocked his hips, pushing further into me as I met him stroke for stroke. The pleasure was intense as he filled me completely. Our bodies joined as one. As he thrust in and out of me, our bodies moving in sync, I felt myself on the precipice of release once again. I reached up, grasping Nexion's shoulders as I clung to him, our eyes locking together.

I couldn't hold back any longer, and with one last passionate thrust, I dug my fingers into his back and moaned as my orgasm washed over me, wracking my body with intense spasms of bliss, squeezing around his cock.

With a low growl, Nexion released himself inside of me, his arms holding me tight as our passion subsided. He remained still for a few moments, then carefully removed himself from me, rolling to the side and pulling me into his arms.

"That was amazing," I purred, turning to him and planting a soft kiss on his lips.

"I love you," Nexion replied, cradling my head in his hands. "*You* are my everything."

"And *you* are my life," I said, tracing his lips with my fingers.

"And we will have so many cycles of this to look forward to," he added with a mischievous twinkle in his eye.

I giggled, and he moved closer to me, pulling me tight against him. We lay there together for a long while, silent but happy. I kissed him tenderly, then pushed up against the pillows. I knew it was time to share the other secret I had been carrying. He moved over, resting his head on my lap. He looked up at me with eyes full of love.

I took a deep breath before beginning, "Nexion, there's something I need to tell you," my voice was soft and full of emotion. He shifted, propping himself up on one elbow to look at me more intently. He shifted, propping himself up on one elbow to look at me more intently.

"What is it, my love?" He asked, his voice filling with concern as he saw my expression.

I took a deep breath, feeling my heart race in my chest. "Nexion, we're going to have a baby," I revealed, my voice trembling.

His eyes widened with surprise, and again, he was speechless. Then, a smile spread across his face, "Zara, that's... that's amazing! I can't believe it!"

"But there's more," I continued, my voice growing stronger. "Our child is going to be a girl. We're going to have a daughter."

For a moment, he was frozen in shock. Girls were so rare and precious among Empyreans, and to have a daughter meant we would have a direct heir to our throne. Tears filled his eyes, and his voice cracked. "A... a daughter? A baby girl. Elzaria, I can't even begin to express how happy that makes me. I'm blown away by this incredible gift you've given us." He ran his fingers through his hair.

Nexion pulled me close, his arms enveloping me as he pressed his lips to my forehead. "I promise you, Elzaria, I will do everything in my power to protect you and our child. I will be the best father I can be, and together, we'll raise our daughter to be strong, just like her mother."

Tears slid down my cheeks, overwhelmed by the love and happiness that filled the room. We held each other tightly, our hearts brimming with hope for the future we would share as a family.

As we drifted off to sleep, I knew as long as I was with Nexion, all would be well. With my soul-bound at my side, we would face anything that was thrown our way. Nothing was more important to me than being in his arms or having his love inside of me.

CHAPTER TWENTY

ELZARIA

The low-pitched wailing of sirens we had never heard before tore through the morning's dawn, jarring us awake. The terrifying sound of an attack on Terrastria. My heart pounded as I leaped from the bed, my silk sheet entwined around me like a protective cocoon. The urgency of the moment propelled me toward the balcony overlooking the city.

"An attack," Nexion's voice beside my ear was tight with tension, his eyes mirroring the fear that gripped me. "We're not ready."

As I peered out into the city below, Arcadia lay spread beneath us, a testament to the beauty and ingenuity of the Terrastrian people. But now, the once serene skyline was marred by chaos. Alarms blared throughout the city, their deep and ominous sound striking fear into the hearts of those who heard them. They weren't the typical high-pitched wail that signals a fire or a medical emergency, but a sound that warns of something far more sinister. Trails of smoke wafted up from buildings, and distant sounds of explosions echoed through the air. Panic-stricken citizens fled through the streets, desperately seeking shelter from an enemy they couldn't yet see. Chaos had replaced the once picturesque view, with smoke now billowing from buildings.

"Vaith," I whispered, tasting the bitterness of the word on my tongue. Skarnak had long been a thorn in our side, a constant reminder of the darkness lurking just beyond our borders.

It was a surreal scene, a slap in the face.

"How can this be happening and with no warning?!" I asked Nexion, unable to cover the shakiness in my voice as we stood beside one another. We shared an uncertain glance, the enormity of the situation beginning to sink in. I could see the fear—so uncharacteristic of him—flicker in his eyes, mirroring my own emotions.

"I never thought we would see this day," he admitted, his voice heavy with concern. "Their cloaking tech must be much more advanced than we ever imagined."

His words, though spoken softly, ignited a fire within me, the fear dissipating as fury took its place.

"I knew. These are the nightmares that have plagued my dreams."

Nexion stood beside me, his presence reassuring even in these dire circumstances. I knew his loyalty and love for both me and our people were unwavering, a strength we would need in the battle to come.

"Elzaria," he murmured, "We must go," his hand briefly touching my shoulder before he turned to gather our gear and weapons. Our training as knights included always being prepared to leave at a moment's notice, so we both kept a go-bag ready. Neither of us thought that day would come so soon. I knew he was thinking only about the task at hand. The burden of responsibility was heavy on me, the fate of the citizens of Terrastria and our very existence hanging in the balance.

My hands shook as I gripped the sleek, lightweight battle suit Nexion had tossed to me. I could feel the weight of our impending confrontation, the magnitude of the threat bearing down on our city. The visions of war that The Creators had sent me played through my mind like a dark phantom. As we dressed, our movements were swift and practiced. The urgency of the situation fueled our every motion.

"Nexion, we need to contact the others, mobilize our defenses," I urged, my voice laced with fury. He nodded, his jaw set in grim resolve. We both attached our NeuralComms.

"We'll rally the knights, the military, and our allies. We'll drive these fucking assholes from our world," Nexion declared, the fire of his convictions lighting up his eyes.

As Nexion busied himself with preparations, I couldn't help but let my eyes wander back to the besieged city below. My heart ached for the innocent lives being torn apart by this senseless violence.

Once dressed, our weapons in place, we raced from our chambers, our boots pounding against the stone floors as we sprinted through the labyrinthine of corridors within the castle. My breaths came in short, sharp gasps, my heart pounding in my ears. As we turned a corner, we nearly collided with my father and Adelaide, both of whom wore expressions of shock.

"Father, Adelaide, gather Mother and everyone you can and get to the spaceport now," I said, struggling to keep my voice steady. "The Vaith have attacked Arcadia. Do what you have to, but get there quickly. This is war! Oh, and Adelaide, I'm entrusting you with the most important task for saving the future of the Empyrean people. You must retrieve the Codex Conscio and deliver it to our quarters on the Resolute."

Without hesitation, they jumped into action, their faces etched with grim persistence. We hurried through the castle, barking orders to the royal guards and servants, sending them to rouse the rest of the household and prepare for the coming onslaught. Nexion and I both communicating over our NeuralComms with those in our line of command as we ran.

The scent of smoke and the distant sounds of destruction grew stronger as we neared the castle's entrance, where our most trusted military advisors awaited us. The air was thick with tension, the gravity of the situation hanging over us like a shroud.

"Your Majesties, we have already begun deploying our forces to protect the city," Loren reported, his voice steady despite the chaos unfolding around us. "We have sent word to our allies, requesting their help in repelling the Vaith."

"Good," I replied, my gaze sweeping over the assembled officers and advisors.

As one, we moved into action, each of us taking on the responsibilities we had trained for. As I geared up for the fight, my crown was a heavy reminder that I was responsible for the safety of my people, my family, my husband, and our unborn baby. This gave me a newfound strength as I headed into battle.

With each step we took towards the inevitable conflict, I felt my resolve harden. I was Queen Elzaria, leader of the Empyrean Alliance, and I would do everything in my power to protect those who looked to me for safety.

The frantic pace of our journey to the spaceport left me breathless, my heart pounding in my chest. As we arrived, the scene before us was a maelstrom of chaos and panic. The deafening roar of engines and the frenzied movement of personnel filled the air as strike fighters prepared for takeoff, their sleek forms gleaming like predatory birds in the light of the burning city. All around us, military personnel and civilians alike scrambled to find safety and defend their homes from the relentless onslaught of the Vaith.

"The attack on Arcadia is devastating," one officer reported, his voice barely audible over the surrounding cacophony. "We've already lost a significant portion of the city's defenses, and the Vaith are closing in fast."

Nexion's jaw clenched, his eyes hardening. "We need to launch a counterattack. We can't afford to lose any more ground."

I nodded in agreement, knowing that every moment we wasted meant more lives lost. "We need to join the battle. We must drive the Vaith back."

Nexion and I would take control of the Phantom Resolute while my mother and father would command the Hellfire. The ship my father commanded before he met my mother.

Having returned eleven days ago, the crew made quick work of preparing the Resolute for battle. The vessel trembled as its engines roared to life. Rising into the air, I cast one last glance back at the burning city of Arcadia and shivered, sensing that I would never return. The morning sky lit up with fire as our ships engaged enemy forces. The city of Arcadia, its once-pristine skyline now marred by destruction.

"Your Majesty, we've received word from the front lines," one ship's commanding officer reported, urgency in his voice. "The Vaith are advancing rapidly, and our forces are struggling to hold them back."

Nexion's grip on the tactical console tightened. "We need to give them air support. Get all ships in the air. Let's go, let's go."

As our ship raced towards the heart of the conflict, we monitored reports coming in of the Vaith's fleet and their actions, the voices of our brave soldiers stoic, the reality of the situation not yet being realized. We issued orders to our forces, coordinating their movements trying to anticipate the Vaith's next move.

The survival of Terrastria and our way of life hung in the balance, and we knew we had to fight with everything we had to protect them.

As the Resolute hovered above the battlefield, we had a clear view of the chaos unfolding below, a painful reminder of the brutality of war. Strike fighters soared through the sky, their engines screaming as they engaged the enemy in fierce aerial combat.

"Your Majesties," my father's voice came through the comm system, his tone grave. "We've evacuated the palace."

"Good, now get on the Hellfire and get the hell out of there. Go to Grymrock, it's near the closest transport portal." I replied, my voice firm. "We're staying at Terrastria to fight the Vaith. Use Grymrock as a rallying point and then you must go to the Aurora 33 galaxy and seek refuge from Queen Cassia, the leader of the Xanthra Alliance. I just met with her, and I trust her."

"Will do. See you soon" his transmission ended.

As the battle raged on, Nexion and I worked tirelessly to coordinate our forces, our focus unwavering. We knew that every decision we made was life or death. It was clear that we were in for a long and difficult battle if we were to survive this initial attack.

As our forces rallied, the tide of the battle shifted. Our initial shock at the Vaith's sudden assault gave way to fierce bravery, and the Empyrean military fought back with renewed vigor. Our ground forces activated the defense systems, creating a network of barriers and shields that slowed the Vaith's advance.

"Your Majesty, we have successfully intercepted and destroyed a Vaith warship," reported communications specialist Ganthion, his voice brimming with pride. "Our defenses are holding, and we're regaining control of the city."

"Excellent, Ganthion," I said, hoping that this would turn the tides in our favor. "We must grab those bastards by the balls and castrate them."

Surrounded by my advisors, I pored over maps and tactical data, devising multiple strategies based on the possible outcomes of the battle. We meticulously crafted each plan, anticipating the Vaith's tactics and countering them with our own strengths. Based on a long-ago prepared doomsday evacuation plan, I gave directions for an updated doomsday retreat if we had no other way out.

Meanwhile, Nexion led the knights and the military in carrying out specific offensive objectives. His strong, confident voice rang out over the comm system, directing our forces with the skill and precision of a master strategist.

"Do not back down in the face of the enemy," Nexion bellowed, his words galvanizing our troops. "Our people depend on us, and we will not let them down."

Under his command, the knights and military personnel executed a series of daring maneuvers, penetrating the Vaith's defenses and dealing them significant blows. Their relentless drive began to turn the tide in our favor.

"Your Majesty, our forces have successfully repelled the Vaith in several key sectors," one of my advisors informed me, a note of relief in his voice. "We're gaining the upper hand."

"Good," I replied, my gaze fixed on the tactical display. "We must continue to press our advantage and drive a wedge between their strike fighters and warships."

As the battle raged on, Nexion and I worked in tandem, our combined efforts bolstering our forces and slowly pushing the Vaith back.

I knew we needed to take immediate action to ensure the safety of our people. I turned to General Theron, my voice firm. "We must order the citizens of Terrastria to prepare for evacuation in case we cannot sustain this drive against the Vaith. Have them seek shelter in the designated safe zones near spaceports across the planet, such as the one at the Citadel of Avendel."

"Your Majesty, are you certain?" One of my advisors questioned, concern etched on his face. "This will cause widespread panic."

"I understand the risks," I replied, my gaze staunch. "But the safety of our people is our top priority. We must act now."

With a nod, General Theron sprang into action, relaying my orders to the military and civilian authorities. They coordinated the evacuation efforts, organizing transport and resources to help our citizens flee besieged cities.

As they carried the evacuation orders out, reports trickled in from other planets in our system. So far, the Vaith had only attacked Terrastria, but there was an unease that they might soon turn their sights elsewhere.

"Your Majesty, we've received reports from our neighboring planets," Ganthion informed me, his brow furrowed in concern. "They're on high alert, but there have been no signs of Vaith forces approaching their worlds... yet."

"We must remain vigilant," I said, my heart heavy, knowing that other worlds could soon share our plight. "Coordinate with our allies and ensure that they have all the information we can provide. We must stand united against this threat."

As the people of Terrastria's cities fled their homes, seeking refuge in safe zones and boarding evacuation ships at the spaceports, I couldn't help but feel that I had somehow failed them as their queen. Despite my efforts to prepare for war, the events that unfolded still surprised us.

With Nexion leading the military and me coordinating our strategy and evacuation efforts, we worked tirelessly to combat the Vaith invasion. Hours ticked off like seconds.

As the battle waged on, our forces continued to push back against the Vaith, refusing to allow them to claim our world as their own. But we knew that the road to victory would be long and difficult, and the fate of Terrastria and its people hung in the balance.

The Vaith's relentless pursuit of the Empyrean civilians was unfathomable. They had tasted blood and were hungry for more. With rage in their hearts, they doubled down and set their sights on Terrastria once again. They launched a massive assault as new enemy ships arrived, reinforcing their flagging numbers.

As I watched from the bridge, the Vaith ships descended upon our world like a swarm of wasps, raining down plasma laser fire and bombs upon our military bases. "Hold your ground!" I shouted to our troops through the communication channels.

The defenses held at first, but the sheer force of the Vaith attack was overwhelming. They pushed our lines back, broken by the sheer numbers of the enemy. I clenched my fists, anger and frustration boiling within me.

The Vaith had learned from their initial attack and brought in massive ground troops to secure the planet. They landed on the surface, deploying drop pods and landing craft across the planet. Our soldiers fought valiantly, but they were outnumbered and outmatched. Even our telekinetic powers were no match for the Vaith. The enemy had superior technology and weapons, and they used them with deadly precision.

The contentment of long-held peace had bred a lack of preparedness on our part.

"Your Majesty, we must consider our options," Loren said, his voice strained as he surveyed the military theater. "We need to regroup and come up with a new strategy."

Nexion grimly nodded in agreement. Knowing that our current tactics were failing, he ordered, "Have our forces fall back to the designated rally points. We'll regroup and plan our next move."

As our soldiers retreated, hand-to-hand combat was brutal and unforgiving. Empyrean soldiers faced off against the Vaith troops in vicious clashes. Their weapons were razor-sharp and deadly, cutting through armor and flesh alike.

As I turned to my advisors, I knew we were facing an enemy unlike any we had ever encountered before. The Vaith were ruthless, and their intent to conquer Terrastria was dogged.

"We need to find a weakness, something we can exploit to turn the tide of this battle," I declared, my frustration clear. "We can't afford to lose our world to these monsters."

As we strategized and coordinated our efforts, Nexion led the knights and military on the front lines.

The battle for Terrastria was far from over. The Empyrean spirit wouldn't be broken. We would stand united against the Vaith onslaught.

"Elzaria, I'm going to join our warriors fighting above Terrastria. I'm one of the best pilots out there and can't sit by when I know you've got command of the Resolute. Permission to leave?" He asked.

Dammit to hell, I hated it, but knew it was the right thing to do. "Granted. You had better come back to me." I demanded.

"The bridge is yours." He paused only long enough for me to see the intensity of his love before turning and leaving the bridge.

"General Theron, assume the Knightlord's responsibilities," I ordered.

"Yes, ma'am," he replied and immediately returned his focus to the ongoing onslaught. Axian Theron was a renowned General who my parents trusted. I knew Nexion's duties were in expert hands.

As Nexion prepared to join the fight aboard his strike fighter, I could see the tenacity etched on his face. We needed every warrior. He was ready to lead the elite Empyrean strike fighters from the Resolute into battle against the growing Vaith forces. My heart ached with fear for my husband, knowing the danger he faced, but understanding his duty to the innocent people of Terrastria.

"Be careful, Nexion," I whispered, into his NeuralComm.

"I'll return to you, Elzaria," he promised, his voice confident and brave.

On a monitor of the hanger below, I watched as he strode towards his fighter, my heart aching with a mixture of pride and worry. I turned my attention to the bridge's tactical display, where my advisers and I monitored the ongoing battle.

Nexion's strike fighter roared to life, the powerful engines propelling him into the fray alongside the other Empyrean pilots.

From the bridge, I kept my eyes on Nexion's fighter, watching as he engaged the enemy with skill and precision, as he quickly destroyed two Vaith fighters. A group of three Vaith fighters targeted him, clearly recognizing his abilities as a threat.

Nexion deftly maneuvered his craft, evading their incoming fire while returning his own barrage of plasma laser blasts. He was a skilled pilot, and I could see the Vaith fighters struggling to keep up with his rapid movements.

"Your Majesty, Nexion is engaging multiple enemy fighters," one of my advisers reported, concern in his voice.

"I see that," I replied, my eyes never leaving the scene unfolding before me. "I have faith in him. He can handle this."

Nexion's fighter danced through the sky, weaving between the incoming fire from the Vaith fighters. He expertly targeted one of the enemy crafts, his plasma laser fire connecting with its engines and sending it spiraling in a fiery explosion.

With the first Vaith fighter eliminated, he pivoted his attention to the remaining two. They continued their relentless pursuit, firing on him from all angles. Nexion's fighter sustained a few hits, but he avoided any actual damage.

In a daring move, Nexion accelerated and swooped behind the two enemy fighters, catching them off guard. He unleashed a barrage of plasma laser fire, striking one of the Vaith crafts and causing it to explode in a brilliant burst of flame. The final Vaith fighter, now alone and outmatched, attempted to flee, but Nexion was brutal. He pursued the enemy craft, his fire connecting with its fuselage, and it too erupted in a fiery blaze.

"Your Majesty, Nexion has successfully destroyed the enemy fighters targeting him," my adviser confirmed, relief clear in his voice.

"Thank you," I replied, my voice filled with pride.

As the wreckage of the three Vaith fighters floated out into space, I let out a breath I hadn't realized I'd been holding. Nexion had prevailed.

Our battle against the Vaith was far from over, but victories like Nexion's gave us hope.

The battle raged on, the skies and space above Terrastria filled with the deafening roar of engines and the crackle of plasma laser fire. From my vantage point on the Resolute, I could see the devastation being wrought upon our once-beautiful world.

Vaith fighters cut through our defenses, their advanced weapons systems tearing through the air with lethal precision. Empyrean strike fighters were being picked off one by one, their pilots struggling to outmaneuver the unrelenting onslaught.

As I watched the chaos unfold, I couldn't help but feel a cold, sickening dread settle in the pit of my stomach. The situation was dire, and our forces were suffering heavy losses.

"Your Majesty," one of my advisers reported, his voice tense, "Vaith forces have breached our outer defenses. Their plasma laser weapons are causing significant damage to our infrastructure and military installations."

I clenched my fists, my jaw tightening as I took in the horrifying scene before me. The devastation was immense—they had reduced entire city blocks to rubble, their once-towering structures now nothing more than twisted heaps of debris. Fires raged, their hungry flames consuming everything in their path, while thick plumes of smoke choked the sky, casting an eerie pall over the planet.

"Our forces are attempting to regroup and counterattack, but the Vaith are pressing their advantage," my adviser continued. "If we don't halt their advance soon, the entire planet will be at risk."

I gritted my teeth. This wasn't the time for hesitation or self-doubt—my people needed a leader, and I would be the one to guide them through this dark hour.

"Order our remaining strike fighters to focus on targeting the Vaith's heavy artillery and command ships," I commanded. "Coordinate with ground forces to establish a defensive perimeter around key military installations and population centers."

My advisers nodded, quickly relaying my orders to the appropriate channels. I knew that this wouldn't be easy—the Vaith had us on the back foot, and their superior technology gave them a significant advantage. But we were resilient people, and we wouldn't go down without a fight.

This was no longer just a battle for our planet—it was a battle for our very survival. The stakes had never been higher, and I knew I would do whatever it took to ensure the future of the Empyrean people.

From the Resolute, I stared at the view-screen, my heart aching as I watched the horrors of war unfolding on Terrastria. Through transmitted communications from our ground forces and embedded reporters, I bore witness to the devastation and suffering our people were enduring.

Buildings, once symbols of our architectural prowess, burned and crumbled under the assault from the Vaith. Their plasma laser weapons sliced through concrete and steel, leaving trails of destruction in their wake. The sky was a chaotic whirlwind of fire and debris, as pieces of wreckage rained down upon the planet's surface, creating yet more devastation and loss.

The images on the screen were a stark reminder of the human cost of this brutal conflict. The people of Terrastria were caught in the crossfire, their lives forever changed by the sudden and brutal invasion. Terrified civilians filled the streets, fleeing from the destruction that seemed to follow them at every turn. Desperation and fear etched on their faces as they sought refuge from the nightmare unfolding around them.

Families clung to each other; their eyes wide with terror as they tried to navigate the ruined streets of their once-idyllic city. Empyrean soldiers, their armor battered and scarred, fought valiantly to protect the innocent from the Vaith onslaught. The sounds of gunfire, screams, and the unmistakable crackle of laser fire filled the air.

I continued to watch the suffering of the people scrambling for their lives. I was their queen, and it was my duty to protect them, to keep them safe from harm. But in the face of such an overwhelming enemy, it felt as though there was little I could do to shield them from the horrors that surrounded them.

A sudden burst of static filled the communications channel, followed by the strained voice of one of our officers on the ground. "Your Majesty, we're doing everything we can to evacuate the civilians, but the Vaith forces are persistent. We need reinforcements to hold them off and buy us more time."

My heart clenched at the soldier's words, the desperate urgency in his voice a painful reminder of the reality Terrastrians were facing. "Understood," I replied, my voice steady despite the turmoil churning within me. "I will coordinate with our forces and send reinforcements to your position."

With a grim resolve, I turned to the bridge and ordered some cover for the position that the soldier requested. We needed to act swiftly if we were to have any hope of saving the lives of those caught in the crossfire.

As I watched the ongoing carnage on the view-screen, I steeled myself for the tough decisions that lay ahead. This war had thrust me into a role I had never envisioned for myself, one that required me to make choices that would impact the lives of countless people. But I knew I could not—would not—let the citizens of Terrastria down.

Amid the chaos and destruction, I would find the strength to lead my people through the darkness and into the light. For Terrastria, and for the future of the Empyreans, I would do whatever it took to see us through this terrible conflict.

The situation on Terrastria grew increasingly hopeless. The Vaith continued their assault, pushing our forces back at every turn. I could see the weariness on the faces of my advisers and military commanders as they reported the losses we had suffered. It was becoming clear that we were fighting a losing battle.

With our backs against the wall, I made the hardest decision of my life. I gathered those on the bridge, informing them of my plan. "We have no choice," I said, my voice heavy with the weight of my decision. "We must activate the doomsday retreat."

Faces around the bridge reflected the gravity of the situation. Our ancestors created the doomsday retreat plan hundreds of cycles ago, in case of a catastrophic attack on our world or global cataclysm. Early in the battle, we had reviewed it as a possibility. It was a last resort, a desperate measure designed to save as many lives as possible.

I issued the order for all remaining Empyrean ships to prepare for evacuation. They were to take as many of our people as they could to remote planets, dividing up and heading in different directions to ensure the survival of our Terrastrian people. The objective of all forces was now to protect and give cover to our fleeing people.

As the evacuation began, there was a massive surge to board transport ships and leave. The ships lifted off from the planet's surface, carrying the hopes and dreams of the Terrastrian people with them. Our once proud planet now reduced to refugees, fleeing from the fierce pursuit of the Vaith.

The Vaith weren't content with simply conquering our world; they pursued our fleeing ships with a cruel obstinacy. They fired upon us mercilessly, their weapons tearing through the void of space as they sought to kill those fleeing.

Our ships split up, each taking a different path in an attempt to lose their pursuers. They navigated treacherous asteroid fields, using them as cover to evade the Vaith's relentless attacks. It was a desperate flight, our ships full of innocents weaving and dodging to avoid the deadly rain of enemy fire.

Aboard the Resolute, I continued to watch the chaos unfold on the view-screen, my heart aching. I could only hope that our desperate plan would succeed in saving as many lives as possible.

"We'll regroup and rebuild, Your Majesty," Loren reassured me. "The Empyrean people are strong, and we will survive this."

His words didn't comfort me. I knew that the road ahead would be long and fraught with hardship. We were a people without a home, our world lost to the cruelty of the Vaith. But somehow, we would survive. We would find a way to endure and rebuild, to ensure that the Terrastrian legacy would live on.

As I watched the evacuation unfold, my heart caught in my throat as I spotted Nexion's fighter on the view-screen, engaged in a fierce altercation with several more Vaith fighters. He was a skilled pilot, but the odds were against him.

"Nexion, you need to disengage and return to the Resolute!" I ordered through our secure communication channel, my voice firm and laced with concern.

"I can't, Elzaria," he replied, his voice strained. "I need to buy more time for people to escape."

As I continued to watch, my worst fears were realized. A powerful blast from a Vaith warship struck Nexion's fighter, crippling it. The enemy warship closed in, capturing his damaged craft in a magnetic tether, quickly pulling him on board.

"No!" I cried out, gripping the edge of the command console. The thought of losing Nexion was almost too much to bear, but I had a duty that I couldn't forsake.

The bridge was silent, all eyes on me as I struggled with the decision I knew I had to make. I took a deep breath and addressed my crew, my voice steady despite the turmoil within me.

"We must continue with the evacuation. Our people need us to keep the Vaith off their backs so they can escape. We can't risk the lives of the many for the sake of one."

My advisers and commanders nodded, their faces grim. They knew as well as I did that the fate of our civilization depended on the success of their escape.

"The last of the evacuation transports have left, Your Majesty." General Theron notified me.

"Prepare for breaking orbit and our ascent into space," I ordered.

As the Resolute prepared to leave orbit, I stared out of the view-screen, my eyes locked on the Vaith warship that held Nexion's captured fighter. I knew that by leaving him behind I was sentencing him to an uncertain fate at the hands of the Vaith. But I had a greater responsibility, and I couldn't let my love for Nexion cloud my judgment.

With a heavy heart, I gave the order to depart, and the Resolute joined the rest of the fleet in their desperate flight from Terrastria. My heart ripped in two as we hurtled through space. I bit back the bile threatening to make me puke, grateful I'd not eaten since this all started. How long had it been?

Even though I had to leave Nexion behind, I vowed I would never stop searching for him, never give up hope that one day we would be reunited. It was a promise I made not only to myself but to the man who had fought so bravely for our people, the father of our unborn daughter.

Reports from Terrastria flooded the Resolute's communication center as our fleet continued its retreat. I listened intently; my heart was heavy as I took in the devastating news.

"Your Majesty, our latest intelligence estimates indicate that over 60% of Terrastria's infrastructure was destroyed," Loren reported, his voice somber. "The Vaith have targeted our military installations, communication networks, and power grid, leaving the planet in chaos."

I nodded solemnly, steeling myself against the pain of hearing the damage done to my beloved home world. "And the civilian casualties?"

"Initial estimates put the number in the tens of thousands, Your Majesty," Loren continued. "But we've been able to save a significant portion of the population through the doomsday retreat."

I exhaled, trying to focus on the lives saved rather than the ones lost. "What about my parents?"

"Your parents are safe, Your Majesty," Loren reassured me. "The Hellfire has joined with Commander Zyrana Velor's fleet, and they're currently in route to Grymrock."

"Thank the Creators," I breathed a small sigh of relief, grateful that they had been spared the Vaith's wrath.

As we continued to receive updates, we discussed our next course of action. It was clear the Vaith were determined to see us wiped from existence, and we would need to devise a plan to ensure the people of Terrastria's survival throughout our galaxy.

"Your Majesty, while the doomsday retreat has saved many lives, we must now focus on regrouping," General Theron advised. "We must establish a secure base of operations on one of the remote planets and begin planning our counterattack."

"I agree," I said, my resolve hardening. "We can't let the Vaith's actions go unanswered. We must regain our strength and strike back."

"Captain Selene, set course to Grymrock."

"Yes, Your Majesty," Captain Selene added, "our forces have successfully evacuated millions of our people, and we have coordinated with the other ships in our fleet to ensure that they reach the designated safe planets."

"That is encouraging news, Captain," I replied, allowing myself a brief moment of relief amidst the turmoil. "We must continue to work together, ensuring the Empyrean people remain united in the face of this crisis and safeguard the other Empyrean Alliance worlds from the Vaith, so this war doesn't spread."

As the hours passed, I continued to receive updates on the situation on Terrastria and the progress of our fleet. Despite the losses we had suffered, it was heartening to see that our doomsday plan had largely safeguarded our citizens.

I spoke to those on the bridge with a somber voice, "Our once-great planet may have been reduced to remnants, but the Empyrean spirit remains unbroken. We will rise from these ashes, stronger and more resilient. We will take back what the Vaith have stolen from us."

"Captain, Selene."

"Yes?"

"The bridge is yours. I'll be in my quarters if you need me." I needed some time alone to formulate a plan to strike back at the Vaith, rescue Nexion, and protect my unborn child; all immediately important. The door slid open, and the memory of Nexion bringing me here when I first snuck onto the ship hit me hard. It seemed like a million cycles ago.

CHAPTER TWENTY-ONE

ELZARIA

I don't know how she did it, but Adelaide had managed to have all the ordinary day-to-day things I would need brought to my quarters during the chaos of our departure. The lock-box containing the Codex rested in the center of the table. Thank the goddesses for Adelaide. I shoved my palm onto the scanner, feeling the familiar prick testing the nucleotides of my DNA and the box opened, revealing the Codex. The ancient tome was a cross between a book and a data storage center. Each page held billions of data packets. Only the royal family could connect to a page and read them, a mixture of text and symbols. I flipped through the pages, looking for anything that might give me guidance. Emotionally and physically exhausted, I rested my head on my hands on top of the open pages.

I drifted off into a light sleep, allowing my mind to rest. From the furthest reaches of the universe, I felt a fine thread of energy nudge at my awareness. The Creators directly connected to me. It was a warm, reassuring presence.

"Elzaria, the Vaith have ignited war across the universe once more. The flame of jealousy and greed is spreading uncontrolled. You must extinguish the head of the fire while those who follow you snuff out the embers."

"Tell me how." I implored.

"When you awaken, you will have the knowledge of how to destroy a space-time portal. We will send to another the knowledge of how to build one. Each of you in your own time will do your part."

And just like that, they were gone. But, dammit, what did their cryptic message mean? I awoke gasping for air. I called for Loren to come to me and help make sense of what The Creators wanted me to do. He would be the only one who would believe me, and he had devoted much of his studies and research to that of the construction and operation of the portals.

Loren came rushing through the door almost immediately. "What's happened, Elzaria? You sounded so distraught.

I explained to him what The Creators had shared with me. As Loren and I reviewed holographic images of the space-time portals, my mind was flooded with details of how to destroy them. The Creators had implanted the knowledge in my memory themselves, and I understood what they expected of me—to obliterate a portal, or even multiple portals. I didn't yet know exactly how I was to go about executing the task. Maybe The Creators are guiding me to destroy portals leading out of the Maffei galaxy. But we would have to figure out how to destroy them and still be able to use the wormhole to escape and return to our allied parts of the universe.

"Do you remember the Dracorians who visited us asking for help because the Vaith were stealing the tritanzium from their planet?" I asked Loren.

"Sure, we've sent a small fleet to monitor the shipping channels. From what I understand, that shut down the Vaith's operation."

"Yes, and there is a portal located close to Dracore. If we can get out there and destroy that portal, it would shut the Vaith out from direct access to Andromeda and other galaxies along the F1R3X wormhole. They may still have access to other wormholes, but none with direct access to us. The ability to destroy a portal would also send a clear message that we have a power that no other people have. That would act as a deterrent for the Vaith and any other bad actors."

"That's a good idea, except we don't know where Skarnak and all his ships are. We would have to develop a plan for how to fight Skarnak if his fleet is still on our side of the portal. It would also require that we execute a covert operation that is stealthy enough to evade detection by the Vaith." Loren cautioned.

"It will require careful planning and help from our Xanthra allies, but it's doable."

"Elzaria, you and I both know how speculative this plan is."

"I know there are a lot of obstacles, but we need to get moving before they attack other Empyrean worlds. Even if Skarnak is still lurking in our galaxy, we could cut him off from his people and his supplies. I also know only the Phantom Resolute can take on the challenge. As a descendant of The Creators, only I or my mother can access the weapons we will need if we have any chance of making this plan work. The former queen has no battle skills. She's a competent politician but can't take the Resolute to face the Vaith. Also, a lone ship won't appear nearly as suspicious as a fleet. I can reduce the crew to only those absolutely necessary."

Loren nodded solemnly, understanding the gravity of the situation. "As you wish, Elzaria. We will do everything in our power to ensure the success of your plan."

As the weight of responsibility bore down upon me, I realized Skarnak wouldn't rest until he had hunted down and destroyed the royal family because we are the direct descendants of The Creators and his greatest threat. To ensure the survival of our lineage, which stretched back thousands of cycles, I made the most heart-wrenching decision of my life.

I summoned my personal physician, various scientists, and my most loyal guards to join Loren and me in a secret meeting in my quarters. With a heavy heart, I informed them of my plan.

"I must confront Skarnak." I began. "Loren and I have discussed the strategic details and you must know that there is a high likelihood that I won't survive. I know this is the will of The Creators and I believe my plan is the best way to protect our galaxy from the Vaith's scourge."

This plan will also require great sacrifice from many of you. I won't force any of you on this mission, for it is a mission that you most likely won't return from.

Everyone was silent.

"The future of the Empyrean people and the continuation of the royal family whose blood is tied to The Creators lies in the hands of my unborn child," I told them. "We must take drastic measures to ensure her survival."

"You're with child?" Dr. Kellan Stellatyro, my father's brother, inhaled sharply, taken aback by the news, as the others in the room reacted with a mix of shock and curiosity.

"Yes, Nexion and I are going to have a daughter." I shared as a couple of people gasped. Loren's eyes grew large, and he started shaking his head no.

Reaching over to my dear friend, I squeezed his hand. "There is no other option. As a knight, I took an oath to follow the *Celestial Creed* and live by its principles. *The Creed* demands we live a selfless life. As knights, we are called to put the needs of the many before our own. Our duty is to protect and serve our people, even if it means putting ourselves in harm's way. Knights are willing to make the ultimate sacrifice for the greater good, knowing that our actions will ensure a better future for those we leave behind."

I carefully looked at each of those gathered, my voice unwavering. "I am a knight. It is my duty to protect the Empyrean people, no matter the cost. We can't sit back and watch as the Vaith continue to threaten the Empyrean people and our way of life. We must act. Our mission is to protect the innocent and defend our home, no matter the cost. And I am willing to pay that price, no matter how high."

Everyone nodded solemnly, understanding the gravity of the situation. With Captain Selene at the helm, I knew that there was no time to wait.

I requested a team of capable and trustworthy volunteers to take a research vessel from the Resolute to an unknown planet in the outer rim of the uncharted universe. To a planet where they could establish a colony of Empyreans and keep my daughter hidden and safe from the claws of the Vaith. They had to keep the direction they were heading a secret from everyone, including me.

Knight Valdorion stepped forward and broke the silence.

"My Queen, it would be an honor to serve you in this mission."

Then, one by one, they all volunteered to go.

The others affirmed their agreement. I nodded, my throat tight with emotion. My heart rejoiced as I looked upon the brave volunteers that had answered my call.

"Thank you for your courage and loyalty," I said, forcing back the tears. "I vow that none of you will be forgotten. Your names will live on in history."

Following my orders, we dispersed as each member of the group prepared themselves for their mission. Dr. Stellatyro carefully removed my unborn child from my womb, cryogenically freezing the tiny life within a secure capsule. He carefully placed her, so small and vulnerable, in stasis, and my heart ached as I watched. I prayed I would be reunited with my daughter one day.

"Thank you, Uncle Kellan. Knowing my daughter will be in your care for this journey means everything to me. I know you will take good care of her. I will be sure to let my father know of your great sacrifice for our family."

"Maybe this will help make up for Seraphean's behavior and the great shame she has brought our family." He replied, hugging me tightly before he left to make his preparations for the mission.

While the capsule holding my daughter was being readied, I retrieved the Empyrean Codex Conscio, the ancient tome that The Creators filled with their secrets and writings. This sacred artifact was said to hold the details of unimaginable weapons, but only The Creators could completely access its knowledge. In my dreams, they had given me a glimpse of what it contained, and I understood its value more than anyone. I knew it was crucial to protect the Codex and pass it down to my daughter.

With the capsule, my baby girl, and the Codex secured, I entrusted them to my most loyal and skilled guards, scientists, and my uncle, Dr. Stellatyro. They understood they were embarking on a mission from which they most likely wouldn't return. Their task was to find a safe, unknown planet far away, along the outer rim of the Laniakea universe, where they would hide my unborn child and the Codex Conscio. I held onto the hope that one day she would return, and we would be reunited.

I addressed my loyal protectors one last time. "I'm entrusting you with the future of the Empyrean royal lineage," I told them, my voice breaking with emotion. "Our survival depends on your success. May The Creators watch over you and guide you on this perilous journey."

Tears streamed down my face as I watched their ship, the Stellavara, depart, carrying my daughter and the hope of our people towards the unknown. In my heart, I knew that this was the only way for the war to end someday, in the distant future. My grief was immeasurable, but I held onto the hope that one day, my daughter would rise to reclaim the Empyrean throne and bring an end to the Vaith's tyranny.

As the small research ship disappeared into the vastness of space, I turned my attention back to the present. The fight for our people's survival was far from over, but I had set in motion a plan that could bring about our salvation. With renewed determination, I vowed to lead the remnants of the Empyrean people through these dark times and to avenge the fallen.

My heart ached with the absence of my unborn child and my soulmate. The weight of the war threatened to crush me. Yet, through the haze of sorrow and loss, a single thought burned in my mind—I had to save Nexion. He was my rock, my love, and my partner in this fight. I wouldn't abandon him to the Vaith.

Despite being weakened from the surgery, I summoned all my strength. The war had begun, a conflict that would stretch across the universe and possibly lead to the deaths of billions. I knew the grim reality of our situation—the fallout from the Vaith's attack was only the beginning. It could take hundreds of cycles before we restored peace, if ever. But I had a duty to each and every Empyrean, and I would not falter.

Our greatest asset in this fight was the Phantom Resolute, the most sophisticated battleship ever created by the Empyrean. Its technology was a relic from the ancient wars, designed by The Creators themselves. They had made the Empyrean royalty swear an oath to only use the ship's full capabilities in the direst of circumstances. That time had come.

I had been infatuated with the Resolute since I was a child, studying its history and design with great enthusiasm. The ship's advanced neural technology and AI allowed it to connect with its commander in ways still not possible to replicate, becoming a seamless extension of their very being. In essence, the ship was virtually alive.

With the Resolute at our disposal and a fleet of smaller fighter craft, I set a course for the planet Grymrock. The remote outpost would serve as a rallying point for our remaining forces and a base from which to plan our retaliation.

CHAPTER TWENTY-TWO

ELZARIA

I stood on the bridge of the Resolute. My heart ached for Nexion, held captive by the ruthless Vaith Supreme Commander, Skarnak. I was surrounded by the remnants of the once-proud Resolute's fleet, reduced to a desperate rebel force. Our Empyrean people scattered across the universe, and our home planet of Terrastria devastated.

My parents had taken refuge on the remote planet of Grymrock, waiting for us to join them. When we finally arrived, their relief at seeing me alive was overshadowed by the news of Nexion's capture. It was a crushing blow, and the weight of the situation weighed heavily on us all.

I gathered my advisers, military commanders, and Grymrock officials in a makeshift war room within the spaceport at Astralys. It was time to plan our retribution against the Vaith and regain control of our destiny. We knew we couldn't do this alone, so we reached out to our allies within the Quindarian Federation.

The Xanthra, our most loyal allies, pledged their support without hesitation. However, the Zayin, once united, were now divided and consumed by infighting. The Quadran, a collection of underdeveloped worlds in the far reaches of the universe, were unable to take sides and were largely ill-equipped to help.

I knew that if we were to succeed in our mission, we needed to unite the outer rim planets and launch a strategic campaign against the Vaith. My plan was to form a lasso, ever tightening around the Vaith forces, trapping them and cutting off their supply lines. To achieve this, we needed to gain control over the space-time portals that granted access to the traversable wormholes. And as Loren and I had discussed, destroy the portal on the wormhole near Dracore that allowed the Vaith easy access to the F1R3X wormhole leading to our galaxy. This portal would be the linchpin in deciding the outcome of the war.

Pacing across the front of the war room with my hands behind my back, I stood before them, feeling the weight of their gazes upon me. Their faces were a mix of courage, fear, and grief. But they all stood ready to serve and protect Empyrean lives.

Loren and I had formed a plan that we hoped could turn the tide in our favor against the Vaith. I could feel the weight of their expectations as they looked at me.

"My fellow Empyreans and our loyal allies," I began, my voice steady and strong, "I'm going to be direct; the Vaith chose now to attack because they thought we were weak. You and I both know I'm young and newly crowned. I may have completed our most prestigious Empyrean Knight's Training Academy, where I learned a great deal, but it wasn't enough. Skarnak knew that our long-enjoyed peace made us soft and unprepared for war. Recently, there were signs of Vaith unrest, and we began making changes, but it was too little too late and now the most innocent among us have paid the price with their blood." I slammed my hands on the table in front of me. "And with the suspected treachery of Seraphean, they were successful in their initial attack."

The room was silent. Everyone knew the truth of what I said. I paced, burning mad.

"I won't let those who have died and continue to suffer do so in vain. The Vaith have signed their own death warrant and I'm here to collect." I shouted.

In response, a frenzied war chant thundered across the room with increasing ferocity. A battle cry of epic proportions ripped from General Theron's lungs as he bellowed his rage out to the heavens.

"Today, we face the greatest challenge in our history," my voice resonated through the hall. "The Vaith have attacked us, and they won't stop until they have destroyed everything we hold dear. We must stand together and fight back."

I could see the fire in their eyes, the spark of defiance that refused to be extinguished. We would not go quietly into the night—we would fight to save our people, our world, and our way of life. This was only the beginning of an arduous war, but as long as we stood united, we would find a way to overcome the darkness.

"The key to our victory lies in a long-ago forged technology from the time of The Creators. I'm speaking of the space-time portals that grant us access to the traversable wormholes."

As I spoke, Loren activated a holographic projection of a portal and its inner workings, bringing the ancient marvel to life before their very eyes.

"These wormholes utilize threads of energy drawn from the very fabric of the universe, allowing us to travel vast distances in the blink of an eye. Tens of thousands of cycles ago, The Creators, devised a way to access the wormholes through the construction of these portals."

The room was silent, hanging on my every word as I continued. "The technology behind the portals has been a closely guarded secret of the ancient Empyreans. It was almost forgotten, but my advisor, Lorentzian, a renowned Empyrean scientist and historian, has studied the technology behind the portals in great detail. We must use this knowledge to our advantage."

I gestured to the hologram, which now displayed a map of the universe with the locations of the space-time portals. "By controlling these portals, we can control access to the wormholes and, ultimately, control the universe. The Vaith understand this as well, and they will stop at nothing to seize control of these gateways."

"We must secure and defend these portals," I declared, "for they are the key to our survival and the restoration of peace. With them, we can outmaneuver the Vaith, strike at the heart of their empire, and reclaim our rightful place. We can cut them off from our local group of galaxies."

I scrutinized the room, noticing the thoughtful expressions and small nods of agreement as everyone grasped just how immense an advantage controlling the access points would be for us.

"We must act swiftly and decisively," I demanded. "We can't allow the Vaith to solidify their hold on our galaxy or allow their disease to spread beyond their own Maffei galaxy."

There were murmurs throughout the room, most nodding in agreement, each of them knowing the immense challenges that lay ahead.

"Your Majesty," General Theron spoke up, "if we are to succeed, we must be prepared for great sacrifices. It won't be an easy path, but we will stand by your side, come what may."

The room erupted in agreement, and I could see the courage in their eyes.

Ganthion cleared his throat and abruptly changed the holographic projection. The sound of an incoming previously recorded transmission interrupted my words. It was over an open channel, broadcast across the universal transmission system for all to receive. I could feel the tension in the room as everyone looked at me, their eyes filled with concern.

Ganthion quickly brought the transmission up on the main screen, and my heart sank as I saw the face of Skarnak sneering back at me. Beside him stood my cousin Seraphean, her expression cold and defiant, confirming that she was the spy and traitor we had guessed. The sight of her betrayal felt like a dagger to my heart.

But what pained me, even more, was the sight of Nexion, battered and bruised, almost unrecognizable in his beaten state. On his knees, he was cuffed and collared like an animal. The sight of Nexion in such a demeaning condition caused my heart to burn with anger and despair. Unable to bear witnessing him in such a state, my fists clenched tightly, and my nails dug into my palms as I fought to control my emotions. The tears welled up in my eyes, yet I refused to let them fall. Strength became imperative—for Nexion's well-being and the welfare of our people.

I turned to those assembled, my voice steady. "We can't let them get away with this. We must rescue Nexion and bring Seraphean to justice."

"Queen Elzaria," Skarnak's voice echoed through the room, "I have a proposition for you. Surrender yourself to me. Come be my pet, and I will spare your precious Knightlord. You have one day to respond. If you refuse, I will make sure you witness his slow and agonizing demise."

The transmission cut off, leaving the room in stunned silence. I could feel the eyes of everyone on me, searching for a sign of what I would do next.

My mind raced, knowing that replying to Skarnak's demand now would give away our location. I couldn't risk the lives of everyone here, but neither could I abandon Nexion to this fate. I took a deep breath, trying to steady myself, and addressed the room.

"We will not give in to Skarnak's demands," I said, my voice resolute. "Our mission is too important, and the fate of the universe rests on our shoulders. I understand the risk this poses to Nexion, and it breaks my heart, but we must press on."

Solemn nods passed among my advisers and commanders, their understanding of the gravity of the situation obvious. We wouldn't be swayed by the Vaith's cruel tactics. We would continue our fight, for Nexion, for the Empyrean people, and for the countless lives that hung in the balance.

I silently vowed that I would save Nexion without compromising our mission. I wouldn't allow Skarnak and Seraphean to win, and I wouldn't let Nexion's sacrifice be in vain.

Then, as if by divine intervention, the answer struck me. I paced back and forth as the room remained silent while I formulated my ideas. Loren watched me carefully, knowing how my mind worked.

I cleared my throat, taking a moment to gather my thoughts before beginning to outline my new plan to the others. My voice was confident, filled with conviction. "Skarnak and his fleet have proven to be formidable adversaries, but I have come up with an idea of how we can break their hold on us and rescue Nexion. A somewhat different plan than Loren and I had devised earlier that we can act on immediately."

Loren raised one eyebrow, giving me the look that he always did when I was about to do something headstrong.

"We will lure Skarnak's fleet to the next galaxy beyond ours, along the F1R3X wormhole. There is a portal along the outer arm of an as-of-yet unexplored spiral galaxy. We will use our ship, the Phantom Resolute, as bait. Skarnak would love to get his greedy claws on it because my guess is Seraphean has divulged some of its secrets. We will release fake intelligence convincing Skarnak we are running there to hide the ancient technology contained within our vessel. There is only one portal to this galaxy, and once Skarnak's fleet is there, we will destroy the portal, trapping them and us in the far reaches of the universe with no means of return. This, my friends, will cut the head off the snake. Queen Elindra and Prime Minister Helion will launch an assault on the Vaith forces left leaderless in our Andromeda galaxy. We will divide and conquer."

The council members exchanged worried glances, but I continued, "Once the portal is destroyed, we will launch a full-scale attack on Skarnak's fleet. The destruction of the portal will catch him off guard and we will use that brief distraction to dock with and forcibly take Skarnak's ship. We will bring the fucking battle to them and rescue Knightlord Nexion. I want Skarnaks's head on a pike! I know this plan is incredibly risky, and success isn't guaranteed, but it is our only option to get Skarnak and rescue Nexion."

My father spoke up, his voice heavy with concern. "Elzaria, are you certain about this? The consequences of failure are dire. No one has ever destroyed a portal. There is no way you'll be able to rebuild it, either. Elzaria, this plan could have catastrophic consequences, including the loss of life for you and everyone on the Resolute. At best, you will never return."

My mother added, her eyes filled with tears, "I cannot bear the thought of losing you."

I looked at them with a mixture of sadness and courage. "I understand the risks and the pain this decision may cause you. However, I can't stand idly by while Terrastrians suffer and Nexion remains captive. Skarnak wants me. He wants to use me as leverage against the Empyrean people. I must do what is necessary for the greater good. I swore an oath to The Creators themselves to dedicate my life to upholding the *Celestial Creed*.

I can't forsake my *Creed* or my knighthood. If we don't uphold what is righteous, then we are no better than the Vaith we revile."

My parents nodded solemnly, understanding the gravity of the situation. I knew I wasn't just fighting for Nexion or the Empyrean people, but for the future of the entire universe.

With a deep breath, I ordered, "We must begin our preparations immediately. The Vaith will not wait for us. We will set this plan in motion and stand together, united against our enemies. It may forever divide some of us from those we love, but so be it."

The council members rose from their seats. It was time to take the battle to the Vaith. I knew that the road ahead would be fraught with peril. But I also knew the Empyrean spirit was fierce and that together we could overcome even the most insurmountable odds. This was only the beginning.

"Your orders are clear," I told my commanders. "We move swiftly, giving Skarnak no time to consider our plan. We strike hard, and we strike fast." The commanders saluted and dispersed to inform their teams.

As we prepared for the upcoming battle, the atmosphere on Grymrock was one of tense anxiety. The crew of the Phantom Resolute and the strike fighter pilots checked and rechecked their equipment, knowing that our chances of success hinged on every detail. I issued my last orders, making it clear that only the Phantom Resolute and the ships we could store within its hangar bay would take part in this risky operation.

Across the spaceport, preparations for the battle continued unabated. Skarnak had given me one day to respond, so we had no time to waste. Everyone did their part as the crew loaded weapons and meticulously inspected the strike fighters, searching for any signs of weakness. The pilots and crew steeled themselves for the mission ahead, seeking solace in one another's company and trying to find moments of peace in the calm before the storm.

As night fell, I ordered everyone to get a full night's rest. "Tomorrow, we face our enemy. Rest well, for we will need all our strength and clear heads."

The quiet murmurs of agreement echoed through the halls as most retired to their rooms. I found myself alone in my private quarters on the Resolute. The weight of the upcoming battle and the decisions I had made came crashing down upon me. My heart ached for Nexion, my brave and loyal knight, and for the unborn daughter I had sent away in a desperate bid to protect her and the descendants of the Royal House's future.

In the solitude of my chamber, I allowed myself to truly feel the overwhelming grief and loss. Tears streamed down my face as I collapsed to my knees, my body wracked with quiet sobs. I knew I had to stay strong, but at this moment, I couldn't help but mourn for all that I had lost and all that I might still lose. For now, I let my tears fall, a testament to my personal sacrifices and the love that still burned fiercely in my heart.

As the night wore on, I eventually found a restless sleep, filled with dreams of Nexion, our daughter, and the battle that lay ahead. When morning came, I rose. My resolve hardened once more, ready to face the Vaith.

I stepped into the bustling hangar with a sense of purpose, knowing the challenges that lay ahead. I could see a throng of people working diligently to prepare the Phantom Resolute for the journey that awaited us. There was a somber determination in their eyes, a quiet understanding that this was a one-way trip.

I watched as they loaded the ship with everything we would need to start new lives in the unknown reaches of the universe. Food supplies, tools, medical equipment, and any remnants of our culture and history that we could carry were carefully packed into the ship's cargo holds.

As the preparations continued, my parents approached me, their faces etched with worry. My father spoke first. "Elzaria, we must discuss Seraphean. Her betrayal is a terrible blow. She was always jealous of you, but we never thought she would go so far as to join Skarnak and bring such death and destruction upon her own people."

My mother added softly, "We failed to see the darkness growing within her. We should have done more to help her, to guide her away from this path."

I shook my head, my expression unflinching. "We can't dwell on the past. Seraphean made her choice, and we must face the consequences of her actions. We won't let her betrayal define us. I will see that Seraphean is served justice."

My parents nodded, their eyes filled with sorrow. "We know you will lead our people to a brighter future, Elzaria," my father said, embracing me tightly.

As we stood together, my parents and I continued our discussion, focusing on the fight against the Vaith on their side of the portal. My father spoke with vehemency, "Elzaria, with Skarnak and his fleet trapped within the next galaxy along the wormhole with you, we will take responsibility for continuing the battle against the remaining Vaith forces. The Xanthra Alliance will stand with us, and together, we'll begin finding and snuffing out the Vaith."

I felt a sense of dread as I nodded in agreement. "I trust that you and Queen Cassia will weaken the Vaith from within, eventually restoring balance to your side of the universe. Mother, Father, you have my complete faith."

Before we parted ways, I had to reveal the secret I had been carrying. "There is something I must tell you both before I go." Barely able to speak the words, they pulled me close, giving me the support I needed in this moment. "I was pregnant with Nexion's child, a baby girl," I said, watching as their eyes widened with shock. "In order to protect our daughter and ensure the survival of our Empyrean lineage, I sent our unborn baby girl to a remote planet far from the reach of the Vaith."

The news shocked my mother. "Oh, my dearest Elzaria, what a horrible decision you had to make. I know you did what was best for your sweet daughter. Protecting her from the many unknown outcomes of the war the Vaith have wrought. It must be unbearable for you. I can only imagine what it cost you—my heart aches for your loss."

My pain gutted me as my mother embraced me, her tears mingled with mine. Briefly, we allowed ourselves to mourn the loss of my daughter. The pain was tangible, and we held onto each other, seeking comfort in our shared grief.

As we pulled away, I wiped away my tears, my resolve hardening once more. "I won't let our sacrifices be in vain. We will survive, and the people of our galaxy will know peace once more."

My father added, "We will do everything in our power to ensure that, one day, our grandchild will know the sacrifices that were made to protect her and to restore peace."

As we embraced, I felt the weight of our decisions bearing down on all of us. We were each making sacrifices, fighting for the future of our family.

"Father, there's something else you need to know. Uncle Kellan went on the mission to protect my daughter. He told me he hoped it would help make up for the great shame Seraphean has brought our family. I don't know if he knew about her treason, but he wanted to help. He was the only doctor I trusted enough to take my baby from my womb and ensure her safety."

I saw the loss in my father's eyes as I told him. He understood it meant he would never see his only brother again. "War brings pain to us all. May his sacrifice not be in vain." He sighed deeply.

My voice was firm as I continued. "There's more, and it's crucial. You must promise me that if my daughter survives and if she returns, she will have the authority to rule over the Empyrean Alliance, no matter how many cycles it takes. We must ensure this through our dictates and any other means necessary."

My father nodded, understanding the gravity of the situation. "We will take every measure to ensure her rightful place as our future leader. We will instill in our people the importance of her return and her connection to The Creators and pass laws in order to maintain her claim to the throne."

My mother added, "We will do everything in our power to pave the way for her so that when she returns, she will have the authority to lead the Empyrean people."

The time had come for our last farewells, and the reality that we would never see each other again hit us hard. Tears welled up in our eyes, and my mother pulled me into a tight embrace. "Elzaria, you are the bravest and strongest person I know. We are so proud of you, and we love you more than words can express. Always remember that."

My father hugged me next, his voice cracking with emotion. "Elzaria, we have faith in your ability to overcome any obstacle that lies ahead. You have our unwavering support and love. May the stars guide you and The Creators protect you on your journey."

With a heavy heart, I stepped back from them, my eyes locked onto theirs. "Thank you both for everything you have done for me, Nexion, and my baby. I love you both so much, and I will carry your strength with me always."

I turned toward the Resolute, refusing to look back. As we parted ways, the emotional weight of our last goodbye was nearly unbearable.

As they completed the final preparations, I took one last look at Grymrock, knowing that I would never see it again. With a heavy heart, I boarded the Phantom Resolute, ready to face the challenges that awaited us in the distant reaches of the uncharted universe. Our mission was clear. We wouldn't let Skarnak, or the traitorous Seraphean, dictate our fate.

CHAPTER TWENTY-THREE

ELZARIA

I stood on the bridge of the Phantom Resolute, watching as the magnificent ship rose from the surface of Grymrock, leaving behind my grieving parents and the remnants of our once-great world. As we ascended into the vast emptiness of space, my heart pounded, heavy with the weight of responsibility and loss.

"Initiate FTL sequence, Captain Selene," I ordered, my voice steady despite the turmoil within me. "Our journey to the space-time portal must be swift."

"Aye, Your Majesty," Captain Selene replied, her fingers dancing over the control panel as the neural link wrapped around her wrists, activating our FTL drive. In mere moments, we were hurtling through space at unimaginable speeds, the star light streaking past us in blurred lines.

We neared the space-time portal, and I couldn't help but marvel at the ancient Empyrean technology that allowed us to traverse the universe so quickly. These portals accessing the wormholes were a testament to the brilliance and foresight of our ancestors, The Creators.

As I prepared the Resolute for its journey through the wormhole, I felt a mix of anticipation and anxiety. I, along with the crew members, strapped into our stations. The atmosphere within the ship was charged, knowing that we were about to embark on a journey that none of us would ever return from.

A warning alarm rang through the ship, notifying all on board we would soon enter the wormhole.

"Engaging portal in 3... 2... 1..." Captain Selene announced, and the ship lurched forward, entering the swirling vortex.

The sensation of traveling through a wormhole is difficult to describe. As the Phantom Resolute was pulled into the maw of the cosmic tunnel, the ship seemed to stretch and contract, distorting both space and time. The walls of the ship seemed to shimmer and waver as if they were made of liquid.

The noise was unlike anything I'd ever experienced. It was a deep, resonating hum that seemed to come from all directions at once, vibrating through the hull of the ship and into our very bones. The sound was so powerful that it was almost tangible, like a physical force pressing in on us from all sides.

As we traveled through the wormhole, the view outside the ship's windows was a kaleidoscope of colors and patterns, constantly shifting and changing. It was beautiful, although disorienting, and I had to force myself to focus on the task at hand, rather than getting lost in the mesmerizing display.

The sensation of weightlessness grew stronger, and I felt as if I were floating inside the ship, tethered only by my seat straps. The crew members struggled to maintain their stability, some clutching onto their consoles for support.

Despite the disorienting sensations and sounds, I kept my focus on the ship, ensuring that we stayed on course for our destination. As the exit portal came into view, I braced myself for the transition back into normal space.

"Prepare to exit down to hyper-speed," I commanded, my eyes fixed on the portal, a shimmering gateway suspended in the vacuum.

With a final burst, the Resolute emerged from the wormhole and into the star-speckled void beyond. The ship shuddered as it re-entered normal space, and the crew members let out a collective breath, relieved to have made it through the treacherous passage.

The Resolute slowed, smoothly transitioning from hyper-speed, and we held our position near the exit portal.

"Your Majesty, we have arrived at the designated location," announced our chief engineer, Tarkis. "The team is ready to install the explosive devices."

"Proceed," I responded, my voice firm. "Remember, timing and placement are crucial. We have only one chance to execute this plan."

I watched as the crew members donned their space suits and disembarked from the Resolute, floating gracefully near the portal to set up the fission explosives. These explosive devices targeted specific points on the portal, causing a localized explosion that would destroy it without causing excessive damage to the surrounding area. With meticulous care, they positioned the devices in the precise locations required to render the portal unusable and block any further access. This ensured that Skarnak's fleet would be trapped with us in this unexplored galaxy.

As they set each explosive in place, my heart raced. The success of our mission hinged on this critical step, and I knew we couldn't afford any mistakes.

"Your Majesty," Tarkis reported, returning to the bridge, "they have successfully installed the explosive devices. We await your orders."

I took a deep breath and prepared a broadcast message, the same type we received on Grymrock that wouldn't only challenge Skarnak but hopefully enrage him enough to take the bait. I signaled to Ganthion, and he nodded, opening a universal transmission for all to hear.

"Commander Skarnak," I began, my voice dripping with sarcasm, "I must congratulate you on your brilliant plan to use Nexion as a hostage. It truly showcases your intellect and strategic prowess. It's a shame that it won't be enough to provoke my interest in turning myself over to you. Nexion is a knight, a true military man. He would never be so foolish to think a trade like that would happen." I laughed, shaking my head.

I paused for effect before continuing, "You see, I will never bow to your demands. The Phantom Resolute and her crew have tolerated enough of your insolence. You may have caught us off guard, but your simpleton band of pathetic pirates is no match for Empyrean forces."

Even though I couldn't see Skarnak's face, I knew it would be contorted with rage as I continued. "And as for your vile attack on Terrastria, it's laughable how you think it will break our spirits. We are resilient, Skarnak, and our vengeance will be swift and merciless."

The moment had come to bait the trap. "But perhaps you already know that. We know you're desperately seeking our location and can't find us, but we see you. Enjoy your last meal and while you're at it, give your nasty whore, Seraphean, a good fucking. It will be your last pleasure."

I let the silence hang for a moment before ending the transmission.

The entire bridge crew stared at me, their eyes wide with a mix of shock and admiration. They knew I had just thrown down the gauntlet and there was no turning back now.

"Loren," I leaned over to him, "You're sure you hid a data packet with our location for them to find."

"Yes, ma'am, I made sure the encryption was difficult enough to break, but still manageable for their comms experts, so they won't suspect it was planted."

"Let's hope they're not too stupid."

"Prepare for Skarnak's fleet to arrive," I instructed, my voice steady and fueled with anger. "Position the Resolute on the other side of that asteroid a quarter-parsec out. That will ensure they're too far from the portal to disrupt our destruction or slip back through. When they come, we'll be ready to spring the trap."

We waited with bated breath, our nerves on edge for Skarnak's arrival. The minutes stretched on, turning into hours, and I couldn't help but wonder if our bait had failed.

"Ma'am, still no sign of Skarnak's presence." Captain Selene reported. "Do you think it's possible they haven't traced us yet, or worse, they have a cloaking ability we can't detect?"

"Hold fast," I ordered. "I'll take over the helm. Get some food."

Strapping into the captain's chair, I took the helm of the Phantom Resolute for the first time. I had studied the ancient ship and wondered if it would recognize my royal DNA. I knew how to fly a strike fighter, but had never flown a warship. Studied it, yes. Flew it, no. For some pilots, there were historical accounts of The Creators mind linking with them and downloading the knowledge to operate the vessel. I hoped that would be the case for me rather than having to rely on Captain Selene's training. Also, according to the Codex, the ship previously had weapons more advanced than those in use today. I wondered if The Creators would allow me to access them if they still existed.

The ship's advanced neural interface awaited my connection. Nervously, I placed my hands on the panels and the connective bands wrapped around my wrists. A sudden rush of energy surged through me. I felt the tiny threads pulsing through my mind and body. I became one with the Phantom Resolute, our thoughts and actions in perfect synchrony. The ship recognized my royal lineage, my direct connection to The Creators. It seemed to awaken something powerful within both the vessel and me.

For a couple of minutes, my brain burned with intense pain. I shut my eyes in a feeble attempt to block the white light that radiated inside me. Soon, it was gone, leaving behind all I needed to know to fly the ship. It was incredible.

As I navigated the Resolute, I could feel new abilities and knowledge bubbling to the surface of my consciousness. The ship and I shared an intimate bond that allowed me to tap into its deepest secrets and potential. It was then that I discovered an extraordinary weapon, one hidden away for eons.

This weapon, a result of the combined knowledge and power of The Creators, was unlike anything the universe had known in hundreds if not thousands of cycles. Its energy seemed to pulse and resonate with the very fabric of the universe itself. The potential for destruction was immense, but I knew I had to wield this power carefully, responsibly.

As I directed the Resolute towards our looming confrontation with Skarnak and his fleet, I couldn't help but wonder how this newfound ability would change the course of the battle. The stakes were high, and the odds were against us, but with this ancient weapon at my command, I was more confident than ever that we could secure a future for our people and avenge the countless lives lost to the Vaith's attack.

As I sat at the helm of the Resolute, the extraordinary weapon pulsing with unimaginable power, I couldn't help but feel a gnawing sense of doubt. I knew this weapon had the potential to turn the tide of the battle in our favor, to give us the upper hand against Skarnak and his relentless Vaith forces. But at what cost?

My thoughts turned to Nexion, held captive and suffering at the hands of our enemies. If I were to unleash the full force of this ancient weapon when we first confront Skarnak, I wouldn't be able to save him.

I discussed my concerns with those on the bridge, their faces etched with worry. "Your Majesty," Loren said, his voice heavy with responsibility, "this weapon could be our only hope of defeating Skarnak. But we understand your hesitation. Nexion's life hangs in the balance, and we must tread carefully."

As we debated our options, I knew I had a hard decision to make. On the one hand, I had the power to potentially end the conflict, risking no more lives. On the other, I would lose the man I loved, one of our greatest knights.

I finally made my decision. "We won't initially use this weapon," I declared. "We will find another way to confront Skarnak and rescue Nexion. I refuse to let this power determine the fate of one of our knights, the man I love, without at least attempting to rescue him."

My advisors nodded in understanding, knowing that our task had just become infinitely more difficult. But we were all united in our commitment to saving Nexion without resorting to the use of this ancient weapon. We set our course and prepared for the battle that lay ahead, armed knowing that the fate of our people, and of Nexion, rested on our shoulders.

Just when it seemed that Skarnak wouldn't come, our sensors picked up his fleet approaching.

"Your Majesty, Skarnak's forces have emerged from the portal," Loren informed me, his voice tense. "They're moving toward our position."

Skarnak's fleet neared, and I knew it was time to enact the irrevocable part of our plan. "Initiate the detonation sequence for the portal explosives," I ordered.

"Your Majesty, are you certain?" Loren asked, his voice betraying a hint of concern. "Once destroyed, there's no way back."

"I am," I replied, steeling myself for the consequences of my decision. "We can't risk Skarnak escaping through the portal. Proceed with the detonation."

The tactical officer nodded in agreement. "Understood, Your Majesty. Initiating the sequence."

I directed the Resolute toward Skarnak's position. As we closed in on his ship, I watched the view-screen as the countdown for the detonation ticked away. Every crew member held their breath.

The detonation rocked the surrounding space, followed by an immense explosion of blinding light and searing heat. Once a shimmering gateway to distant galaxies, the space-time portal was closed. The shock wave buffeted our vessel, causing it to shudder violently, but we maintained our course, barreling towards Skarnak's ship.

With the portal gone, we were well and truly trapped in this distant corner of the universe, but I refused to let that knowledge weaken my resolve. We would save Nexion and defeat Skarnak—there could be no other outcome.

Skarnak's attention drawn to the destruction of the portal was our smallest of opportunities to latch onto his ship before he fired at us. With a last burst of acceleration, the Resolute locked its docking clamps onto Skarnak's flagship. The point of no return was upon us, and I steeled myself for the battle that was about to begin.

"Prepare for boarding maneuvers. Once docked with Skarnak's ship and the airlock opened, the strike team is ready to move in." General Theron informed the bridge.

"Find Nexion and get him out of there fast." I demanded.

The crew of the Resolute executed my orders with swift precision, and within seconds, they were forcing their way into Skarnak's massive Vaith vessel as I watched through their neural links.

General Theron led a team of our most elite knights and warriors, storming through the corridors of the Vaith ship with deadly efficiency. The Vaith forces were caught off guard, and we cut through their defenses with ease. However, despite our swift progress, there was no sign of holding cells or of Nexion.

"Split up," General Theron ordered, his voice firm and commanding. "Search every corner of this ship. We won't leave without him."

The troops broke into two units. General Theron headed for the bridge while Ganthion led a small contingency into the depths of the vessel. My heart pounded in my chest as I desperately watched for any sign of Nexion. The ship seemed to be a never-ending maze of hallways and chambers, and with each passing moment, my hope of finding him waned.

Finally, after what felt like an eternity, Ganthion stumbled upon a heavily guarded cell block. My instincts told me that Nexion had to be held there, and I steeled myself for the battle that lay ahead. With a nod to his fellow soldiers, Ganthion charged forward, engaging the Vaith in a fierce firefight. But even as they fought their way deeper into the cell block, Nexion remained elusive.

Their search continued, and seconds rolled off the clock as my heart grew tighter and my confidence began to falter. Would they be able to find Nexion in time? Or would our daring rescue mission end in failure, with Nexion still trapped in the clutches of our merciless enemy?

The team's search for Nexion was relentless, and as they rounded a corner, they finally found him—battered and bruised, but still alive.

Without a moment's hesitation, Ganthion ignited his Empyrean Knight's saber, its blade a lethal fusion of ancient metal and crackling energy. With a swift, precise strike, he severed the restraints binding Nexion to the wall.

Nexion slumped forward, panting, but there was no time for words. Vaith warriors still surrounded the team, and their fight was far from over. Ganthion tossed his saber to Nexion, who caught it deftly and rose to his feet, his eyes burning with rage.

Nexion wasted no time launching himself into battle alongside our warriors. He moved with fluid grace and deadly skill despite his injuries, his saber cutting through Vaith soldiers. As much as I wished I was fighting by his side, I knew my duty was here on the bridge.

"Your Majesty, we need to get back to the Resolute!" Ganthion shouted over the chaos, his voice strained with urgency.

"General Theron, Ganthion has him. Withdraw, withdraw, withdraw." I shouted.

As the teams fought their way back to the Resolute, I heard the sounds of our troops engaging the Vaith forces. It was a whirlwind of destruction. They fell foes left and right, but time was running out.

Some of the guys had been separated from the others and were returning through the airlock. The fierce fighting, screaming, and sounds of weapons made it impossible to determine what was happening with our warriors as they battled to make their way back on board.

I had to start the undocking process, all while keeping my eyes trained on the screen showing the airlock, praying for Nexion and the others to make it back in time.

"Update on the evacuation team," I ordered.

"Eight souls on hostile ship. Airlock secured by rear guard and waiting." A young Ensign whose name I couldn't think of in the chaos responded.

"Hold final closing sequence." I commanded.

The seconds felt like an eternity, each one stretching out as I held off on sealing the airlock shut.

I watched as General Theron and three others ran through the airlock.

"Four souls on hostile ship." The Ensign updated.

"Ma'am, hostile strike fighters' weapons are ready to fire. We've got to separate to engage."

"Have our strike fighters' weapons ready and engines hot. As soon as we disengage, launch all birds. Expedite."

Turning to my right, I ordered, "Tactical, on board weapons at the ready. Light them up as soon as airlock is engaged."

With no other choice, I inhaled sharply.

"In 10, we activate the lock-down protocol. 10... 9... 8..."

Just when it seemed as though Nexion and the three others wouldn't make it, he appeared—sprinting through the closing gap and diving into the ship with the others on his heels.

"Lock-down, lock-down, lock-down."

"Seals verified?"

"In 2... 1... Verified."

Relief washed over me, but there was no time to celebrate. I wrenched the Resolute away from the Vaith ship, putting as much distance between us as possible. We weren't in the clear yet—the Vaith had launched a counterattack.

Their weapons' fire slammed into the Phantom Resolute's shields, each impact rattling the ship and its crew. I gritted my teeth and focused on evasive maneuvers, weaving through the incoming fire as best I could.

"Shields at 80 percent and dropping!" Tarkis called out.

"Keep us moving!" I barked, my hands gripping the controls tightly. "We can't afford to take any more hits!" With the portal destroyed and our fates sealed, there was no turning back.

Out of the corner of my eye, I saw on a small screen Nexion collapse onto the floor, his body trembling from the strain of his injuries. He was covered in blood. How much was his I didn't know. Dr. Xanderian, rushed to his side, quickly assessing the situation.

"Elzaria, Nexion's been badly injured. I'm taking him to the medical bay now!" Dr. Xanderian called out, worry unmistakable in his voice.

"Copy that, doc." I responded, trying to maintain my focus on the ongoing attack.

With every ounce of my concentration, I piloted the Resolute, attempting to put more distance between us and the Vaith fleet. We needed to be far enough away to safely use the ancient weapon without causing harm to our own ship.

"All birds, this is command. Immediate RTB, we're prepping for FTL jump. Disengage on the double!"

The situation grew increasingly dire as the Vaith fired an unknown, powerful weapon at us. Its impact was overwhelming, leading to significant damage and stripping our shields. The ship rocked, and the sound of alarms filled the air. Crew members struggled to regain their footing, fear painted on their faces.

"Shields are gone! Hull breaches on multiple decks!" A crew member shouted.

My heart raced, but I forced myself to remain calm. "Seal off the damaged areas and evacuate the crew from those sections!"

As the Resolute limped through space, it seemed like all hope was lost. But just when I thought we were finished, the ship's ancient weapon came online. I could feel the immense power surging through the neural connection, and I knew this was our chance.

"What the hell?" Tarkis shouted as he watched the ship's energy divert to a weapon's system deep in the Resolute's belly.

"All birds in the nest, Commander. We're clear to proceed."

With a hate-filled glare, I targeted Skarnak's ship and fired the ancient weapon. A brilliant beam of energy never seen before shot forth, striking the Vaith vessel with overwhelming force. The enemy ship erupted into a massive explosion, its debris scattering across the void, taking out most of his surrounding fleet vessels. Then suddenly, everything was silent. The only sound was the humming of the Phantom Resolute's engines as we drifted through space, victorious but battered.

I let out a deep breath, feeling a small amount of tension leave my body. We had made it through, but at what cost? In the fierce battle, Nexion and several other crew members sustained severe injuries. It was a bittersweet victory.

A collective sigh of relief swept through the Resolute. We had narrowly escaped certain destruction. The tactical officer ordered our strike fighters to engage the remaining Vaith ships.

Relief washed over me as the last of them were destroyed.

With the Vaith ships gone, I collapsed into my chair, exhausted, but relieved. We had won the battle on our side of the portal. We had several good warriors down and now stood alone in the far reaches of the universe. The Resolute had suffered significant damage. But at least we were alive and had accomplished our mission.

I made my way to the medical bay, my heart heavy with worry. I had been so focused on the battle that I had barely registered Nexion's injuries. Now, as I stood before him, I could see the severity of his wounds. His body was covered in bruises and cuts, and his breathing was shallow. I could feel the tears prickling at the corners of my eyes as I took in the sight of the man I loved lying there, broken and battered. Dr. Xanderian huddled over Nexion, his expression grave.

"How is he?" I asked, my voice barely above a whisper.

"He's stable, but his injuries are severe," Dr. Xanderian replied, his voice grim. "It will take time for him to recover."

"Thank you, Dr. Xanderian. Please do all you can for him."

As the days passed, the doctor tended to Nexion's wounds, and the crew repaired the Resolute. I spent many sleepless nights at his bedside, watching over him, praying he would recover as the others had.

CHAPTER TWENTY-FOUR

ELZARIA

Now safe and the ship repaired, it was time to find a new home. I gathered my officers around me, their faces unsure.

"We must find a suitable planet for us to live and start again," Loren said. "The conditions must be just right—enough resources to sustain our people and provide ample protection from outside forces." The officers nodded in agreement as Loren continued. "We need a planet with an atmosphere capable of supporting human life, lush vegetation, and plentiful water."

The crew set out on their mission to locate the perfect planet. Loren was particularly excited, envisioning this as some grand science experiment. It took days of scanning the stars within this mostly unexplored galaxy before they finally came upon an ideal candidate—a world full of promise and hope.

We set a course for this new planet. It would be our new frontier.

Interrupting a planning meeting, Dr. Xanderian requested I come to the medical bay. After many days where Nexion's condition had been touch and go, I couldn't help the panic rise in my chest at his request. Although the automated medical nanobots and advanced cellular regeneration technology had pieced him back together, returning Nexion's body almost as good as new, he had remained unconscious. Dr. Xanderian explained to me how the brain can shut down from emotional and mental trauma and that it would be impossible to predict for how long.

The doors slid open, and I entered the room. Nexion was sitting up in his bed, his eyes slowly focused on me as I approached.

Barely able to contain my excitement, I ran to him, throwing myself into his arms. I held Nexion tightly, tears of relief streaming down my face. "I was so worried about you," my voice breaking with emotion.

Nexion held me close, rubbing my back soothingly. "I'm okay, Zara. You don't have to worry about me."

"But I do worry, Nexion," I said, pulling back slightly to look at him. "You were so badly injured, and I thought I was going to lose you."

Nexion's expression softened, and he reached up to brush a strand of hair from my face. "I'm sorry for scaring you. But I'm here now, and I'm not going anywhere."

I could see a few scars that remained, a testament to his ordeal.

"Nexion, I'm so glad you're awake. I didn't know how long it might take," I replied, trying to hide my distress. "The medical team said it could take a while for your brain to heal, and that your mind needed time to recover from the horrific abuse you suffered as Skarnak's prisoner."

He nodded, slowly. "I can feel it, the lingering effects of what they did to me. But the Empyrean medical technology is truly remarkable. I never thought I'd be able to move after what I went through."

I leaned in to kiss him, feeling his arms wrap around me as we deepened the kiss. But as the kiss ended, and we pulled back, I couldn't help but notice the haunted look in Nexion's eyes.

"What's wrong?"

Nexion hesitated for a moment before speaking. "There's something you need to know, Elzaria. About what happened when I was captured by Skarnak."

My heart sank at the mention of Skarnak. "What is it, Nexion?"

Nexion took a deep breath, his eyes flickering with pain. "He... he did things to me, Zara. Things that I can't even begin to explain." He trailed off, his voice unsteady.

The pain reflected in his eyes shattered my heart as I realized the extent of what Nexion had endured. I took his hand, squeezing it tightly. "You don't have to explain anything, Nexion. I'm here for you, no matter what."

He looked at me, his eyes almost a dull gray like the misery had sucked the emerald intensity I loved out them. His eyes brimmed with unshed tears. "Thank you, Zara. I don't know what I'd do without you."

We sat there in silence for a long while, just holding each other. The weight of what Nexion had endured was heavy on my heart, but I knew we would get through it together.

"I love you," I sighed, leaning in to kiss him again.

"I love you too."

As we lay there, wrapped up in each other's arms, I couldn't shake the feeling that Skarnak's shadow still loomed over us, and that our battle was far from over.

Dr. Xanderian told us that Nexion could return to our quarters to finish his recuperation. He was weak but made it with my help.

I scurried around, fussing over his pillows and making sure everything was just right.

"Stop, I'm good. Come to bed and tell me what I've missed. How many days was I out?" His memory was still shaky as he asked some of the same questions over and over.

"Almost a lunar. Don't worry, I'll catch you up."

I brought him a tray of food and his favorite drink, still trying to pamper him. We snuggled up together, and I recounted every detail from the moment he flung himself through the airlock as we undocked to the planet we were heading for as our refuge.

He was particularly interested in the neural connection between me and The Creators' weapon used to obliterate Skarnak's ship. Having me recount every second and feeling I experienced while connected to the ancient technology.

I played him a recording of Skarnak's message to me on Grymrock as well as my return message once we were on this side of the portal. We talked about the daring plan to trap Skarnak's fleet on this side of the wormhole, the Vaith ships we had destroyed, and the search for a new planet to call home.

"You had some balls baiting him like that and trapping us along with his fleet beyond the reach of our people." His eyes flashed with pride. "I guess I made a kickass knight out of you, after all." He said, laughing. It was the first glimmer of happiness he had shown since his ordeal.

Days later, we were resting on the bed, and Nexion seemed to be doing well, considering his harrowing experience. Our conversation turned to our new planet, a place that held the promise of a fresh start for all of us.

As we talked, Nexion reached over and stroked my belly, a loving smile on his face. "Our daughter," he whispered. "I can't wait to meet her and hold her in my arms."

I felt a sudden wave of panic wash over me, realizing I hadn't yet told Nexion the truth about our unborn child. Taking a deep breath, I tried to explain. "Nexion, there's something I need to tell you. Out of an abundance of caution and worry for our daughter's life, I... I made a decision before I left Grymrock. I didn't know if any of us would survive on this side of the portal with Skarnak, nor did I know how the Vaith planned to attack the other side."

He looked at me in alarm. "What are saying, Elzaria? What happened?"

I hesitated for a moment, then continued. "I had our family doctor remove the baby from my womb and sent her off with a crew of the very best doctors, scientists, and warriors. We cryogenically froze her, Nexion. Waiting in suspended animation until a time when she can be safe. The team's mission was to find a safe planet to keep her hidden and protected until it's secure for her to return."

Nexion's eyes widened, and he struggled to process the information. "But, why? Why would you do that?"

Tears welled up in my eyes as I explained my reasoning. "I couldn't bear the thought of our child being born into a universe of danger and uncertainty, with enemies all around us. I didn't know if my plan would work, and if I would survive. Skarnak had already captured you and I didn't know if you were alive or dead. I was terrified that she would end up orphaned and hunted. I had to do something to ensure her safety, even if it meant making that gut-wrenching decision." My body shook from the torment of telling him.

Nexion exhaled, running his fingers through his hair. "I guess I understand why you did it, but it's still hard to accept. Our daughter... out there somewhere, without us."

I reached for his hand, squeezing it gently. "I know it's dreadful, Nexion, but we have to trust that she's in the best hands possible. And one day, when the time is right, we'll be reunited with her. Until then, we must focus on our mission and building a future for her to return to."

Nexion's expression changed. His face lit up with a new purpose. "You're right, Zara. Our daughter is out there, and I'll do whatever it takes to find her, to make her safe."

I nodded, feeling a surge of love for the man beside me. "We'll do it together, Nexion. We'll find her and bring her home."

He trailed reassuring strokes up and down my back as I laid my head on his shoulder.

We spent the next hours discussing our plans and strategies, working together as a united front. We talked about gathering intelligence on the locations where our daughter's crew might have settled and about the world we wanted to build for her.

As we talked, I couldn't help but feel a sense of hope growing within me as well. Our love for our daughter, even though she was far away, was a powerful force that brought us even closer together.

"We'll need to be cautious, Zara," Nexion said, his voice focused. "We can't let our enemies know about her, or they might try to use our daughter against us."

I nodded in agreement. "We'll be careful, Nexion. But we won't let fear hold us back. We owe it to her and to ourselves to do everything in our power to find her."

As we continued to discuss our plans, we knew that the road ahead would be filled with challenges and uncertainties, but we also knew that we were in this together.

313

CHAPTER TWENTY-FIVE

ELZARIA

A couple of days later, we reached our frontier planet. Upon arriving, further scans confirmed its suitability, and we sent down scouts to make sure the planet could sustain our people's needs.

They soon returned with enthusiastic reports of rich soil, abundant wildlife, freshwater, rivers, and lakes, and plenty of fertile land that we could use for farming. This was it—the new home we had been searching for. We quickly prepared to move our entire population down onto this wondrous world; excitedly making plans for how best to establish our new society among these alien surroundings.

It didn't take long to discover that the planet had underdeveloped human populations.

We had long known that The Creators, the orginal beings, had populated the universe, scattering the seeds of humanity out from its center. These human seeds began as one race. Over hundreds of thousands of cycles, humans developed at different rates and in different ways. The Empyreans evolved quickly in the cradle of the Andromeda galaxy. As we and many others developed, our evolution made us different. These differences developed into rivalries and conflict which led to the ancient wars. Following those wars, we had thrived in relative peace until now.

At the same time, there were many of the original human seeds that were just now developing the intelligence and desire to look out from their own worlds to those across their galaxy, or even further afield to the greater universe.

This planet's humans, however, were primarily agriculturalists, who cultivated crops and raised animals for food. They also engaged in simple trade and commerce, exchanging goods and services with neighboring communities. They lived in small, self-sufficient villages, with a hierarchical social structure led by chieftains and warriors.

These humans were becoming skilled artisans, who produced a variety of decorative and functional objects, such as pottery, jewelry, and tools. They were skilled metalworkers, who created intricate designs on their weapons and tools, as well as produced figurines and sculptures indicating high intelligence.

Their religious beliefs, which often involved the worship of natural forces and deities, led them to build stone circles and other monuments, likely used for religious and ceremonial purposes. They also buried their dead with grave goods, such as pottery, jewelry, and weapons, suggesting a belief in an afterlife or spiritual realm.

We were about to supercharge their evolution.

The transition to our new home world was swift but not without challenges as everyone worked long hard days together cultivating crops, and establishing laws while exploring all the secrets this mysterious world offered us—from vast plains where herds of wild beasts roamed free in search of food under an azure sky that glistened like a sea of diamonds at night when two moons gracefully rose in the horizon to underground caves filled with exotic creatures. Most of the crew found this new way of life exhilarating and embraced all it offered.

After an entire cycle of living on the planet we now called Terrainitium, Nexion, and I never felt settled. We worked diligently in every aspect of our lives to support the success of our crew. But our hearts were unsettled. We tirelessly reviewed every direction and place to see if we could locate the crew that had taken our daughter. Not having access to the space-time portal, our communications had been cut off from our known parts of the universe.

The Phantom Resolute remained anchored in orbit off of Terrainitium. Nexion and I spent most of our time on board the ship, maintaining its functions and monitoring for any communications or threats. We would receive archaic snapshots from developing worlds from within this galaxy, some of which we found hilarious, while others were horrifying depictions of war and violence. It was as if we were watching ancient history unfold before our eyes.

Nexion and I spent many nights lying in our bed, staring out of the large windows into the vastness of space. We couldn't help but become philosophical as we worried about the daughter we had never known. Where was she? Was she safe? Was she loved? Together we realized that no matter how evolved humans were, we had basic traits that were a part of our DNA and controlled how we related to others. At the most basic level was a survival instinct coupled with an innate sense of right and wrong. Humans, like the universe in which we live, are suspended between the light and the darkness. The best any being can hope for is to give and receive more good than bad; more light than darkness.

One day, standing on the bridge running routine systems checks, a strange highly encrypted communication came through. We both knew in our bones that this was from the crew that had spirited away our baby girl, but it used encryption we couldn't decipher. Out of frustration and desperation, I linked with the ship neurally, hoping that it might break the encryption. It had been a long time since I had felt the warmth of the ancient energy pulse through me; it felt like home.

"Ship, open and translate communication ID νέοξεκίνημα." I requested.

Nexion and I waited breathlessly for what felt like forever when the message began scrolling on the screen in front of us.

To Queen Elzaria Eridani or her future representative:

This message is to confirm that we, the crew of the Stellavara, at your direction, have successfully completed the mission you ordered. Using our advanced cloaking technology, we slipped through the Vaith's perimeter unnoticed. Fleeing the chaos and destruction of the Vaith assailants, we flew to a small remote blue and green planet at the border of the Laniakea and Perseus-Pisces superclusters within a spiral galaxy using the F1R3X wormhole. The planet is in a small solar system containing nine masses that exhibit enough self-gravity to overcome rigid body forces so that they assume a hydrostatic equilibrium shape surrounding a medium size yellow-dwarf star. This small planet lies within a spiral galaxy that looks milky from a distance. It is approximately 27,000 light cycles from the galaxy's center. This planet was unknown to the Quindarian Federation.

It is a planet very similar to Terrastria in condition and resources and has one moon. The undeveloped inhabitants near the landing site call this planet Elohi and themselves Aniyunwiya. They're an intelligent and peaceful people who value the environment and all creation. We plan to assimilate with them and protect our precious cargo.

In an effort to protect our ship's limited resources, we will have no means to return to space travel. We have devised a plan that will allow the cargo we protect to be directed toward the nearest space-

time portal within this galaxy. Sometime in the future, when we hope it will be safe from the Vaith, the cargo will use our ship on a one-way ride to return. Upon the launch of our ship from its current resting place, it will trigger a beacon which you can access from the Phantom Resolute. We don't know how, but just before we exited from the Resolute, this digital beacon's mechanism was entered into our data systems with instructions for its use.

We have complied with our orders to the best of our ability and have automated the return procedure. We pray to The Creators that the cargo we protect will be returned safely.

Farewell,

Commander Risenhold of the Stellavara

"Zara, you know what this means." Nexion shouted. "We're in the same galaxy!"

"Yeah, but finding the exact planet could take who knows how long."

"The message said that as soon as the cargo, our daughter, can launch the ship, it will trigger a location beacon. We just have to wait."

"Wait for her to be born, wait for her to make it to a spacecraft that is completely foreign technology to her, wait for her to activate and launch, wait to receive the beacon, wait..." My words tapered off into a sad sigh.

Nexion paced with his hands behind his back for so long that I gave up and went to bed.

I awoke to the gentle stroke of Nexion's fingers along my arm.

"I've got an idea. I think I figured out how we can be there for our daughter, no matter how long it takes."

I turned over, my breath hitched in my throat. "How did I get so lucky to be bound to such a gorgeous, smart, loving man like you?"

Nexion smiled and dragged his fingers down my cheek and to my collarbone. "It can wait until we awake. But now, I want to make love to you until our bodies are spent." And he did.

Nexion bounded awake with the energy of a wild beast. His words shooting out like a high-speed laser cannon.

"Get up. Get dressed. I've already asked Loren to shuttle up and meet us on the bridge. He'll be here in five. Let's go. He will know how to turn my ideas into an action plan."

I rushed to shower, dress, and drag a brush through my tangled hair. I didn't take long, but Nexion had already left for the bridge. When I entered, he and Loren were poring over a holographic projection filled with charts and formulas.

"We've got it figured out!" He told me with the brightest smile I've ever seen him have, those emerald eyes brilliant once more.

"We can use the beacon not only to track her ship, but also as an activation device. We can enter cryogenic sleep and the beacon can awaken us with its signal. The Resolute can stay in orbit until our sleeping beauty awakens. Then we'll go meet her ship and figure it out from there."

"What..." I wanted to argue, but my brain was still trying to wrap itself around the idea. "Loren, is this possible?"

"Believe it or not, I think it is. I'm working on the math and logistics as we speak. Of course, there's a lot that could go wrong, but it could definitely work."

I had to sit down.

I connected to the ship and asked for it to analyze the probability of this plan working.

"61%" It replied.

"Those odds are better than nothing. I'm in." I told the guys.

The next few days we visited Terrainitium and explained our decision to our people, said our goodbyes, and readied the Phantom Resolute for our cryogenic sleep.

We worked closely with Loren, who would be the last person we would see before our sleep. We didn't know how long it would take. Nor did we know if our loved ones would still be alive when we woke up. Loren promised me he would protect the Resolute for as long as he could and automate its maintenance. He also swore he would figure out how to rebuild the space-time portal, using the information provided by the ancients through my special connection to the ship. He also told me about a strange dream he had where The Creators spoke to him.

"Elzaria, you're not going to believe this, but I think The Creators not only spoke to me in my dream but also downloaded an enormous amount of technical knowledge about the construction of the portals. I feel like they connected to my brain."

"Exactly! Now you know how I've felt. The Creators only speak to you when they're directing you for their purposes. This is such an amazing thing, Loren." I grabbed him up in a hug. We all pledged to do whatever it took to find our daughter and to create a safe, peaceful world for her to return to. Together, Nexion and I would face whatever came our way, united by our love for our daughter and our determination to be with her once again. It was a promise we made not just to each other, but to the future we were fighting for. And it was a promise we intended to keep, no matter the cost.

It was time.

"Loren, I pray I'll see you again." I tightly hugged him for a long time. "Love you." I whispered.

"Love you, too, Elzaria." He said as he stepped back from the cryogenic sleeping chamber.

Nexion was steadfast in refusing to acknowledge any potential danger in our plan. We held each other silently, rocking back and forth. I couldn't hold back the tears. He cupped my face in his massive hands and brushed the tears from my cheeks.

Then, he helped me lie back in the chamber. The last words I heard him say were, "If she never rises from her protective sleep, then we will never rise to greet another day. If she were to wake and join us in the world of life, then we will be forever liberated by the light of her hope... Sweet dreams, my little knight."

Find out if Elzaria and Nexion's unborn daughter survives the perils of an unknown planet and whether they are reunited in the next book of the *All is Fair in Love and Galactic War* series:

ABOUT THE AUTHOR

What can I say, I was born a moonchild, not only a Cancer but also during a full moon. They say "it makes me a unique and curious soul whose mind is always out of this world."

Growing up during the space age, science fiction, especially movies and books, captivated me. I remember watching The Jetsons' cartoon and TV series like Star Trek and Lost in Space, movies like Star Wars, Alien, Mad Max, Moonraker, Blade Runner, War Games, Dune, The Terminator, Back to the Future, Planet of the Apes, Interstellar, The Martian and so, so many more. They inspired all kinds of questions about the universe and the possibilities of what could be out there. The idea of civilizations existing on other planets and what life would be like for them intrigued me.

As a Certified Professional Photographer, I'm enthralled by astrophotography and can't get enough of NASA's James Webb Space Telescope pictures. Images of the II ZW 96 galaxies twisting and melding into each other, the light of a new star being born in the shape reminiscent of an hourglass, to the Pillars of Creation are just a few of the awe-inspiring pictures sent back to us mere earthlings. The vastness of space boggles my mind and inspires me to think about who all might be out there.

Combine always having my head in the stars with the love of a good romance book and I have found myself irresistibly drawn to writing stories about space adventures. The best kind of alpha alien male is one who's met his match with an even stronger-willed, independent female from Earth. I hope to craft stories that inspire the reader to believe in the possibilities of the universe. I think the best stories are about people succeeding against all odds.

HOPE YOU ENJOY MY BOOKS!
LORI

I'm a passionate author and I strive for excellence in all my projects. Despite my best effort, however, typos and errors can sometimes slip through the cracks. That's why I'm seeking the help of my readers—if you spot anything that needs to be corrected in this book, I would be very grateful if you could let me know. Your feedback is invaluable and helps me improve all future editions of my work. Whether it's a typo, inconsistency, or other error, I would appreciate your help. Please don't hesitate to contact me at Lori@LoriLind.com with any corrections you find. Your support means the world to me, and I can't thank you enough for taking the time to read this book and improve its quality. Thank you!

WHERE TO FIND ME

LORILIND.COM

FACEBOOK
LORI LIND

INSTAGRAM
@LORI.LIND.AUTHOR